The Witch's Market

Also by Mingmei Yip

Secret of a Thousand Beauties

The Nine Fold Heaven

Skeleton Women

Song of the Silk Road

Petals from the Sky

Peach Blossom Pavilion

The Witch's Market

Mingmei Yip

KENSINGTON BOOKS
www.kensingtonbooks.com

KENSINGTON BOOKS are published by

Kensington Publishing Corp.
119 West 40th Street
New York, NY 10018

All Kensington titles, imprints, and distributed lines are available at special quantity discounts for bulk purchases for sales promotion, premiums, fund-raising, educational, or institutional use.

Special book excerpts or customized printings can also be created to fit specific needs. For details, write or phone the office of the Kensington Sales Manager: Attn. Sales Department. Kensington Publishing Corp., 119 West 40th Street, New York, NY 10018. Phone: 1-800-221-2647.

eISBN-13: 978-1-61773-324-6
eISBN-10: 1-61773-324-5
First Kensington Electronic Edition: December 2015

ISBN-13: 978-1-61773-323-9
ISBN-10: 1-61773-323-7
First Kensington Trade Paperback Printing: December 2015

10 9 8 7 6 5 4 3 2 1

Printed in the United States of America

To Geoffrey

Even the *Book of Changes* could not have predicted
a better life together than the one we have

ACKNOWLEDGMENTS

Writing a book a year taxes mind and body. However, I have only gratitude that I have been given the privilege of doing this over and over.

Without the support, encouragement, and generosity of many people, none of my novels would have been written. First, I must thank my husband, Geoffrey Redmond, himself an excellent writer who has published seven books, including the newest *Teaching the I Ching (Book of Changes)* (Oxford University Press).

Geoffrey is my most enthusiastic reader, honest critic, and most important, he supports me as a writer even though this means his wife, instead of serving him home-cooked meals, depends mostly on take-out, especially when meeting deadlines. Fortunately, living in New York City, most food is only a phone call away.

I have to thank all the wonderful staff at Kensington. My editor, Martin Biro, who gives useful suggestions, and is ever thoughtful and supportive. Others include publicists Karen Auerbach and Vida Engstrand, designer Kristine Mills-Noble, who graces my books with beautiful covers, and Jacqueline Dinas, who has succeeded in having my books published in ten countries so far. And, of course, Kensington President Steven Zacharius and his son, Adam Zacharius, who have made me able to fulfill my dreams year after year.

Many readers have friended me on Facebook, bought my books, and cheered me along the way. I owe them my sincerest gratitude.

Dear Reader,

About two years ago I read an article by my favorite Chinese author, Echo, about her trip to the Witches' Market in Bolivia. Though it is a very short article, somehow the title captured my imagination and inspired me to write this novel.

However, instead of setting my novel in Bolivia, I decided to make it happen on the Canary Islands. These seven islands are guarded by goddesses who are also safe keepers for the hidden golden apples of Aphrodite. Sailors seeking the legendary golden apples were lured to their doom by beautiful goddesses.

This novel, besides Echo's article, was also inspired by an incident I experienced years ago. Once at a concert I was so annoyed by the performer's pretentious style that I stared at her instrument's strings and willed them to break. Surprisingly, a few seconds later one of the strings broke, forcing her to stop in the middle of her performance. Rather than being happy, I was frightened that I might possess some strange power. I never tried it again; the possibility that it might work was too scary, maybe even unethical. Instead, I put this experience into *The Witch's Market.*

I follow Confucius' famous advice to respect the spirits but keep them at a distance.

I beat you little man, so your breath has no place to vent!
I beat your little hands, so they can't draw money from the bank!
I beat your little feet, so wearing shoes will make them bleed!
I beat your little head, so fortune will leave you sad!
I'll beat your little tongue, so you can't chew meat
and might as well be a monk!
I'll beat your little heart, so your life is like the bitterest tart!

—*Beating the Little Man*
Ancient Chinese folk custom for getting
rid of petty troublemakers

Nothing stains me with the world's dust
Wherever I go, cares do not follow me.
When it rains, I just wait for the rainbow. . . .

—*Qiusi (Autumn Thoughts)*
Lu You (1125–1209)

I dream, forgetting I am just a trespasser on life.
Now, after an evening's stolen pleasure,
Alone, resting against the fence
The rivers and mountains going all the way to infinity,
It's easy to part, harder to meet again.
Spring is gone, like flowing water and fallen petals. . . .

—*Lang Taosha (Waves Washing Away Sands)*
Li Yu (937–978)

PART ONE

Prologue

When I turned thirty-three, I decided it was time for a big change in my life. It was time to become a witch.

I have to admit that I was not sure if this would be a good idea.

My name is Ai Lian, "love lotus" in Chinese, or Eileen Chen in English. Although I was Western-educated and lived in the modern era, I believed somewhere inside me there lived a witch, at least in spirit. I grew up in a family who believed in anything metaphysical, however implausible.

Both my mother and grandmother were "witches," or what the Chinese call *wu,* "shamaness." Sometimes *wu* are also referred to as *fangshi,* people who have mastered the way and thus have the power to manipulate reality.

Both my mother and my grandmother could predict the future, visit the past, see auras, and talk to invisible beings. Unfortunately, Mother had died young in her forties, to the great grief of myself and her own mother, my grandmother, Laolao. Because she had lost her daughter, Laolao wanted me to be a shamaness to carry on the family lineage. Besides healing, casting spells, going into trances, and taking on animal powers, she organized underworld tours. Laolao would also cast the *daxiaoren*—"beating the petty people" spells. These spells would ensure that the trivial, touchy, gossipy, jealous little men and women who cause us endless troubles got what they deserved.

From my mother and grandmother, I'd learned the basics of witchcraft—empowering amulets, concocting healing herbs, casting spells, communicating with the dead. And the great Chinese tradition of *feng shui*—finding out if a residence, whether *yin* for the dead or *yang* for the living, had good placement and energy flow. Though I was forced to study these skills, I'd never really practiced them. I prided myself on being a modern woman, not an old-fashioned or superstitious one. So, instead of becoming a shamaness like Mother and Laolao, I'd become a scholar of shamanism.

After I'd gotten my Ph.D. in shamanism, I'd started working as an assistant professor at San Francisco State University. Four years had passed and I desperately needed to get a book published in order to get tenure and a promotion to associate professor. The head of the anthropology department, Timothy Lee, had advised me to add a section on Western witchcraft to my dissertation, then publish it as a book. It was an excellent suggestion. However, while I deemed myself pretty knowledgeable about Chinese shamanism, my understanding of its Western counterpart was mainly secondhand from books.

What is a witch anyway? Do they really exist? Are they just ignorant, crazy people who try to scare you to get your money?

I decided that the only way to really know about witches would be to become one myself.

Was I scared? Of course. But I had to write my book, or otherwise I might lose my job. Timothy had hinted that he'd highly recommend me for the promotion—but only if I got my book published. He always deemed me the best candidate because of my cultural background, which was filled with tales of fortune-telling, witchcraft, shamans, vengeful gods, voodoo, juju, and whatnot, actively practiced for 3,000 years from the Stone Age into the electronic era.

Did I really believe in witchcraft? Sometimes yes and sometimes no. I was of two minds. Part of me believed I was a witch born into a long family lineage. Another part, my academic self, kept insisting that I was not a witch, but a normal woman studying witchcraft scientifically.

Either way, I needed to write this book. And to write it I needed to do fieldwork. So I decided to take a year off to look for witches, gather materials in order to write about them, and then, once I had tenure, relax and enjoy life.

At least this was my plan.

1

A Birthday Gift for a Witch

It was my thirty-third birthday. In Chinese culture, three is an extremely lucky number, because it is synonymous with the word *alive,* or "prosperous." Needless to say, thirty-three is double good luck. So I wanted a special celebration for my once-in-a-lifetime thirty-third birthday.

My birthday fell during midterm exam week, leaving me stuck grading papers. So I was very grateful when my younger sister, Bao Lian—"precious lotus" in Chinese and Brenda in English—offered to organize the party for me. At twenty-nine, Brenda was already a real-estate lawyer aggressively climbing the relentless legal ladder toward partnership. My little sister's success was in part due to her knowing how to use her charm—especially with men. I suspected Brenda had volunteered to host the party so that she could flirt with my guests—perhaps even my on-and-off boyfriend, Ivan Collins. Her flirting was indiscriminate—anyone male, from her boss and senior colleagues to waiters, doormen, bartenders, taxi drivers, delivery guys.

Whenever I criticized her for this, she'd wink, and say, "Relax, Eileen. Life should be a big party with us all enjoying ourselves!"

* * *

As an assistant professor, of course I didn't have a large apartment to invite friends over to. Luckily, Ivan said we could use his big luxury condo in Pacific Heights as long as we cleaned up afterward. Brenda and I had no problem with that, as we'd both cleaned houses and apartments to work our way through college.

Of course Ivan had only said this as a joke. An investment banker, he could well afford a cleaning lady. Divorced for several years, Ivan had been looking for the right woman and seemed to think that I was the one. I appreciated him for his hard work and generosity but wasn't comfortable with his take-no-prisoners, overly ambitious approach to life. Nor did I want his hyperactive, jet-setting, breakfast-in-London and dinner-in-Paris lifestyle.

Of course, like most women, I didn't mind having a rich boyfriend. For some reason I just couldn't love Ivan back completely and that bothered me. While I felt attracted to his intelligence and success, I found his constant boasting about how much money he had made that week tedious. And so we drifted apart. Since he never complained about our on-and-off relationship, I guessed he must have other women on the side. Or maybe he just hoped that one day I'd come around.

Right now we were in a separation phase, as he put it, to give each other more space and time to reflect on our future. Or maybe it just gave him more space and time for other women. I believed Ivan truly loved me, but I knew he was also aware that if things didn't work out between us, he could have almost any woman he wanted.

When I talked to Brenda about my intermittent romance, she said, "Eileen, why don't you just marry Ivan and enjoy a luxurious life? After a few years, if you want, you can get a divorce and live off a big alimony check and child support. So you really have nothing to lose. Listen, big sister, only a crazy woman would let go of such a once-in-a-life-time catch!"

I gave her a dirty look. "Brenda, when did our parents teach us to be so practical and materialistic?"

But she ignored my question. "Trust me, Eileen, you've everything to gain and nothing to lose by marrying Ivan. Period."

I wished I could pass Ivan on to Brenda, but there was no chance of that. At least if he was with Brenda the money would still stay with us—as Brenda wished—and not be wasted on some unknown women. But unfortunately my little sister was too much like the other women Ivan knew—climbing the corporate ladder, chasing after designer clothes, luxury cars, trendy restaurants, and exotic vacation spots—to interest him.

I think Ivan liked me because I was not money and status crazy. He knew I cared more about the other world than this one. With me, he could glimpse a life utterly different from his own. But I worried that Ivan would get tired of me when the initial excitement of having a witchy, professor girlfriend wore off. Anyway, I was not yet ready to take the plunge. Since I was a child, I'd been waiting for something unusual, or big, to happen in my life. Life with Ivan was not it.

For my birthday party, Brenda and I had sent out over thirty invitations to friends and colleagues. But no students were included, because in case the professors got drunk, I didn't want gossip flying back to the university administration. There was always the risk that when faculty and students got drunk together, remarks would slip out that would later be regretted.

Brenda suggested that the theme should be witchcraft and offered to do the decorations.

I told her, "Fine, but everything should be innocuous, absolutely no creepy stuff like fake corpses or severed hands and arms."

"At your order, ma'am," she said. "After all, Halloween is months away."

Since I had a late-afternoon class to teach on my birthday, I didn't arrive at Ivan's apartment until six. Entering his living room, the first thing I noticed was red candles lining the walls, giving the place a cozy, but also eerie, feeling.

Brenda dashed toward me, screaming, "Eileen, happy birthday!"

I eyed my little sister's long-sleeved red dress. The plunging neckline revealed quite a lot of her bosom. The whole effect was multiplied by her bright red necklace, earrings, and bloody-looking lips. She would get plenty of male attention tonight.

"Thanks, Brenda. Everything's ready?"

"Of course. You can always count on me, big sister."

"Good." I exchanged nods with a few early arrived guests, then turned to Brenda. "Now I need to change."

Inside Ivan's marble bathroom, with its gold-rimmed mirror, I took off my pantsuit, refreshed my makeup, and put on my shamaness's gown. I had decided not to dress in a Western witch's outfit because I didn't want to wear black on my birthday. So instead I wore a pink Chinese dress, accessorized by a chunky silver necklace with Daoist motifs: bats for good luck, pears for immortality, and goddesses for beauty and compassion. After piling my hair into a bun and decorating it with a silk pink lotus, I looked at the mirror and was happy with what I saw. A mysterious, exotic shamaness—ready to play tricks or cast spells.

Was it a real witch staring back at me from the mirror? The answer was yet to be found out.

When I went back out to the living room, most of the guests had arrived. They came up to greet me with the obligatory Chinese sayings Brenda had probably just taught them:

"Happy birthday, Eileen! May your good fortune
be as deep as the Eastern Sea and your longevity
as high as the Southern Mountain!"

"May every year be as wonderful as this one,
And every birthday like this birthday!"

"More wealth, more years, more fame,
More light, more pleasure, more luck!"

After greeting me, people gathered in small groups to talk or, with a glass of wine in hand, walked around to appreciate Ivan's luxury apartment and his collection of modern paintings, handcrafted ceramics, Indian statutes, and exotic Mexican masks.

Soon Brenda materialized by my side, took my hand, and led me to a table set up as an altar. "It took me a few hours to set this up. I hope you like it!"

I was relieved that my little sister had kept her promise and hadn't displayed anything creepy. There were candles, crystal balls, a deck of tarot cards, jars of colorful "medicine," small plates of exotic herbs, a witch doll with a comical face, a witch bracelet with miniature charms, and a Ouija board for conjuring. The table-turned-altar was bedecked with a floral shawl with long black tassels. To complete the scene, Ivan's black cat, dressed up by Brenda in a witch's cape and hat, posed regally on the altar as if she were the real boss of this party.

Just as I was about to complain that there should also be an altar for a Chinese witch, Brenda smiled mysteriously.

"Eileen, come."

She led me past a few guests toward the other end of the living room before she stopped in front of another display. To my delight, this one was decorated with Daoist talismans: gourds, a long string of prayer beads, a small drum, a bronze mirror, a ceramic mortar and pestle, a small three-legged cauldron, and a Prussian blue string-bound book entitled *Jade Lady's Feminine Fist.*

Chinese shamans are expected to have great longevity, heal diseases, undergo otherworldly journeys, practice internal and external alchemy, and, of course, cast spells and curses. *Jade Lady's Feminine Fist* is a manual for the practice of achieving internal *qi* energy. Chinese people believe that if you have strong *qi,* you can practically do anything—levitate, knock people to the ground without even touching them, stay alive without food, survive severe cold without clothes, even be buried alive and emerge a few days later.

My little sister, despite our family's heritage, had never shown any interest in either Western or Chinese witchcraft. She only cared for practical things, which was not a bad thing, but I believed that people should also cultivate their spiritual side. So when disaster strikes, as it always does sooner or later, you have something to fall back on.

I was amazed by my little sister's efforts, and I said, "Thanks, Brenda. How did you know about all these things?"

"I read your papers and dissertation for ideas."

"But then where did you buy everything?"

"Haight-Ashbury." She chuckled.

Just then my off-again boyfriend Ivan materialized. He draped an arm over Brenda and me.

"Girls, everything going well?"

Like me, Ivan had had to work late, but unlike me, he had to sweet-talk the big wigs and sign seven-figure contracts while I lectured, graded papers, and met with curious students. I suspected my students' enthusiasm to meet me after class was due to rumors that I was a real witch. They wondered, though wouldn't dare ask, if I burned old socks on my lover's side of the bed so he'd stay faithful. If I'd put my menstrual blood into my boyfriend's soup for the same reason. If I could concoct a brew of exotic herbs to mend a broken heart—or to break one. I had no one to blame but myself. For, in order to attract more students to my class, I often hinted that I was a witch.

"Yes, Ivan," Brenda and I said simultaneously.

"And thanks for lending us your place," I added.

"My pleasure."

Later, when all the guests had arrived, Ivan made a public display of affection—even though I wasn't his girlfriend at the moment—by holding my waist and kissing me on my lips.

"Happy birthday, my dear Eileen."

Everyone raised their glasses and toasted. "Happy birthday, Eileen!"

Ivan stared at me lovingly. "Eileen, you look very beautiful and exotic. But please don't put anything into my soup or drink tonight, promise?"

Everyone laughed.

That was why I liked Ivan—despite his driving ambition, he had a sense of humor. He looked particularly attractive tonight with his well-shaped nose and strong jaw. At forty-three, he possessed a muscular physique due to his relentless gym visits. He was a charming man even without the overflowing bank account.

He whispered in my ear, "Can you spend the night with me tonight, please?"

I cast him a mock dirty look. "Ivan, aren't we sep—"

He cut me off. "Eileen, it's cold tonight and I'm lonely. . . ."

"Okay," I said, and smiled, "I can spend the night. But since I promised not to put anything in your drink, then you can't put anything in me."

He made a face, whispering back, "Ah, can't outsmart a woman, especially one with a Ph.D.—in witchcraft, no less."

Enjoying being the center of attention, dressed in my exotic costume, I floated around the apartment greeting people, all the while imagining myself as Xiwang Mu, Queen Mother of the West who reigns over all the immortals. And Ivan as if he were the King Father of the East, casting me protective, or controlling, glances as he chatted with his friends. A friend of mine strummed a guitar, providing soft background music for the partygoers.

In a corner next to the altar, Brenda talked with one of the male guests, her delicate hands and fingers, never having practiced nonattachment, lingered on the man's arms and shoulders. Brenda always told me that a little flirting never hurts, for all men like it, even gays and grandfathers.

After all the greetings, Ivan came back to me. We took food from the table and sat down on a couch to eat. My department head, Timothy Lee, came to sit with us.

Downing a big gulp of Ivan's expensive wine, Timothy smiled. "Happy birthday, Eileen. How are you?"

"Busy teaching and writing, as you know."

"Have you considered my suggestion?"

"Yes, but I'm not strong on Western witchcraft. . . ."

"Then you should do some serious fieldwork."

"I thought of that, but—"

"Eileen is not going anywhere. I need her here," Ivan said.

I gave him a disapproving look.

Timothy ignored Ivan's remark and went on. "Fieldwork is the way to make your work credible."

Now my boyfriend, maybe soon to be ex, put his arm protectively around my shoulder. "No. What about if Eileen gets sick or even captured by natives?"

Timothy smiled. "If Eileen is a witch, I'm sure she'll find a way out. Or if she's a shamaness, she'll be in another time and space before anything happens, ha!" With that, he winked at me, stood up, and began to talk with one of the professors.

Soon there was the sound of metal hitting glass. The room went quiet and Timothy spoke to the crowd. "Let's ask our birthday girl, Eileen Chen, to entertain us all with some witchcraft!"

Laughter and applause burst out.

Red-faced and probably half-drunk on Ivan's free-flowing, expensive wine, Timothy went on excitedly. "We all know that Eileen is a . . . let's put it this way, Eileen is a professor of Chinese and Western witchcraft." He turned to me. "So could you show us some tricks?"

People cheered as Ivan cast me an encouraging look. Now that I was on the spot, I wished I really did possess supernatural powers, such as to break a glass—specifically the one in Timothy Lee's hand. Or simply disappearing for a quick mystic journey to the other world. Unfortunately I didn't have such abilities. But I had to admit to myself that if my colleagues thought I did, it was my fault because I had so often dropped hints of having special powers.

The guests were not going to take no for an answer.

"Yes, let's see some witchcraft on your birthday!"

"Open our eyes!"

"Eileen, bring some excitement to our tedious lives, please!"

I decided that all right, I'd try. If I failed—and of course I would—my excuse was that I was too tired from work.

My reluctant feet dragged me to the middle of the living room. I meditated, then circulated my internal energy the way my mother and grandmother had taught me. My eyes searched the room for an easy object upon which to exercise my supposed power. Seconds later, they landed on the guitar strings.

I asked the guitar player, who was my colleague, "John, can you play the 'Spider's Dance'? You played it at last year's Christmas party."

I gathered up my courage, and announced, "I'm going to break the third string."

A round of applause exploded in the room.

John looked a bit puzzled, but nevertheless obliged. In no time the room was filled with a frantic tune and every one nodded or jumped to the rhythm. I was just hoping that John would play so fast and exert so much strength that the string would break.

Now I was on the path of "no return." My mother had always insisted that I possessed supernatural power, if I would just let myself believe. Her proof was an incident that occurred when I was a child. She had just taken away my glass of Coke, which she deemed toxic. So I focused my anger on the glass in her hand, which fragmented, spilling the soda and staining her dress.

Either my mother had made up this event, which I had no memory of, or she desperately hoped that her elder daughter was born unusual. My mother said a lot of strange things, most of which I did not take seriously. Like all children, I had known better than to believe what adults told us. In any case, I did not remember the incident, and so it did not tempt me to explore my supposed unusual talents. As a scholar, I needed to maintain objectivity about my subject.

I could tell that a few of Ivan's stuffy colleagues were expecting me to fail and become a laughingstock. I knew many of them, mostly self-satisfied jerks who enjoyed seeing others fail.

I didn't expect to succeed, but I was going to try my best. So I concentrated and stared fiercely at the third string. Three minutes into playing, when John was furiously strumming, there was a loud snap and he stopped, looking totally shocked.

Ivan's cat, who had been sitting lazily on the altar, watching the drama with arrogant, wicked eyes, now jumped, emitting a loud screech as if it had seen a ghost.

Ivan was the first to speak. "What happened?"

"Yes, what's happening?" someone asked.

John looked at his guitar, then the guests. "A string broke, the third one." He frowned as he looked at his instrument.

Now everyone turned to look at me, some curious, some a little scared. It was as if I'd suddenly transformed into a witch, complete with black cape, broom, pointed hat, long bloodred nails, and was perhaps about to burst into delirious laughter.

Adding to the collective shock, the doorbell suddenly rang loudly. Since all the invited guests were already here, who could be at the door? An angry neighbor? Brenda dashed to the door and came back with a big beribboned package, which she handed to me. Tucked under the red ribbon was a card with the words ***Happy Birthday to a Witch***.

My heart skipped a beat.

A jealous expression flitted across Ivan's face. "That's a big birthday gift, Eileen. Let's see who it's from."

What he really wanted to know was if someone had sent me something more expensive than he had. I doubted that, since Ivan had earlier given me a very nice pearl necklace.

Ignoring my birthday guests' curious stares, I excused myself and walked toward the bathroom. Somehow opening gifts in front of an audience has always been embarrassing to me. Brenda and Ivan followed me, however.

I gave Ivan a disapproving look. "Ivan, a gentleman does not follow a lady, let alone two, to the bathroom."

Reluctantly, he turned back toward the living room.

Inside the washroom, with Brenda beside me, I quickly tore off the shiny silver gift paper, which seemed to make a despondent sound as it ripped. Next I peeled through layers and layers of tissue paper before my eyes landed on something strange. It was an animal skull, probably that of a monkey. It was stark white and I couldn't tell if it was real or not.

Both Brenda and I fell silent. *Why would someone send me a gift like this on my birthday?*

"Who delivered this?" I asked.

"I don't know—when I opened the door, it was lying on the floor."

"Very strange." In fact, it was more than strange, it was scary. But I didn't want to alarm my little sister.

She looked worried anyway. "You think it's bad luck?"

"I'm sure whoever sent this wants to make me feel uncomfortable."

"I'm so sorry, Eileen. Who would want to do that?"

"I don't know. Someone must be trying to send me a message."

"What's the message?"

"I don't know, but it can't be anything pleasant."

Maybe, I thought to myself, *I really have to become a witch to fight the unknown, evil force that might be coming my way.*

2

Signs from Heaven

When Brenda and I reentered the living room, people were still chattering about my "supernatural" power.

Then Ivan brought up the question I had to avoid. "What's that gift you and Brenda are so mysterious about?"

"It's a cookbook for my birthday," I lied.

He didn't inquire further. He was pretty tipsy by this point.

Ivan planted a kiss on my forehead, then looked around proudly at the other guests. "See? Eileen is a witch! She's awesome. Impossible to find another girl like her, right?"

I could smell alcohol from Ivan's breath, mingled with his expensive cologne. Would he still want me if I really was a witch with supernatural powers? But he didn't look scared.

"Eileen, how did you do that?" Timothy asked suspiciously.

I smiled. "Nothing special. It was just a coincidence."

No one seemed to believe me, so I added, "If we *really* pay attention, we notice coincidences happen all the time. But some are more than coincidences . . . synchronicities."

John made a face. "Then how do you explain my third string breaking?"

"I asked you to play the 'Spider's Dance' because it's fast and the third string would be plucked aggressively. So it broke, as I'd hoped."

He didn't look convinced.

"You think I really possess this kind of power?" I asked, wondering myself.

"Maybe. I did pull very hard on the third string, though," said John. But he still didn't look convinced.

I was so preoccupied with this strange event that the rest of the evening was a blur. I talked with people without knowing what I said and ate without savoring the food. What occupied my mind was my suddenly acquired "supernatural" power and the bizarre birthday gift, the small skull. Long ago, my mother had told me that after my previous life I was supposed to descend into hell, but instead I had fallen into this life.

Mother always joked that I must have been a hungry ghost before I reincarnated into this world because the day I was born, according to the Chinese calendar, is when the Gate of Hell is opened. This is done out of compassion for all of the ghosts, who are allowed to enter the *yang* world for a brief stroll. But all the ghosts must return to hell before midnight. Mother said that because I liked to eat so much I was still looking for the next meal, well past midnight, and missed the chance to go back to the *yin* sphere. So I'd been stuck as a human. Anyway, here I was. Maybe because I'd been born at the edge between *yin* and *yang,* I was half witch and half human. *Yin* and *yang* mean "female" and "male," but also the world of the living, full of strong *yang* energy, and the world of the dead, teeming with *yin* spirits.

Mother also told me that when I was little, some ghosts followed me around. One pinched me when I was not paying attention, another knocked down my rice bowl when I was about to eat, yet another tripped me when I was trying to learn to walk. Apparently, they didn't want me to grow up but instead come back to the other world—hell. But I grew up anyway because my parents always kept lots of cash and change with them to donate whenever we ran into monks or nuns. This was to generate merit for me so the Buddha would protect me from the ghosts. Therefore, miraculously, I actually did grow up. Once you go through puberty the ghosts lose interest, so I was safe after that.

No sooner had the party ended and everyone was gone, than Ivan and I were naked, entwined in his spacious bed. Though I wasn't in the mood for sex, Ivan wouldn't take no for an answer and I felt too tired to resist. It was my birthday treat from him, he insisted—even though we were supposedly in our trial separation. Didn't he fear that I'd break part of him like I'd broken the guitar string? But it seemed that instead the idea of making love with a witch had turned him on.

After we were done, Ivan put his arms behind his head and looked at me admiringly. "You have to tell me, Eileen, how did you snap that string? Just coincidence, some sort of magic trick, or are you really a witch?"

"You're the one to decide."

He didn't respond but kept staring at me.

Finally, I said, "Do I or don't I look like a witch?"

Instead of answering, he reached out to hold me.

"If you want to turn into a real witch, you know you'll have my full support." He smiled.

Was this a joke? Or maybe he really did care about me.

Why was I attracted to Ivan? The question made me think of what the famous novelist Cheung Ailing said in her novel *Lust, Caution*:

A man conquers a woman through her yin tunnel and a woman captures a man through his stomach.

In Ailing's story, a woman spy seduces a Chinese man who is a traitor to the invading Japanese. But it is she who becomes sexually besotted with him, leading to his escape and her death.

So sex could bind a woman, maybe even a witch as well, against her will.

Although I had enjoyed playing the role of witch at my party, in truth I was more shocked by what had happened than my guests.

For weeks, I tried to put the snapped guitar string and the peculiar gift of the skull out of my mind. Yet like cancer cells, these memories just wouldn't leave me alone. So I took a break from preparing lessons to research the symbolism of skulls. What I discovered was not what I'd expected. Traditionally a skull evokes terror, but it can also celebrate the memory of the dead. After all, the skull is the part of the body that remains after death.

But my research could not shed light on my biggest question: Who had sent the skull as a birthday present, and why? Was it good luck, bad luck, or merely an unpleasant prank? Maybe the strange object was somehow meant to lure me away from my humdrum life into unknown realms that, perilous or not, held my destiny.

But I was baffled about what to do with my suddenly discovered possible power. It was even scarier than the skull. My pretense about being a witch was simply to lure students to enroll in my course. Did my will really break the string, or was it just a coincidence? I was clueless.

So I tried a little experiment in my office by focusing my concentration on a teacup on my desk. In a moment it seemed to slide back a fraction of an inch, but it did not crack. Was I just fooling myself?

That night I had a dream. Dressed in a witch's outfit complete with black cap, pointed hat, and a broom, I wandered around an island covered by ancient ruins. Instead of flying, I was sweeping the ground. Disturbingly, the more I swept, the more I discovered that the ground was made up of human skulls. As I was wondering why this was happening, a towering, thousand-year-old tree, no doubt the only living witness to whatever massacre had produced the skulls, suddenly spoke.

"Miss Chinese Witch, you seek to know the deep mystery of the universe."

I put down my broom and looked up at him—if a tree can be a "him."

"Listen carefully," said the tree. "You're now on an island off North Africa. This is the city of virgin witches. . . ."

I cast a curious glance at the faceless faces below me. "How can you tell from the skulls that they were virgin girls?"

"Because I witnessed the ritual carried out here nearly a thousand years ago."

"What ritual?"

"Be patient, young Miss Chinese Witch. The virgins were to accompany the King in death. Deeper down are the rest of their skeletons."

When I was about to sweep away the soil under the skulls, there was a loud crack of thunder, followed by drenching rains.

Lord Tree's sonorous voice was almost indistinguishable from the hissing rain. "You will awake now. Find this island and come to it. There you will find answers."

As I saw the rain trickle down the tree bark and onto the skulls I jolted awake, the sheets soaked with my sweat.

I knew that dreams held knowledge because my grandmother Laolao had been an expert dream interpreter. But was this a real premonition, or just the result of reading too many strange books in the university library? I turned the bedroom light on and took several deep breaths, but the dream seemed no less real. Surprising myself, I decided I would follow the talking tree's advice. But how was I to find the island—and did I really want to? An island of sacrificed virgins . . . did it make sense to follow a nightmare?

The next day I went to the library to find information about North Africa. If the dream island was real, I figured that it must be part of the Spanish *Carnarias Archipelago,* or the Canaries in English. These islands are just off the north coast of Africa, close to Morocco.

I mouthed the exotic names of the seven islands: La Gomera, La Palma, Hierro, Tenerife, Fuerteventura, Lanzarote, and Canaria. I could not imagine any reason why I would have dreamed about such strange and distant places. How foolish to trust a dream. And yet, the dream had been very specific, about a place I'd never imagined even existed, let alone thought of traveling to. Yet Laolao had believed in dreams and quite often she was right about what they meant. According to her they held the mysteries of fate.

As I read more, it all seemed even stranger. These islands had been conquered in turn by the Dutch, British, French, Portuguese, and Spanish, and through all these changes had been the hiding place of vicious pirates. And, it seemed, there were also witches, though exactly what they did my sources did not reveal.

The indigenous inhabitants, a white-skinned and blue-eyed tribe, were either killed by invaders or sold into slavery. But I imagined that some of their secret knowledge had been passed on and somehow survived despite the bustle of trade and tourism.

3

The Lineage of the Shamaness

Whenever I was worried about the future I felt again the pain of losing my grandmother, Laolao. When she was alive, I relied on her advice about all sorts of things. Now I wished I could ask her to predict my future with Ivan. Would we, despite my reservations, end up marrying, having kids, and living happily ever after? Or would we marry and eventually head for divorce? Either he would have an affair or I would tire of his constant money craziness. Brenda always pointed out that if I were divorced from him I'd get plenty of alimony and child support payments. But I was not going to marry someone just to get alimony.

I'd trusted Laolao's prediction, for she'd enjoyed a reputation among the Chinese for accuracy, based on her skill with the *I Ching,* the ancient 3,000-year-old *Book of Changes*.

As a shamaness, Laolao had many supernatural talents: *feng shui,* fortune-telling, mind reading, even accompanying people on journeys to the underworld—or so she'd told me. Another talent she was hired for was *daxiaoren,* beating the petty people. When we lived in Hong Kong, Laolao supported all of us by performing this ritual. Her "office" was a deserted space under the Goose Neck Bridge in the Wanchai area that was occupied mainly by the poor: coolies, street vendors, construction workers, even prostitutes serving British sailors. Probably wanting to keep us away from her rough clients, Laolao never allowed Brenda and me to go with her. But one time we secretly followed her to her "office." But instead of finding her rituals scary, we found them funny.

Around six, my grandma Laolao sat on a small wooden stool under the Goose Neck Bridge and waited for the workers pouring out from the nearby buildings, factories, and restaurants. We could hear as they told her their problems, often about petty people spreading malicious rumors about them or otherwise stirring up trouble. Many were getting a hard time from family members. Brenda and I had to suppress giggles when one man, a particularly handsome one, said he had a mistress who was pushing him to leave his wife. He couldn't decide if he wanted Laolao to "beat" his wife or his mistress—so either one would leave or leave him alone.

Laolao had explained to us that "beating the petty person" is a very old Chinese tradition. Implements used in the ritual included a small stool, writing paper, paper cutouts resembling human figures, a pair of shoes (preferably the owner's), pork fat, green beans, sesame seeds, duck eggs, and a small tiger statue.

Laolao would ask her troubled clients to put their enemies' name and age on a piece of paper. Then the victims would tell their grudges to Lord Tiger, known to be the protector against evil spirits, demons, villains, as well as the bringer of good luck and wealth. To bribe the tiger, she would grease the statute's mouth with pork fat, then offer him the duck egg. Laolao would sprinkle the tiger with green beans and sesame seeds to symbolize the falling away of problems. After that, she'd use her wooden clog to beat the paper figure, representing the petty person, as she cursed, loudly calling out the villain's name and saying:

> I beat you little man, so your breath has no place to vent!
> I beat your little hands, so they can't draw money from the bank!
> I beat your little feet, so wearing shoes will make them bleed!
> I beat your head, so fortune will leave you sad!

I'll beat your little tongue, so you can't chew meat and might as well be a monk!
I'll beat your little heart, so your life is like the bitterest tart!

The next day, more often than not, the client would find that petty person—a gossiper, backstabber, troublemaker, or husband stealer—was in trouble or had fallen ill. By helping others in this way, Laolao also helped us by being able to bring home an extra dish for dinner—soy sauce chicken, pepper and salt shrimp, glistening roast duck. If business was extra good, the dish would upgrade to my favorite—crispy suckling pig that made a *crack, crack, crack* sound when I chewed on it!

Eventually Laolao was able to quit her honorable profession of "beating the petty person." She had become a rich and successful shamaness with a real office in Causeway Bay and upgraded her business to the less sordid one of communicating with the dead. Laolao boasted that not only could she see those "no longer existing," the respected dead, she could also charge people basically for talking to the air. But when I asked her if she really possessed the *yin* eye, her answer was always evasive like this: "How do you think I raised your mother into such a big woman to give birth to you and your sister?"

So the secret of what she believed about her *yin* eye, she carried with her to the *yin* world.

Her new "office" was indoors, under a staircase instead of under a bridge. In old, dilapidated buildings in Hong Kong, spaces below staircases were mostly used as storage areas, stuffed with discarded furniture, worn-out clothes, and bags whose contents were long forgotten. Sometimes the landlord would clear this space and rent it cheaply to a single man as residence or to a family to be used as their dining room. In Laolao's case, it was for meeting with clients.

In this cozy—from a child's point of view—little area, Laolao set up a small, round, wooden table with three stools and a lamp. On the walls she pasted lurid pictures of Daoist gods and goddesses.

Here Laolao summoned the loved ones of the bereaved. Blindfolded with a red cloth, she'd tilt her head to show she was listening very carefully, then repeat messages in the loved ones' voices.

As word got around regarding Laolao's talent of speaking for the dead, her business thrived. Because people would get sore muscles very quickly in the cramped space, they'd quickly pay and leave to make room for the next customer.

When the dead spoke through Laolao, their words were always simple and curt. Her explanation was that she couldn't let the dead dwell in her for too long since that would exhaust her and endanger her health. She emphasized over and over that, though paid, she was in fact doing her customers a huge favor by renting her body to their dead relatives and friends.

Laolao had once told me about a young woman who had come to her to find her deceased lover. But this was one of the rare times that Laolao couldn't speak for the ghost. The woman got very angry, calling Laolao an imposter and demanding her money back.

I asked my grandmother what had happened, and she said, "It's not that I couldn't reach her lover; it was because the man was a murderer and I didn't want to deal with him!"

Before I had a chance to ask more, Laolao continued. "Of course I could still let him talk to her through me. But I'd found out he was a con man planning to kill her to get her money. But then he put the poison into her mother's soup by mistake. She should have told me that he'd been caught and was executed—she was lucky to be rid of the bastard.

"He reincarnated as a cat and was hit by a bus. You know, Eileen, I couldn't possibly let my customer talk to a cat's ghost."

"Why not?"

"Am I supposed to just sit here and meow?!"

I never found out if Laolao made this all up for fun or really believed it.

And soon after that, Laolao died.

It happened on a day when my grandmother was seeing a customer as usual. A Mrs. Song had asked Laolao to speak to her stillborn baby. But the negative *qi* emanating from Mrs. Song's body made Laolao extremely uncomfortable. However, since Laolao had already meditated and been paid to open her *yin* eye, she felt obligated to continue. All at once, she clutched her throat and her face turned paper white as she exclaimed, "Ahh . . . Ahh . . . Ahhhh . . ." as if choked by invisible hands. Under the eyes of waiting customers, she slid to the floor, dead.

Laolao had never seen a doctor in her life, so I had no idea about the state of her health, or what caused her to die so suddenly. The only explanation I ever received was from Laolao's friend, who told me it was Mrs. Song's dead baby who'd taken Laolao's life.

"But how, since he was a baby and dead at that?"

"Ghost babies can be very powerful. You know parents have to appease their baby's ghost by giving a proper burial and hiring monks to chant sutras for its soul. Sometimes people adopt ghost babies to harass their enemies."

"How can that be?"

"It was after Mrs. Song learned that her husband had been cheating that she lost the baby. After the baby died, she secretly fed her baby's ghost with all kinds of goodies so his *yin qi* built up and he could go out to harass her husband's mistress."

"Then what happened?"

"The mistress felt her body being pierced by hundreds of needles—the ghost baby used her body as a target for throwing daggers. The pain became so severe that she couldn't have sex, so finally the man left her and went back to his wife, Mrs. Song."

"You really think this is what happened?"

"Oh, I know these things." She paused and went on. "Then this ghost baby also killed your grandmother."

"Why?"

"That was when Laolao tried to talk to him. Somehow the baby ghost mistook your grandmother for his father's mistress and scared poor Laolao to death."

Even though this sounded like complete nonsense, it was still very scary. So, despite Laolao's wish, I decided not to carry on her lineage as a shamaness but instead to study it safely as a scholar.

* * *

One time before her death, when I asked if the dead really spoke through her, Laolao's answer was, "Just because a person is dead doesn't mean he or she turns mute!"

"But do they really speak through you?"

"That's not for me to decide. I'm only doing my job as a medium." She cast me a chiding glance. "It's impossible to find out, so don't even try."

"Why not?"

"Because the answer lies beyond this world."

Dissatisfied with my grandmother's evasions, I decided to find out for myself, by becoming a scholar and researching shamanism and witchcraft.

Laolao did not approve of my choice of profession. "Why be a professor lecturing to bored students? Why not be a shamaness like me? Besides, I make more than a professor."

"I like to teach—" I began.

"Can you teach about the dead?" She rolled her eyes. "Dead means dead, period!"

"Then how come you talk to them?"

"I don't. They come to me. I just lend them my body."

"So, is what you do real or not?"

"Everything in this world and the other is real." She knocked hard on the table, then my head. "See? Things and people exist. The dead are the same people; the only difference is that we talk about them in the past tense."

I didn't understand her logic, so the argument ended. She never gave me a straight answer and so this woman with whom I spent much of my early life remained a puzzle to me.

PART TWO

4

Journey to the West

Timothy Lee and the dean granted my request of a one-year leave and found some grant funds to modestly support me. Hearing the good news, I immediately called Ivan to discuss my tentative plans to travel to places I'd never even known existed until a few weeks ago.

He paused for a moment before asking, "Eileen, you really want to go to this non-place—why not Paris, or at least Madrid?"

I couldn't tell him that it was because of what a tree had told me in a dream.

"I need to do fieldwork so I can write a book. Otherwise, no tenure and no job."

"Then marry me and I'll support you."

I raised my voice. "I'm not joking, Ivan!"

"Neither am I. But what exactly are you going to do there? When will you be back?"

"Maybe in a year. I need to find witches, interview them, learn what they do, collect some of their juju stuff. Then I can write my book on comparative witchcraft. Maybe I'll learn how to put a spell on you too."

"You know I'd wait forever for you. But a whole year? Geezzzz!"

"Ivan, I don't expect you to wait." But I stopped short of telling him he would be free to pursue any woman he wanted—or that I might find a new man.

I figured all women were as selfish as I. Even though he's your ex, you still want him to think about you, be ready to dash to your side if you need help, and ideally, remain single the rest of his life nursing his broken heart, because he will never find your equal. Or secretly hope you'll change your mind someday and return to him.

I could not suppress a giggle.

"What's so funny?"

"Nothing, Ivan, it's not about you. Anyway, I'll come back. Maybe you can visit me there."

"What gave you this crazy idea?"

"Well, it's hard to explain, but it started with a dream. . . ."

Now he sounded a bit angry. "So, you decide to leave me and go to a few strange islands you know nothing about all by yourself. All of this because of a dream?"

"Sorry, Ivan, but I've already booked my ticket."

"All right, then. I know how stubborn you are."

There was a pause before he spoke again. "Will you be safe there?"

"I'll be very careful. I speak Spanish, remember, so at least I can ask around if I get lost."

I actually felt a little disappointed that all of sudden Ivan wasn't persuading me to stay. Was this a sign that we really were breaking up, this time for good? That while I was away, Ivan was actually going to look for another girl? It would be my fault, not his.

I decided to put Ivan and our uncertain relationship out of my mind and busied myself preparing for my trip to the Canary Islands.

There seemed to be lots of supernatural stories about the islands. They were even mentioned in Homer's *Odyssey*. Legend recounted how, borne on gentle breezes, many had sailed to their doom on these islands, believed to hold golden apples hidden in a cave. The cave was supposedly guarded by beautiful nymphs who were actually wild animals ready to rip the sailors apart.

I wasn't worried about wild animals but wasn't sure how safe the countryside would be for a foreign woman traveling by herself. So I decided to stay on the Grand Canary Island first, since it seemed the most modernized. Then I'd figure out the rest of my itinerary.

Between shopping trips, I went to the gym to build up my muscle strength and stamina for what might be a physically demanding trip. I tried to eat well and sleep well. I did have sex a few times with Ivan, though he always wanted more. I told him this was my farewell gift to him—in my opinion, much more generous than anything I could afford to buy him.

Looking for real witches was not the only reason for my trip. Since my string-breaking I wanted to test whether I really possessed special powers. And, of course, advice from a tree is unusual enough that one needs to consider it seriously. But I also needed a break from Ivan. Over the four years of our relationship, I felt that my spirit was confined by his overly money-conscious one.

The trip would be an escape, during which I could perhaps figure out what I really wanted in life—and in love. Did I need to be spoiled rotten with material things? Or was it adventure and mystery that I really craved? For Ivan, travel was just another chance to flash his wealth. I won't say I didn't get enjoyment from this, but I feared it would soon seem hollow. I also feared he would tire of me—or any other woman—after a few years. I did not want to end up like poor Mrs. Song.

But for now I'd set it all aside and focus on my goal. I wasn't sure if the trip would be a good move, but because of my dream I'd come to believe it was part of my destiny. I wondered if my journey would be like that of the three heroes in the famous Chinese novel *Journey to the West*. In the story a monk and his companions, a pig and a monkey, travel west from China to India in search of mystical truth in the form of Buddhist sutras.

On the way they cross treacherous seas and encounter endless adventures such as climbing the Flaming Mountain, passing the Water Curtain Cave, entering the Entangled Silk Grotto inhabited by spider seductresses, even plunging to the pit of hell. Most dangerous of all were the many demons along their journey, all of whom wanted a chunk of the high monk Xuan Zhuang's flesh because they believed that eating it would give them immortality.

Braving all these dangers, the four made their way safely back to China with the sutras. I was not so arrogant as to compare myself to these intrepid travelers. I only hoped that, like them, I'd survive whatever adventures awaited me and bring back not soul-saving sutras but a humble book to gain tenure with. And, if I was lucky, a collection of stories to entertain my grandchildren during my old age.

Ivan promised to see me off at the airport, but at the last minute couldn't make it; he had to participate in an international conference call with several rich clients. To compensate, he paid for a fancy limo for Brenda and me. But of course I'd rather have had his company—and his help with my luggage.

I slept fitfully during the long overseas flights, alternating worrying about what I was leaving behind and what awaited me. I wondered if I was being courageous or stupid. Brenda certainly thought the latter. For her, leaving behind a rich boyfriend was simply crazy.

Just before I'd boarded the plane, she'd said, "Sister, you're hopeless, but I still care about you. So be careful not to fall into a volcano in any of those islands! Or end up cooked in a witch's cauldron!"

We both laughed and hugged. She waved as I stepped onto the plane.

When the plane finally touched down on the Grand Canary Island's runway, I felt a huge jolt both on my bottom and in my brain. At that moment I wished I were back in my familiar surroundings with my sister and maybe even with Ivan. According to Brenda, this would be the biggest mistake I'd ever made.

However, I was happily surprised that the Aeropuerto de Gando airport on Grand Canary Island was clean, spacious, and quite modern. After going through immigration and passing by people jabbering in Spanish and other exotic languages, I went up to the hotel booth and booked a rather expensive one—Santa Teresa—in the capital, Las Palmas.

The taxi drove along the highway with the sea on one side and hills on the other. Red-roofed and white-walled houses were scattered along the edge of the hills. There were many buildings with huge pipes jutting up, I assumed for converting seawater to fresh, as I'd read about in the guide books.

The weather was as pleasant as the books had promised: soothing breezes under a warming sun. Strangely I felt a subtle familiarity, as if I'd been here before. But I also felt anxious, wondering what sort of strange things went on in the wooded hills.

Finally the taxi pulled to a stop in front of my hotel. I paid, got my luggage, registered at the counter, and then entered my room—all in one swift motion, like running-style calligraphy. Despite being fatigued from the long flights, I forced myself to unpack and take a shower. Feeling somewhat refreshed, I went down to the lobby and approached the concierge desk, behind which stood a bearded young man in a neat gray uniform.

I tried out my Spanish, a little rusty since college. "Señor, I've just arrived here; can you recommend anything worth seeing?"

Of course I did not ask him where I could find witches.

He eyed me curiously. "From China, señorita?"

"Chinatown, San Francisco."

He studied me with curiosity. "You speak Spanish well for a foreigner."

"Gracias."

"How do you know Spanish?"

"Because as a child, it was my dream to marry Picasso, not knowing that he's already married—and dead."

He laughed, his teeth gleaming under the lobby's bright lighting. "Yes, he was the greatest artist of all. Señorita, if you're going to stay longer, you should definitely see all seven islands. However, I recommend you go to Tenerife Island tomorrow if you can."

"Why Tenerife and why tomorrow?"

"Don't you know that Tenerife is called the Jewel of the Atlantic and is the most popular of the seven islands? It's paradise there!"

"Of course I've read about it in guide books, but why tomorrow?"

"Believe me," he said, and his eyes shot out some mysterious sparks, "go there tomorrow and you won't be disappointed. I promise.

It's our famous carnival. Then you can come back here. If you take the express ferry, it's only about an hour's ride, an easy trip."

He pulled out a small book. "My advice is to get the round-trip boat tickets now, since they're almost sold out."

"All right." I was eager to catch the carnival. For me, the best way to learn about a place is to visit its markets and holiday events. You learn a lot about a place by seeing how the inhabitants enjoy themselves.

Along with my ticket he handed me a brochure on Tenerife Island. "Don't forget to bring a big hat and sunscreen. It's very hot during the day."

Back in my room, suddenly overcome by jet lag and exhaustion, I collapsed on the bed. I awoke after dark and, after calling Ivan and Brenda to tell them I'd arrived safely, I decided not to go out, but rather to eat a good meal at the hotel's restaurant and then have a full night's sleep.

Awakening early the next morning, I went down to the small hotel café for breakfast. Whether it was jet lag, or the sea air, or something else, I was ravenous and ate everything in sight: fresh-squeezed orange juice, rolls, yogurt, muesli, a cereal with raw rolled oats, grains, fruits, seeds, and nuts mixed with milk, fresh-baked bread, fruit salad, pungent coffee, and a bowl of *gofio,* a local cereal made from barley. Since Laolao always said that a good breakfast is the best start to a good day, I felt happy and hopeful.

An hour later, I was among other tourists on the boat to Tenerife Island. There were about twenty people, casually dressed in T-shirts, jeans or shorts, and sneakers or flip-flops. Most wore wide-brimmed hats. Looking excited, they busied themselves snapping pictures of their family and friends against the background of the turquoise sea and the gray sand of the beach. Next to me were two young men with serious expressions, talking in English. One phrase caught my attention: "You know I had another of my premonitions—my sixth sense tells me that something bad is going to happen."

The other one chuckled. "So you think this boat will sink, or a volcano will erupt?"

"Ed, it's no joke, something tragic is going to happen." He

pointed to the sky. "It may come from up there"—he pointed to the ground—"or down here."

I had the feeling that the friend was used to his companion's prognostications and did not take them too seriously.

He replied, somewhat jocularly, "Then maybe it won't affect us. 'Cause we're both going to Tenerife and back by boat."

The guy with the sixth sense remained silent, looking very somber. Despite the bright sun, I felt a chill. I had come here expecting to find strange events, so I thought I should talk to them to find out more. But then I dismissed the premonition as idle talk and turned to look around at the other passengers.

Besides these two men, only one other person attracted my attention. She was a Caucasian woman, about twenty, but somehow seemed both familiar and unusual. She wore long sleeves that flapped in the breeze. Elbow against the rail, she gazed into the distance of the empty sea. Unlike the others, instead of tanned, her face appeared ghostly pale. A distinct feature was the mole between her brows. She carried no camera, not even a purse. But what really contrasted with the lively crowd was her lugubrious expression. Was she pondering the sadness of life and the inevitability of death? Would hers be the tragedy the English-speaking man had just predicted? Suddenly I felt a wave of fear that she had taken the boat ride so she could jump into the sea.

No one seemed to share my anxiety for her. Though her pretty face and mournful expression stood out among the boisterous and excited tourists, only I seemed to notice her. Not even the young man with his ominous prediction.

Finally the ship arrived at Tenerife. No sooner was the boat made fast to the dock than the passengers poured off and dispersed in all directions. I searched in vain for a sight of the pale-faced girl but could not find her in the dense crowd.

Locals and tourists alike were craning their necks and snapping pictures, as policemen frantically blew whistles to control the traffic. Along the shore came a procession of people in colorful masks and costumes, dancing to cheerful, boisterous music. From the windows of the buildings lining the street people leaned out, cheering. Revelers released large balloons, turning the sky into a sea of huge, colorful bubbles. On a TV bus, crews with intense expressions aimed their cameras at the parades.

The marchers moved slowly, but with animation. Along came brightly made-up clowns, gun-toting soldiers, pirates wearing wide-brimmed hats and long swords, kings in ermine robes, half-naked, curvaceous women singing and swaying, drums banging out loud tattoos, maybe to scare away evil spirits. Following them was a seemingly endless cast of characters: cowboys, bare-chested Indians, the Statue of Liberty, and to my delight, Chinese kung-fu fighters striking intimidating poses, and yelling, "Ooh! Aaah! Aiiiya!"

I held up my camera, my fingers rapidly pressing the shutter button, its *click, click, click* pleasing to my ears.

In front of the street stalls, customers lined up to buy ready-made costumes, colorful wigs, and painted masks, both comical and scary. The drinks and snacks looked colorful and tempting: sugared apples, stir-fried wheat noodles with scallion, grilled fish with pepper, chunks of meat emanating enticing aromas, rows of yellowish corn, looking like babies swaddled in green blankets. I bought a sugared apple, savoring its sweetness as I let myself be carried along with the flow.

A big fellow dressed as King Kong lumbered in front of me, pretending to snatch at my apple.

I made a scared expression as I screamed in Spanish, "Please don't take away my forbidden apple!"

He laughed, struck a fist high in the air, and then disappeared into the crowd.

I was feeling relaxed and had all but forgotten my need to do fieldwork when I spotted a small group of women wearing black capes, tall conical hats, and carrying brooms—witches. I didn't know if they were ordinary people dressed up as witches for the festival or if they were the real thing—if one can even tell a real witch by how she dresses. I'd come in search of real witches. Could I have found them so quickly?

There were four of them, their ages ranging from twenties to fifties. Faces painted, they were chanting strange, eerie songs. It seemed that nobody paid them any special attention. The onlookers probably thought they were ordinary women in costumes. I suspected otherwise; I wasn't sure why.

The oldest one noticed me staring at her and to my utter surprise, squeezed through the crowd to approach, her small entourage following. I tried to back away, but before I could they were already right in front of me.

"Come join us," the head witch said, quite abruptly.

"Join you?"

She flung her head back and laughed. "We're witches. And you're one of us."

I felt my scalp tingle. "How can you tell?"

She smiled. "We know our kind. Even though you're yellow and we're white."

"What do you want?" My voice turned angry.

"I've never met an Asian witch, so maybe we can teach each other—you know, juju, strong magic."

With a swift movement of her crooked hand, she took out a piece of paper, scribbled on it, and then thrust it into my hand. I snatched it like a lost traveler grabbing a glass of water in the desert. A quick glance revealed the name "Cecily" and an address. Before I could ask another question, the entourage had already disappeared into the sea of tourists and performers.

Was this a joke, one of the festival's pranks? A real witch handing me her name and address? Feeling dizzy, I lost interest in watching the parade and went to sit at a nearby street café. I ordered black coffee to clear my head. Was the dark color of my drink an omen? Sipping the bitter liquid and watching the parade go by in a blur, I heard the sound of English next to me. I turned and saw the same two young men from the boat. This time they noticed me.

The older one smiled. "Tourist?"

I nodded, returning a smile. "And you?"

"Yes, we're from the U.S." He hesitated, then continued. "If you need company, you're most welcome to join us. We'll be here for a while. By the way, I'm Kyle and this is my younger brother, Ed."

I shook my head, smiling. "Kyle, may I ask you a question?"

"Of course, go ahead."

"We were on the same boat from Grand Canary. I overhead you talking to Ed about a tragedy coming—either in the sky or on the ground. Were you serious?"

Kyle looked a bit uneasy. "My mom always said I have a sixth sense."

"Why did she think that?"

"Sometimes I seem to see things happen before they actually do."

"Hmm . . . but do those things *really* happen?"

He smiled. "Fortunately never the way I envisioned them."

"What do you mean?"

He took a sip of his drink. "Sometimes they did occur, but much later. Actually it's a burden. Because I always worry that a tragedy is about to happen. Wherever I go, I see signs. . . ."

"Are you frightened by these signs?"

"I'm used to them." He shrugged.

I was wondering if I should tell them about my breaking of the guitar string but decided to keep it to myself. No reason to make them think that I was crazy.

So I changed the subject. "What are you two doing here?"

"Scuba diving. What about you?"

"I'm here to find witches."

The two men laughed. "You mean like those costumed ones in the parade?"

When I didn't respond, they exchanged glances.

Ed took a small paper package from his knapsack and opened it. "They pushed us to buy this."

He pulled out a vial of colorful liquid floating with herbs. Or animal parts?

"Pretend witches selling us pretend medicine!" He made a face. "But at least the stuff is interesting, isn't it?"

I was pretty sure this was real witches' medicine. I'd learned something about ancient Chinese medicine from Laolao—not only herbs like ginseng and goji berry, but also gecko tail, snake bladder, bear bile, deer antler, rhinoceros horn, tiger penis. . . .

Now Kyle spoke. "Take this if you want. It's of no use to us."

After a moment's hesitation I accepted the vial.

"Anyway, they said they sell this in the Witches' Market."

"Witches' Market?" My ears perked up. "Do you know where that is?"

Kyle took out his map and pointed with his finger. "I believe it's somewhere here in the south of the island."

"Did they tell you anything more about the Witches' Market?"

He thought for a while. "We heard that it's open on the first Saturday every month—and that it's not on any map."

I was anxious to control my excitement so I stood up, and said, "Well, I have to go. Thank you for the information. Maybe I'll see you again."

"Sure. See you around. We're at the Santa Catalina Hotel."

"Okay. I'm staying at the Santa Teresa on Grand Canary."

We waved good-bye to one another. I decided that I'd had enough carnival for the day and so took the next ferry back to my hotel.

5

Maiden Fortress and Heartbreak Castle

The next morning I went back to the hotel café. This time I ordered the traditional Spanish breakfast. The plate arrived piled high with cooked ham, chorizo sausage, cheese, and jamon Serrano. Although it was more than I could eat, I had wanted to try the *plátano* ("banana") *flambé* served with orange segments and sprinkled with demerara sugar. After that, wishing I could eat more but feeling stuffed, I had another cup of the strong Spanish coffee.

One more week remained before the next Witches' Market, so I decided to visit Cecily. I was nervous about this—she might be an evil person—but I'd come to meet witches so I felt I had no choice.

After I signed the bill for breakfast, I went to the reception desk and handed Cecily's note to the same bearded young man who'd helped me before.

"Could you tell me how to go to this place?"

He looked at the paper, then took out a map and studied it. Then he said, his expression puzzled, "Señorita, I believe this is in the south of Tenerife Island, not the Grand Canary. Anyway, why this place?"

"Something wrong with the address?"

"It . . . looks like it's in some remote area. Tenerife's south is very barren, nothing like the pleasant north." He cast me a worried look. "I don't think it is good for you to visit there."

I was not going to tell him the real reason why I wanted to go there, so I said, "I have a friend there. I am sure it will be safe to visit her."

"Sorry, señorita. Maybe she should meet you here. This place is in the middle of nowhere. Besides, it has a story. . . ."

"Can you tell me the story?"

"I don't really know it, only that it's something strange with a sad ending." Now he looked at me curiously. "Your friend should come here."

This man was getting rather annoying. Did he think he was my father? "Don't worry about me. But thanks for your concern," I said.

The next day I was back on the ferry to Tenerife, this time bringing my hand luggage with me. The carnival had ended yesterday and so I'd had no trouble booking a hotel room. I'd taken a nap and overslept, so I had to hurry to dress and get started on my journey to meet the witches.

I had to ask several taxi drivers before finding one who was willing to take me to the address on the slip of paper. His taxi was a rickety old Ford, and I sensed that the driver, barely out of his teens, agreed to take me only because he was desperate for business.

When we were on our way, I asked, "Have you been doing this for long?"

"Not long. This car is my uncle's, but he was busy today. I substitute for him."

My heart sank. "You think you can find the way?"

He lifted up a torn, stained map. "See? I have this. Señorita, relax. Take a nap. When you wake up, we'll be there."

Maybe he knew witchcraft, too, because I quickly fell into a deep, dreamless sleep. It seemed but a moment had passed when I felt a light touch on my shoulder.

The kid had already opened my door. "We're here, señorita. What time you want me to come back?"

I got out, stretched my limbs, and looked around. In front of me was a huge grassy expanse. At the end of a narrow footpath was a huge mansion. It was really a castle, with terra-cotta walls, dark green leaded glass windows, and a peaked slate roof. The crenulated towers, or turrets, stood like giants on guard. Though imposing, there was a pathetic air about the place. If an object could have feelings, then it definitely was not feeling well.

I turned back to the kid. "Can you come back before sunset?"

"No problem."

"Where are you going now?"

"To get something to eat and take a nap. Don't worry, señorita, I'll be back."

"All right." I paid him for the first trip plus a generous tip, hoping he'd come back in pursuit of another fare and an even more generous tip.

"Good luck," he said, and smiled, then went back inside the car and started the engine.

I watched the car until it disappeared down the road, then turned around to face the castle. A sudden fear gripped me. What was I doing here by myself? To see witches, really? Maybe at this very moment they were concocting soup mixed with menstrual blood. Or cooking the human flesh of their most recent visitor. Or perhaps the place was deserted and I was the victim of an elaborate practical joke. Or some sort of kidnapping. But it was too late to back out, so I braced myself and began to walk toward the castle to begin my witch-hunting.

In the far distance, patches of ocean showed between the thick tree trunks. To the right of the castle, behind a low fence, stood a white horse, its mane swaying in the breeze, the only sign of life in this strange place. I went up to the haughty creature to stroke his nose and long mane. He stared at me with what I interpreted as kind, though sad, eyes. I was sure he could tell a moving story—if only he could talk. Unfortunately I was not like the Confucius' student Gong Yechang, who could understand animals' thoughts.

Just then the horse raised his head and neighed, as if trying to tell me the secrets of the castle. If he was trying to tell me something, I couldn't tell what it was, so I just stroked his beautiful mane once more and resumed my walk toward the castle. When I stood in front of it, I felt its surrealistic aura even more strongly.

A signboard painted in red read:

MAIDEN FORTRESS

A strange name. Did it mean that all those who dwelled within were young women? After my knocks on the door elicited no response, I decided to walk around the edifice to better sense its *qi,* to feel whether it was positive, negative, or even haunted. Peeking through the narrow windows, I could make out some forlorn-looking furniture, colored vases, dingy oil paintings, and knickknacks that looked more like burdens than decorations.

I circled the building completely without seeing any signs of a living human. I decided to explore the grounds a little. After wandering for nearly an hour I passed beyond a thicket of trees and spotted a pond sparkling under the afternoon sun. As I approached I saw four heads bobbing on the jade green water. Not sure how I would be received, I hid behind one of the nearby tree trunks. After intense scrutiny, I recognized the heads as belonging to the witches I'd encountered during the carnival.

The four women were singing, laughing, and splashing water on each other. After a few minutes, they stood up and started to the shore. All of them were stark naked. In front was Cecily. Though middle-aged, she was surprisingly attractive, with long red hair, full breasts with nipples like two large berries, curvy hips, and dense vegetation between her thighs. The woman behind her was somewhat less voluptuous, but still shapely. The other two were younger, probably a few years younger than me, and looked very much alike, possibly twins. Both had lithe, muscular figures and strong legs.

The four didn't pick up any clothes to cover themselves with—there apparently weren't any close by. I moved back around the tree trunk to watch them as they walked through the thicket and then sat down together where a large picnic cloth had been spread out. Cecily started to unpack a straw hamper, bringing out bells, purple candles, wineglasses, and jars of herbs. Together the women arranged the objects around the cloth. One of the twins took candles from a box and handed them to her sister, who lit each one, then placed it on the ground to form a circle. The light gave out a mysterious glow accompanied by a subtly intoxicating scent.

It was then that I realized that the sky had begun to turn dark. I guessed the driver had already left, if he'd even had any intention of coming back for me. Anyway, I could not pull myself away from the sight of these strange women.

Now the four women stood in a circle, closed their eyes, and seemed to meditate. They intoned a strange song. Next they dipped twigs into jars of water and sprinkled it in the air. Then, holding hands and raising them heavenward, they began to dance. As they circled the cloth, their breasts swayed, waists twisted, and legs kicked suggestively. After a few minutes they paused, swept the ground with small brooms, and lifted the bells to resume their rhythmic dance.

Ending their ritual, they hugged, kissed, and downed some dark liquid, either wine or some homemade concoction.

Then, suddenly, Cecily spit fire from her mouth!

"Oh my!" I blurted out.

The women all turned toward me. Instead of looking surprised at the intrusion, they smiled.

"Hey, señorita, welcome to the circle of witches!" Cecily said.

I stepped away from the tree I was partially hidden behind and approached them cautiously.

"You're the Asian witch we met at the carnival. What are you doing here?"

As if in a trance, I told them my name and that I was Chinese, though lived in America.

Cecily extended a long-nailed hand. "Come, Eileen, let's dance, chant, and drink to celebrate life!"

Before I knew what was happening, they had come up to me and swiftly pulled off my top, sneakers, and jeans. They then dragged me into their circle. Next they picked up their twigs to flick water onto me. I found myself drinking their strange concoction and joining them in dancing and chanting. Though I had no idea what the chant meant, it was pleasing to my ears. I felt myself gradually slipping into another universe. . . .

When I woke up the next morning the sun was filtering through lace curtains. I shaded my forehead and looked around me. A plain, fortyish, and slightly plump woman sat by the bed, reading a newspaper. I lifted my head from the pillow.

Before I could saying anything, she yelled, *"Qué bueno!"* and dashed away.

Seconds later, she hurried back. Accompanying her was a robust, broad-shouldered, fiftyish man with a rugged face, a straight, high nose, and intense eyes. Before I could say anything he spoke to me in accented English.

"Señorita, I'm glad that you're awake. Welcome to Heartbreak Castle."

Heartbreak Castle. Why would someone give his residence such an unlucky name? Anyway, wasn't it called the Maiden Fortress?

"Señor, who are you? I don't know where I am. Have we met?" I said in Spanish.

I realized I'd spoken abruptly, and that I was an uninvited guest, or intruder, in this man's place. But he looked delighted.

"Qué bueno, usted habla Spanish!" Good, you speak Spanish.

I smiled and apologized for my rudeness.

He smiled back. His teeth were neat and white, contrasting nicely with his tanned skin.

"Señorita, my housekeeper, Maria, found you some distance from my castle, by the pond. You were so drunk that you could hardly walk, so she came back to get me and I carried you here. Are you feeling okay?"

I took stock of myself. I didn't feel great, but everything was intact, so I replied, "I have a headache, but otherwise I'm fine, Señor. . . ."

"Alfredo Alfrenso. And you are?"

"Eileen Chen, I'm from San Francisco." He was being polite, but I suddenly felt embarrassed. "Señor Alfrenso, I've already troubled you and Maria for the whole night, so I think I should be on my way." I tried to sit up but felt a wave of dizziness.

I remembered that the witches had taken off my clothes before I danced with them and I was suddenly mortified. Was I still naked? I lifted the bedsheet and was relieved to see my body in a loose gown. I hoped it was Maria who'd put the gown on for me and not her master. Fortunately I was far enough from San Francisco for anyone there to hear about my current state of affairs.

Maria handed me a glass of water, which I gulped down as if stranded in the desert.

"You better stay with us for a day or two until you're fit to go home," Alfrenso said.

"No, I'm feeling better," I said, but just then I had a coughing spell.

"Eileen, I'm afraid you can't. You caught pneumonia and I had my doctor come give you an injection of antibiotic. Here in Spain we believe in hospitality. You were nearly unconscious for a while. I must keep you here until you've completely recovered."

I had pneumonia? I coughed again and realized he must be right.

He went on. "You need to eat. Maria will fix you something,"

He seemed to be a very kind man, so kind that I wondered if he hoped to take advantage of me. But this Spanish gentleman seemed quite refined, not at all that kind of man. I thought he must be rich to live in this castle and therefore could find plenty of women, so he had no need of me. I felt relief wash over me. And actually I wasn't helpless. As a shamaness, or at least someone from a shamanic lineage, I knew all sorts of supernatural arts, or at least thought I did, in case I needed to handle this older man.

Later, after I woke up from another nap, Maria helped me change out of my nightgown and into a dress. I couldn't help but wonder whose gown it was—Señor Alfrenso's wife's? A mistress's? But I was too hungry to speculate further and so allowed myself to be led into the kitchen. It was quite roomy, larger than the entire apartment in which I'd spent my Hong Kong childhood. There was a long, sturdy table, a metal-covered counter, an ancient-looking stove, and even a chandelier.

Maria leaned over her pots while Alfrenso sat across from me, sipping his coffee and looking pensive. I wondered if someone entering the kitchen and seeing us together would imagine that we were lovers, enjoying breakfast together after a night of passion.

"Señor Alfrenso—"

"Please just call me Alfredo."

"Alfredo." I took a sip of the chilled, fresh orange juice. "I think this place is called the Maiden Fortress? But you said it is Heartbreak Castle. . . ."

"Yes, I changed the name. I just haven't gotten around to changing the plaque outside."

"Oh . . . I . . ." I almost said that I was sorry to hear about the "heartbreak" but feared it would be impolite to ask.

Some silence passed, punctuated by my coughing. When I had cleared my throat, he said, "Eileen, can you tell me how you ended up here?"

I was at a loss as to how to answer him. Would he believe my convoluted story of coming here to find witches and ending up dancing naked with them? What would he think of me if I told him? But surely he must know about the witches, as they carried out their rituals near his castle.

"I came to the island to do research for my book," I said rather timidly. "I'm a professor of anthropology at San Francisco State University."

He cocked his head. "Professor! It's an honor to have a professor as my guest." He paused to sip more coffee. "Tell me why you came all the way to Tenerife Island and ended up at my castle. Do you expect to find happiness in a heartbreak castle?"

"Heartbreak Castle or not, we're all looking for happiness, aren't we?"

He eyed me with great curiosity. "Yes, we all are, whether we find it or not. It's the journey, not the destination, right?"

It was as if I'd just engaged in a Zen conversation with a high monk somewhere on a deserted mountain.

"What is your research about?" he asked.

I didn't want to say that my field was witches and shamanism because I did not want to sound too strange or scary. But the rugged man in front of me didn't seem as if he would scare easily.

I decided to change the subject. "Alfredo, do you live alone here?" It was none of my business, but my curiosity won out.

"Yes, I mean except for my housekeeper, Maria. I also have a driver and gardener, but they don't live here."

"Do you have woman friends?" I couldn't help but ask.

I suddenly realized this sounded like I was trying to find out if he had a wife, or girlfriend, or mistress. And that if he did not, that I was available. He might think that anyway since I was the woman who had slept in his bed uninvited!

Alfredo didn't really answer my question, but replied, "I don't have many friends, unless you consider my staff and my horse my friends." He gave me another intense glance. "You still haven't told me why you are here."

I couldn't think of a good lie quickly enough, so I said, "Oh . . . I heard there was a nice castle here, so I came to take a look."

"And instead of knocking on my door, you went and got drunk by the pond?"

"No, I didn't get drunk. I fainted from exhaustion and hunger."

Of course he knew better, because he must have smelled the alcohol on my breath. And no one takes off her clothes because she is hungry.

Alfredo looked amused but did not press me any further. "I need to go away for a few days. Please stay until you feel well enough to travel back to your hotel. Maria will take good care of you. While you were sleeping we checked your pockets and saw that you're staying at the Santa Teresa. In fact, Maria has already canceled your reservation and Adam, my driver, is on his way to pick up your luggage.

"I am afraid you will find it boring just staying in this old place. I suggest you do some sightseeing. Adam can take you around and bring you back to the city when you are ready. If you ride horseback, you can take my horse Lonely Star—we call him Lonlon—to explore the beautiful ruins around here. You are welcome to stay as long as you want. It would be my pleasure to see you again when I return. It's lonely here. I did have a wife, but she passed away many years ago."

"I'm so sorry."

"Thank you. But life goes on for those of us left behind."

I nodded. "When will you be back?"

"A few days. Maybe a week. You can come and go. If you ring the bell loudly, Maria will let you in, even in the middle of the night. We do keep the doors locked even though there's nothing here worth stealing, except maybe my heart. Don't worry, no one will come here to trouble you."

How was he so sure? What about the witches? And the old castle was just the kind of place that harbors ghosts. Alfredo Alfrenso was not worried about leaving a stranger here by herself and he seemed to trust his servants completely. Strange. Here was a man who was quite handsome and seemed to have money, but said he had no friends and nothing but his heart to steal. Yet the few rooms I'd already seen were filled with antique furniture and old paintings. Perhaps Alfredo simply did not care; he seemed to be a sad man who took no joy in his possessions.

"Eileen, make yourself at home. When you feel better, you can explore the castle if you want. Some of the rooms are sealed off—it's a big place and we can't use all of it. You won't get lost.

"Maria has already cleaned and prepared a room for you. Everything you need should be there. If you need anything else, just tell her. You can help yourself to food, but Maria will cook your meals, if you tell her what time you want them."

I was astonished. Last night I'd slept outside—though not by choice—and now I was living in a luxury I'd never imagined. And it seemed I really was welcome to stay as long as I wanted. But I had no idea of what life would be like here or how long I would feel comfortable with this stranger.

"Alfredo, thanks for you hospitality. But it can't be very convenient for you to have a guest."

"No inconvenience at all."

He started to get up and I knew this was my last chance to ask the question that had really been on my mind.

"Alfredo, do you know the witches?"

He cocked his head. "Witches?"

Obviously he did not want to discuss it, so, lest I offend my host, I let the matter drop.

6

Sculptor in the Ruins

After Alfredo left, Maria came to the kitchen, cleaned up the plates, and showed me to my guest room. She took out a flashlight and a bell and put them on the bedside table.

"If you need me, just ring the bell as loud as you can," she said.

"*Gracias,* Maria, I will." I smiled.

After Maria left, I took a shower before dozing off. When I awakened I felt pretty much back to normal. I decided that my first priority was to explore the castle and its surroundings. With the owner gone, I could wander freely around the strange building. It seemed that I knew even less about the place now than I had when I first spotted it from the road. I didn't even know why Cecily had given me Alfredo's address, and why Alfredo claimed to have no idea of the witches' existence.

Although the place was called a castle, it was not a huge fortress with a moat, drawbridge, portcullis, and tall watchtowers. I counted about fifteen rooms, many concealed behind thick, padlocked doors. There was a main hall with leaded glass windows, and from the high ceiling was suspended a row of dim chandeliers. Thick wooden chairs with dusty upholstery were scattered around. I guessed that the room was once used for parties and balls, but the current owner didn't seem the type to host such events. Indeed, the dusty, tattered upholstery and stale air suggested that it had not been used for a long time.

Next to the main hall was a series of smaller rooms. There was a music room with an elaborately carved harp and a huge grand piano set against the stone wall, with music scores in uneven piles on the floor underneath it. The two instruments were silent, looking like sexless mistresses long deserted by their lovers.

I wandered into the master bedroom and three other guest rooms. Judging from the austere décor of the master bedroom, I was sure that Alfredo Alfrenso didn't have a woman in his life, at least not now. He was rich, manly, and seemingly a warm, generous person, but if he had any women, where were they hiding? Or was it him who was hiding? But from whom?

I went deeper into the castle's womb, feeling oddly anxious. There was an eerie buzz in my ears, as if the walls were trying to tell stories of what they had seen over the years. Some happy, some sad, some ghostly. Now I was using my flashlight and could see more doors down the long corridor, but I had no courage to look any farther. Alfredo had told me that some parts of the castle were sealed off, but he didn't say why. Maybe there was nothing in all these rooms, but I wasn't going to push my luck.

Lonely like its master, the castle nonetheless radiated an intense *yin* energy. Feeling a chill, I tightened my thin jacket, then hurried back to my room. I sat by the writing desk, took out a pencil, and from memory drew a simple map, in case I wanted to explore further. I also wrote down the events of the last few days, especially my encounters with the two brothers, the witches, and Alfredo Alfrenso. I wondered what other adventures I would have to write about before I found my way home.

The next morning I awakened to the mouthwatering scent of bacon and coffee teasing my taste buds and stomach. When I arrived in the kitchen, Maria smiled warmly, revealing a few irregular teeth. Soon I was heartily devouring bacon, scrambled eggs, and fried potatoes, washing it all down with the strong coffee and sweet orange juice. Eating and drinking, I kept raising my thumb in appreciation of Maria's kindness to the hungry traveler.

When I was finished, I told the housekeeper I'd be out and might not return until evening. Though I didn't mention it to Maria, my hope was that I would run into the witches again.

"The whole day, señorita? Maybe that's not a good idea." The housekeeper looked concerned.

"Don't worry, I'll be very careful."

"You have the bell with you?"

I nodded. However, if I did run into mishap and ring the bell, I doubted she'd hear me. I planned to walk as far as necessary to find out more about this peculiar place.

Outside, the sky was covered with dense, dark clouds, the morning sun sneaking through to cast long, surrealistic shadows. My feet propelled me forward as if they had eyes of their own that saw something in the distance. Soon it started to drizzle, the tiny raindrops pricking my face like gnawing ants.

I ducked under a tree and sat on a rock, looking and listening. Why did Alfredo choose to live in this lonely place? I saw something moving in the distance, veiled by the drizzle. As it approached me, I saw that it was Alfredo's white horse, Lonely Star. The animal lowered his head and looked at me tenderly as if I were his lover. Did any women ever fall in love with a horse? Or harbor intense romantic feelings? If so, they would never admit to this secret love for a beast.

I went up to the horse and reached to caress his muzzle and smooth his mane. Full of tender feelings for the animal, I asked, "Dear, do you want to tell me something?"

To my utter surprise, the horse neighed and tossed his head.

"You want to take me somewhere?"

He neighed again as if saying yes.

Ivan had taken me for riding lessons, so I knew something about horses and could ride short distances. However, even though Lonely Star looked friendly, I wasn't in the mood to ride, not today. I caressed his muzzle again, telling him, "I'm fine sitting on this rock."

He kept looking at me, refusing to budge.

"All right, then, be gentle. Don't hurt me or throw me off, all right?"

I rose up from my rock, stood on it, and climbed onto the horse. I had never ridden bareback, so I leaned over and clung to his neck as he began a leisurely amble. Then his hooves picked up speed, and though I shouted at him to stop he kept going until we arrived at a deserted ruin. He stopped by a low wall and I climbed off only to see him gallop away.

"Wait!" I yelled. "Don't go away! How will I get back?"

I had been so busy holding on during the ride that I really had no sense of where I was. I looked around and was relieved to see someone in the distance.

It was a white-haired man, busy working with his hands, but I couldn't tell what he was doing. The bizarre thought crossed my brain that he might be digging up graves to rob them. Then I drew closer to watch, hiding myself behind a boulder. At first I thought he was doing something with a knife, perhaps skinning an animal. My heart skipped a beat.

However, when I strained my eyes to look more carefully, I saw that he was chipping at a stone with a chisel. Since he was completely immersed in his work and looked too old to be dangerous, I took a deep breath and went straight up to him. To my surprise, the old man didn't even raise his head to look at the approaching stranger.

Besides the one in his hand, there were five or six other stone sculptures scattered on the ground. One was an odd-shaped abstraction, its surfaces twisting and winding, as if embodying the mysteries of space itself. Another was a simple figure but somehow a visual poem. Keeping silent, I took in this haunting scene, with the wrinkled hands of an old man giving birth to smoothly modulated surfaces.

Had I not seen the sure movements of his hands, I might have thought that the old man himself was just another statute. Whether he was oblivious to my presence or deliberately ignoring it, I could imagine that he'd been here almost as long as the stones upon which he worked.

My eyes fell upon the carving in the old man's hands, that of a voluptuous woman with a baby's head making an agonizing exit from her life-granting vagina. The mother's expression was of joy and pain, nirvana and samsara.

I gasped before I could stop myself.

The old man looked up and stared at me for a few seconds before returning to his role as midwife. Although our eyes met for only a split second, I could tell that he was slightly crazy. Crazy because he lived not in this world but another, one more perfect than the one I lived in. He might be starving, but he wouldn't notice the urging grumbles of his empty stomach, nor care. A genius in art but a fool in life, like van Gogh.

The old man's hands stopped. He put down the statue, took his scarf from his shoulder, and wiped his hands, his neck, and his dripping face. He then tenderly wiped the mother-birthing-baby figurine with the same filthy cloth. With an expression of satisfaction, he caressed the baby's head while smiling and making funny faces at it.

I realized that this meant he was finished and would leave mother and baby at the intense moment of life beginning. Setting his creation down, he took a cigarette from his pocket, lit it, and started to blow smoke in concentric circles. I watched the circles disappear into the air for a few moments, then looked down at the other works that were spread out on the ground.

There was a boy holding his penis, peeing. A brood of snakes engaged in a choreographed dance on a goddess's head. A big fish, in the mouth of which perched a smaller fish, in the mouth of which was an even smaller fish. A baby with a mischievous smile, sitting cross-legged on a big flower, his chin supported by his hand, lost in thought.

But I wasn't satisfied just by looking; I wanted to keep one, or more than one, of these modest but evocative creations.

I dropped onto my knees. The old man tilted his head slightly to squint at me, then went back to blowing smoke rings. He paid me no more attention than if I were one of the many solitary ghosts that had wandered all the way from ancient China to this deserted land.

Without asking permission, I reached to pick up the fish-within-fish and the birthing mother. My tone was pleading like a toddler anxiously asking his mother for a huge pink marshmallow. "Señor, would you let me buy these, please?"

He lifted his head to stare at me again with his seemingly bottomless eyes. I was certain that this man was truly insane. His mind was not in the real world, only in the realm of art.

"Can you please sell these to me?" I pleaded again.

Now he looked at me as if I were the crazy one, trying to purchase his work, which was probably worthless in the commercial market. But still, he didn't respond.

Desperate, I fished out a wad of pesetas and laid them on his lap. "Will that be enough?"

This time he studied me curiously, still without uttering a word.

We stared at each other like two cats trapped in a narrow alley.

"This is not enough?" I did not want him to think that I was trying to cheat him.

He still didn't respond. On impulse I quickly stuffed the two statutes inside my pocket and hurried away, my heart screaming as loud as an alarm clock.

Alas, in a few seconds, I heard footsteps chasing me from behind.

"Please let me have them," I muttered. "I gave you a lot for these two small statutes!"

But I knew that just grabbing the statues without his consent was downright wrong. So I stopped and turned to face the mad artist, to see if he was willing to part with his stunning creations. Or if he wanted more money—maybe a lot more. But instead of trying to take back what I had grabbed, he surprised me by stuffing two more statutes into my hands—the snake-headed goddess and the peeing toddler.

"You're selling these too? How much more do you want?"

He shook his hand vehemently, and said, "Ah! You take!"

I pulled out more bills and showed them to him. "You want me to pay you more for all these? Just tell me how much. But I'll have to go back to my place to get more money."

He gave me a vigorous, dismissive wave of his hand, then laughed heartily, displaying a toothless mouth that reminded me of the capacious vagina he'd just created. Suddenly I realized that, just as I thought he was a crazy old mute, he must think me a deluded woman. Only a crazy person would pay such an astronomical amount for a few pieces of stones shaped by a toothless old man living alone among ruins on a remote island.

But to be sure, I waved the bills. "How much more should I pay you?"

He shook his head.

"So you want to give me these two statutes as gifts?" I asked.

This time he emphatically nodded. I almost burst out laughing at my good luck.

Letting out a long, relieved exhalation, I smiled. "Thank you so much, great master."

I put my hands together and bowed. After that, I dashed away, fearing he might change his mind and ask for his treasures back.

It turned out that I was less lost after my horseback ride than I'd feared. To get my bearings, I climbed a small hill and was able to spot the castle off in the distance. Tired after the long walk back, I sunk down on my bed and spread out the four stone sculptures to examine them more closely. First I appreciated them from above, then picked up each in turn and examined it closely. This had been an extremely lucky trip, one that allowed me to acquire these wonderful objects.

I glided my hands over the statues one by one, outlining their subtle contours, grainy textures, and oddly artistic shapes, sensing their creator's unfathomable soul within. Did he foresee the final shape of each work even before his chisel made the first incision? Did his hands have an unspoken philosophy as they made their arduous journey?

Though all the sculptures were exquisite, I liked the mother and half-born infant the best. It reminded me of a relief sculpture I'd once seen in a museum. It told the story of a young mother who had just died of an incurable disease and was sent to hell along with her newborn. Unwilling to renounce her life, she defiantly clung to the Life Gate while trying to reenter. But her efforts would soon be gone like a trace of smoke, for pushing against her on the other side were two giant armored guards.

The baby, though tiny like a thermos, seemed to have sensed the awaiting catastrophe from his mother's agonized cries and the dark, tremendous force pulling her onto the other side. The baby clung tightly to her chest, his tiny face distorted from his hysterical crying. I could almost hear his bawling. The baby's desire to live was so powerfully depicted that I could feel the waves of desperate energy crashing over me, tightening my throat and triggering my tears.

My attention went back to the old man's creation as my finger caressed the baby's tiny head as it seemed to emerge from his mother. Like the one in the museum, would he succeed in pushing through the gate back to life? Or would his head be forever stuck in between? What was the old man trying to express?

"Shhh . . . little one," I said, kissing the to-be-born's bald head, "everything will be all right, just be patient. Your mommy loves you and will protect you from all evils."

I sighed, then picked up the next figurine, that of the fish within fish within fish. Life within life, or if you looked at it from the opposite side, death within death. For each fish was being devoured by a larger one.

I gently put down the fish and picked up the snake-headed goddess. The nine snake heads were all different from each other, some with open mouths and forked tongues sticking out, others with sharp fangs exposed, as if ready to strike. One with eyes closed as if meditating—or more likely just hibernating. I wondered if each was symbolizing a different aspect of life.

Finally, I picked up the peeing toddler. In comparison to the other statutes, this one seemed relatively banal. However, when I looked more carefully, I noticed that a small bird was perching on the boy's head, watching the other little birdie pee.

Appreciating the sculptures made me think of a birthmark that I had. The shape of it was something like a baby in the fetal position, and it was near my own intimate part. My mother had told me that it was the trace of a she-ghost's jealousy of my birth. During Mother's pregnancy, the ghost kept kicking her womb, hoping that I'd end up stillborn. Fortunately, I was saved by Laolao, who concocted a special demon-quelling herb soup to soothe her daughter's pregnancy. And so I came into this world.

I once asked Mother if she knew whose ghost it was and why she was so jealous of me.

Her answer was, "She was an ancestor who had only boys, but all were as hideous as Zhong Kui, the brilliant scholar who committed suicide because he was so ugly. She desperately wanted a beautiful girl. By killing you she could take possession of your body."

Even when I was young, I knew this was total nonsense, especially because everyone knows ghosts envy boys, not girls. So I asked Mother, "Don't all Chinese want boys?"

"Yes and no. Remember the famous Concubine Yang? She became the emperor's favorite woman and brought endless glory to her family."

"If this relative was dead, how would I become her daughter?" I challenged Mother again.

"Because then she could reincarnate!"

It was because of such silly superstitions that I did not want to continue my family's shamanistic lineage, despite Laolao's wishes. Looking at the half-born stone baby reminded me again of my "baby"—the birthmark right next to my vagina. Ivan loved it. He liked to kiss it before we made love, sighing. Once he said, "Ah . . . so sexy. Eileen, you may not be a witch, but you are definitely a born seductress."

"How's that?"

"Because you're born to draw attention to here. . . ." He kissed my birthmark again, then moved farther down. "It shows you are very fertile."

"What does my birthmark have to do with fertility?" I was moaning and asking at the same time.

"Don't you see that it's a baby?"

Back in the present, I just stared at the stone baby in my hands, at the moment happy with art rather than life. I wondered how I had happened to encounter the old man—had Lonely Star intentionally led me to him?

Wondering, I fell into a deep sleep.

PART THREE

7

The Witches' Market

The following morning I woke up feeling confused and disoriented. Already during my short time in the islands, I'd had distinctly odd experiences: the carnival, the mysterious brothers, the nude, dancing witches, Alfredo and his Heartbreak Castle, the crazy old sculptor. What else would I run into? The more, the better as it was all material I could use to write my academic book, and maybe even have enough left over for a novel.

As I pondered recent events, I suddenly realized that today was the first Saturday of the month—reminding me that it was the day of the Witches' Market, what I had traveled so far to see. I gulped down coffee while Maria explained how to find the bus stop.

I walked for about two miles until I finally saw the rusted sign. I waited restlessly for about twenty minutes, until finally the bus pulled up. I climbed aboard and was on my way to another adventure.

I looked around at my fellow passengers as the antique vehicle rattled along the pothole-filled road. Most looked like farm families, their faces leathery from the years spent under the bright sun, dressed in worn, baggy clothes. There were a few hippie world travelers, one sneaking a joint that he hid in between tokes. Animals made up a significant portion of the passengers: chickens, no doubt about to provide a family meal, a few bedraggled dogs, and one cat, bits of its ear missing from previous fights and pink skin showing where his fur had fallen out. Although I was somewhat entertained by the contrast with the buses I rode in San Francisco, I was relieved when I finally arrived at the marketplace.

The Witches' Market was adjacent to the main public market area but somewhat hidden behind the back of a huge building, so that people were unlikely to find it unless they knew where to look. Although I had a general idea of where it was, I wandered around for a while before I found it.

The first thing that struck me was that all the vendors, and nearly all of the customers as well, were women. Though many fit the stereotype of wrinkled old crones, some were young and pretty. A few even had a young child in tow. Women vendors were mostly dressed in what seemed to be the regional costume of long skirts, tasseled shawls under wide-brimmed hats, and short boots or sandals.

Offered for sale were vials of colorful medicine and herbs, packets of seeds for medicinal or magical plants, pendulums and other paraphernalia for divination, amulets, paper charms for good luck—and probably also for curses.

A few people cast me curious glances, but none expressed hostility toward the exotic stranger intruding upon their territory. I wondered if there was something about me that other witches, like Cecily, could sense. Though I looked different from them on the outside, we were comrades.

Besides witches' supplies, more ordinary items were on display: fruit, vegetables, cans of soda, batteries, as well as beads, plastic jewelry, bolts of hand-dyed fabric and piles of ready-made dresses, animal skins, small carpets, even ordinary household items like pots, thermoses, mirrors, toys, and plastic flowers. It was an odd assortment of traditional handicrafts and prosaic, manufactured items.

Though most of the crowd was obviously local, besides myself there were a few other tourists. They stood out in their shorts and sandals with large cameras hanging over their T-shirts. The tourists particularly attracted the attention of beggars with vacant eyes and blank expressions, squatting behind chipped bowls. Children ran around chasing the tourists with constant giggles and dirty, outstretched hands. At a corner, a bedraggled man of indeterminate age was blowing notes from a flute, sometimes disjointed, sometimes smooth—just like life's journey.

Anxious to obtain documentation for my book, I took out my camera and furiously snapped pictures of everything in sight. After that, I sat down at the corner of a building, took out my notebook, and wrote down my impressions.

When I looked up I noticed that children were crowding around one particular stall. Somehow this seemed to be pointed toward my possible destiny, so I stood up and headed over to the stall. A woman dressed all in black was laying out brightly colored tarot cards on a black velvet cloth. She was obviously a witch, or pretending to be one. Seemingly in her forties, she had a cunning look with a high nose and equally high cheekbones.

Her table was more decorated than most of the others, with a bowl of fresh roses as well as a scattering of crystals of varied size, shape, and color. As if to match her decorations, her face was heavily made up. She noticed me right away, perhaps because I seemed to be the only Asian person in the market. Her half-gloved and many-ringed hand shooed the children away, then signaled me to sit across from her. As if under a spell, I obeyed.

Since everything that had happened recently was entirely unlike anything I'd previously experienced, I thought it would be a good idea to have my life mapped out. As I looked at the cards laid out on her table with their strange figures, they suddenly seemed to have a story to tell me, something about my life that had been hidden from me up until now.

The woman stared into my eyes intensely. "Señorita, the cards are waiting for your question."

I felt stupid. Supposedly a shamaness myself, shouldn't I be able to foresee my own future? Or was I like a doctor who could diagnose others' maladies but not her own?

"Do you want to know about love, money, relationship with Mother Earth, the stars?" the woman asked.

"How about all of the above?"

"Pretty greedy I would say, to ask the cards for so much," she muttered as her gloved hands continued to rearrange the cards.

"All right, then, what about my immediate future—what will happen to me here as a Chinese stranger in this land?"

"Chinese?"

"Yes, but I'm from America."

"Then maybe you should go meet the owner of that restaurant over there."

She pointed to a small eatery at the end of the market. "He's old and lonely and doesn't have any friends left. There aren't many Chinese here." She sighed. "A person is cursed to have a short life, and equally cursed to have an extra-long one, isn't that so?"

She paused to scrutinize me before speaking again. "From your face, I can't tell if you'll live a long life, but I can tell that your life will not be an ordinary one."

"In what way?"

"You really live only half in this world—and half in another one."

I felt a jolt of alarm. "What do you mean?"

"Your destiny is not an ordinary one, unlike your American boyfriend's. You find yourself in remote places. Be prepared to deal with very strange people. All you can do is go with the flow and embrace your fate. Your life will not be easy, but it will be satisfying."

"That doesn't sound too bad."

She looked down at her cards and remained silent for a while. Then she looked back up at me. "Go to see that Chinese man. Because he is old he is a man of knowledge. He can see things that are hidden from me. After all, you share the same ancestors." She tilted her head and laughed. "Maybe even from five thousand years ago!"

"I'll go there after we finish. In the meantime, can you tell me more?"

"All right, I can look at your near future." She gathered up her cards, shuffled them, and spread them out again.

In the past, I'd never paid much attention to tarot cards. Now, as I looked at the spread she had created for me, I sensed that they had many stories to tell, all mysterious, some scary. Even the cards' soft swish as she dropped them onto the table seemed to be an invitation into a world as yet unknown to me.

She studied the cards with a serious expression. "Hmmm . . . complicated."

"How?"

"Your inquiry was not clear and so the cards are not clear." She pointed to a card depicting a man hanging upside down. "Ha, the hanged man. Your life is in suspension. You've been feeling that you're in the middle of nowhere, right?"

I nodded, trying to digest her words.

"Oh! Here's the Ace of Pentacles! You want wealth to come to you from the sky! You must be here to seek the legendary golden apple."

I realized she was referring to the Greek myth that five goddesses dwelled on the island. One guards a golden apple, but the other four lure passing ships and their sailors to their destruction. I'd come here to find witches but wouldn't mind a golden apple as a bonus—but maybe she was warning me not to be lured to my own destruction.

Obviously there were no golden apples. It must be a symbol, but of what? A fortune from Heaven? A loving man? An important discovery? Tenure?

The witch's sibilant voice rose to my ear. "You have two sisters—"

"No, only one."

"No, two, but unfortunately one died." She looked serious. "She might not be a birth sister, but a spirit sister."

I had no idea what she was talking about, but her firm, no-nonsense tone made me wonder if I really did have a second sister somewhere in this world or another.

"All right, if you say so. But what about me *now?*"

She looked back at the cards, holding one up to me. "This is the High Priestess. See, the goddess is draped with many layers of white silk."

I nodded.

"Isis is the goddess who knows all that is hidden. See the sun and moon on her head and the veils behind her? If we could lift them, we would know all, even the secrets of death."

"What if there's nothing behind the veil?" I thought out loud.

"Maybe you are here to find out."

I sighed inside. Suddenly I wasn't sure what I knew—or didn't know.

She pointed to the bird perching beside the goddess on the card. "See the owl?"

I nodded.

"Your vibration led me to pick the High Priestess. Only my card has the owl with her. This shows that she is a witch, like us. She comes because you are her kindred spirit."

The day was growing hotter and I was beginning to feel a little dizzy, a little unsteady on my stool.

"You have been brought here to discover yourself and your spirit sister. And these will reveal your future. They always do."

Though feeling almost faint, I tried to act cool. "I came here to gather material about witches for a book."

She laughed. "Of course you have. And this is the right place! We're all witches here, like you. You can even write yourself into your book."

I needed to change the subject to something more normal. "I came to the market to look for Cecily. Do you know where she is?"

"Cecily? I think I know who she is. But she doesn't come often; she mostly makes her stuff at home and other witches sell it for her. Anyway, they are not here today."

"You know where she lives?"

"No, they keep to themselves. Selfish and secretive. We don't like her and her friends. We don't want to deal with them."

"How's that?"

"They think they're better than us."

It was clear she would say no more about it, so I decided to take my leave. She then demanded a much larger payment than I'd expected. Her pretext was that I would make lots of money from my book, so the extra payment was her share of the royalties in advance.

It must be witch's logic—the logic of no logic. But I paid what she'd asked rather than face an unpleasant scene.

She smiled as she took my money. "Don't forget to see the old Chinese man."

After I left the tarot card reader's stall, instead of further exploring the Witches' Market I decided I would follow her suggestion and meet the old man. I found his restaurant easily, as it was a straight eight-block walk from the marketplace.

Despite its grand name of Oriental Garden, it was a dingy little place with plastic tables, chairs, and handwritten menus taped on the soiled white walls. I sat down at one of the empty tables and looked around. The only other customers were an elderly couple and two middle-aged women whose long, flowing skirts suggested that they were witches taking a break from selling at the market. The old couple cast me a nonchalant glance, then went back to suck up their greasy noodles. The witches were gesturing wildly, too engaged in their own conversation to pay me any attention.

I didn't see the old man. Instead, a young Chinese waitress materialized in front of me. Holding a small notebook and a pen, she gave me a curious once-over, probably surprised to have a Chinese patron. I was more curious than hungry, so I ordered only a pot of jasmine tea and a plate of shrimp dumplings.

When the food came, I asked the waitress in Cantonese, "Is the owner of the restaurant here today?"

"You mean Uncle Wang? He's retired and moved to Grand Canary Island."

"Oh . . . not here?"

"He's ninety-three! His friends here are either gone or in nursing homes."

"No children, grandchildren, even great-grandchildren? No one can take care of him?"

"Uncle Wang never got married, so he decided to spend his last years with a few leftover friends on Grand Canary. He always joked that he needs to be close to the volcanoes to warm his chilled, arthritic bones." She smiled. "He won't admit it, but we think he hopes to meet aliens from a UFO before he dies—he thinks they have the secret of immortality. That's where they land—Grand Canary. Not this little hick place."

"And you are his . . ."

"Youngest niece."

"Since he has you here, why didn't he—"

"We get along okay, but I'm third-generation Chinese, so not as interesting to him as his old friends. Besides, I don't care about volcanoes or UFOs. What I like is fashion, watching TV, and Hello Kitty." She pointed to her shoes, which were pink and adorned with Hello Kitty faces.

She wrote on a piece of paper and handed it to me. "Here's Uncle Wang's address on Grand Canary. Please visit him. I'm sure he'll be very happy to meet a Chinese from America."

"Thanks. I certainly will."

She cast me a curious look. "But why do you want to see Uncle—to talk about volcanoes and UFOs?"

I smiled. "Ah, no. I heard he knows everything about this place and I want to learn more about the island for a book I am writing."

"Yes, he knows all about that old history stuff."

Glad to have gotten the address so easily, I left a big tip for Uncle Wang's niece and headed for the bus stop to go back to Heartbreak Castle.

8

Underground Witches

I slept so deeply that when I awoke it was already noon. Maria fixed me a late breakfast and while I was gulping it down, she asked me what I wanted to do for the day. I'd actually been thinking about visiting the Witches' Market again, but it wasn't open today and I wasn't going to tell Maria about this anyway.

"Señor Alfrenso wants you to stay longer. I can tell he likes you." She smiled mischievously.

I deliberately didn't ask how could she tell, but said, "Hmmm . . . I don't know what to think about this."

She shook her head, still smiling. "You think too much—not good for pretty young woman. Señor said stay, then you like to stay. No?"

I realized that I'd come to like staying in the castle and had no wish to go back to my hotel. Plus, staying at the castle was free.

"All right," I laughed, "maybe I should. Maria, I'm sure Señor is just being hospitable to me."

She shook her head. "I can tell by his eyes. He looks at you differently than he does other women."

"He has many other women?"

"Of course, he's rich and not bad looking."

I did not want to give Maria any more ideas, so I dropped the subject.

My recent adventures kept running through my mind—Maiden Fortress or Heartbreak Castle, Alfredo, Maria, the stone sculptor, the witches, the Chinese restaurant, even the white horse. . . . At moments I feared that all of these were but figments of my imagination.

Though I'd been on the island for only a few days, I had come to feel affection for the people I'd met. It was almost as if I'd lived here during a past life. But I was also apprehensive about staying. Though they seemed nice and harmless, I knew almost nothing about these people. They were strangers, after all, and belonged to a different culture.

I decided I would stay two or three more days at the most, then reconsider. That way I could see the stone sculptor and the witches again, and explore more of the castle. I wanted to know why the name of the castle had been changed from Maiden Fortress to Heartbreak and why Alfredo chose to live by himself in this strange place.

After finishing breakfast, I returned to my room and gathered up my flashlight, whistle, knife, camera, pen, notebook, and jacket. Then I went outside and began to stroll around the castle's stone walls, hoping the fresh air would relax me and help clear my mind.

In the distance, I spotted Lonely Star, the white horse, who trotted right up to me. I gently stroked his mane, then whispered in his ear, pleading for him to take me back to the old sculptor. I climbed on and a few minutes later he stopped, but not at the same place he'd taken me before. I alighted and climbed up a low rock wall, hoping to spot the sculptor. To my disappointment, the old man was nowhere to be seen. When I turned around, the white horse was gone as well. As before, he seemed to just disappear.

I continued to walk, still hoping to run into the old man. Under the pigeon gray sky the field was covered with ruins, of what sort of buildings I could not tell. Oddly shaped rocks seemed to resemble human faces, some happy, others sad. Bare branches formed artistic shapes like the elegant, but pained limbs of dancers. I found myself fascinated by this strange, nearly empty landscape. I wanted to stay longer in the castle so as to be able to fully explore its surroundings. But what if Alfredo and Maria were not as they seemed? I needed an escape plan.

I sat on a rock to rest while enjoying the desolate scene. I noticed a gap between some bushes and, underneath it, rocks circling what looked like a burrow. Curious, I went up and pushed aside the branches. As I looked down into the hole I was taken aback to see a ladder leading underground. As so often during the last few days, I could not help but wonder if I was just imagining things. But when I pressed on the ladder it was quite firm.

I knew it was foolish to climb down, but my curiosity overcame me and, despite all the strange experiences of the last few days, nothing bad had happened. In the back of my mind was the idea that the cave might be the home or studio of the old sculptor.

Gingerly I climbed down. When I reached level ground, it was quite dim, illuminated only by the light above. I could see large slabs of rocks arranged as chairs and table, but I couldn't walk far because it would be completely dark.

"Old señor, are you here?" I called out.

Silence.

I swung my flashlight around. Besides the table and chairs there was a large slab of stone on which was placed a thin mattress, blankets, and pillows. In an alcove was a stove with a propane tank, a stack of dishes, and cooking utensils. On a rickety wooden table were candles, piles of clothes, and a well-thumbed book. I shined my light on the book and could read "Herbs and Decoctions" on the cover. Was the old sculptor also an herbalist? Maybe he wanted to concoct his own elixir of immortality. I hoped so, for then he could sculpt even more of his beguiling figures. I took out my camera, turned on the flash, and snapped everything I could see.

"Anyone here?" I called again. "Old señor, it's me, the woman who bought your statues!"

My call was answered only by eerie echoes. I was beginning to feel very nervous, wondering who really lived in this place. I sensed a strange vibration—perhaps from the other realm—and decided it was time to leave. Just as I was about to head toward the ladder, I heard footsteps clambering down. Immediately I turned off my light and hid behind a boulder. When I saw their faces, I had to press my hand across my mouth to stop myself from screaming.

It was Cecily and the other three witches!

Once they alighted, they went over to the table and lit the candles. The space was immediately filled with flickering light, casting shadows across the wall like wandering ghosts. The four women sprawled on the rock seats, talking and laughing, while Cecily went to the stove, turning the valve to light it and producing a swoosh sound. She had brought a sack down the ladder with her and from it she produced some meat, carrots, and onions. With deft movements she sliced the meat, cut the vegetables, sprinkled them with herbs, and threw it all into a big metal pot.

Minutes later the space was filled with a mouthwatering aroma. After pushing away the blankets and pillows, the witches put plates, bowls, glasses, and condiments on the big slab of stone now used as a table. Soon they were eating and drinking ravenously as I watched and salivated. My stomach rumbled and I feared it would give me away, but they were too absorbed in their repast to hear.

I knew I couldn't possibly hide behind the boulder forever, so I gathered up my courage and walked out to show myself.

"Hello, everyone, sorry to intrude. . . ."

Cecily used her knife to point at me. "Who's this?"

"Please put your knife down. You know me—we've met twice."

Finally recognizing me, they seemed to relax.

"All right," Cecily said, and smiled, "you are welcome in my humble home, even though you are uninvited." She pointed to a stone chair. "I remember you danced with us. Now have a seat and eat."

The three other women shifted to make room for me.

"Maybe we should now properly introduce ourselves. You know I'm Cecily," said the head witch. Then she pointed to the fortyish, big-boned woman next to her. "This is Lucia. And the tall ones are Mimi and her twin, Angie."

"Glad to meet you all. I'm Eileen Chen." I could tell my voice sounded stiff and nervous.

"Relax, Eileen, no one will harm you here. We only do healing and magic," Cecily said.

"What about casting spells?" I asked.

"Of course, that too."

I looked around, then asked, "Cecily, you really live here—underground?"

She cast me a condescending glance. "That's part of the tradition of witches. Do you know about the ancient Black School?"

I shook my head.

"They chose to live underground and I like the idea."

I doubted this was the real reason she lived underground, but it wasn't the time to ask her.

Mimi and Angie continued to gape at me as if I'd just landed on earth from outer space. Our hostess poured me a glass of red wine, picked up a plate, and plopped a piece of meat onto it.

"Eat," Cecily ordered, sounding just like all Chinese mothers and grandmothers.

With a rumbling stomach and no hesitation, I began to gulp my wine and shovel the meat and vegetables into my mouth.

"Are you Japanese?" Lucia asked, lifting beans into her red-painted mouth.

"No, I'm Chinese."

"So you're a Chinese witch here to dance and dine with us. What an honor!" said Lucia.

"Why did you say that I'm a witch?"

She smiled. "My horoscope said I'll have a witch visit from the East, and here you are."

I asked no one in particular, "Are you all witches?"

This time Cecily answered. "Yes, but there's no need to be afraid."

But I was afraid, remembering how they had drugged me the last time we met. Cecily cast me a mischievous glance, then refilled my glass. "Relax, my friend, and have more wine."

I took another sip and then immediately regretted it. Would I be drugged again?

As if reading my mind, Cecily said, "Don't worry, it's not poisoned. Our concoctions are only to heal."

"So you do healing?"

"Of course. What do you think witches do? As I said, we heal, cast spells, tell fortunes, connect with nature. We celebrate life . . . and of course death as well, the other side of the coin." She downed more wine, then added, "We're women of power and we'll make you one too."

Women of power! But stuck living underground like homeless people?

"How do you make your living?" I asked.

Cecily flung her head back and laughed. "What a question! I'm not a homeless beggar, if that's what you think. I chose to have my home here, because it's close to nature."

"Really?"

"My home is rooted in the ground and hidden from intruders by shrubs, not suspended in midair like those hideous glass and concrete skyscrapers! I am a free woman and I help others to be free."

"Who are your customers?"

"They're all over. We travel for house calls."

"Do you have a phone here?" I cast a suspicious glance around the place.

She laughed again. "Ha! Those who need me can find me. Anyway, Lucia, Angie, and Mimi all have their own places and phones, so sometimes they book appointments for me. And people meet us at the Witches' Market where we sell the stuff that we make."

I felt more and more intrigued by these self-proclaimed witches.

Soon we finished eating and plates, knives, and forks were moved away and washed in a small bucket. Despite my curiosity, I thought I should leave while there was still some light outside.

I stood up, and said to the women, "Thanks for the delicious food. I should leave."

"No, you're not going anywhere," Cecily said, her face serious.

"What?" I asked, and my heart started to pound.

"Yes, stay with us," Angie and Mimi both chimed in high-pitched tones.

"Since you came uninvited into my place, you should join us for our ritual," their boss added.

She ignored my protests and went on to light more candles, arranging them in a circle. Lucia, Angie, and Mimi spread out dishes of herbs, a bowl of water, a plate of salt, then placed a thick candle in the middle. Then the two twins grabbed my hands and pulled me into the circle. I was too scared to try to escape.

Cecily lit incense and led us first in whispered prayers and then silent meditation. Ten minutes later, she announced in a resonant voice, quite different from her usual tone, "Now I'll call upon Baal, Belial, Astaroth, Orias . . . and all the spirits of earth and sky and the four elements to sanctify this circle of light."

She dissolved salt into the water and sprinkled it inside the circle. Next she picked up the candle and called on fire. Then she shook a small bell to call on metal.

After the rather ominous-sounding invocation, the four women began to chant some unintelligible words and danced around as if controlled by some unseen force—a good or evil force I couldn't be sure of, but I was drawn into its vibrations and found my legs and arms swaying as I joined their dance.

I don't know how much time passed before the witches slowed down and we all seemed to come out of our collective trance. Cecily motioned for us to sit and called us to another silent meditation.

When finished, wiping sweat from my forehead, I asked, "What is this ritual for?"

"Purification and illumination."

That didn't really explain anything, but at least I was still conscious, so they hadn't drugged my wine or cast a spell on me.

I realized that it was dark out now and I was worried about finding my way back to the castle, so I thanked Cecily for the food and the dance but told her I had to leave.

"Why not stay with us for a day or two? There is enough space for everyone," Lucia said.

There was room—but only if everyone was going to sleep on the ground.

"I need to get back."

"Stay, so we can exchange knowledge," Cecily said matter-of-factly.

"Knowledge of what?"

"Witchcraft, of course. Where do you live?"

"The Maiden Fortress." Somehow I didn't have the heart to use the castle's other name, fearing that I might divulge some secret tragedy.

Cecily scoffed. "You mean the Heartbreak Castle? I figured. Lucky girl, how do you know the owner?"

I told them what had happened and that Alfredo Alfrenso was still basically a stranger to me.

"He is a stranger to everyone." Cecily's statement came as a surprise.

"You know him?'

"Ha, everyone knows him, but he doesn't know anyone!"

I didn't know how to respond to this, so I changed the subject. "Why do you live so close to Alfrenso's castle?"

"Maybe I'll tell you later. When the time is right."

I repeated my intention to leave and this time they made no effort to dissuade me but invited me to visit again anytime I wanted.

"Anyway, maybe we'll see each other at the Witches' Market. I am sure it is our destiny to meet. You can teach us some of your Chinese witchcraft," Cecily added.

Both Angie and Mimi chimed in as they waved good-bye. "Yes, teach us Chinese witchcraft!"

The next day I slept restlessly, dreaming of being trapped in a deep, dark hole. I woke up quite late. I wondered if I was turning into a night person. It seemed that I was still tired from the ritual with the witches in Cecily's underground home. Instead of going to the kitchen for breakfast, I stayed in my room to write down my encounter with the witches while it was still fresh in my mind. Just when I finished writing, there was a quiet knock on the door. I called for Maria to come in.

Once she entered my room, Maria said, "Señor Alfrenso has returned early and will have a big party this evening. He hopes you will join him and his guests at the ball. I didn't want to wake you before since you were so soundly asleep. But señor says that his guests will be very pleased to meet his beautiful young lady from America."

"A ball? But I don't have a decent dress to wear!"

"No worry. We have many dresses here. Come and I will show you."

I followed the housekeeper down long corridors, past cavernous empty rooms, and around corners until I had no idea where I was. We finally entered a small room that clearly served as a wardrobe. One wall was covered with drawers and shelves, the others had long racks from which hung a multitude of gowns and dresses. Except in a department store, I had never seen such a large assembly of women's clothes in my life. And in the home of a bachelor. I was already confused by all the twists and turns that had brought us to this section of the castle and began to have a headache.

As I massaged my temples, Maria pulled open a huge closet revealing row upon row of silk evening gowns in a rainbow of colors, trimmed with lace and adorned with beads, pearls, and sequins. Styles varied: sleeveless, off the shoulder, plunging neckline, bare back, bare midriff.

Tucked into cubbyholes were matching accessories such as shawls, handbags, and shoes. There was no jewelry to be seen, which I guessed was because it was locked away somewhere.

Of course I was dying to know whose clothes these were, so I asked Maria, "Did these belong to Señora Alfrenso?"

Maria avoided my question, and instead said, "You can choose whatever you want to wear for the evening."

The immense collection of clothes made me more eager than ever to find out more about Alfredo's wife. Hoping to get Maria to tell me more about her master's wife, I said, "She must have been very beautiful and had many parties to wear all these gowns."

Maria's only reply was, "Yes, very beautiful and she loved parties."

The few days I'd been here, I hadn't seen any other woman besides Maria. So where was Mrs. Alfrenso? Was she really dead? Or had she tired of her extravagant existence in this non-place and absconded, perhaps to the bright lights of a sophisticated city like Barcelona. I hoped she'd simply escaped, otherwise I would be wearing a dead woman's dress for her husband's party. Was I about to play a role in this man's perverse fantasy involving his absent wife? Suddenly I wanted no part of this strange household, nor the fancy ball at which I would be a guest.

While I was still surveying the dresses, Maria pulled one out and handed it to me. It was rose colored, with white lace trim, a little young for me but still a very pretty dress.

"Señorita Eileen, this one is perfect for you."

When I looked at it more closely I realized that the neckline plunged a lot lower than I was comfortable with. I never thought of myself as prim, but not as loose either. What would the men at the ball think of me?

Seeing me hesitate, Maria said, "I know all these dresses. Believe me, this one is perfect for you. No need to look more. It's begging for you to wear it."

"I'm afraid it's too long."

"I can size it quickly."

"And the shoes are too big."

This time she laughed. "I'll just stuff them with a little tissue paper."

"Can you also sew up two or three inches of the neckline?"

"Don't worry about that. Please try it on and then I can make alterations."

Fortunately when I tried on the dress it almost fit. The neckline was low, exposing quite a bit of breast. But the bodice was loose; Señora Alfrenso must have been a busty woman. Maria took me in front of a gilded mirror, put a few pins on the dress's hem, and then made a few measurements with a tape. After that, she suggested I relax in my room while she worked on the dress.

I spent the afternoon in my room writing notes for my book and napping. At six, Maria reappeared and helped me wash my hair, apply my makeup, and fit myself into the dress. It left my shoulders bare and fit perfectly around my waist, but Maria had not kept her promise to sew up the low-cut neckline, so I stepped into the ballroom with more skin showing than I'd wanted.

9

The Ball

The dust-covered and run-down ballroom had undergone an amazing transformation since I'd first seen it. Help must have been hired to clean and decorate it while I'd been away with the old man and the witches. Now, instead of looking like a gloomy-faced first wife, the room shone and glittered like a beautiful, newly favored concubine!

Small lightbulbs dangled from the high ceiling and perched on walls like glowing vines. High on the ceiling, more lights were blinking against a dark purple background, as if the ballroom were open to the stars.

Elegantly dressed couples were already seated at small, round tables, chatting, sipping wine, and drawing on cigarettes. Two musicians played animatedly, resurrecting the harp and piano that must have lain moribund for months, if not years. Bejeweled women were either talking to tuxedoed men or twirling with them on the polished dance floor to the enticing rhythms. The intoxicating tones of the instruments under the shimmering lights had turned the previously empty chamber into a dreamscape. I felt that I was now living in a fairy tale. Was I to be the princess for whom the prince was searching?

A waiter passed by with a tray of champagne glasses and I

helped myself to one. The liquid was sweet, but the bubbles bit at my tongue. I wondered why Alfredo was now hosting this lavish party in his ballroom, which had lain fallow for so many years.

I saw that Alfredo had spotted me and was approaching from across the crowded room. He smiled enigmatically as he surveyed the scene he had created along with his hired help. Suddenly this empty castle seemed to remember its decadent past, one I was curious to know about.

The castle's owner, imposing in a crimson silk tuxedo jacket, lifted my hand and kissed it, then clinked his glass with mine. "Eileen, you look absolutely gorgeous!"

"Thanks, Alfredo." I was about to return his compliment by saying, "You look handsome too," but swallowed my words, lest they be misunderstood.

"Maria told me you spent some time away from the castle—was everything okay?"

I nodded as he extended his hand.

"May I?" he asked.

I noticed that all eyes were on us as the castle owner led his exotic guest onto the dance floor. I felt like I was impersonating his wife by wearing her designer dress and shoes. I started to wonder if it was possible that he'd planned the ball just for me.

My host didn't say much as we danced, but rather focused on swinging and twirling me with elegantly sensuous movements. As Alfredo pressed me closer against him, I was aware of his subtle cologne. He was aware of me, too, particularly the plunging neckline that Maria had somehow forgotten to fix. Did she intend to aid him in seducing me? It seemed likely. But while I was enjoying dancing in the exotic atmosphere of the ball, I had no wish to share his bed.

While he was quite different from my Ivan, I did not like where romance with Alfredo would lead. I appreciated his European poise and aristocratic bearing, which were quite unlike Ivan's aggressive American manner. But it seemed to me that Alfredo, no longer needing to be ambitious, was becoming melancholic in his later years. I felt I was too young to share someone else's decline.

Despite his world-weary demeanor, I sensed a relentlessness in

Alfredo. Perhaps a long ago trauma had introduced some compassion into his nature. But I did not want to count on that. Ivan might learn compassion someday, but for now he was totally focused on his own success. I hoped to find a man who was capable, but kind, not a calculating, moneymaking machine.

Ivan must have hurt a lot of people—colleagues, associates, partners, clients, even friends—on his way up. I never asked him about his business. Not only that I was not interested, but I feared I'd see a different Ivan, one even worse than I'd imagined. Was he completely ruthless, not hesitating to harm others if it would bring him an extra buck? I just did not want to be around that sort of thing.

I thought of the famous Chinese saying, "The path to a general's victory is paved with ten thousand skeletons."

Another one: "The winner of a battle stands amidst corpses begging at the Gate of Hell."

But now I was far away from it all, so I pushed thoughts of Ivan and my life in America out of my mind and glanced around at the other couples on the dance floor. In the dim light it was a sea of movement, limbs coming and going rhythmically like waves on the beach.

I remembered the novelist Cheung Ailing's famous line: "Dancing is but civilized wantonness." Underneath all this beauty and glamour were greed and lust. Sex and money. It was pretty obvious that my host was expecting the former.

His gentle voice rose next to my ear. "Eileen, what are you thinking about?"

"I'm thinking how wonderful this room is and how beautiful your guests are. Do you hold parties like this often?"

"Oh no. This is something special to welcome you."

"But, Alfredo, we hardly know each other!"

"Don't worry. I feel as if I've known you for a long time. I think God brought you to my castle for a reason."

I had nothing to say to this. I certainly didn't come here to sleep with him. I did enjoy his company, but that was it. The music stopped and Alfredo took my hand and led me back toward the tables.

Suddenly a woman's harsh voice called out, "Señor Alfrenso, how are you doing?"

My host looked shocked when his eyes landed on a late-fiftyish woman wearing elaborate makeup that was trying to hide the fact that she was past her peak. Her garish purple gown revealed even more of her breasts than mine did.

"How did you get in here?" Alfredo asked with irritation in his voice.

"Relax, Alfredo," the woman said, "I'm as good as you at going in and out of places. . . ." She waved her red-nailed hand. "Please sit with me for a minute." She cast me a curious glance. "Your exotic friend too."

Reluctantly, Alfredo pulled out a chair for me.

After we sat, the woman turned to me. "I'm Sabrina Sanchez. Alfredo and I are old friends. Sometimes enemies, too, hahaha!" She then gestured to a young, bland-looking man next to her. "This is Diego, my new friend."

Sabrina turned to Alfredo. "When did you meet such a pretty *young* woman?"

"This is Eileen Chen from America. She's a professor of anthropology."

Our host looked proud when introducing me. But then he leaned toward Sabrina, not bothering to hide his anger, and simply said, "Now leave me alone."

Sabrina smiled, taking out an ivory holder into which she inserted a cigarette. Her young friend immediately lit it for her. She inhaled deeply, then breathed out smoke like strokes of agonized calligraphy.

After her nicotine hit, she said, "Haven't I done that for twenty years? We can chat and catch up on things."

My host patted my hand as if to reassure me that this woman would not be a problem. He turned to his apparently uninvited guest. "All right, Sabrina, what do you want to talk about?"

Even though Sabrina was obviously intruding, I felt instant pity for her. She might be the same age as Alfredo, but in looks they were many years apart. There is a Chinese saying that states, "The setting sun is beautiful, but twilight is brief." Sabrina was clearly in her twilight—try as she might to conceal it.

Sabrina cast Alfredo a sexy smile. "Come on, Al, how about a dance for old time's sake?"

Before Alfredo could refuse, Sabrina stood up and took his arm. So as to not embarrass her, he had no choice but to be led to the dance floor. Diego eyed his partner stoically as she pressed her half-exposed, busty chest against Alfredo's. Eyes fell on them as they began to move. Sabrina clung on to Alfredo as if he were a branch floating on turbulent waves.

After watching the pair for a few moments, Diego turned to me, shaking his head. "My friend likes men."

I didn't quite know how to respond, so I smiled. "How long have you been together?"

"Not long. We met in a bar. Sabrina says she likes bars because she can get drunk and forget her sadness. She also says that a sad woman never plans, because it's useless."

"Hmmm, so, do you . . . try to comfort her?"

I immediately regretted asking such an insinuating question. What Sabrina and Diego did—especially behind doors—was really none of my, or anyone's, business.

"I believe she's inconsolable. I guess something very bad happened to her."

"Did she tell you what?" Now my curiosity was piqued.

He shook his head. "I'm just a passerby in her life, and I'm sure she's had many like me. Maybe someday she'll tell you about herself."

During the ensuing silence, I quietly sipped my champagne and watched Sabrina and Alfredo dancing among the other guests. There was some strange chemistry between the two. While Alfredo looked awkward and uncomfortable, Sabrina danced with abandon. She pressed her breasts against him, seemingly trying to both excite and annoy him. Alfredo was definitely annoyed, but seemed unable or unwilling to extricate himself from her grasp. He didn't look very happy, but it was pretty obvious that he was excited also, even if it was against his will.

Finally the music stopped and Sabrina dragged a reluctant Alfredo back to our table. As they sat down, Sabrina waved her many-ringed fingers.

"Why don't you two gentlemen go ask other ladies to dance? I'd like to talk to Eileen."

This was a strange request since I didn't know her, even Alfredo, really. Maybe this bluntness was a Spanish trait.

To my surprise, Alfredo went along, perhaps anxious to avoid a scene at his own party. I wasn't sorry at this interruption because it seemed that Sabrina would be the person to finally tell me about my enigmatic host's past.

10

Sabrina Sanchez

After Alfredo and Diego left, Sabrina smiled at me insinuatingly. Under her heavy makeup I could see little red veins on her nose and cheeks. The skin of her upper breasts that she was so generously revealing was freckled from years in the sun.

She smiled flirtatiously. “I love parties, but then I get bored quickly—isn’t that strange?”

I shrugged. “It’s okay.”

“My whole life is a bore. My husband’s long gone. I’m getting old and I’ve been sleeping around too much for too long. Diego is my new conquest—the best I can do at this point in my life.”

Before I could respond to her surprising outburst, she spoke again. “I picked him up in a bar. Half my age, but he’s willing to hang out with me. You know why?”

I was pretty sure I knew what he was getting from her. But I was curious, so I shook my head.

“Let me tell you. Men, especially someone like Diego who doesn’t have much going for him, think they can find paradise in an older, sexually experienced woman like me. You know, men’s eyes will bleed when their nose smells free sex.”

I was surprised by her frankness, but I realized that her several glasses of champagne might have something to do with it.

"I'm a bad woman and I could never settle down with just one man," she continued. "Believe it or not, I used to be so beautiful that heads would turn whenever I'd pass. Now I only want to have a little more fun before my time is up."

"You're still beautiful, Sabrina."

It wasn't a complete lie. I could only comment on her beauty, but not her time left. I thought she might attract better men if she did not come on so strong and left more of herself to their imagination.

"You think so?"

I nodded. Staring at her big, watery eyes, I felt I had to be reassuring to this troubled woman. But I thought to myself that she was more sexy than beautiful.

"Thank you. I like you, Eileen, you're very kind. Not many people are kind these days, especially women. I tell you, there's no sisterhood, not in the past, now, or in the future. It's always been every woman for herself, ha!"

Her sisterhood remark led me to think of Empress Dowager Ci Xi, China's notorious ruler in the late nineteenth century. The real empress, An, kept a note from the emperor allowing her to kill Ci Xi, should she become a threat. But Ci Xi was tender and supportive to the lonely empress.

One day when she was sick, Ci Xi supposedly cut off her own flesh and put it in healing soup for Empress An. In gratitude, Empress An burned the note giving her the power to have Ci Xi killed. From that day on, Ci Xi was relentlessly cruel to the empress, who died of poisoning not long after.

I didn't think most women were evil like Ci Xi, but I did know that Sabrina was not the sort of woman who is appreciated by other women.

"Eileen, I'd like you to be my friend, so tell me about yourself," said Sabrina.

I explained that I was a professor here to research witches but offered nothing about my personal life.

"Impressive! A learned woman and a writer!" she said, then scribbled on a napkin and handed it to me. "I live a little south of this castle, not too far. Please come visit so we can talk more."

"I'll try." But I was not at all sure she was someone I would want as a friend.

She cast me a pretend irritated look. "Please! For God's sake, won't you?"

"All right, then, I will."

"And don't wait too long!"

"I'm not sure how much longer I will be here."

"Don't ever lose a chance to make friends. Trust me, I'm an old woman speaking from experience. Be sure you'll keep your promise—life is short and I don't have much of it left."

"What about Diego?"

"He's just a pet. You know what I mean. I have a sad life."

I was starting to tire of her self-pity, but I was also curious to know more about the dead husband she'd just mentioned, and of course also her relationship with Alfredo. But I felt I should wait until she was ready to confide. It turned out that I did not have to wait long.

"My husband killed himself, my only daughter died, and my only son disappeared."

Now I really was sorry for her—so many tragedies in one woman's life.

She gulped down more wine, sucked at her cigarette, then went on. "If you're willing to come visit a lonely woman and keep her company over a glass of wine, then I'll tell you the rest of my story." She winked, adding, "And about Alfredo and me."

My ears perked up. But I feared I was neglecting my plan to gather material on witches and witchcraft. However, I was intrigued by the woman and did not see any reason to refuse her invitation to visit.

"Don't think about it too much, just come. Now my limbs feel itchy, so I need to find someone to dance with. Hopefully a stud, ha!"

Sabrina stood up abruptly, and, after throwing me a lopsided smile, went to search for her next mark.

Alfredo soon returned without Diego. His mood was much more subdued and I felt sorry that his party had been spoiled by this intruder. But his interest in me seemed to have grown during even this short absence. I knew I would disappoint him and tried to think of a way to let him down gently. All I could do was say that I was still jet-lagged and, while I'd enjoyed his lavish party, the music and champagne had given me a headache. I thanked him for lending me the gown and told him I needed to sleep.

The next morning I awoke to Maria's loud knocking.

"Señorita Eileen, breakfast is ready. Please come with me. Señor Alfrenso is already waiting."

When we entered the kitchen, Alfredo was pouring juice and buttering toast. The coffee grinder made a pleasing sound as the smell of the exotic beans reached my nostrils. After Maria left, Alfredo gestured me to sit and shoveled scrambled eggs and sausage onto my plate.

"I hope you enjoyed the party—sorry you were not feeling well and had to leave early. Do you feel okay now?"

I nodded. "Just jet lag and being in a new place."

Sipping my coffee and munching my toast, I could not help wondering about Sabrina. I had no reason to believe she was one of the witches, yet I felt I was under her spell. She was not easy to like, yet I was curious to know more about her—her youth when she turned heads, her relationship with Alfredo, the tragedy with her husband and children.

Since Alfredo's interest in me was getting more apparent, I didn't feel entirely comfortable staying with him any longer. I decided to speak up.

"Alfredo, you've been very kind to me, but I fear I am imposing. Anyway, I need to work on my research."

My host looked disappointed as he put down his coffee. "Why are you in such a hurry? You know you're most welcome to stay as long as you wish. This castle is at your disposal, not to mention that I greatly enjoy your company."

I smiled warmly. "I appreciate that, but I came here to write my book." *And not to have parties and befriend an older man,* I thought to myself.

"Why not stay here while you are writing your book? You know, there are many rooms we don't use. You can pick any one you like and I'll have Maria fix it up for you."

It was a good idea, especially because it would be free.

"But, Alfredo . . ." I searched his eyes.

"What are you afraid of? You know I'm a gentleman."

"But . . . we hardly know each other."

"I understand," he said, and then, after thinking for a while, added, "Of course you must have someone back in the States, right?"

"Yes and no." I sighed. "I'm here for research. My personal life is back in California."

"Yes, of course, you're a very smart and capable young lady. I've gotten very fond of you. How could I not?"

He kept leading back to where I did not want to go. So as much to change the subject as anything else, I said, "I chatted a little with Sabrina. Can you tell me more about her?"

My host didn't look happy. "She's an old acquaintance. I didn't invite her; she crashed the party. The woman is nothing but trouble. My advice is stay away from her."

It was pretty obvious that he did not want to tell me anything about her. But I still tried to coax a little more from him.

"Sabrina told me she has had a sad life. She said her husband killed himself and that she lost her son and daughter."

"She told you all this? Eileen, don't believe a word coming from that woman's mouth. She's a witch anyway."

My ears perked up on hearing the word *witch.*

"So what she told me isn't true?"

Alfredo's expression turned serious. "Some things are better left alone."

"All right, Alfredo. You know, I really think I should go back to the hotel to work on my notes. There are too many distractions here. I also need to rest and explore other places. After that, I'll come back for a visit. How's that?"

"Well, if you must leave, I know a small hotel nearby. They always have rooms available. I'll have my driver, Adam, take you."

I was sure Alfredo still had hopes of something more from me, but a nearby cheap hotel seemed like the best answer, so I thanked him and went up to my room to pack.

* * *

My new room at the hotel was small and threadbare, but it was clean and quiet. So much had happened in just a few days that I welcomed the chance to be left alone and clear my brain. As I lay on the sagging bed, I kept thinking of my recent encounters with Alfredo and his oddly named Heartbreak Castle, the dancing witches, the old sculptor, the pathetic Sabrina and Diego, her "pet." I decided I would definitely pay Sabrina a visit, but not right away. I needed a break and also wanted to organize my notes and pictures. After that, I'd take it easy for a day or two.

11

Signs from the Cracked Earth

The next day, after a quick shower, I went to the hotel lobby and asked the receptionist for directions to the nearest village market. I felt the need for fresh, wholesome food after drinking too much wine and eating too much meat at the castle. After a short walk I arrived at the market and strolled around, admiring the food and watching the other customers.

I bought some grapes, strawberries, a bag of nuts, and freshly squeezed orange juice in a tall paper cup. Tables were clustered at the edge of the market under a tall tree. I sat down and ate while watching the people around me.

As I was finishing, I noticed two young men walking in my direction. They looked somewhat familiar, but I couldn't place them right away. Soon they sat down at a table not too far from mine, ordered, and began to eat and drink with gusto as soon as their food arrived.

When they noticed me staring, one of them leaned toward me and smiled. "Miss, how are you? Do you remember us? We met on the ferry to Tenerife Island, then at the café near the Witches' Market. I'm Kyle and this is my younger brother, Ed."

I hit my head. "Yes, of course! I'm Eileen Chen. I'm surprised to see you two again."

The two exchanged a meaningful glance.

The younger brother, Ed, rounded his eyes. "Oh, Eileen . . . maybe you haven't heard . . ."

"Heard what?"

"Something very strange . . . a couple of days ago . . ."

Something in his tone made me anxious. "What happened?"

"A man and a dog. Lhasa Apso, a rare breed. We were just walking along and right before our eyes . . . the road seemed to crack open and they fell in."

"Who?"

"The man and the dog."

"You saw this?"

"Yes, a woman saw it too."

"What happened?"

"The earth closed back up. It was as if they'd never been there. It was terrible. Hard to believe—but we both saw it."

"This really happened?"

"Yes—about twenty blocks north of here in a deserted park."

His brother went on to explain. "I think the man is homeless, so there's no one to report him missing. There's been nothing in the papers or on TV either."

"Hmmm . . . Maybe you should report it to the police. . . ."

Kyle shook his head. "They'll probably think we're just crazy. Or think we did it and arrest us."

"Arrest you? But you didn't do anything."

Both Kyle and Ed nodded emphatically.

"Exactly. You know us, but the police don't. The police here have a bad reputation. Better to stay away from them," said Kyle.

"Anyway, we'll be gone from here soon and who knows if we'll ever be back," Ed added.

"What about the woman who also saw it—maybe she reported it to the police?"

"I don't know. We think the dog was probably hers, but instead of trying to look for it, she just hurried away."

Kyle took out a pen, wrote on a small piece of paper, and handed it to me. "Here's our hotel number if you want to call us.

Maybe we'll run into each other again. It's a small world, after all. Good to see you again, Eileen. Enjoy your breakfast."

With an odd feeling lodged in my chest, I continued to think as I finished my breakfast. Every day I spent on this out-of-the-way island made it seem stranger. The brothers themselves seemed odd. I half suspected that they'd made the whole thing up, but why would they bother?

Because of Laolao's profession, I'd grown up around weird people who told weird stories. Some of the stories may even have been true—but normal people didn't believe them. I knew from experience that there is another realm, a metaphysical one. Maybe that's where the man and dog ended up. Somehow my instincts told me what the brothers had seen was real. Things happened on the island that didn't happen back in San Francisco. Why, I had no idea.

I finished my healthy fruit breakfast and sat for a while trying to make sense of everything. Finally I gave up trying to figure things out and decided I would take up Sabrina Sanchez's invitation to visit her.

Sabrina's home was perched on a pleasant hill by the sea. It was one of a row of wooden houses similarly decorated with white walls, green roofs, and yellow fences. The small yards were filled with flowers and lush vegetation, creating a storybook atmosphere. I climbed the hill slowly until I reached the middle house that bore a small sign that said SANCHEZ.

After a few knocks, the door swung open, revealing my new friend's face, still slightly puffy from her earlier indulgences at the party. She was wearing full makeup as if she'd been expecting visitors. I wondered if she was one of those women who would never let herself be seen without makeup. Seeing me, she smiled expansively, revealing the deep wrinkles beside her mouth.

"Eileen! What wind blew you here?"

"It's a very pleasant day, so I decided to pay you a visit. Besides, I'm a girl who keeps her promises."

"Good, I'm bored and was hoping an honorable guest would arrive to keep me company and entertain me. Please come in, Eileen."

I followed her into the living room, which was small but nicely decorated with oil portraits that must have been of Sabrina when she was young and fresh, as well as peaceful landscapes and rural scenes. Her furniture looked antique, or at least old and well-crafted. The carpet was large with a faded floral pattern, and a yellowed leopard skin was placed in front of the fireplace. Glazed figures struck ballet poses inside a glass-fronted cabinet. A bookcase had old leather-bound volumes on the bottom shelves and brightly colored best-sellers on the top. In a corner, a white baby grand piano sat silently, as if awaiting caressing fingers. I suspected that the cozy house was to help her survive a life that was all but unbearable.

I was surprised. The décor was feminine but without the overstatement of Sabrina's dress and makeup.

"Sabrina, your house is beautiful!"

She raised her fingers, still covered with rings, to smooth her black-dyed hair. "Thanks. Most of what you see is antique, including me . . . hahaha!"

She was wearing a long blue floral dress with a matching long-tasseled shawl. Perhaps she hoped that the slightly undulating tassels, together with her dangling gold earrings, would animate her tired face and body.

Not knowing how to respond, I smiled. "You look lovely. Where's your friend from the party?"

"Oh"—she made a face—"you mean my puppy. Diego has wandered off somewhere. I'm not his mother nor his nanny, so he's not my problem. Here in my house, people freely come and go, like vaginas in a whorehouse. Ooopps!" She rounded her artificially lashed eyes. "Sorry about my vulgarity. Anyway, he'll come back if he needs me, or if I want him. Make yourself at home. I'll be right back."

My hostess returned bearing a tea tray with a pitcher of iced tea, glasses, a bottle of brandy, and two little bowls filled with flan. Soon I was sipping iced tea and taking little bites of flan with the small spoon Sabrina provided. She, however, took little interest in the tea or the sweets, instead consuming the brandy rather rapidly.

I couldn't help but stare at the brandy bottle. "Sabrina," I said, and pointed to her glass.

She cast me a sad glance. "This is me. You must have noticed that during Alfredo's party I drank like a fish and smoked like a chimney." She took another gulp. "Like many women of a certain age, I drink to forget."

Forget what I dared not ask, fearing a swarm of snakes would dart out between her brightly painted lips to poison me.

"But, Sabrina, your health . . ."

She laughed. "Ha. Health. For what? To get back my youth?"

"You're still beautiful and you would be even more beautiful if you took good care of yourself."

Also, I thought, *if you got rid of your gaudy clothes and makeup.*

Her response surprised me. "Maybe I drink to kill myself on purpose."

"Surely you don't want to kill yourself!"

"All right, all right." She turned to stare at the vast expanse of sea outside the window for a few seconds, then said, "You know, I had many lovers."

I cast her an inquisitive look. "Yes, you told me that. You've been fortunate." What else could I say?

"Fortunate?" She flung her head back and laughed. "Ha, you bet, all sorts of rich men used to line up to ask me out, politicians, rich businessmen, gangsters, officers, athletes. . . ."

"So . . . was Alfredo one of these men?" I ventured to ask.

"Of course."

She walked to the window and gestured for me to join her. "Look over there—what do you see?"

I strained my eyes. "Stones?"

"Gravestones. After I die, I'll be buried there."

I felt I should say something comforting. "But you're not old. . . ."

"No? I'm older than you think! Soon I will join my daughter."

"What do you mean?"

She pointed. "Over there, there's where she's buried."

"I'm so sorry." I remembered that she'd told me her only daughter had died and her son disappeared. "How did that happen?"

"She looked like you, at least to me. You two could have passed as sisters, but of course she didn't have dark eyes like yours; her eyes were green like mine."

I doubted I really looked like her white daughter, and I certainly didn't want to be compared to a dead person.

She ignored my discomfort and went on in a different direction. "Eileen, my liver is giving out. But I'm not afraid. . . ."

"Oh, Sabrina, stop this. Chinese don't like to hear bad-luck talk."

She was silent for a moment. Just then I saw a framed picture nearby—my friend smiling and holding a dog.

I pointed to the picture, and asked, "A Lhasa Apso?"

"Yes, a rare breed."

I wondered if this was the same dog that had been swallowed up into the earth.

"It had an accident."

Before I could say anything, she went on. "It was my daughter's dog. She inherited it from Alfredo's wife, Penelope."

"How come?"

"Alfredo gave the dog to his wife as a gift. But she was too lazy and arrogant to take care of a pet, so he gave it to my daughter instead."

"It was swallowed up by the earth?"

Sabrina's eyes bulged in surprise. "How did you know?"

"There was a man, too, right?"

"How do you know all this?"

"I was told by two young men I met in a café."

"What else do you know?"

"That's it. I'm curious about what happened, but it has nothing to do with me. I'm only a tourist here and will go back to the States soon."

"Maybe you'll stay, you never know."

"I don't think so."

"Nothing is for sure in life, except death—and evil."

"Sabrina, you are a pessimist."

"The world is filled with evil forces; witches know about them and can control them."

"You know about this? Do you know any witches?"

Now she looked at me curiously. "Are you a witch too? Is that why you're interested!?"

"I'm here to find material about witches. I'm a professor and plan to write a book."

"Hmmm . . . a witch disguised as a professor!" She cast me a sharp glance. "I bet you have your own gift. You should learn to use it."

"Why do you think that I have a gift?"

"You can see things, just like my daughter."

"What did she see?"

"She saw everything. Not like those who claim to be witches now."

"If she saw everything, did she even foresee her own death?"

"She probably did, but she never told me. I guess because she didn't want to break my heart in advance. Who wants to know anyway?"

"How did she die?"

"Drowned in a lake. She was an underwater photographer."

Could there be some connection between her drowning and the earth swallowing up the man and dog? I was no geologist, but it sounded something like quicksand. However, Sabrina's daughter's death and the incident with the man and the dog had happened years apart.

"Where's this lake?" I asked.

"I can't tell you. It would not be good for you to go there."

At first I'd simply felt sorry for Sabrina, but now she was a little frightening. Maybe her eerie talk was due to her alcohol intake, but it was giving me a headache. I decided it was time to leave.

"Sabrina, thanks for the tea, but I need to leave now."

"Please have lunch with me. Or at least another flan."

"Maybe next time. I'm not feeling well right now."

"You can rest here if you want."

"Thanks, but I need my medicine back in the hotel."

"I can fix you some herbs."

The last thing I wanted was some strange concoction from this woman.

"Well, thank you, but I'll just head back."

"Suit yourself. Please come back again and I'll tell you more about my daughter." She continued in a dark tone. "She was attracted to death like a fly to honey."

"How so?"

"She was too pure and innocent for this evil world. Some people live their lives longing for their own demise."

What was that supposed to mean? But I didn't feel like asking.

Back in the hotel I lay down, planning to nap, but I couldn't quiet my mind. Who was Sabrina, really? There were hints that she was more than just a loose woman in her declining years. She'd had a daughter who saw everything, even her own death, or so she'd said. Was all this something I needed to know about or something I should stay away from?

It seemed that my journey to the west had been much more interesting than I'd expected. I thought of the supposed ancient Chinese curse, "May you live in interesting times." So far the trip had been successful in producing material I could use for my book. But at what price to myself? Somehow, Sabrina's mysteries and her talk of death seemed to be the last straw. Now I was really frightened.

I wished Laolao was here so I could consult her. Ivan and Brenda, the people closest to me, were so practical and materialistic that they were of no use at all with metaphysical matters. Since my arrival, I'd only called them twice. I had no reason to worry about them, but of course they were probably worrying about me.

Despite my apprehensions, I wanted to visit Sabrina again to find out more about her mysterious and tragic daughter.

But my intuition told me to stay away from her.

12

Laolao and the Meaning of Dreams

The next day I went to the spot where Ed and Kyle claimed that the earth had swallowed up the man and the dog, presumably Sabrina's dog.

The carnivorous earth was north of the open market, in a deserted park filled with trees with long aboveground roots like claws. Moss hung down from the branches like hair hanging over a ghost's face. Approaching the spot, I became aware of an odd odor, perhaps of death.

From a distance I could see what appeared to be wide cracks in the ground. This must be where the brothers had witnessed the bizarre disappearance. Looking at the cracks, I was reminded of the 3,000-year-old oracle bones used by the Chinese to tell their fortunes. But anything foretold by these cracks would be calamities.

Laolao had told me about the bones, pressed with a red-hot poker to produce future-revealing cracks. In ancient China, the three most important things the Sons of Heaven divined about were illness, war, and sacrifice. No important decision was made without consulting the cracks. Military decisions were particularly critical, as the losers were likely to be sacrificed themselves. Weather was another important matter because no rain meant no crops and no food.

The characters brushed on these ancient records are the earliest known examples of Chinese writing. Laolao had me copy them when I was learning to write. She told me that these were secret ways of writing that were never taught in school.

"These are little pictures, but they can reveal the future. Chinese have many ancient arts to know the future and make decisions," she'd said.

"Then why did China have such a terrible history?" I'd asked.

She had ignored my adolescent skepticism, saying, "That's how Chinese know what they should or shouldn't do. What is auspicious and what is virtuous. Which path to take and which to avoid. We Chinese always practice *chuiji bixiong*—go for fortune and avoid disasters at all cost."

I was young but starting to question what I was told. "Laolao, why does China still have so many tragedies?"

Laolao had looked at me and smiled. "Eh! You think you're pretty smart, don't you? So let me tell you. If you don't ask Heaven's guidance, you'll be even worse off! You think the gods have nothing better to do than watch out for you? Sometimes you have to figure things out yourself! The gods can help you, but you have to ask."

I lacked Laolao's naïve faith in these unnamed gods and thought that even if they existed, their advice was probably not very reliable.

That was the main reason I decided to be a scholar instead of a shamaness like Laolao. Professions like fortune-teller or *feng shui* master have a mixed reputation at best. Many despise them as con artists at society's margins. Among Chinese, those who make accurate predictions and earn their clients big fortunes are highly sought after and command big fees. They have earned the title of *gaoren* ("nobles").

They are respected because they claim knowledge of happenings in the other realm. The unwary client is intimidated by pronouncements like, "I can see a black cloud hovering above your head. A disaster will strike soon if you fail to do something to neutralize it."

The "something" involves paying the master hefty sums to carry out prayers, spells, incantations, rituals, or who knows what, to dissipate your impending bad luck. When I was younger, I felt confused about Laolao's work, because it seemed that while some people respected her, others called her a charlatan.

But she had always said, "These people are just jealous that I make good money. Remember this—in ancient China, a shaman was put under the category of 'Ritual Expert.' Even emperors respected them and took their advice very seriously." She'd also told me the best shamanesses were virgins, but having had my mother did not seem to have held her back in her career. Perhaps there were not enough virgins to offer serious competition.

However, as I grew older I could not help but notice that most of Laolao's clients did not seem to have become rich by following her advice. Rather they were mostly ignorant and superstitious losers who hoped to change their fate, not through hard work but by bribing their dead ancestors or one of the numerous Chinese money gods. Despite their supernatural expertise, only a few shamans are lucky enough to make a lot of money. Most barely get by. Fortunately for us, Laolao was one of the lucky ones.

She had always assured me, "Eileen, you don't need to worry about money because you will attract money. Rich men will chase you. But unfortunately, this isn't true for Brenda, even though getting rich is her life's goal. That's because life teaches us all different lessons. Some people's karma is to be thrust on the opposite path of what they desire."

Would I get rich as Laolao had told me? Would the path I was treading lead to fulfillment of my desires? I stared at the cracks in the earth, wondering if they, like the ancient oracle bones, could foretell my future. I knew that some recorded human sacrifices and wondered if somehow the earth had claimed the man and dog as victims.

But the only logical explanation was that it had been due to some sort of geological oddity. Anyway, the cracks that were visible now were far too small to swallow anyone up. Still, I could not help but fear that I might be the next victim.

Just in case, to appease my fears, I walked around the area and whispered a prayer to any gods or ghosts that might be dwelling nearby. Then I quickly left to go back to my hotel.

Even safely back in the hotel, visiting the cracks in the earth left me shaken up for the rest of the day. So I stayed in my room, lying on the bed. I dozed off and dreamt that I was seeing Sabrina's daughter, who looked like the Spanish version of me.

"You belong here," she said, her tone serious.

"How are you so sure?"

"It's why you came here, of all places. I'm dead, but you're alive, so you can do for me what I can no longer do for myself."

"What do you think I can do? Why me?"

"I need a living witch's magical power."

"But I'm not a witch."

"Yes, you are, but you're still in your denial phase. There's a hidden lake a few miles north of where you were today. You must go there to find out about your life. And mine too."

"My past or my future?"

"First your past, it's what leads to your future."

She began to recede into the distance, saying in a fading voice, "Whatever you do, you must go to the lake. It will show you what you seek."

I wanted to ask her why I should be interested in a dead person and a forgotten lake, but it was then that I woke up, soaking wet.

Could I believe a dead girl in a dream?

With a chill, I suddenly realized that the woman in my dream was also the girl I'd seen on the boat ride to Tenerife! No wonder nobody on the boat had seen her, for she didn't exist—not in our realm! I wasn't sure I believed in such things, but it seemed that this phantom woman must have something important to tell me, coming to me first on the boat and now in my dream.

My grandma Laolao had never tired of discussing dreams. She had studied the "Duke of Zhou's" famous *Book of Dreams* and was highly skilled in interpreting them for her clients.

Laolao had often told me, "Dreams are other realities. Haven't you heard of Zhuangzi's Butterfly Dreams? The scholar's dream of a butterfly was so real that when he awakened, he could not decide if it was Zhuangzi dreaming of being a butterfly or a butterfly dreaming he was Zhuangzi.

"Don't dismiss anything metaphysical; there is more to reality than just the physical. You understand?"

I nodded while she went on with increasing vehemence. "Dreams make the invisible visible. What you are confused about in your life, look for a sign in your dreams. Dreams can shake us up, but they tell us what we need to know. That's why I use dreams for divination. Life is so uncertain, we need ways to foresee our future. So, remember, don't just discard your dreams like old calendars!"

I'd never imagined that dreams had any importance. But Laolao seemed pretty confident about it, so I was confused. Were dreams a powerful way to knowledge—or were they just dreams, bubbles that pop as we wake up?

Laolao said, "Doctors can even tell from dreams if you're sick. However, only Chinese doctors know how to do this."

"I've never heard of this."

"Easy. For example, if you often dream of demons or ghosts, that means your body is afflicted with evil *qi* entering your organs. If you have confusing dreams, you're weak, always feeling dizzy and faint. Dreaming of boats and drowning means your body lacks water, your kidney *qi* is declining, and your health in serious trouble. But if you dream of strong fire, that shows you have a strong heart. Listen, dreams tell your internal balance, which in turn comes from the cosmic balance."

"*Wah,* that's amazing! Laolao, how do you know all this?"

Laolao patted my head, smiling proudly. "Because I had a very learned mother—your great-grandmother."

Great-grandmother. She must be a dinosaur, or anyway a long-buried mummy!

Laolao winked. "My mother made me memorize the *Duke of Zhou's Dream Manual;* that's why I'm such an expert on dreams. I can even reinterpret my interpretations. So when people come to me with a bad dream, I can always turn it into a good one."

"Laolao, so you're lying to people about their dreams, cheating them?"

She laughed. "Of course not, silly girl. I'm helping them. You know, anything is possible in dreams, so anything is possible in their interpretations."

Laolao paused, then continued. "Believe it or not, dreams can even solve murders. . . ."

"Murders?" My ears perked up. I'd read many thrillers and detective novels, but never about dreams solving murder mysteries. Being a dream detective would be an easy job—just sleep until you dream the solution.

Laolao's voice could sound as mysterious as the murder mysteries. "You know the famous Judge Bao?"

I nodded.

"Bao is the most revered judge in Chinese history because he was completely impartial. There was never a case he couldn't solve, sometimes by dreams."

I kept very quiet so as not to interrupt Laolao telling the story about Judge Bao, the Chinese Sherlock Holmes.

"Que raped and murdered Madame Wei, but the perpetrator vehemently denied it, claiming that he didn't even know the woman. One day Madame Wei appeared in Judge Bao's dream, telling him how she'd been murdered by Que. In the dream, she showed Bao a love letter written by Que to seduce her. With just this evidence from a dream, Bao confronted Que, telling him he had his love letter to Madame Wei. Though Judge Bao had never seen the actual letter, this was enough to scare Que into confessing."

I said, "I hope my dreams can solve my problems too."

My grandmother looked at me affectionately. "Eileen, you'll live a great life." She smiled. "Anyway, don't forget your dreams, they'll tell you whatever you need to know."

"But, Laolao, I can't control if I'll dream or not!"

"Of course you can! People used to perform rituals for the dream god to enter their sleep."

She added, "Don't worry, when you need a dream it will come to you. You might even have a dream within a dream. If you are so lucky, you'll be enlightened beyond the dimension we're living in."

Before I had time to figure out what all this meant, Laolao

spoke again. "However, Zhuangzi said, 'The highest sage has no dreams.' "

"What did he mean?"

"The truly enlightened don't need dreams, because nothing troubles them."

Even though I didn't always fathom her profundity, I thought Laolao was the most intelligent person I'd ever known, certainly more than any of my teachers at school.

"So, Laolao, do you too have dreams?"

She laughed. "Of course. How many people do you think can reach this dreamless state? The answer is none!"

"Not even the sage Zhuangzi?"

"That I don't know, because I still haven't found a way to have him enter my dreams, not even as a butterfly."

Just then, I awakened from my reverie and wished I had Laolao with me to explain Sabrina's daughter entering my dream. Could I trust a deceased stranger telling me I would find my future in an isolated lake?

13

A Meeting in the Graveyard

I knew I should visit the witches for my research, but I was more curious about Sabrina and especially about her deceased daughter who had come all the way from the other realm to seek my help. Also, when Alfredo had called Sabrina an evil witch, I didn't know whether he was just being spiteful or literal. I was resolved to find out.

So I found myself back at Sabrina's front door, which this time was opened by a fiftyish maid with an apron tied around her bulging waist. I was holding a small bouquet of carnations that I had bought at a bodega at the bottom of the hill, as a gesture to show sympathy for the unhappy woman.

"Señora Sanchez has been waiting for you. Please come in."

Why was Sabrina so confident that I'd visit again?

After the maid had ushered me into the living room, she pointed out the window.

"Señora Sanchez is outside. She wants you to meet her in the cemetery over there. She's is waiting for you with Isabelle."

"Who's Isabelle?"

"Her daughter."

"But isn't she . . . dead?"

"Yes, of course. Please . . . señora is anxious to see you now."

I suddenly wondered how it was that Sabrina could afford a house and a maid. "I didn't see you when I was here before," I said.

"I only work here part-time. Señora needs help. She's not been well." The maid held her hand up to her mouth. "She drinks too much."

"Her health is in decline?"

She nodded. "Cirrhosis. Haven't you noticed that her feet and face are swollen? But if she can't get a drink, she trembles. Your visit cheered her up, so I hope you can come here often."

She leaned over, and whispered in a conspiratorial way, "We don't know how much time she has left."

"I'm sorry to hear that. I will try."

She didn't answer me, but went to open the door.

After walking under the hot sun for a few minutes, I reached the cemetery. There were only three rows of graves, all marked with small bone-white stones, some decorated with crosses, others with winged angels who looked tired and forlorn, as if trapped on the cold stone to mourn the inanimate occupants—or perhaps trying to rein in some very animated ghosts! Some of the graves seemed well-tended, but others were overgrown with weeds.

I spotted Sabrina, sitting on the grass and reading by herself near one of the gravestones. She could almost pass as one of the stone angels, only she had no wings to lift her body—or her mood. Hearing my footsteps, she raised her head and our eyes met.

"*Hola*. I've been talking with my daughter and waiting for you."

"That's good," I said, but immediately regretted it. What was so good about talking to the dead?

I handed her the bouquet. Surprised, Sabrina smelled it, then placed it on her daughter's grave.

"Gracias," she said, patting the grass next to her. "Come sit with us for a minute."

After I sat, she went on. "Actually, I've been reading to my daughter—"

"Isabelle?"

"Yes, she liked metaphysical books and ghost stories. Since she was a little girl, she firmly believed that life would continue in another dimension after death."

Well, that was novel—reading ghost stories to a ghost. I would have thought a dead person would have wanted something more cheerful. If the ghost could hear, would she be bored, frightened, or more likely, laugh at this ridiculousness? Just then a breeze blew from the southwest—the direction from which Chinese people believe ghosts appear. Despite my skepticism, I felt a chill, wondering if Isabelle really had arrived to join us.

"I miss Isabelle," Sabrina continued. "So I'm glad that you have come to me, even during the twilight of my life. Seeing you makes me feel like I'm seeing my daughter again."

She may have thought this would please me, but I didn't want to be the substitute for her dead daughter. But staring at Sabrina's sad, swollen, face, I did not want to disillusion her. So I simply nodded. She responded by smiling sadly.

"Sabrina," I said, "do you come here often to talk to Isabelle?"

"Sometimes. She's been dead for twenty years. I miss my daughter. She was so smart and beautiful—just like you."

My friend pulled a photo out from her purse and handed it to me. I was startled because, seeing Isabelle's face close up, I thought she really did look like me. She wasn't Asian, of course, but her somewhat sloping eyes, high cheekbones, and full, determined lips did remind me of myself. She had a tiny strawberry-colored mole between her brows, like a third eye—just like the she-ghost I'd seen on the ferry. . . .

"Maybe she's reincarnated in you. That's why you came all the way here to comfort me," Sabrina said.

I was thirty-three and Isabelle had died twenty years ago, so the timing was wrong. I didn't comment on this because I did not want to deprive Sabrina of what little comfort she had.

"We do look alike, so maybe we have something in common."

I thought to myself, *Like cousins or sisters in one of our past lives.*

"If Isabelle were still alive, I'm sure she'd have achieved a lot, just like you. Do you ever think about life after death?"

Of course I did, because it was one of Laolao's most common

subjects of conversation. But, casting a glance at the graves and involuntarily imagining the rotten corpses underneath, I really would have preferred to talk about something else. So I said nothing.

"I think about it all the time. Because Isabelle is dead and I'm dying," said Sabrina.

"Please. Chinese consider talking of death unlucky."

"Lucky or unlucky, we will all face death someday. So, why can't we face it now, eh?"

"What makes you think you're dying?"

She held up something from her handbag—a metal flask covered in leather. "This. It's been destroying me."

"Then why don't you stop?"

"Ha! You think anyone can stop death? It's my fate."

Isn't it everyone else's?

"Does Alfredo know about this? I mean you're . . ." I couldn't say the word *dying.*

"He doesn't want to deal with me—in fact, he stopped giving a damn about me a long time ago. And why should he care? I'm old, ugly, and dying." Her eyes wandered to a grave at the far end of the row. "But he used to be crazy about me."

"It's no surprise, because you're a beautiful woman, Sabrina."

She cast me a curious glance. "You mean *were.*"

"Sabrina, please. You're still attractive," I said, swallowing. What she said next startled me.

"It's true I was beautiful, but it helped that I hired a witch to cast love spells on him."

Now my curiosity was aroused. "A love spell by a witch? Did it work?"

"I believed that my beauty alone would have lured Alfredo. The spell was just to be sure."

This was getting really interesting. "Did she really do the spell? Maybe she just took your money."

"No, I watched her do it. I told her I needed a love charm, so she asked for pictures of Alfredo and me together; then I had to write down all sorts of things about us—birthdays, interests, favorite foods, where we'd traveled, what colors we liked. I wrote down singing and dancing as my hobbies, but I didn't know Alfredo's so I wrote down that it was making money. I could have added seducing women, ha!

"Finally, Nathalia asked me to put my wish in writing, so I wrote, 'Please make Alfredo love me and give me money forever.' Ha, you think I'm greedy? But that's me, I'm just being honest!

"When everything was ready, Nathalia asked me to focus my mind on capturing Alfredo's love. Then she waved her wand to purify the space and began dancing and chanting. After that, she lit the papers and pictures with the candle, then burned them to ashes in the cauldron as she continued to chant."

"What's the chanting about?"

"Something like, 'I call upon the Universe to keep Alfredo Alfrenso by Sabrina Sanchez's side and make him love her forever. Make him do whatever she desires and love no other woman, not even his wife. . . .' "

This surprised me a little—it was the first time a wife entered into her little romantic melodrama.

I couldn't help exclaiming, "That's a very selfish spell!"

Now my friend cast me an are-you-stupid-or-something? look.

"You think love is so generous that you'd share it with others? Selfless love is only for church!"

"But . . . Alfredo was married, right?" I asked, though I already knew the answer.

She nodded, looking annoyed. "Anything wrong with that?"

"Maybe not. So . . . where is his wife now?"

"She's been dead for a long time."

"How did she die?"

"What is it to you? I said it's been a long time. So what does it matter now?"

Some silence passed before I asked, "Where's this witch Nathalia now?"

"I don't know—maybe also dead. I don't care about her, only that her spell worked. My advice is that if you have a boyfriend you want to keep, you'd better hire a witch."

I remembered my mother had told me that one of her girlfriends had used a Daoist spell to capture her man. It had also worked. Laolao had told her about it, a love spell called *hehe jiang,* charm of the harmonious union. Actually, this spell was pretty complicated. She got a picture of two immortals that Chinese believe help women capture a man. She put up the picture in her bedroom, bowed, and made offerings of betel nut and dried oyster. Then she asked the immortals to bless their marriage—and also, most important, stop the men's, even the women's, wandering eyes. Afterward, the picture would be burned to send it to the immortals waiting in the other world.

I didn't know the details of Sabrina's spell, but the Chinese ones I learned from Laolao were quite mild and harmless, though complicated. But I knew that there were plenty of bad ones she'd never mentioned to me, like the love spell—or more accurately, love curse—practiced in Southeast Asia. The ritual involves preparation of curse oil, maledictions, and the burning of talismans, incense, and paper money. Curse oil is made by burning a deceased virgin's maidenhead, then rubbing it on a man's body.

Miraculously, the man will lose all his judgment, find the woman irresistibly beautiful, and all others ugly and repugnant. Unfortunately, sometimes this love charm can be reversed by a more powerful shaman.

Sabrina's voice rose in the air, pulling me back from my thoughts. "When Alfredo was madly in love with me, he showered me with money and jewelry. I saved as much as I could and that's how I've survived till now. Unfortunately I don't have much left. But I won't need much more, because I am dying."

Not knowing how to respond, I remained silent.

"But now Alfredo has a new love," Sabrina said.

"Who?"

"Who else? The one right in front of me."

"You mean me! What makes you think that? Anyway, I have no romantic interest in him."

"But that doesn't stop him from fancying you."

"But why me?"

"Who needs a reason for love? You're pretty and daring—also, you look like Isabelle!"

I had assumed that Isabelle was Alfredo's daughter.

As if guessing my thought, my friend said, "Isabelle was not Alfredo's daughter, she was my late husband's."

Before I could respond, she added, "During the five years Alfredo and I were together when he was completely in love with me, he treated Isabelle like his own daughter."

"So he married you?"

She laughed bitterly. "Hardly. He was still married to his wife, Penelope."

"So you were having an affair . . . ?"

She rolled her eyes. "Eileen, you're so naïve! This happens every day."

"Yes, of course," I said, feeling stupid.

"Alfredo didn't legally adopt Isabelle, he did it by having a witches' ceremony. "

"A witches' adoption?"

"A ceremony to merge their blood, so they became blood relatives. Alfredo and his wife didn't have children and Isabelle had lost her father. She was very pretty and flirtatious, so they attached to each other instantly. Isabelle even called Alfredo Dada. When Alfredo left us, Isabelle became depressed and bitter."

Sabrina stared at the stone angel guarding her daughter's grave, her eyes sad. "After they'd become father and daughter, strangely Alfredo seemed to lose interest in me. So I paid Nathalia to cast more spells, but they stopped working. Alfredo didn't care about me anymore."

"So he went back to his wife?"

"Not really. Since he'd never actually left her."

Sabrina sighed, her eyes looking far away over the gravestones to where withered branches from an ancient tree stretched agonizingly toward the sky.

"I haven't told you the worst of it. Alfredo fell in love with Nathalia, the witch whom I hired to keep him in love with me!"

"How could that happen?"

"Nathalia became so jealous of me and Isabelle that she took away my lover and patron! She left me and Isabelle helpless, loveless, and penniless. A heartless, evil woman. Hateful!"

"But Alfredo gave you jewelry and cash, right?"

"After he left, there was no more coming in, so I had to be very thrifty. I'm a high-maintenance woman. I shouldn't have to pinch pennies."

It looked like she was still high maintenance despite being supposedly penniless.

"Now I'm old, so I need to pay for company. You think Diego would stick around otherwise? I've turned from a beautiful woman pursued relentlessly by men to an old hag relentlessly pursuing men. . . . Hahaha! Karma, isn't it?"

Her self-denigration was getting tedious.

"Sabrina, stop putting yourself down—please!"

I shivered as a chilly wind gusted over the cemetery.

Sabrina looked up, her eyes tired. "I'm sorry to bore you with an old woman's sorrows. Eileen, tell me more about yourself."

I didn't think she was really interested, but I told her anyway about my grandmother, Laolao, my teaching job, and about my on-and-off relationship with Ivan. I ended by saying, "My life must not sound very interesting to you."

But when I looked up I saw that her eyes were round like two shiny coins.

"No!" she said. "I envy you. What a fulfilling and adventurous life! I hope you'll marry this rich Ivan and have lots of children. I also pray that I'll live long enough to visit you two in America."

"You'd be most welcome. But right now Ivan is just a friend, not my boyfriend. I'm not sure I really want to marry him."

"Of course you should! Eileen, don't be stupid! You've got a rich man, hang on to him! I won't let myself die until I get your wedding invitation, how's that?" Then she sighed heavily. "But if you put the day off too long, I won't make it."

I patted her swollen hand. "Don't be so pessimistic, my friend. You never know, life is full of surprises, right?"

"Sorry, but there will be no surprise about this." Her eyes looked even hollower in the lengthening shadows. "I won't be around when it happens, but I am sure that you'll successfully write your book and get tenure. But I know that someday you will accomplish something even bigger and better."

"Like what, is being a professor and writing books not good enough?"

"I don't know what it will be, but it will be something completely out of the ordinary."

"Maybe . . ."

"I'm sure. But it's getting chilly out here, so let's go back to my place, now that you two are acquainted."

"Me and who?"

"You and Isabelle, who else? Trust me, she's been listening."

Maybe the dead do listen to us, but whatever they may think about us, they keep to themselves.

Back at Sabrina's home, after we'd sat down and been brought snacks and drinks by the maid, Sabrina handed me a notebook.

"Isabelle's diary. Take a look so you'll have a better idea of her."

Of course I was curious to read the thoughts of this woman who had died young and whom I'd never met—except somehow we had met, first on the ferry and then when she came into my dream. But it made me a little uncomfortable that Sabrina was so eager to introduce her dead daughter to a stranger from a far-off land. Maybe all mothers love their daughters so much they must share them with the world, whether beautiful or plain, vibrantly alive or long dead.

I caressed the pages of the diary with my hand. "You're not afraid that I'll lose it?"

"No, I can tell you're a very careful person who values what is important. But you needn't worry, because this is only a copy. The original is locked in my safe. Believe it or not, I haven't read all of it, so maybe there are things I don't yet know about Isabelle."

"Aren't you curious?"

"Of course. Maybe someday I'll read all of it, but it's too painful now."

By my estimate, twenty years had passed. So when would she be ready? Probably never.

"Soon I will be in the place where everything is forgotten," said Sabrina. "But you will still be here to remember her."

"But why me?"

"Because I feel that you two are connected in some way. I don't want you to miss out."

"Miss out on what?"

"I'm not sure, exactly. But I know that whatever it is, it will be very important for you."

I was glad for this time with Sabrina because I'd learned more about witches and about her departed daughter. But being around her was spooky, too, with all her talk of how I was connected to the dead girl, who seemed to have decided to haunt me in my dreams.

I'd come to the island to have strange experiences, but I seemed to be getting more than I'd bargained for. Maybe Laolao was right and my destiny was to carry on the family tradition and become a shamaness—whether I wanted to or not. If there is such a thing as destiny, it is chosen for us. It just seemed particularly odd that I had to learn about my own destiny from dead people.

14

Isabelle's Diary

After I left Sabrina's house I walked to the bus stop and waited almost half an hour for the bus back to my hotel. I was extremely eager to read the diary, but somehow I did not want to take it out where it could be seen by others.

Once I was back in my room, I sat on the bed and immediately opened Isabelle's diary to the first page.

> Dear Diary:
>
> Even when I was young, I felt that I was old. I didn't know why I thought this until one day I figured it out. It must be that I've lived before, in another time and place—probably in ancient China. Everyone who thinks she was reincarnated believes she'd been a beautiful princess, so maybe I was too. That's what I like to think when I look at myself in the mirror.
>
> When I was little I knew China was on the other side of the world, so I thought I could see my ancient palace if I could dive deeply enough under the sea.
>
> When I saw an illustration of the famous city of

the Tang dynasty—Chang'an—I decided that is where I lived as a princess, more than a thousand years ago. I was particularly fascinated by the story of Princess Precious Jade.

When the princess reached thirteen, a barbarian king, having heard about her beauty, asked for her in marriage. But her parents had no heart to send her away to the cold, desolate far north. So they told the barbarian king that the gods would severely afflict any man who took their daughter away.

To hide her in case the barbarian invaded, her parents had a lavish temple constructed for her. Every day she made offerings to the deities and recited sutras. During the evening, she'd invite eminent monks, famous scholars, and poets to gather in the temple's courtyard. Strolling among the odd-shaped rocks and exotic flowers, the princess and her guests would drink tea brewed with snow from flower petals, while reciting poetry, viewing paintings, and doing calligraphy—flirting all the while.

Her lovers included a handsome Buddhist monk and Li Bai, one of China's greatest poets. So great was the poet's love for the princess, that when she died a peaceful death inside the temple, the great poet died the same evening. But the monk was not as lucky, for he was soon executed.

I wished I could live like Princess Precious Jade. I like to imagine living as a recluse in a mountain temple, sipping fragranced tea while conversing with artists and poets. But alas, I am not a princess.

However, now anytime I want I can dive under this noisy world into one of silence and strange visions. The sea has become my temple. Here I feel I really am a princess, the recluse of the sea. . . .

* * *

That evening, Isabelle came into my dream again. At first she stared silently at me with her sad, curious eyes, as if we were under the sea together.

"Why do you come to see me?" I asked her.

"I'm your spiritual sister."

"I already have a sister. Her name is Brenda and she works as a lawyer in San Francisco."

"That doesn't matter. We might even have been real sisters during the Tang dynasty one thousand years ago. So you must do something for me."

"What's that?"

"Go to the lake near the small village. Then you'll know."

"Know what?"

"How I died."

"You don't know yourself? You drowned, remember?"

"That's what people say, but I think . . ."

"What?"

"There's this lake near a village."

"What lake and what village?"

"The village nearest my dada's castle. And there's the lake where I supposedly drowned."

"Who's your father?"

"You know who. My father. And my lover."

Just then she vanished and I woke up, feeling distressed. What if the dream was true? Even if Alfredo was not her biological father . . . I didn't want to think about it.

Though I would never have admitted to anyone that it was because of a dream, I decided I would go to the lake, in case I really could learn something.

The next morning, after having breakfast at the hotel, with the dream still lingering in my mind, I saw an article in the local newspaper.

PRIEST TO PERFORM EXORCISM

The mayor, in response to widely circulated rumors about the ground swallowing up a homeless

> man and a dog, has decided to engage a priest to perform an exorcism. This was at the behest of area residents who are convinced something supernatural is involved.
>
> No one has yet reported a missing person or dog, and no eyewitness has come forward.
>
> The police continue to investigate.

After hearing this news I decided to postpone my trip to the lake and instead go see the exorcism. Fortunately, as usual on the islands, the weather was pleasant with a light breeze blowing from the south, the most auspicious direction. When I reached the area where the crack had occurred I saw that a small crowd had already gathered under a nearby tree. Its roots extended deep into the ground, as if they were trying to offer comfort to the vanished man and dog. Among the crowd were several men snapping pictures, either reporters or just tourists. Parents held on to tugging children, already bored with waiting.

Finally, a small procession of solemn-faced men in exotic robes approached the area. The head priest, dressed in a white and gold robe, kept dipping a brush into a silver vessel and sprinkling the water on the ground. As he approached I could hear the priests chanting in low, resonant voices.

Soon the simple ritual was over and onlookers began to disperse. To my surprise, however, no one, neither the priests nor the audience, seemed to have paid any attention to the faint cracks on the ground. Somehow I felt I could read them, and they seemed to say:

Shamans dance by the lake
Holding a maiden and a handicapped boy to sacrifice

I wondered if I was having hallucinations, so as a young man walked by I stopped him, and asked, "Señor, do you see those cracks on the ground?"

He looked puzzled. "What do you mean?"

"Don't you see those cracks over there?"

"Hmmm . . . yes, señorita, but cracks are everywhere, so what's so special about these?"

He cast me a strange look, then sauntered away, shaking his head. I realized I was going to have to get used to seeing things that other people could not. I sensed that my crack readings—real or imaginary—were telling me something important. But what?

I decided to return to my hotel because I wanted to finish Isabelle's diary so I could give it back to Sabrina. Though I was fascinated by this thin book, it also evoked fear. I was peering into the soul of a dead person.

Back in my room, I poured a glass of mineral water and braved myself to continue to read Isabelle's diary. I opened the notebook at random and came upon:

> Dear World,
>
> Recently I've been having horrible dreams, as if someone is about to die. In one of them I went to answer the door to find a coffin lying on the ground. Inside was a middle-aged woman crying and smiling crazily. She might have looked like my mother, but I wasn't sure because it was too dark. In another dream I was diving and under a rock I spotted a severed arm with what looked like my mother's watch on the wrist.
>
> But of course I didn't tell any of this to Mother. So I have to keep it to myself, which is extremely painful.

I flipped to another page and read:

> It's my birthday today. At breakfast, Mother told me that after Alfredo left she'd had to work as a stripper and a prostitute to keep food on our table.
>
> Why did she choose to tell me this on my birthday?
>
> Mother said it was only when she threatened to tell Alfredo's wife that he gave her any money.

> Mother said Alfredo is filthy rich so the pittance he gave her was a slap on the face!
>
> I decided to take matters into my own hands and went to Alfredo, demanding more money. But he turned me down! So much for fatherly feeling. He even cursed at me.
>
> Maybe I'll tell his wife myself. Then he'll be sorry.

I was eager to discover what happened after the confrontation, so I skimmed through the rest of the diary but found nothing more about it. On the final page I read:

> I keep having these bad dreams. Is God trying to tell me something? I'll go for a dive—maybe I'll find an answer in the quiet of the undersea world.

It sounded like she was leading up to more unhappiness and I wanted to sleep this night at least without disturbing dreams. So I set the book aside and turned out the light.

The next day I was once again on the rickety bus to Sabrina's home. She welcomed me and prepared a pot of tea while I waited on her worn couch. I took a few sips of tea before gathering up my courage.

"Sabrina, I need to ask—how did Isabelle die?"

"I told you, she drowned." She looked down at her hands that were tightly clasped. "I never liked her diving, but it was her passion. She sold some of her photographs to magazines but never made very much."

"But she must have been an experienced diver. How could she have drowned?"

"She was too smart to have drowned by accident." Sabrina took a gulp of brandy and grimaced. "I almost have the feeling that Isabelle didn't want to live in this evil world. I always suspected . . ."

"What?"

She sighed. "Isabelle was pure and innocent. She wanted to believe everyone else was as good as she was. She didn't belong here."

I struggled to digest what she'd just told me.

My friend stared at me, her eyes full of misery. "If it wasn't an accident or she didn't kill herself, there's a third possibility."

"Which is?"

"That she was murdered."

I shook my head. "Oh no! Why would anyone have killed her? What would be the motive? Did the police investigate?"

Sabrina didn't answer but just looked down, shaking her head. I thought of Isabelle, setting out for a dive to calm herself and then never returning.

I knew Sabrina did not want to say any more, but I pressed her anyway. "Do you think the culprit might be . . ." But I just couldn't say his name.

"You've met him," she said.

"Who?"

This time she didn't respond. I sipped my tea and watched her pour herself more brandy.

Finally, she spoke. "Eileen, I'm so happy that we met. I hope you can find out how Isabelle really died."

"Isabelle has been gone for two decades. I'm a scholar, not a detective. Sometimes even experienced divers drown. Just like good drivers can have accidents."

I feared I had been insensitive, but Sabrina looked unperturbed.

Suddenly it occurred to me that hearing of my dreams might be of some comfort to her, so I said, "Isabelle came in my dreams a couple of times."

Her eyes brightened. "Did my daughter say anything?"

"She told me to go look for a lake here on Tenerife Island."

"Yes, that's where it happened. Please go there and see what you can discover."

Thinking of the lake, I was reminded of the cracks in the earth. Rationally, I knew I should ignore this, but Laolao had fed so much metaphysics into my mind that I could not dismiss such thoughts. I always remembered my grandmother's constant warnings: "Don't dismiss signs! Pay attention to them or you'll never know what you missed. If you really listen, the world is full of voices that you need to hear."

I couldn't tell if Sabrina felt better or worse after talking about her deceased daughter. I did not want her to become despondent, so I promised I would visit the lake and tell her what I found.

Back in the hotel, I bought a map of the area, hoping to get a better idea of where things were. I saw Heartbreak Castle, and the pond where Cecily and her fellow witches had danced. Then, farther away, there was another blue area, labeled "Past Life Lake."

15

The Village Carpenter

Past Life Lake was near a small village seemingly not too far from the castle. I decided to visit the village first. Perhaps the villagers could tell me something useful about the lake, or maybe even about Isabelle.

Before I set off on my "past-life" journey, I bought food that I could give as gifts to the villagers: candy, tea, coffee, canned fish, dried sausage, even some simple medicine like aspirin and poultices. I hoped this would help me befriend the probably impoverished locals.

There was no public transport to the village, so with the help of the hotel's concierge, I hired a car. After a tedious drive through empty land punctuated only by low bushes and trees, the driver pulled up beside a small path.

"This leads to the village."

"Why can't you just take me there?"

"Sorry, señorita, the road is too narrow and bumpy; it might damage my car. It's better you walk. It's only about two miles."

I sensed that there was no point in arguing, so I paid, got out, and began my journey. Possibly to nowhere, but maybe to somewhere or even everywhere. A perfect April day—impossible not to be in a good mood, with the sky clear and blue, and the path smooth, though narrow. Rustling leaves and the occasional chirping of birds kept me company. With my senses opening to the fresh air and the pleasant smell of vegetation, I felt as if I were stepping back into a past life, or a fairy land.

The palm fronds were a mixture of green and yellow, and the sun's rays sprinkled gold dust over the foliage. Everything seemed to be gilded with magic. I had no idea what awaited me at the end of this path, but just concentrated on enjoying the fleeting moment before it vanished—or turned into a nightmare.

After walking for about a half hour, I spotted a few houses off in the distance. As I approached I could see that all were flimsily built, as if pasted together by mud and vulnerable to being blown away by the next strong wind. Yet they had a strangely alluring fairy-tale quality, like immortals' dwellings.

I entered the village clearing, walked up to the nearest house, and knocked.

"Quién está?" Anyone here? I called.

There was no answer so I went around to the back of the house. In the distance I saw a young, muscular man splitting wood with an ax. Under the bright sun, this fresh-faced man flexing his muscles was a pleasant, sensuous sight. He was quite absorbed in his task so I enjoyed watching him, unnoticed. After a few minutes he put down his ax, looked up, and finally saw me. He smiled warmly like the morning sun.

"*Buenos días.* I've come to this village to find a lake," I said.

"*Hola, señorita. Yo soy* Luis. Welcome to our little village. You must be thirsty after the long walk here. May I bring you a drink?"

I must have lived a toxic city life for too long, because I found myself worrying that he might put poison in the drink, or try to lure me into some trap. After all, I'd already been drugged by the witches. Then I felt guilty being suspicious of this friendly, innocent village man.

I smiled back warmly. "Yes, please, that'd be lovely."

The young man quickly disappeared into the house, then came back with a tray. He gestured for me to sit at a wooden table. Then he placed an earthenware teapot, two cups, and a plate of bananas and dried grapes on the table in front of me.

My long walk had left me hungry and thirsty, so I eagerly sipped my tea and helped myself to the fruit.

"Señorita, where are you from? What brings you to our village?" he asked as I ate.

"My name is Eileen Chen. I'm Chinese, but I live in San Francisco in the U.S."

"My goodness, that's really far away. Both China and America."

"Not all that far. Just a plane trip."

"I've never been in an airplane." He looked embarrassed.

"Surely you will someday."

"I hope so."

I looked around at the other houses scattered like chess pieces on a chessboard. "Luis, this is a small village to be found on a map."

"They must have sold you an old map."

"How's that?"

"This village used to be much bigger, but people keep moving out."

"It's so peaceful here. Why would people leave?"

He sighed. "It's a long story."

I noticed that around his neck was a silver chain. I somehow felt I should not ask him about it, so instead I said, "Do you know about a lake near here?"

"Señorita Chen—"

"Please call me Eileen."

"We don't like to go to the lake, Eileen."

"May I know why?"

"It's nicknamed the Ghost Lake. It's such bad luck that some say it's actually a pool of tears disguised as a lake."

"Who says that?"

"I've heard that since I was a child. Everybody here knows it."

"So something happened there?"

"They say that sometimes one can see people." He lowered his voice into a whisper. "Not people but ghosts—dwelling deep underneath. Sometimes people can see their past and future lives unfolding under the water."

"That does sound scary. But also like complete nonsense. Are you sure this wasn't just made up to scare the children and tourists?"

"It's why people have been moving away from here over the years. Only Father Fernando's church and three families are left, and only because we're too poor to move." He smiled dreamily. "But I kind of like it here. It's so calm. Besides, I grew up here and don't know any other places. Sad, isn't it? I'd like to see the world someday. I've read a lot of books about faraway places. Someday I hope to visit China and America."

"That's good, Luis. The Chinese say, 'Read ten thousand books and travel ten thousand miles.'"

"Yes, yes, that's exactly what I think!"

I found Luis's enthusiasm and innocence quite touching, yet I doubted that a man stuck in this poor village with mostly ghosts for company could have a chance to see the world.

"Have you been planning to leave?" I asked him.

"Yes! I've been saving up money. I make furniture and sell it. This table here—I should be able to get twenty thousand pesetas for it!"

This sounded like a lot, but when I did a quick conversion in my head it was only about one hundred and thirty dollars. Not much toward an airplane ticket.

"So you're a carpenter?"

He nodded. "It's quiet here so I have plenty of time to work and think."

"What do you think about?"

"My future, Grandpa, the village, the lake . . ."

"What about this lake?"

"I guess you better ask Grandpa. He'll be back for dinner. Grandpa knows everything."

I was curious to learn more about the ghost lake but was not sure I should wait until dinnertime. I also wasn't sure if it was a good idea to go to the lake with Luis, a man I'd just met.

As I hesitated, he asked, "Eileen, are you an educated woman?"

It was an odd, yet appealing question. I couldn't help but smile at this seemingly guileless young man. He had high cheekbones, a high nose, and a square, but expressive face. His physique was muscular but was the result of real work, not from lifting weights in the gym like the men I knew in San Francisco.

"I guess so," I answered. "I'm a professor, and I've come to gather material to write a book."

"Wow, a professor! You must have read lots and lots of books?"

I nodded.

His face lit up. "I'd like to be a learned man someday, but for now I just read books when I can."

I suddenly felt tempted to offer to teach him but swallowed my words. There was no need to raise a young person's hopes since I was only a passing tourist.

"You speak well—do you still go to school?" I asked him.

"Yes, it's about an hour's walk from here. But now I don't have to go every day because Father Fernando gives me lessons in the church. And I read a lot—Father Fernando lends me books." He stood up and beckoned me to follow him inside the house.

It was a small place but warmly decorated with rock figurines, wildflowers, and some rough-hewed wooden furniture, in shapes that made me think of rock formations or even a waterfall. Above a long wooden chair hung a plaque inscribed **GOD IS LOVE**.

"Who made all of this?" I said, pointing to the furniture.

"I did. Do you like them?"

"They're beautiful. You're very gifted."

"You really think so?"

"Who taught you?"

"Grandpa. He's very good with his hands."

"Do you ever think of going to the city to start a career?"

"I don't have the money. Besides, I can't just leave Grandpa behind. He's old and needs me."

"You're a very decent young man, Luis. I love your house."

He smiled happily. "I like to make things." He paused, then spoke again, blushing. "I also hope to have a family someday."

I didn't know what to say to this, so I went up to look at the spines of the books on a nearby shelf. They were mostly novels but also some poetry.

"Where did you get these?"

"Some I bought secondhand in the city market. And some are from my school library."

"Chinese call stealing a book an elegant offense."

He seemed a little discomfited by this. "I will return them eventually."

"That's good. But finish reading them first. How old are you, Luis?"

"I'm not sure, I think at least twenty."

"I'm thirteen years older than you!"

"So you're thirty-three?"

I nodded.

"But you don't look it, not at all."

"Then how old do you think I look?" I asked, hoping he'd say at least ten years younger.

"I think how long you live on this earth is irrelevant. Maybe you're a goddess. You're beautiful too."

"You don't know anything about me."

"But I can feel it in my heart." He put his hand on his chest.

"Young as you are, you've already developed a glib tongue," I said with a laugh.

"I only say what I feel," he said, looking very serious.

"How come you live with your grandpa? Where are your parents?" I asked, trying to change the subject.

"I've never met them. They both died when I was young. Whenever I ask Grandpa, he talks about something else. I guess he doesn't want to tell me, but someday when I have some money I'll try to find out what happened to my parents."

"Then what about your grandpa?"

"I hope he'll still be around and I can bring him along. And I hope I'll run into a special girl . . . maybe someone like you."

We went back outside and sat at the table again. Luis begged me to tell him about China and America. It seemed to be his only way to explore the world outside his tiny village. We sipped tea and chatted as the sun descended to the horizon, dyeing the village a rich orange. Then I heard footsteps approaching. Luis dashed up to go greet an old man.

"Grandpa!"

He helped his grandpa to sit on a chair by the table. To my surprise, Grandpa was none other than the crazy old sculptor from whom I bought—or took—the four sculptures!

I turned to the old man and smiled. "*Hola,* Grandpa!" I explained to Luis how I first ran into the old man.

Luis looked surprised and amused at the same time.

Grandpa cast me a nonchalant glance, then said to Luis, "I'm hungry, cook me something to eat."

I was shocked again that the old man was neither crazy nor a mute!

I asked. "Grandpa, sorry that I thought you're—"

"Mute and deaf? Hahaha! When we met earlier, you acted so crazy that I was too scared to talk!"

Was that so? Just as I thought he was crazy he had been thinking the same about me.

"Did you work well today, Grandpa?" Luis asked.

The older man shook his head, then took something from his pocket and handed it to Luis. It was a well-crafted horse's head. But nothing special, nothing like the sculptures I'd bought from him.

"It's not yet finished," said Luis. "Are you tired?"

"No," the old man said, casting me a dirty glance, "when this dark-eyed, yellow-skinned woman took my best works, she also stole my inspiration."

I felt alarmed to be accused of being a thief in such a horrible way.

"Grandpa, I certainly don't want you to lose your inspiration," I said. "I did pay you. Do you want me to give you your sculptures back?" My heart ached at the thought of departing with my treasures.

He caressed his white beard and thought for a while, then said, "No, it's too late. What is done can't be undone. Maybe God is telling me that it's time for me to stop my rock carving. Anyway, what are you doing here in my village? Seducing my grandson?"

What a thought! I almost laughed out loud but bit my tongue to suppress myself.

"Grandpa, please stop talking nonsense again. Señorita Eileen and I have only been talking," said Luis.

With his cloudy eyes, Grandpa gave me an intense once-over. "Señorita Eileen, I'm sure you can tell my grandson is a nice-looking lad and he's also a skilled furniture maker. So many women, young and old, especially the widows and their daughters, are infatuated with Luis. I only hope you're not one of them. I can't afford to lose my only grandson to a dark-eyed woman from a far-off land!"

Instead of being offended, I laughed out loud.

"Grandpa, please stop embarrassing me! Eileen and I have really only been talking!"

"All right, then stop talking now and go fix me dinner!" He patted his protruding belly. "Can't you hear my stomach rumbling?"

Luis swiftly disappeared into the house and soon I heard the banging of pots and pans, pouring water, and sizzling oil.

"You have dinner with us and stay overnight here. Now come inside," the old man commanded.

"With pleasure, Grandpa."

I couldn't believe that I had just gladly accepted such a rude invitation from a grumpy, racist old man.

16

Past Life Lake

Luis, besides being a skilled carpenter, turned out to be a very good cook. Surrounded by plants and Luis's woodwork, we helped ourselves to simple but tasty dishes of yellow rice with chicken, black beans, onions and green peppers, tilapia al ajillo, and big, soft slices of freshly baked bread.

Wiping his sauce-smeared beard with a worn cloth, Grandpa tossed me a question. "Why did you come here?"

"To see the lake."

"That lake is not a place for a young woman. But if you really came all the way from America, I'll take you there after we have coffee. But whatever you see, don't say anything because if the ghosts hear you talking about them, they'll become real."

This sounded silly—but I was still scared. Would I actually see my future below the water? Or would I see ghosts? But isn't everyone's future to eventually turn into a ghost?

"Can we go in the morning?" I asked.

"Not if you want to see *things,*" Grandpa said mysteriously.

The witch in me definitely wanted to see something ghostly. But the woman in me might not be able to take these ghostly sights.

"It'll be dark by the time we're there, so how can we see anything?" I asked.

"Haha! The dark is when they appear. But even if you don't see them, they will see you. And when they see you, you'll 'see' them by feeling their presence. Don't worry, Eileen. If they want to take someone with them it'll be me, not you. Your time is far from being up."

That was reassuring. But what if the ghosts here are like Americans, totally youth-oriented? Anyway, I might not have another chance. The old man was notional and might change his mind.

After we had drained our coffee cups and cleared the table, Grandpa went inside and returned with two flashlights. Handing one to me, he told Luis to stay and watch the house until we got back.

"But I want to see the lake too," Luis protested.

"No, it's not for you. It will suck out a young person's energy. Stay here till we come back."

I actually wanted Luis to come along since I wasn't sure I could trust the old man. But he took my arm and pulled me along. Despite his frail looks, his arms were powerful, as was his determination.

As if approaching a sacred place, neither of us spoke as we walked down a murky path, the sky hidden by overhanging trees. The flashlights cast narrow, flickering beams. The shadows were filled with ghosts by my overactive imagination. They seemed to keep pace with us as we made our way along the path.

Finally, we entered a clearing and the lake appeared, gleaming faintly in the moonlight. There was nothing else to see except the dark boundaries of the trees, as if I had left the normal world completely behind.

Approaching the water, I felt a chill, though in a pleasant way. In the moonlight, the ripples on the lake conjured up tiny, sparkling reflections, like stars scattered on a dark sky. Grandpa signaled me to kneel down with him and put my hands together in a prayer gesture. Eyes closed, he mumbled something I couldn't understand, all the while remaining motionless. It was as if the sculptor had turned into a sculpture himself.

As he mumbled on I became impatient. "Grandpa, why are you closing your eyes—are you going to be like this the whole time?"

"At ninety I've seen enough. And right now I don't want to see anything I'm not supposed to. I will die soon and then I'll see nothing but ghosts, so there's no reason to look for them now. I'll just close my eyes and wait while you contemplate the lake. You can look into the water as long as you want."

Suddenly I wondered why I had come to this surreal place rather than staying home in San Francisco. My heart beating like a metronome in presto, I turned my gaze back to the lake. Staring at its gleaming, silky surface, to my surprise, instead of fear I felt a wave of tenderness surge inside me. The vast expanse of water looked clear, but the bottom was obscured, like a beautiful woman's face covered with a veil. As I stared into the water, I felt myself slipping into a trance.

Minutes later, I sensed a presence surrounding me. Now I was scared, and froze in place, not daring to move even my lashes and quieting my breathing. Gradually from the surface of the water I began to hear intense whispers seeming to reveal ancient secrets, if only I could make out what they were saying. My eyes and ears seemed to open up to things I had never before seen and sounds I had never before heard. It was in a language I could almost, but not quite, understand.

I turned to Grandpa, wondering if he also heard the voices, but he was nowhere to be seen. He must have stealthily escaped through the brush back to the path. Or, quite possibly, he knew another way back. It seemed impossible that he would have abandoned me here. Yet, he was gone. The chill that had felt good before now raised goose bumps and I could feel my adrenaline surge. Suddenly my legs felt like jellyfish, yet as if rooted to the ground by some hidden force.

I told myself not to panic but instead to concentrate on my breathing. Perhaps because of my intense emotion, I began to feel as if my soul were escaping from my body and sinking into the depths of the lake. I was diffused in the water, joining the spirits that had dwelled there from time immemorial up to the present. I saw—or thought I saw—a small group of people, like that in a small village, chatting, eating, working, strolling . . .

A face seemed to float by me, starting to come into focus but still blurred by the water. I saw—or imagined—that it was Sabrina's long-dead daughter, Isabelle. Her mouth was moving and soon our eyes met. I strained to hear her words, but they were lost in the vast expanse of water.

Seeing that I couldn't hear her, Isabelle began to gesture desperately. Then, an older woman, less distinct but resembling Sabrina, approached as if to comfort her. . . .

All at once I found myself back in my body, looking at the lake that seemed as calm and bright as before. But now it was just an empty lake once more.

This brief experience had exhausted me and I decided to return to the village. After an anxious search I found the flashlight that the old man had had the decency to leave for me. I followed our footprints back along the mushy ground until I was back on the path. Despite my fear I was able to reach the house to find Luis waiting. He'd thoughtfully fixed his room for me and announced he would sleep on the long chair in the living room.

"Are you all right, Eileen?" His voice was filled with concern.

"I'm okay," I said, my voice trembling. "When did Grandpa come back?"

"Not long after you two went to the lake. He said he was exhausted by all the dead energy and had to go to sleep early."

"So he just left me there to take in all the dead energy by myself?"

"I'm so sorry about this. But Grandpa's an old man and he does as he pleases. I was very worried, but he said you're a very strong and brave woman. I would have come for you, but I don't know the way and he wouldn't tell me."

"I didn't feel very brave on the way back. It's pretty scary. What makes him think I'm so brave?"

"Because most people want to leave this village, but you came here, all by yourself."

I felt my lids drooping, so I thanked Luis, went inside his room, and collapsed on the narrow bed. Though my body instantly fell asleep, my unconscious mind kept whirling like a merry-go-round. How could my consciousness leave my body and enter the lake? And my visions—I could make no sense of seeing Isabelle and Sabrina underwater, one long dead, the other still alive.

When I woke up for a moment I realized what had happened—my third eye had opened, allowing me to see beings in the other realm. I was beginning to believe that I really had inherited Laolao's powers. First by making the guitar string break, then this out-of-body experience. Maybe it really was my destiny to be a witch or shamaness.

When I thought about Isabelle I felt distressed by her obvious desperation to communicate with me. Was she trying to tell me the truth about her death? I felt unable to move, even a bit sick.

Laolao always told me that when a person is ill, evil forces can take this as an opportunity to enter your body and wander around sucking up your *qi,* playing with your mind, or even break things. Now I could tell that my *qi* was weak, so I felt completely helpless against beings whose nature was beyond my comprehension.

In my confusion I wished for Laolao's calm explanation of the ghosts and other terrifying phenomena. Now in my peculiar mental state I wished that she were here to explain what was happening. And just as I wished for her help, she seemed to be in my room, not in the flesh but as a warm presence. Her voice was weaker than it had been in life, but her gentle concern was unmistakable.

Laolao smiled, and said to me reassuringly, "Eileen, just as our body breathes, the mountains and lakes breathe too. It is for you to align your *qi* to the divine pulse. This will bring you into harmony with the universe and extend your powers. In San Francisco you wasted too much time with that fool Ivan. Now you are back in nature. So you should practice until you can follow your breath into the core of the Dao."

I asked, "Laolao, why did you come to me now, after all these years?"

"So you can be prepared."

"For what?"

"There is a mystery that must be solved. I cannot do it because I no longer have a body. So you must."

"What's the mystery?"

"Heaven's secrets are not revealed until the time is right. Everything in life is about situation and timing. Whatever you do, choose the right time.

"You're my granddaughter. Your powers will continue to increase. But you must promise Heaven to only use them for good, and not for petty things like making a buck or scrying into people's bedrooms. Will you promise me this?"

"Yes." But Laolao had definitely used her powers to make a buck. That was what had supported our little family.

"Sometimes," she continued, "good people can be blinded by situations and make wrong choices. But sometimes a bad choice is the only one.

"You will go on living in this dusty world for many more years. One day you will come to the other realm, so there is no point in my telling you about it now. In the meantime watch out for greed and lust. There is no end to desire. It isn't easy to stay rooted, but you must, no matter what happens.

"Promise me," she implored in a fading voice.

I whispered, "I promise," but I wasn't sure if she could hear me, or whether she'd even actually been here.

I dozed off, then half woke up again, trying to make sense of what my grandmother had said. I had another vision—or was it a dream?—this time of a young woman by my bedside. Indistinct as she was, she seemed to resemble Isabelle.

"You came to the lake," she said. "Now you're one of us. This is where you belong. Even if you go back, part of your consciousness will remain here. You must accept this."

After that I slept dreamlessly until I was awakened by the sound of wood being sawed. Bright sunlight streamed through the window and I was back in the normal world. Yet in the daylight, I felt more perplexed than ever by my strange visions. They seemed more than dreams, perhaps hallucinations induced by some miasma at the lake.

I could not escape thinking that my *yin* eye had really opened, just as Laolao had told me would someday happen. What would it be like perceiving the invisible realm? It seemed like a good thing to have developed a new ability—but it was also frightening. Like Luis's grandpa had said, why see ghosts before you become one yourself?

It was a relief when my eyes landed on Luis in the distance. I leaned out the window and waved to him.

He smiled back, and announced, "Morning, Eileen! Wait for me in the kitchen. I'll be right there to fix breakfast."

Soon we were sipping milk, chewing bread, and eating scrambled eggs with hot sauce. Grandpa did not join us.

"I hope my bed wasn't too uncomfortable for you," said Luis.

The bed was fine, but the dreams weren't. But I was not going to tell him about my nocturnal encounters with two dead people.

"I hope you don't mind my simple cooking. Eileen, we like you, so you are welcome to stay with us as long as you like," Luis said hopefully.

Since my arrival on the island, it seemed that nearly everyone I'd met wanted me to stay with them. Were they lonely? Bored? Or was there some other plan they had for a solitary woman traveler? Perhaps a collective conspiracy?

"Is Grandpa still sleeping?" I asked.

"No, he woke up very early and went out to get you something."

"How come? I thought he didn't like me."

"He's just a grumpy old man. In fact, he likes you a lot."

"He doesn't act like it."

"He said you're the only person who appreciates his rock carvings and paid him, even though he did not ask for money."

"I would think his work would be very popular here."

"Grandpa says that most people can't tell beauty from ugliness, refinement from vulgarity."

Now I suspected that Grandpa was in fact a wise man pretending to be crazy. I was reminded of the legend of two famous Chinese monks, Han Shan, or "Cold Mountain," and She De, or "Picked Up," in Chinese legend.

Han Shan got his name because he'd lived a secluded life in a remote mountain where, even in the hottest summer, its snowcap never melted. His friend She De was an orphan abandoned on the street and picked up by an enlightened Zen monk. Both Han Shan and She De were carefree and detached. Day in and day out, they swept leaves, scrawled poems on rocks, played with the village children, and appreciated the moon. They are honored in Chinese legend because they lived simple lives in accord with the Dao—The Great Way. . . .

Looking at Luis, I thought that perhaps he possessed the same clear, bright eyes and sweet smile as the two hermit immortals, and also lived a simple life in accord with the Dao. Perhaps Grandpa, too—enlightened Zen masters were famous for being grouchy.

I was wondering what Grandpa had in mind for me, but Luis wouldn't say. Instead he sipped his milk meditatively.

Just now we heard the old man's footsteps approaching. He strode up energetically and thrust a large bunch of wildflowers onto my lap.

"Beautiful flowers for a beautiful lady," he said with a smile.

I pressed the flowers against my nose to enjoy their fragrance. There was something particularly pleasing about receiving hand-picked wildflowers. Ivan liked to give me flowers, but they were all grown in a hothouse and wrapped in expensive paper and ribbons. The wildflowers were less spectacular, but a gesture straight from the heart.

I hugged the old man, then took out the food I'd brought from the city and spread it out on the table. "Grandpa, this is for you and Luis."

"No," said Luis, "you can keep it for yourself. We have enough food here."

Grandpa gave him a dirty look and waved his hand dismissively. "Stop jabbering and just take it, for God's sake!"

17

Grandpa's Sculpture Lessons

I felt comfortable with Luis and Grandpa, so I decided to stay with them for a few more days. I was curious to see the rest of the tiny village, so together they took me around to the two other households and the little church, where I met the fiftyish Father Fernando and his helper, Juan, a young man who was mute and walked with a limp.

In one of the houses lived a black-clad widow of fifty years. Grandpa told me that she went to church every day to pray that she'd die soon so she could join her husband in Heaven. The rumor was that she feared if she died after she'd become old and ugly, her husband, who'd died young, would fail to recognize her. In the last house dwelled an old man who had come after his retirement so long ago that he couldn't even remember when it was. Once there had been many more residents, but all of the others had left over the preceding decades.

It was only with Luis and Grandpa that I felt any connection. Looking at Luis's youthful face and body, I felt sorry for the young man and wondered why he stayed in this dying hamlet, his only company being old men and women and a God disinclined to show his face.

Nevertheless, I liked the village, at least for the time being. Luis and Grandpa were unlike anyone I knew back in the States and, though the thought made me apprehensive, I wanted to visit the lake again. I hoped to better understand why it'd had such an effect on me. I'd gone back there in the daylight, but then it just was a lake, nothing obviously mystical about it. I realized that if I was to have another out-of-body experience there, I would have to return at night, but I was not quite ready for this. I wanted my mind to be on an even keel for a while first.

One morning Father Fernando stopped by and invited me to take a walk with him in the woods. We strolled in silence under the towering palms before he spoke.

"Señorita Chen—"

"Call me Eileen, Father."

"Eileen, may I ask you your real reason for visiting our village? There's no life here for a young woman like you, nothing to do, no chance to make any money."

This priest was no fool. He knew I must have a reason for being here, and was not shy about asking me what it was.

"Father, I came here because of a dream. A young woman told me that if I could find a lake near here, I could learn about my past and my future. Something about her too."

Of course I didn't tell him that the young woman was a ghost.

He cast me a curious glance. "Young as you are, I doubt you have much of a past."

"The Chinese believe we have many past lives. Some can even remember details from a few of them. Anyway, I'm not as young as you think; Asians look younger. I'm thirty-three."

He laughed. "That's still pretty young to me! I'm fifty-six. Past lives . . . that's interesting. I don't reject this possibility, but we Catholics don't believe in past lives, only a future one—in Heaven, or Hell, that's up to God's judgment. Anyway, have you found what you've been seeking?"

"Somewhat." I made my answer vague because I feared that a Catholic priest would disapprove of my mingling with spirits and witches.

"Some woman in a dream told you to look for a lake and so you decided it was ours, which is not even on most maps. May I ask if you saw anything unusual in our lake?"

I didn't think I should tell a priest about what I'd seen, especially not about the opening of my third eye.

"Well . . . yes. But now I am not sure what it was."

"This woman in your dream, does she have a name?"

"Her name is Isabelle, Father."

"A common name here. Eileen, you shouldn't take dreams seriously. They are just the workings of your subconscious. They don't come from God. People think they see things in the lake. But for you, I think it's just exhaustion. Only Jesus and the saints possessed supernatural powers. Our Savior walked on water and divided five loaves of bread and two fishes to feed a whole village. But this came from God."

I felt like a deflated balloon. He was a priest, so he must know about spiritual things. And he lived near the lake. Maybe he was right; my newly opened third eye was merely in my mind, a hallucination. But Isabelle did come in my dream and then the lake turned out to be real.

"Father Fernando, is it true that someone drowned in this lake?"

He looked surprised. "This lake has been here forever, so there must have been the occasional drowning. I've been here about ten years—I came when Father Ricardo died. However, I won't be needed here for much longer. Everyone leaves if they can and those who remain are nearing death. Except of course for Luis, Juan, and hopefully myself."

"It's sad that the village is declining—I really like the quiet and friendliness here."

"Friendliness yes, but the quiet can become oppressive after a while."

He paused, then seemed to know who I was thinking about because he said, "Luis is a smart, good kid, so he'll do well elsewhere. Juan is the one whom I worry about."

"I only met Juan for a few minutes. Why can't he talk?"

"Nobody knows. We think he was born that way. Maybe his parents couldn't cope with his handicap, so they abandoned him at the church. Father Ricardo found a local woman to take care of him. Then, when he was older, Father brought him to work in our church. Anyway, Juan's past is taboo. People here think that foundlings are bad luck, so anyone old enough to remember won't talk about it.

"Unfortunately Juan can only express himself by writing and he knows only a few words. However"—Father Fernando looked up toward the sun shining through the treetops as if he were seeking the Almighty—"God looks after Juan. Father Ricardo took good care of him until he passed away."

So Juan, though handicapped, was not entirely unlucky. Without the two priests, the poor lad might have ended up like a broken piece of furniture, no longer used but not thrown away either, simply forgotten.

"I'm sad to say that Juan's condition will only get worse." Fernando sighed. "Luis and Juan are about the same age, but Luis is smart and poor Juan is slow. Sometimes I wonder what God's plan is."

I didn't respond, because I didn't think much of God or his plan. Laolao had taught me to believe only in karma, the cause and effect of one's actions. I wondered if Juan's parents had done something bad. Then I immediately felt guilty. After all, Juan was innocent and shouldn't be blamed for his misfortune.

Father Fernando's melancholy voice rose again in the palm-scented air. "As I said, this village will be abandoned very soon. Juan will probably end up in an institution. Grandpa is getting old, and once he returns to God, Luis will leave to pursue his dreams."

I felt sadness welling up inside me. This idyllic hamlet, abandoned, all because of rumors about a lake.

"As Christians, we do not believe in ghosts, yet this lake has caused great harm. It's best you don't go back there," the priest continued.

I suspected Father Fernando knew more about the lake than he let on, but I could tell he would say no more about it. He was a kind man, but in thrall to his church's teachings.

Later that day, Grandpa, Luis, and I were sitting together, finishing our coffee and watching the sunset.

When Luis got up to clear the table, Grandpa said in a serious tone, "Eileen, I've decided to teach you to sculpt. You have my best statutes now. So all I have left to pass on to you is my skill."

Wah, how kind! But I doubted I was a suitable student. "But, Grandpa, what about if I don't have any talent?"

"Bah! You think the great artists in the world knew they had talent before they started lessons?"

Maybe I did have talent and maybe I didn't. But I was here to research a book, not learn to sculpt.

Grandpa went inside the house and returned with a stained canvas sack, from which he took his tools: knives, hammers, chisels, charcoal pencils, and blocks of wood.

He spread everything on the table, then sat next to me. "Sculpting rock is too hard for a beginner, so we'll start with wood. I'll carve something simple—a bird. Watch how I do it."

I frowned, doubting that I could really learn.

He cast me a disapproving look, then picked up a small block of wood. "Now stop fretting and just watch."

An hour later, a small bird had alighted, perching on a twig. Next, seemingly with only a few strokes of his chisel, the face of an ancient Mediterranean goddess appeared, with two round holes for eyes and a protruding bulge for a nose. When finished, Grandpa looked very satisfied, caressing his creations, then viewing them from different angles.

From that day on, Grandpa gave me lessons in carving. Luis would watch sometimes, but he was usually busy in the yard, making the furniture that brought in the small amount of money they lived on. My lessons could stretch out to two or three hours. The rest of the time I would jot down notes for my book and go for solitary walks when restless, often bringing my sketchbook and drawing the sights that had become so familiar.

Around six in the evening, Luis would come back inside to prepare our dinner. I helped by washing clothes, feeding the chickens, and tidying up. Grandpa would always protest, telling me I was their guest and should not do chores.

One day, more than two weeks into my lessons, Grandpa pressed a piece of wood into my hand. "All right, now you carve something by yourself."

Under his intense, no-nonsense gaze, I felt as if I were going into a trance. My hands moved about with a mind of their own as scraps of wood fell to the ground. Finally the work was finished and I set it down as if guided by a superior power from above—or a ghost below.

Carved onto the wood was the face of a young woman above waves.

Grandpa looked startled. "I think I know this girl. Can it be that you knew her as well?"

Now back to my normal state of mind, I looked at my own creation—the girl looked like Isabelle. In a way I knew her—but only in my dreams and visions.

"You've never met this girl. She's been dead for many years." Grandpa's quavering voice rose again.

My eyes met Grandpa's cloudy ones. "You knew her?"

"It was pretty big news at the time. She drowned in the lake. That's why people stopped going there."

"How did it happen?" I was hoping for information, but I was quickly disappointed.

"She drowned in the lake. That's all that I know." Grandpa pointed to my statue. "Who's this person here?"

I saw that I'd also carved a small figure, a woman with long hair, watching "Isabelle" in the water.

Was someone or something sending me a message through my own hands? Had a woman witnessed Isabelle's death? Her own mother? It wasn't possible!

Grandpa started to say something, but then Luis's happy voice interrupted us.

"Grandpa, Eileen, I'm back and dinner will be ready soon!"

That night Isabelle came into my dream again, smiling sadly. She looked at me for a while, then whispered, "We were close in a past life. Now you must help me."

"What do you want me to do?"

"When I drowned, I'm not sure if I fell or . . . was pushed. I can't really remember that night. Just that I had a headache and felt dizzy from drinking."

"I'm not a detective."

"Keep your third eye open. Use your powers."

I woke up, soaked in sweat. I was getting tired of my obsession with Isabelle, but I suspected the only way to be rid of her was to solve the mystery of her death.

We must face what we fear.

18

God Is Gracious

I ended up staying with Luis and Grandpa for a little over a month. I knew I should visit the witches again to gather material for my book, but I kept putting it off. It was just too comfortable, staying in the little village with Grandpa and Luis, and I was not in the mood for anything unpleasant.

Every day after Grandpa finished teaching, I'd practice on my own, sculpting little things like a cow, a dog, a cup, a goddess, or whatever I fancied. Around six Luis would come home to cook. Once Grandpa had gone to bed after dinner, Luis would beg me to tell him stories about China.

I didn't know many stories, but I certainly knew the most famous Chinese one, *The Butterfly's Lovers.* So I told it the way I had heard it from my mother:

One thousand years ago during the Eastern Jin dynasty, women were not supposed to study, but marry early so they could raise children, do housework, and embroidery. But not Yingtai, a daughter of the wealthy Zhu family. She convinced her father to let her disguise herself as a boy and attend school in the city.

On the first day of school she met the young scholar, Liang. The two felt such intense connection that they took an oath to become sworn brothers.

During the three years as classmates in school, Yingtai fell in love with Liang, who had no idea that his best friend was in fact a woman.

One day Yingtai received a letter from home demanding her immediate return. Liang insisted on accompanying his friend for the first eighteen miles of the long journey home. On the way, Yingtai hinted to Liang in different ways that she was a woman, but none worked. Finally, she told him she'd be a matchmaker for him and her sister, to Liang's great delight. When they finally parted, Yingtai reminded Liang to visit her home to meet the sister.

A couple of months later Liang visited the Zhu family and was overjoyed to discover that the young "sister" was Yingtai herself. But no sooner had the two declared their passionate love than they learned that Yingtai's parents had already betrothed her to a wealthy businessman. Liang fell sick at this terrible news and soon died.

The day when Yingtai and the businessman married, a sudden wind prevented the wedding procession from passing beyond Liang's grave, located along the way. Yingtai dashed to her lover's grave and begged Heaven to open it. With a deafening clap of thunder, the grave opened up and the bride threw herself into it. Minutes later, two butterflies flew out from the grave side by side and soon disappeared in the clear blue sky.

When I finished, I told Luis, "This is Chinese *Romeo and Juliet*."

To my surprise, he began to tear up. Putting on a determined expression, he said, "I'd also die for someone I love."

"Luis," I smiled, "it's nice to think that, but trust me, you're way too young to realize that life is more than just love."

He shook his head. "No, I think love is everything. It gives hope and trust to people."

I could tell that he was enamored with me, so I reminded myself to avoid telling him love stories.

When we were alone, Luis would look at me lovingly, as if I

were his lover, or even his wife. He'd fix me tea or coffee and prepare treats that he'd gone outside the village to get. I was touched by his affection but also cautious because sooner or later I would go back to the States. I didn't want to break anyone's heart. I liked Luis very much, but I knew there was no future for a relationship.

Besides Luis and Grandpa, I also came to spend some time with Juan, Father Fernando's handicapped assistant. Like a vulnerable child, he stirred my maternal instincts. Despite his not being able to talk, there was an understanding between us. He was kindhearted and, in his own way, affectionate. Of course I felt pity for him, though he never seemed to want it. At times I was tempted to ask Father Fernando if he could explain how the young man's afflictions were part of God's plan. But the priest was a good man and I did not want to discomfit him.

One time Grandpa said, "Juan may be slow, but he's very kind. That's why Father Ricardo named him Juan, which means 'God is gracious.' " He sighed. "But his parents abandoned God's Grace."

"How could his parents be that cruel?" I asked.

"Ah . . . the human heart is something that no one can fathom."

This reminded me of the Chinese saying: "Understanding the human heart is like searching for a needle at the sea bottom."

Sometimes when Grandpa and Luis went out, I'd walk over to the church to spend time with "Grace of God."

Juan could utter "Ah . . . Ah . . ." and a few other sounds whose meaning I could only guess. But we could communicate in a halting way by writing on the ground with a stick. When he wanted to tell me something, he'd take me to his favorite place, the church's backyard, where the ground was soft enough for him to write on.

The first word he had written was *Madre,* making me think he missed his unknown mother. But then when he wrote *tú,* I realized he wanted me to be his mother since he'd never known one.

Another time he shocked me by writing the word *puta.*

At first I thought he was trying to insult me, but then I thought he was young and big and must have the same desires as other men, but with no way to fulfill them. Certainly he could not find a girlfriend or wife, so perhaps he hoped I could help him find someone willing, presumably for cash.

I felt sad that he had normal feelings while trapped in an abnormal body. Reluctantly I wrote, *"No es posible."*

He looked crestfallen, making me feel very sad. He put his hand on his heart and made a cradling movement. I guessed that he wanted a woman to hold him, to feel the feminine warmth that he'd never felt, not even from his own mother as a baby.

"Don't worry, you are loved by many," I wrote on the sand.

Juan smiled like the sun had cast its golden rays on a blooming flower. Though he looked and acted like a child, at times his facial expression made me think he was not as "slow" as he seemed. I also noticed that his pinkies were slightly bent inward. I wondered if he'd been hurt accidentally, or beaten up by bullies. However, in comparison to his other "defects," this one was really minor.

When Juan seemed particularly cheerful, he'd ask me to get on a rusty swing and push me. The higher I rose and the louder I'd scream, the happier he'd be. He also enjoyed riding up and down like two giant jumping beans on the seesaw with me at the other end. These simple activities seemed to be his only source of enjoyment. I tried to please him by shouting as loud as I could, while he laughed like a tickled toddler.

Juan also insisted on helping me carry things: a bunch of wildflowers, bucket of water, or piece of wood for sculpting. He'd always insist on walking me back to Grandpa and Luis's house. Then, to say good-bye, he'd suddenly stand very straight, click his heels, and salute, his expression serious. I realized this was his idea of Spanish chivalry.

Juan's face had nice, even features, so I couldn't understand why he'd been abandoned like a rag doll. I assumed that his mother was a teenage girl who'd just had a bite of the forbidden apple and couldn't swallow the result. Likely, his father, whether another teenager or an evil older man, had taken off as soon as he'd found out she was pregnant. I wondered where his mother was now, and if she had ever tried to find her baby.

As the days passed uneventfully, I had a feeling of unreality, as if the tiny village was beyond space and time. Though I'd lost track of the days, one morning I decided that I had to move on. I had to get back to my witch research. And I felt I needed to tell Sabrina about my visions of her daughter, hoping it would give her some comfort in her last days.

Luis and Grandpa urged me to stay longer, but I had to harden my heart and say no. While I enjoyed their simple company, the goal of my trip—to see the lake and glimpse the *yin* world—had been accomplished. Somehow being by the lake had evoked the opening of my third eye and enlightened me to the reality of being a shamaness. I'd realized that I'd been given this gift, if that's what it was, to see something very important. I just didn't know yet what it was.

I'd revisited the lake in the daylight and seen nothing remarkable, but I could not bring myself to return in the dark. I simply did not feel the strength to endure another vision of the *yin* world with its cold and negative energy. I'd quickly realized that the powers of being a shamaness come with a cost. That's why no one wants the spirits of the dead to visit very often.

Before my departure, our little group gathered in the church's backyard for a farewell dinner prepared by Luis. I ate and drank with relish, but the pleasure was bittersweet, since none of us knew if we'd ever meet again. I promised I'd come back to visit, but I doubted any of them believed me.

The previous day, I'd walked to the bus stop and gone to the nearby town of San Luis to buy gifts for the six villagers. After dinner, I presented the gifts that I'd bought. I gave Grandpa sculpting tools. Though he insisted he was too old and that his inspiration had gone, I knew that sculpting was still his passion. Applying his lessons, I'd sculpted four pieces so far—a woman's nude torso, a sheep, a mystical bird, and of course the drowning girl who might be Isabelle. I had no illusions that my work was good, but I was happy to have these mementos of the simple, kindly people and the little village.

For Luis I'd bought a book about China. He was so pleased that he grabbed me and kissed me on my lips in front of the others.

"Eileen, someday I'll go to find you, either in China or the U.S., or anywhere," he said, wiping away tears as everyone clapped.

Father Fernando received a new bible with a gilt edge. I'd noticed that his old one was falling apart, with pages either torn or missing. Although there was hardly anyone ever in the church, I thought it'd be inappropriate for a priest to make mistakes in his reading. Instead of a kiss, he gave me a blessing with his wooden cross.

It'd taken me quite some time to think of what to get for Juan. Finally I decided to give him the book of sketches I'd made during my stay in the village. I hoped that it would evoke happy memories of our time together.

Juan was so happy that he screamed, "Ah . . . Ah . . . Ah!" as he threw himself into my arms. It was a strange feeling to hold a big, grown man as if he were a helpless child.

To the widow and widower, I gave a shawl and a hat, respectively. Both thanked me with tears in their eyes.

I felt sad to be leaving the little group, not at all sure that I could keep my promise to return.

19

The Dancing Widow

As I sat on the rickety bus on my way back to Santa Cruz, my stay in the village already seemed like a fairy tale—the feeling of peace, the two young men, so different like *yin* and *yang* in intellect, yet alike in their naïveté and purity.

But as the sage Laozi taught, when things reach their peak, they'll inevitably begin their decline. So from this seemingly idyllic place I had to return to the messiness of life in the bigger world. I just hoped, despite Father Fernando's telling me that everyone was leaving, that the village would remain the same, welcoming me with open arms anytime I returned.

At last the bus entered the city, which seemed bustling and noisy. I checked into the same hotel as before, reclaimed my luggage from the bellman, and took a shower. I was anxious to see Sabrina since she was ill, but was too tired for more travel. I ate *arroz con pollo,* or chicken with rice, with a glass of local white wine in the hotel restaurant, then went upstairs to sleep.

The next morning I went to visit Sabrina and was ushered in by the maid, who whispered to me that I should try to cheer up her mistress, who had been very sad lately.

Sabrina seemed glad to see me as I sat down in the comfortable living room.

"Eileen, I didn't expect you to come back to see a lonely old woman."

I looked at her with silent sympathy.

She sighed heavily. "These days I have only my memories, and unfortunately they are all sad."

"Sabrina, you are not hopeless. And not so old. When things seem bad, life can surprise us."

"You really believe that?"

I nodded.

"All right, then, let me tell you. The surprise in my life now is that my lover, Diego, has decided to leave me."

It was pretty obvious that this would happen sooner rather than later, but I still felt sorry for her.

"What happened?"

"He knows that I'm almost out of money, plus I'm getting older and uglier by the day."

I felt compelled to say something comforting. "Sabrina, you look great."

"You think so? Then do you want to see me dance?"

I didn't know what to make of this unexpected offer, but I could not very well say no. "Of course!" I replied.

Looking more animated than I was used to seeing her, Sabrina swiftly disappeared into her bedroom. When she reappeared, she'd changed from her plain black dress into a revealing, red lace one. One of her black lace gloved hands held a castanet, its polished surface sparkling. In her other hand was clasped a black lace fan painted with fiery red roses. In an instant, she'd transformed from a half-alive woman with dead-fish eyes into a vivacious one exuding romance and passion.

"You look beautiful! Am I about to hear *Carmen*?" I asked.

"Just wait."

The castanet began to emit crisp, animated sounds like the clacking of ducks. Her legs, shod in black high-heeled boots, gleefully chased and teased each other like a pair of mischievous twins. I imagined I was seeing the sort of sensuous, decadent woman painted by Toulouse-Lautrec. Like those long-gone French ladies of the night, Sabrina lived at the mercy of heartless men. This normally morose woman of a certain age was transformed before my eyes into one filled with sexual energy. In a smoky voice like Juliette Gréco's, she began to sing through her red-painted lips.

Sabrina's eyes were watery and dreamy, her lips parted sensuously, as if waiting for passionate kisses. As her body swayed, her soft breasts jiggled like tofu. I was but a stand-in for a past lover—perhaps the Alfredo of his younger years. Though her voice and body were those of a mature woman who'd experienced life, I could sense in her the young woman longing for romance.

She finished by swinging her leg onto a chair and lifting her arm in a graceful arc.

I clapped enthusiastically and praised her performance. She smiled proudly, wiping her forehead with a white lace handkerchief.

"*Gracias!* Thanks for giving me this chance! I haven't done this for years. I feel I'm young again." Then her tone turned sad. "At least for a few minutes."

"We should enjoy our moments to the full."

"You're damn right!" My friend clapped her hands and the maid appeared with a bottle of wine, two glasses, and a plate of tapas.

Seeing that Sabrina was ready to start drinking even though it was not even lunchtime, I couldn't help but frown. She ignored my expression and filled the glasses. I took a tiny sip just so she would not feel embarrassed. Then I wondered, would I do much better if I were on the far side of fifty and bereft of daughter and lovers?

Sabrina of course noticed that I was not really drinking, but this did not slow her down, and the level of the wine in the bottle fell quickly.

"You know, I worked as a dancer and cabaret singer before I married," she said.

"I should have guessed. You're so good!"

"Once I was very young and very beautiful, and my life was filled with passion. In those days, men pursued me relentlessly. But none of them stayed around. A few were already married, actually.

They just wanted some on the side. I was better than what they got at home. But it ended up that I did the fucking and the wife got the money. Unfair, ha!"

She took another sip of her drink. "That was why when I was older, I decided to marry someone safe, a boring but responsible man who would truly love me. So I married a notary. I quit my decadent life, settled down, and had my daughter, expecting a quiet life. Unfortunately, I soon realized that I was not the housewife type. I needed excitement, parties, and fun with exciting men. Pretty soon I began to fuck around. Of course he caught on. That's when I learned that he truly loved me—he killed himself. I was shocked. I didn't think he had it in him."

"Sabrina, how terrible for you!"

She shrugged. "It's been a long time."

She went on, and now both her expression and her tone softened. "You don't have to feel sorry for me, Eileen. I made my choices and ended up burying the only man who ever truly loved me. And all he left me was my daughter, Isabelle. For a while I had lovers, and now I have alcohol. I'm a sinner, after all. A priest might grant me absolution, but I don't grant it to myself."

She paused to take another big gulp of her wine. "I'm still alive due to the mercy of God—or is it His punishment?"

There was a pause; then she went on. "You've been away. I know because I called your hotel. Were you at the lake? Did you find out how my daughter died?"

I hesitated. My vision had seemed real, but I did not know how I could put it into words that would make any sense. Yet one reason I'd gone to visit the lake was in the hope of finding solace for Sabrina. I had to tell this desolate mother something.

"I did have a vision when I visited the lake. But it was so strange that I haven't wanted to tell anyone about it. But I have to tell you, don't I?"

"Did you see her?" she asked eagerly.

"Yes, well, she looked like the picture you showed me. . . . I don't think I imagined it."

"Please, tell me."

Just remembering what had happened caused an eerie feeling to arise in me. I felt my voice shake as I began to speak again. "All right. I was by the Past Life Lake in the pitch-dark. Someone from the village brought me there, an old man. He got scared and left me alone. Then I saw a woman—I mean the spirit of a woman. I thought she was trying to tell me something, but I couldn't hear. Then I thought I saw someone go to comfort her. . . ."

"Who was it?"

I didn't answer right away. Laolao had taught me that seeing a living person with ghosts means that he or she is about to die. It was a superstition, but I didn't want to add to Sabrina's miseries so I made up an answer.

"You know I have powers of perception. I know the dead have consolation—those they miss will join them someday."

I was a little surprised that Sabrina seemed relieved to hear this.

"Yes, I will be joining her quite soon."

"No, many years from now!"

"Before I die I must tell someone my secrets. And it looks like you're the one."

I like to hear secrets as much as anyone, but hers all seemed too sad to bear. But she needed someone to listen, so I took another tiny taste of the wine and looked toward her expectantly.

"Someone murdered my daughter—but no one will listen to me. Now I know for sure. That's what Isabelle was trying to tell you by the lake!"

She stood up and nervously rearranged the flowers on the table, then sipped more wine and continued. "My husband, the one who killed himself, worked for a Spanish company on the other side of the Sahara Desert. He came home only once a month. Anyway, that's why I began to have affairs. I was pretty mad at him for leaving me alone all the time."

"Why did he work away from home?"

"Because he made a lot more money working in the desert. He loved me more than anything. That's why he killed himself—he found out about all these men I had. He didn't have the guts to kill me, that's why, ha!

"So he left me alone, this time for good. And that's how I ended up being a prostitute."

I wasn't sure I wanted to hear this revelation, but I tried not to look judgmental.

To reassure her, I said, "Well, you had to support yourself."

"My husband left me nothing! Turns out he'd been embezzling from the company. Maybe it was his guilt, and not love, that made him kill himself. He was in debt up to his ears. All the gifts were bought with stolen money.

"Though I never loved him, after he killed himself I regretted being so selfish and spending so much of his money on clothes and everything else. Anyway, I didn't become a prostitute right away. I tried to find work as a cabaret singer again, but I'd lost my voice from smoking. The best I could do was be hired as an exotic dancer. But one day I tripped onstage and ended up on crutches and had to skip work. The club owner, a heartless and money-crazy monster, fired me right away despite my pleadings—and I'd slept with the bastard too!"

She studied me with her blue-shadowed eyes. "Eileen, you despise me now, don't you?"

"The Chinese say 'every family has its own difficult sutra to recite.' Yours has been a lot harder to recite than mine. We all have to survive."

She went on. "I started hanging around hotel lobbies. The best was the Sahara—a fancy place filled with lonely executives with money to burn. Of course I had to tip everyone in sight, but I still made good money. Maybe my clients had stolen it like my late husband, but then it was their problem, not mine. Or their wives' problem, hahaha!" She laughed cheerily. Her two brightly painted red lips looked like two bloody lizards ready for mischief.

She leaned toward me as if about to divulge a confidence. "A few were even my late husband's colleagues who'd been curious about me for a long time. Then I met Alfredo."

"So he was also one of your . . ." I couldn't bring myself to finish the sentence.

"Not only that, he was my richest and most generous customer."

"So he was rich already?"

"Of course! But because of his wife, Penelope. Her father hired him to work in his oil company. Alfredo was actually very good at business. Not just oil, he sold weapons, too, to whomever had the cash."

What she was telling me clashed with my impressions of the man. But of course I barely knew him. Maybe now that he was in his fifties he'd mended his ways.

"But wasn't he married then?"

She gave me an incredulous look. "You think anyone would turn down *pudín diplomático* just because he's had a full meal of steak and lobster?"

I lowered my head, feeling foolishly naïve.

"He told me his wife, a cultured, talented, and beautiful opera singer, wouldn't satisfy him in bed. Merely a year into their marriage, they'd stopped having sex. He told me this was because she was completely pure. He still worshipped her as a saint. The fact is, the man only likes whores. But just in case that was not enough, there is something else—not just the sex, but what I did before."

"You mean making out?"

She laughed out loud, shaking her head. "No, I mean witchcraft."

"You—or that witch who stole Alfredo from you?"

"Yes, it was Nathalia who taught me the spells. Later it turned out she cast them better than I did. But before her treachery, Alfredo was obsessed with me. He liked my curvy body and mind-blowing sex. A lot better than his saintly wife's non-sex, hahahaha!"

I was more interested in the witchcraft than whether Sabrina or the saintly wife was better in bed. "Tell me, what did you do to Alfredo?"

"There are special herbs grown only in a secret place on the island. I paid a high price for them, then mixed them in our wine to boost his sexual desire and my sexual stamina. I also secretly put my hair and nail clippings under his pillow and my photo, scented with my perfume, into a slot in his briefcase—these were to ensure that I was always on his mind and he'd always want more of me than he could get."

"You really believe these things work?"

"Yes, but it's complicated. Are you sweet on someone who's not so sweet on you?"

Actually, with Ivan it was the other way around. My interest in love spells was purely academic—but who would believe that?

"You're too innocent, Eileen. Hiring a witch is like picking a doctor. You need one who really knows her stuff. Most are fakes. Or evil and cast spells that have the opposite effect—making you repulsive to the man you fancy."

I was thinking that this was great stuff for my future book. And it would make me think twice before paying for a love spell—if I ever found someone I really fancied.

"Hmmm . . . then how come Alfredo still left you?"

Sabrina laughed again. "Ha, because that bitch witch's spells overpowered mine, that's why! She was my teacher, so of course she held back her best secrets. So eventually she got Alfredo and I got my heart broken again."

She downed more wine, a bitter expression on her face. "But of course when he was crazy about me, he kept giving me cash and expensive jewelry. The cash is long gone, but I still have some of the jewelry to survive on."

In my few years on earth I'd already learned that if you didn't take your future into account, you will come to heartbreak. It's great to live for the moment, but then the moment is over. Sabrina had given herself too freely, but at least she had gotten something in return.

Sabrina called out to her maid, who brought tea, snacks—and a bottle of brandy.

Staring at Sabrina's swollen face, I put my hand over her glass. "You really should stop drinking."

She lifted my hand off gently. "Please indulge a dying woman. You have your life ahead of you. I just have my memories—and brandy."

As soon as I let her remove my hand she filled her glass and took a big gulp. "I have another secret to reveal. Alfredo made me pregnant with my son," she said.

I vaguely remembered hearing that she had a son. Before I could stop myself I blurted out, "Alfredo had a son with you? What happened? Where is he?"

I had the feeling that I was about to learn of yet another tragedy, since Sabrina had never said much about having a son. I feared he had ended up with his half sister Isabelle, surrounded by ghosts in the *yin* world.

"One evening I'd had a little more brandy than usual and dozed off. Then he was gone. Maybe stolen by witches."

"Stolen? Did Alfredo know about this?"

"Yes and no. When he saw that I was pregnant, Alfredo became cold to me. He rarely visited me; then I found out that he'd fallen for Nathalia the witch. A few days after Oscar was born I wrapped him up and took him for Alfredo to see.

"He took one look at our son, and said, 'You're a fucked-by-a-hundred-men whore, so how do I know he's mine?' "

"Do you have any idea who took him?" I asked Sabrina.

"That witch, who else? She was consumed by jealousy because she was barren. So she stole my Oscar and told Alfredo the baby was his."

"But wouldn't Alfredo know she wasn't pregnant?"

"Maybe, maybe not. She's a witch; she could have faked it. Or cast a spell on him so he imagined she was pregnant. But even Nathalia couldn't fake a baby, so she stole mine. This way if her spells stopped working she could hold on to Alfredo."

"But she didn't. . . ."

She nodded.

"You never found them?"

"No, all I know is that Alfredo eventually kicked both Nathalia and the baby out of his house for some reason. The rumor was that as soon as the little boy could stand up in his crib, Alfredo took a dislike to him. He was ashamed that his son didn't look like him at all and so forced both of them out."

"But he was your baby! Nathalia should have given him back to you."

"Fat chance—then everyone would know she'd stolen him. I tried to find them, but no luck. Maybe she changed her name and moved away. Or maybe she could use a spell to make them both invisible. Or maybe they're in another universe. Anyway, Oscar is gone. That witch, if I run into her again, I'll send her to the other world!"

"Sabrina, better that you don't mess with these people anymore. They've brought you nothing but misery."

"But I deserve to get something back for what I suffered. And you can help me."

"I don't think I can find your son. Or find out what happened to Isabelle. This all happened so long ago."

"Not that—I mean something else."

I liked Sabrina, but being with her was draining and I dreaded hearing what more she wanted from me.

But I asked anyway. "What is it?"

"One evening after sex, Alfredo told me that he had a big stash of cash and gold in his castle."

"So?"

"So I want you to find it for me."

"So you want me to steal from Alfredo for you? No way!" I exclaimed angrily. I was beginning to regret my friendship with this aging, self-pitying alcoholic.

"Wait, calm down, Eileen. Let me finish. Oscar is Alfredo's son and only heir. If I can find my boy, he'll inherit Alfredo's fortune. Then I'll be rich too."

"Sabrina, if you're dying, as you keep telling me, why do you care about money?"

"Everybody loves money, dying or not. That's why I crashed Alfredo's party—to snoop around after the money."

"Did you find it?"

"Of course not. Otherwise I'd be drinking cognac instead of brandy, hahaha!"

I studied her eyes, still flirtatious despite her sagging face. In a way I admired her spirit. Even with her health failing she was still greedy and scheming.

Sabrina smiled, looking at me as if I'd already agreed to be part of her plot. "If you find the money and gold, I'll give you a share."

"But I'm not going to steal from Alfredo. I don't steal, period."

"Not steal, just find them."

Now she'd pricked my curiosity. Maybe I should take a look around the castle. And if I did come across a pile of money . . .

Sabrina sighed, her voice losing hope. "But even if you find the money, it won't bring back my son. And even if it did, Alfredo wouldn't admit it's his."

"But how would you even know?"

"A mother knows."

"In China we have a way of finding out." I'd learned about this from Laolao, but like a lot of what she'd told me I had no way of knowing if there was any truth in it.

"Tell me."

"You put a drop of the mother's or father's blood into a bowl of water, then a drop of the child's. If the two drops merge, they are blood related. If not, they are unrelated."

"You believe in this?"

"I don't know. But this method had been used by the Chinese for thousands of years, long before DNA testing."

"There's another way. Right after Oscar was born, for protection, I put a silver chain with a pendant around his neck. It was a red stone with a sword carved on it. I don't think anyone else has anything like this."

I remembered that Luis also wore a silver chain, but I couldn't remember if it was like the one Sabrina had described.

"But someone else might have a pendant like this, so . . ."

"No, this one was especially made, so it's the only one."

This seemed like a long shot to me. Even if Oscar had the pendant as a baby, it was likely lost long ago. I thought searching for the witch was a better chance of succeeding. After all, I couldn't very well go around checking men's pendants.

"Do you have any clues about the witch who stole Oscar?" I asked.

"Nathalia was very pretty, with a heart-shaped face and big eyes. But that was twenty years ago. I don't know if I'd recognize her now."

That wasn't much to go on, but it was better than checking pendants. I could ask around in the Witches' Market. And if I could locate Nathalia, then I might be able to locate Oscar.

Despite Sabrina's whining, I did feel sorry for her and hoped to somehow reunite her with at least one of her lost children before she died. She didn't look to me as if she was at death's door, but when I watched how she gulped down the brandy I was not optimistic.

I was feeling exhausted from hearing all her tales of woe, so I stood up to take my leave. Sensing that she did not want me to go, I told her I would try to figure out a way to find Oscar.

She took my arm. "Please come back, Eileen. I'll read you some of my poems next. I'll also cook you some Spanish dishes. It's lonely here, you know. . . ."

"Don't worry, Sabrina, I will."

"I'll be waiting for some good news worth postponing my death."

This certainly put the pressure on. "Finding what you asked for will be no easy feat."

"But if it doesn't lead to anything, then I'll accept my fate and die a contented death."

I took a few steps and heard the door close behind me like a long sigh.

20

Revisiting the Witches' Market

It was a relief to get away from Sabrina. I made my way back to the hotel, ate a simple meal, and went to sleep, for once without any dreams. But as soon as I awakened to the sun streaming through the thin drapes, I started thinking of all the mysterious things that seemed to be happening on the island.

Questions popped inside my head like firecrackers. Who was this witch Nathalia? Was Sabrina's son dead or alive? What had Isabelle's spirit strained to tell me? Was the genteel Alfredo actually evil? And would my newly opened third eye help me to understand any of these things?

I wasn't sure about when I should use my third eye because Laolao had always warned me that special talents should be used sparingly, only to help. Each time you use your power, your life would be shortened accordingly. I thought the latter was probably superstition; maybe the whole third eye thing was anyway. But then how to account for my experience at Past Life Lake?

Was knowing too much actually a burden, or even a curse?

Despite all these doubts, I resolved to continue with my plan of visiting the Witches' Market. I could ask around there about Nathalia. After that I thought I might go back to the U.S. for a short break. After my months on the island San Francisco seemed normal by comparison. I could try to make sense of what had happened because I was no longer sure it was my karma to be a scholar of witches rather than a witch.

The next day when I arrived at the Witches' Market, I felt a similar energy from my previous visit, one entirely different from the little village. Probably seeing that I was Asian and a tourist, many vendors seemed curious about me, smiling, waving, and trying to draw my attention to their products. I smiled back, hoping to be on good terms so they'd talk openly to me.

I walked around the various stalls, buying a few cheap items such as amulets, incense, and malodorous herbs claimed to cure any disease. Curses seemed to be selling well, but I avoided buying any because Laolao had always warned me that the bad luck can bounce back to you. I paid for these items without haggling, then asked each vendor if they'd heard of a witch named Nathalia. None admitted to having heard of her, but instead recommended themselves for any magical services I might require.

I spotted a fortyish vendor, wrinkled because of long years in the sun, but of indeterminate age. What caught my attention was not her, but what she had for sale: dried dead animals and their parts.

Repulsive as this was, I felt I needed to record it for my book. I went up and saw an odd-looking creature, perhaps some kind of cat. Its dried-up eyes seemed to stare, as if seeking answers to the question of life and death, or perhaps to discover a secret hidden for hundreds of years.

"What kind of cat is this?" I asked the vendor.

"Hahaha!" The tan-faced woman cackled crazily. "Señorita, you think this is a cat! It's a stillborn baby lamb!"

"*Aiiiya!* You mean like a half-born baby?!"

This time she laughed so hard that her eyes narrowed into two slits. "Hahaha! 'Half-born baby,' I like that!" She looked around at the nearby crowd, then yelled in a hoarse voice, "Come buy, half-born baby for sale! Half-born baby, half price!"

Soon a few young men and women had gathered at her booth. No one seemed to want to buy this bizarre object, but rather they were enjoying this drama between a local witch and an exotic foreign woman.

"Señorita, buy one, very hard find! Very good luck!" she said.

"How can a dead baby, even a lamb, be good luck? I think it's"—I leaned over and whispered so as not to seem to hurt her business—"bad luck?"

"Ah, señorita, you young girl. I wise woman. So you listen. Good luck, okay? Good luck!"

"If it's half alive and half not, how can it be good luck?"

I was definitely not going to say the taboo word *dead* and possibly offend the poor animal's spirit.

Now more people had crowded around to watch the tug-of-war between good and bad luck. A few children had pushed to the front for a better view of the action. Some touched me out of curiosity as to what a foreigner felt like, or for good luck—I hoped I had enough to go around.

The vendor went on, shouting over the crowd. "Only one! Lucky person buys. Bury in your backyard and get big good luck! No more evil!"

She sounded very much like a Chinese fortune-teller—except of course that she was speaking in Spanish. To fortune-tellers, everything for sale is for good luck and provides protection against evil. If anything can unite different cultures, it would be this sort of superstition. Fortune-tellers as ambassadors.

I wanted to know more because this could be an entire chapter in my book.

I asked her, "How does it work?"

"Hey, señorita, you look educated, but you don't understand?"

The crowd erupted in laughter. They all stared at me as if I were from another planet instead of just another country.

The witch, happy to have an audience for her jibes, went on. "She can't even tell the difference between a cat and a lamb!"

There was another round of stares and laughter at the ignorant foreigner; then the witch waved authoritatively for the crowd to calm down.

"This lamb was almost born but failed at the last minute. This means it died for you, taking with it all your bad luck. Just imagine how safe you will be with its powerful, bitter spirit scaring away all evil forces from your door!"

This whole scene reminded me of a Chinese story that Laolao had told me about. If a child dies young, from an abortion or abuse, they become *tongling,* malevolent child spirits. Because of their violent deaths, *tongling* are filled with hatred and bitterness. Their killers live in terror of fatal attacks.

I had once read in a newspaper about a woman whose boyfriend abused her son until finally the boy died. They wrapped his tiny body in a blanket and hid it in a basement closet. Later the woman and her boyfriend got married, had a baby of their own, and completely forgot about the dead child.

One day they opened the closet door and the little dried body fell out. Fearful their new child would find it, they took the tiny corpse to the wilderness and buried it in a shallow hole.

Now that the child had not only been murdered, but evicted from his home, the terror began. One night soon after, the mother and her now-husband were driving home in the dark, when she suddenly saw her dead son sitting next to her—with bruises, cigarette burns, and cuts oozing blood.

He screamed, "Mama, take me back!" then dissolved into the night.

Her husband didn't see anything, but the mother knew her dead son would soon get his revenge. And so it happened—the grandmother greatly missed the little boy and had kept asking for him to visit. Growing suspicious, she notified the police. Not long after, the police came for the murderous parents.

Tongling are believed to have such magical potency in China that a few people still follow the creepy practice of "raising the ghost baby" for revenge. A shaman is hired to find a recently deceased child's grave. At midnight he burns incense at the grave, chants invocations, and casts the notorious "seducing the soul" spell. Finally, he'll plant a tree sprout in the fresh earth at the burial site.

Weeks later when the sprout has become rooted in the ground, he'll return, chant another invocation, and burn talismans to make the dead child's spirit attach to the root. Then he'll pull up the root, carve it into a small figure, brush the child's name and birthday onto it, and put it inside a bottle. Sometimes the black magician will place another figure in the bottle to keep the child company, so he won't feel lonely and escape to the outside world.

Now the ghost baby will be sleeping inside the bottle and waiting for the magician's command. The shaman nurtures the ghost baby with milk, juice, rice, vegetables, noodles, even animal's blood. When it is time to wake up the spirit, the shaman breathes into the bottle and chants incantations. The ghost baby, now fully awake, will do whatever its boss asks. Of course a black magician will use it to commit evil deeds—harassment, revenge, even murder. . . .

My unpleasant recollections were interrupted by the vendor's impatient voice.

"Hey, señorita, are you going to buy this or not?"

Of course I wanted nothing more to do with the repulsive object—or the repulsive beliefs. However, photographs would provide essential documentation for my book, and once that was done I could give the poor animal a decent burial. Also, if the witch thought I might become a regular customer, she might give me more information.

So, hiding my reluctance, I said, "Yes, please. Wrap it up."

She split a big smile. "I knew you were a knowing lady when I first laid eyes on you!"

I waited until she finished business with other clients, then pretended to look for other objects before asking, "Are you all witches here?"

"Of course I am. But most of the others are fakes."

"How can I tell which are the fake ones?"

"Easy, the fake ones' stuff doesn't work. Their spells are made up and what they sell has no magic power. I have everything you will need. Just ask me."

"Wow! Is that so?"

Her pudgy finger pointed to a few stalls in the distance. "Look, all they have over there are fakes, they are selling handmade folk craft, not spirit-made witchcraft. Mind you, I'm a good witch, but some here are evil. So watch out!"

"How can you tell if one is evil?"

"They'll curse you so you get sick and the doctors won't know what's wrong. Or you'll lose things, everything."

I looked around the busy market. "Can you tell me who is evil so I can avoid them?"

"A long time ago there was one here named Natalie, or maybe Nathalia." Scowling, she continued. "Fortunately we haven't seen her for a long time. She was so mean she would even cast spells on her own sister witches. Some got sick and even died."

She went on before I had a chance to respond. "Señorita, you can always get what you need from me. Don't think about this evil woman, as it may attract her attention to you. Anyway, the only one who remembers any of this is the old guy at the Chinese restaurant over there."

She must mean Uncle Wang, who I'd tried to find during my earlier visit. I decided I would need to seek him out after all, but I'd have to wait a bit since I knew he'd moved to Grand Canary.

Back at the hotel, I took a nap and reluctantly lifted the stillborn lamb out of the plastic bag the woman had placed it in. Then suddenly I had an idea. I got out Grandpa's stuck-between-the-womb-and-the-world sculpture and placed the two objects side by side on the floor in front of me. To have two such unusual objects, Heaven must be sending me a message. Or maybe Isabelle was sending me a message through Grandpa and the witch, a message about her life being cut short.

Thinking of this I remembered Isabelle's diary and retrieved it from my suitcase. Flipping the pages toward the end, I found this entry:

> Alfredo seemed to truly care about me, even though he was not really my father. But one day, he abandoned us. Mother said another woman stole him from her. But she wouldn't tell me anything more. Now that we are by ourselves, Mother worries about money every day. She's afraid she's losing her looks and cannot attract another rich man to support us.
>
> I'm only twenty and already have experienced so

much bad luck. Mother told me that Alfredo has hidden lots of cash and even gold somewhere in that huge castle of his. She wants me to sneak in there to look for them. I told her this would be impossible—and could land me in prison. Then she actually suggested I should try to seduce him! According to her, this is how women get ahead in the world.

When I told her that Alfredo was practically my father, Mother got very angry. She said it wouldn't be a big deal to sleep with him a few times since my real father had left us with nothing.

Hoping to placate her, I did sneak into Alfredo's castle, though I doubted I would actually find any treasure. The place is huge and has many secret rooms, cellars, and attics. I couldn't even guess where to start looking for all this supposed wealth. Even thinking about it I felt so fed up that I just went to confront him and ask for my share.

To my utter surprise, this time, instead of cursing and threatening, Alfredo told me he loved me as a real daughter and was willing to discuss this with me over a nice dinner. Maybe he isn't as bad as Mother says.

I hoped Isabelle's diary would reveal what happened with Alfredo's hidden wealth. Before reading more, I poured myself a glass of white wine that I'd bought earlier at the market. I sipped meditatively, hoping the alcohol would free up my thinking. It occurred to me that Sabrina must have already read her daughter's diary. If there were any reference to the location of the treasure, she would have tried to find it herself. Maybe she hoped that I could find some clue that she had missed. No doubt she thought I could have my way with Alfredo, if I wanted.

Feeling more relaxed from the wine, I continued to read.

After an expensive meal at an elegant restaurant, Alfredo suggested we go to a hotel—obviously to avoid his wife—and I agreed. Once we were inside the luxury suite, he took my hand, kissed it, and gently led me to a couch. It quickly became obvious that he did not think of me as his daughter. Soon Alfredo's passionate kisses extended to my neck, and down from there. Then I let him undress me and lead me into bed.

In the end it wasn't as bad as I'd thought it would be, though I wouldn't say I got any actual pleasure out of it.

I promise myself that I won't do anything like this again—I don't want to end up like my mother.

When I got home the next morning, Mother knew. I don't know how, but she told me mothers know these things.

But that was where the entry ended. Isabelle might have gotten something from Alfredo, but I suspected she didn't. She seemed to have lacked her mother's guile.

Staring at Isabelle's handwriting that ended halfway down the page, I had a feeling that something had happened to make her stop writing. Reading these lines, I realized with a start that the date of the entry was around the time she had drowned. I felt a pounding headache coming on. Suddenly it occurred to me that these may have been her last words.

She must have written this just before her death!

My fear that I had gotten myself into matters I would not be able to handle was intensified.

Sabrina had hinted to me that Alfredo had killed her daughter. Somehow I doubted this. That Alfredo was a womanizer was obvious, but that didn't mean he was violent. Certainly, he'd had ample opportunity to take advantage of me, but he had always behaved quite properly.

All these uncertainties were starting to drive me crazy. I decided to pay a visit to meet Uncle Wang, to distract myself. I hoped he really was as wise as his niece had claimed.

21

Wielding the Wand

The next morning I took the ferry back to Las Palmas. I still had the address that Uncle Wang's niece had given me and it didn't take long for the taxi driver to find it. There was a tumble-down wall with ancient-looking houses behind it. They were old, but probably not quaint enough to attract tourists.

I paid, got out, and walked down a bustling pedestrian street surrounded by green-roofed, white-walled houses. Cooking odors wafted from food stalls ornamented with faded red banners, announcing dumplings, pancakes, noodles, and other dishes. Small plastic tables and chairs were arrayed outside. From spice shops came exotic scents, promising the availability of tasty Mediterranean dishes. Barrels of abalone and sea slug contributed the aroma of the deep ocean. There was also a mahjong parlor. Tiles clanged in the background as winners cheered and losers cursed. This was a miniature Chinatown, but for homesick Chinese, not tourists.

Uncle Wang's address turned out not to be a private residence or even a nursing home but a small Daoist temple. Above the building hung a signboard with the characters **LUMINOUS SPIRIT TEMPLE** in gold against a red background.

I climbed up the three steps to the threshold and peeked in. Like all such temples it was dark inside with an overwhelming odor of incense. On the far wall a variety of gods stood on a large altar. In the central place of honor was Daoism's founder, Laozi, a white-bearded old man riding a water buffalo.

In contrast to this gentle philosopher, beside him stood the ferocious, red-faced General Guan, protector of police and gangsters alike—or anyone who makes him a generous offering. The relentless warrior-deity held a halberd, ready to chop in half anyone imprudent enough to annoy him. His loyalty and integrity are legendary, but his real appeal is his ferocity and invincibility. The Chinese believe if they put up General Guan's image and make him generous offerings, their stores and households will be protected against all evil and misfortune.

Chinese like their temples to have many gods, just to be sure to cover all their bases. On either side of Laozi and General Guan, I recognized two more gods: Lu Dongbin, the immortal famous for enjoying life, and Li Bai, one of China's greatest poets. Placed on the altar for these beings were abundant offerings: fruit, tea, mai tai, red-dyed buns, fresh flowers. Hung at the front of the altar were cloths embroidered with good-luck symbols such as bats, lotuses, piles of coins, and the black and white *yin-yang* symbol.

On a long table in front of the altar was placed a shallow box with a smooth layer of sand inside. Next to it was placed a Y-shaped stick. I knew about this from Laolao. It was for calling up spirits of deceased ancestors. I'd never seen it in use, because Laolao had warned me that it could be very dangerous to bring ghosts up right in front of you. I hadn't taken this very seriously when she'd first told me about it, but my experience at Past Life Lake had shaken my doubt.

As I continued to examine my surroundings in the temple, a middle-aged Chinese woman, wearing a Chinese top embroidered with lotus flowers, approached and spoke to me in Cantonese.

"I haven't seen you before, you are . . . ?"

"I'm looking for Uncle Wang."

"He busy now, so you must wait."

"How long?"

"About an hour." She gestured toward the many people either sitting or milling around, looking anxious.

"Uncle Wang will do a very important ritual soon. You can stay and watch but first must buy incense and light it on the altar."

Now a stream of people were entering the temple, all Chinese, and mostly older.

"Many here make big donations," said the woman.

Her message was clear, but I limited myself to purchasing a bundle of incense. I lit several sticks, then went up to insert them into the sand of the bronze burner, inhaling the strong smoke as it billowed from the vessel like question marks.

Just then a very old, small, skeletal Chinese man materialized in front of me, somewhat comically holding a large clock in his hand that was making crisp *tick tock, tick tock* sounds.

The old man stared at me curiously, lids drooping over sharp eyes. "What are you doing here?"

"I'm looking for Uncle Wang."

"You're looking him in the eyes."

"So you're Uncle Wang? I met your niece at the restaurant in Tenerife. She told me you know things."

For a moment I studied this old man, an animated mummy with a head of white hair, a white goatee, narrow face, and radiant eyes. It was as if he were a 300-year-old Daoist immortal stepping out from an ancient Chinese painting, or perhaps descending from a cloud-veiled mountain. I bowed respectfully to this frail but powerful presence.

"I'll be busy for an hour, so talk to me again after the ceremony," he said.

He gave me another nerve-racking once-over. The clock's ticking and tocking didn't do much to calm my nerves. Because of his advanced age, the ticking clock gave me a sense of foreboding.

"I'm Eileen Chen. I came here from America to learn about shamans and witches," I said.

He stroked his white beard with his long-nailed fingers. "Hmm . . . think you're a shamaness yourself?"

"Maybe, but I'd rather think of myself as a professor of anthropology."

"A professor . . . but still a shamaness."

"How can you tell?" I had, after all, opened my third eye, so maybe as a man of knowledge he could tell.

"I feel *qi* emanating from your body. You possess more power than you know."

When I was about to ask him more about this, he waved his hand dismissively. "Because you're a woman of *Dao,* I will let you stay. But you must sit and watch quietly. Any noise might frighten the spirits away. I will now perform *fuji,* wielding the wand. The people here are waiting to learn about their past, future, and all the other mysteries of life."

This must be the ancient Daoist divination method that Laolao had warned me about—but it was too late to pull out now. And I was curious.

He pointed to the clock. "The ceremony must start at two thirty-eight. That's the auspicious time I calculated." He signaled for me to go sit with him on a bench. "Listen carefully. Once the *fuji* starts this temple will be filled with spirits. Are you brave enough for this?"

After all I'd been through—the witches' dance, Past Life Lake—I thought I could manage a ritual in an old temple.

"This is an ancient practice I learned from my master, a hermit who showed himself only to his few students. Wielding the wand is how we invite spirits, ancestors, immortals, even the ancient sages, to reveal what is hidden.

"If they want to contact you, they'll just come. Otherwise, you have to lure them here through offerings like their favorite food, wine, cigarettes, even poems. We call this Inviting the Spirits."

"Dead people," I said.

He cast me a chiding look. "'Dead people' is not a very respectful term, Señorita Chen. They are still alive, but in another dimension. Anyway, this ritual involves a magistrate, which is me. No woman can do it because women's bodies are impure . . . the spirits will be offended."

"Why are women's bodies impure?" I interrupted.

"Ahhh . . . you don't know. Because their great aunt visits every month!"

I must have looked completely puzzled, for he sighed. "Because they have their monthly sutra!"

Just then a woman about my age passed by, and whispered to me, "Uncle Wang means your period," before she walked away.

I laughed out loud, and told the old man. "Ah, you mean falling off the roof!"

Now it was Uncle Wang who looked puzzled. "No one is falling off the roof of my temple. So stop your bad-luck talk!"

I was still laughing while he went on. "With *fuji* absolutely every detail has to be correct. The inquirer must be present, as well as a channeler who transcribes the words of the spirit in the sand using the Y-shaped wand representing the *yin,* or ghost, world. Then a reader of spirit writing dictates to a scribe. All is supervised by the magistrate in charge—that's me. This is how the spirits tell us what they wish us to know.

"The best channeler is an innocent child no older than six. Then there can be no fakery. The writing on the sand is often a poem, but sometimes prose."

"How are you sure it's the words of the spirit, not the channeler?" I asked.

He cast me an annoyed look. "If it's a child, he can't make up a long, complicated poem. When an adult channels, he or she writes in someone else's handwriting and reveals secrets no one knows. Besides, the writing is quick. There isn't enough time to make things up."

Before I had a chance to respond, he continued. "You should know that crossing the boundary between human and spirit realms taxes the energy of the living."

"What about the dead? How can they speak to us?"

"Because the dead possess dark, powerful forces we living cannot understand. Anyway, we should always keep our distance from the dead, so we do not want them to come through for very long. Even your mother or father or lover who is in spirit, no matter how much you love and miss them."

Though this was a lot to take in, I got the basic idea. But I didn't understand why he carried the big clock—was it to set a time limit for spirit visits? So I asked him.

"To remind people that our time in the *yang* world is running out," he explained. "Only the *yin* world is timeless." He laughed, stroking his goatee. "But anyway no one is in a hurry to go there."

Just then a gong began to ring loudly. After suggesting that if I became frightened I should recite a sutra silently to myself, he hurried to his place behind the altar facing the congregation.

I squeezed my way to the front, tried to compose myself, and took out my notebook. Suddenly the chatter stopped as everyone awaited the imminent arrival of the spirits.

Wang made a gesture to signal the beginning of the ritual. A five- or six-year-old boy stepped out from behind his mother and took his place next to Uncle Wang. Then the child picked up the Y-shaped wooden wand and passed it back and forth through the incense smoke. As the celebrants began to chant, the boy's expression changed, as if he was entering an altered state. Moments later, his small hand moved the wand back and forth on the tray of sand, as surely as if he were a virtuoso calligrapher. Excited, the audience pressed forward, trying to see what he wrote.

In a resonant voice, the recitation master read what he saw on the sand as the scribe brushed the characters onto a long scroll. When this was done, the scribe held up the scroll, on which was written:

> Waiting for good news in winter,
> Toward end of Spring, good news is but empty words.
> In Autumn when the cinnamon's fragrance drifts,
> Is when the Moon Goddess descends from the Cold Palace.

The inquirer studied this. Seeing his nervous manner I thought it was pretty likely that he was here to ask about his love life. Maybe he fancied a girl who seemed not to notice him. How the poem related to his love life I had no idea and he seemed not to know either.

Fortunately Uncle Wang read the spirit writing aloud and announced the interpretation.

"My dear friend, this is an extremely auspicious reading. Congratulations! Now you can go home and wait for good news to arrive."

Everyone clapped.

The little boy, no longer the center of attention, slipped away from the altar and went back to his mother. When the clapping died down, Wang signaled me to come forward from the audience.

Smiling, he said in his authoritative voice, "Today we have Señorita Eileen Chen from America. She is a famous shamaness and will invite down her own familiar spirit."

I was quite unprepared for this, but the audience was shouting encouragement so I had no choice but to go up to the altar.

"Don't worry." With his bony fingers, Uncle Wang pointed to the deities on the altar. "We're protected by all the gods here."

"But . . . I don't have anything to talk about."

"We all have doubts in life, so ask whatever is on your mind."

A young man raised his voice among the crowd. "Just go ahead!" The audience followed him in chanting.

Suddenly I was terrified, thinking, *What if the spirit gets inside me and doesn't want to leave?*

Uncle Wang's voice rose again in the packed hall. "Señorita Chen, someone is here in spirit to tell a secret about herself."

Suddenly, I had the same uncanny sensation of being sucked out of my own body that I'd had at Past Life Lake. I found myself walking around to the back of the altar, then standing under the deities, waiting for instructions.

"You have a question in your mind," Wang said. "A spirit has the answer and will come to you." He picked up a cloth and gently covered my eyes. "So you can better focus. Now meditate to still your mind."

I felt my mind relax and could no longer feel my body. There was a sense of peace and beyond that, nothingness. The world surrounding me gradually fell away, leaving me alone in the void. Minutes later I felt a presence, feminine with a troubled *qi*. Although I could not hear or see anything, I felt my hand guided as it moved the Y-shaped wand on the sand. There was nothing but my hand, the wand, and the sand.

I had no sense of how much time had elapsed when my hand jerked to a stop. I looked down at what I had written and saw it was in Spanish, not Chinese. Before I could react, I heard the master of recitation read out the passage I'd written.

"So many unanswered questions in my short life. Please, sister, help me find them in your world. I know you came all the way here for a reason."

Now I found that I had stopped writing, instead attending to a voice within my head. The conversation became more intimate, just between myself and the female spirit seemingly within me.

Can you help me?

I don't know. Why do you keep coming to me?

I cannot rest. No one but you can find out if my death was an accident or murder.

But you were there when it happened. Can't you remember?

Everything's vague where I am now.

Why do you think you were murdered?

Because I've felt evil around me ever since. All because I learned something I was not supposed to know.

What's this secret?

You already know.

How do I find out how you died?

Use your third eye.

What if it doesn't show me what you want to know?

You have this gift for a reason. Just try. If you can't, I will go away and never bother you again.

You are asking much of me. At least tell me your name?

You already know.

When the intense conversation with a being from the other realm had ended, I was suddenly jolted back to reality. I noticed that everyone looked anxious, even scared. A toddler burst out crying in his mother's arms. Maybe they had felt the same presence I had and were reacting to the spirit's intense distress.

"I hope it's not a vengeful ghost," I heard a young man say to a woman.

"It doesn't feel vengeful, only miserable," the woman answered.

I felt myself almost slip away again. People's conversations sounded like bees buzzing next to my eardrums, hurting them. My feet were unsteady and I climbed down from the platform; Uncle Wang took my arm to steady me. He announced to the audience that there would be an hour break before the next reading. Then he brought me to his office at the back of the temple.

It was a small area with a desk, chairs, shelves filled with books, and a high table with Daoist deities. After we sat down, he poured two cups of tea and handed one to me.

"Eileen, you experienced a presence. I can tell. Someone in spirit that you knew when she was alive?"

"No, I know her mother, who told me about losing her daughter. The young woman has been coming into my dreams."

"Hmm . . . dreams may be just dreams, but her descending onto the altar and communicating with you is real."

"You mean that I've just been visited by a ghost?"

"They come here, to our world"—he pointed to the floor—"maybe from the one below. Or the one above. We don't know—yet.

"People imagine that there is an impassable boundary between the *yin* and the *yang* worlds, the living and the dead. That we should respect this boundary and not cross it."

"But you invite these crossings!"

"Only for good reasons, not just from idle curiosity." He pointed to his clock on the table. "See? This is to keep time. I don't want the spirits to stay too long in our realm. But for me, there's not much time left in this realm. Though I've lived a long life, I still feel sad that it's about to run out.

"I do this to help people. . . . They are desperate to hear from their lost loved ones.

"So, Eileen"—he paused and stared hard at me—"what about this presence you felt?"

"Uncle Wang, I didn't ask her; she just came to me."

"But they always come to us for a reason. So this one wants something from you. Something she can't get in her world."

"She died young and maybe was murdered."

"Ah, that's it. This person must have had a horrible death and wants her revenge."

Perhaps he was right. If Isabelle had died in peace she'd have no reason to come back.

"Are you going to seek justice for her?"

I really did not know what to think about this. I had come to write a book, not avenge a murder.

"I . . . don't know. "

"My advice is to try to appease this woman."

"Me?"

"Murder must not be ignored. She chose you to help, so maybe you were friends, or even sisters, in a past life. If you don't help, she will keep coming to you in your dreams, especially when your *yang qi* is weak because you are sick or exhausted."

"What can I do?"

"First, don't invite contact with her anymore."

"But I don't invite her!"

"But you think about her. That enables her to enter your mind."

"I visit her mother and she talks about her all the time."

"Be careful. Too much contact with the *yin* world will deplete the life *qi* you got at birth."

I had planned to ask him about the witches, especially Nathalia, but given this warning, I sensed that I would not get more out of him. Instead, I turned the conversation back to him. "But if it can shorten your life, why do you do it?"

"I'm a man gifted with ample *yang qi.* Most ghosts, especially female ones, can't harm me. After all, they're *yin* beings. But you're a woman. Although you're young and strong, your heart is very soft. Both the living and ghosts can take advantage of that.

"But I'm different." He pointed to his eyebrows. "See? My hair, my goatee, and even my brows all turned white. Their brightness will blind the ghosts so they can't get too close to me, no matter how vengeful. Besides, I'm already ninety-three, so they know they'll have me pretty soon.

"This female ghost is not angry at you. So my advice is, when she comes to you again, try to comfort her. Once she is finally at peace, she'll leave you alone. Don't involve yourself in other people's business, especially not the dead. You are young. Live your life."

It was good advice. I should have followed it.

22

Dinner with the Housekeeper

As the Chinese say, "If one has a ghost on his mind and in his heart, then it is real." Real or not, now I would have no peace until I found out how Isabelle had died.

Even though I wanted to keep searching for the truth, my mind and body told me to wait. I needed a good rest. I needed to eat, watch mindless TV, take a walk along the beach, sip iced tea in a cozy café, or just watch life pass by my hotel window. And catch up on my sleep—hopefully without any dreams.

So I took two days just to relax and refresh. I also took time to write down all the happenings and organize the photos I'd just had developed—Alfredo's castle, the village, the cracked ground, the Witches' Market. I did not take any pictures of the ceremony in the temple, as that was absolutely not allowed.

I decided to call Ivan and Brenda. It had been a long time since we had talked. I didn't know why, but instead of my little sister, when I picked up the phone, my finger dialed Ivan's number first.

Ivan sounded so excited to hear my voice, which, despite myself, made me feel good. Whatever his faults, it was nice to hear a normal voice after all of the strange people I'd been spending my time with.

Ivan complained that I hadn't called and he had not been able to reach me at the hotel. I told him most of what had been happening—the Witches' Market, the village, Alfredo, Grandpa, Sabrina, her daughter, Isabelle, and Past Life Lake. I didn't think someone as practical and materialistic as Ivan would understand or believe in any of my bizarre encounters, so I left out all the supernatural happenings, especially my visions at the lake and in the temple, and the opening of my third eye. To him I'd never have more than two. He'd already told me that I paid too much attention to Laolao's nonsense and read too many New Age books. And of course I was not going to tell him about the wealthy Alfredo and his interest in me, nor Luis's infatuation.

"Do you think about me at all while you're having so many adventures?" Ivan asked, his voice wistful.

"Ivan! We're talking now."

"I know, I know. But I care about you and hope that you also feel the same about me."

"Of course I do." Maybe I did. After all, we'd been together for almost five years.

"Good. That's all I need to know."

"Have you seen Brenda?"

Some part of me wished Ivan and Brenda would become a couple. They seemed really suited for each other and it would solve two of my problems: get rid of Ivan and have my sister married off. And, best of all, it would keep Ivan's wealth in the Chen's family!

Ivan's voice rose again, interrupting my wishful thinking. "Not really. Sometimes we talk over the phone."

"Ivan, have you been having a good time with other women while I'm away?"

There was a long pause on the other end before he replied. "Well . . . not really."

His pause told me the true answer. I could not help feeling a little jealous, even while I hoped he would find someone and leave me alone.

He knew he'd given himself away, so he quickly said, "What about those tall, dark, handsome, passionate Spanish men?"

"Ivan! Of course not."

Since Ivan had no interest in witches, or anything else nonmaterial, there was really not much to talk about, so I soon told him I had to hang up but would call again.

I couldn't tell if deep down I actually loved Ivan, or even if he truly loved me. Feeling strangely discontented, I dialed Brenda.

We chatted about ordinary things before I told her about Alfredo and Sabrina, this time including most of the details. Needless to say, all of her interest was in the rich Alfredo.

"Eileen, wow! Use your charm on this castle owner—better yet, seduce him! Once you're his wife this castle will be yours too! Then we can all come and have a big party!"

"When did our parents teach us to be so materialistic?"

"It's not that. It's about not letting go of opportunities. Sister, this could be a bonanza dropping from Heaven."

There was no point in arguing with Brenda. She had her priorities, and to me she was still my cute little sister, dear to my heart.

"All right," I said, "maybe I'll think about it."

"Yes! That's my big sister!"

My next move was to visit Alfredo at Heartbreak Castle, to see if I could fish something fishy from him. Of course I'd be particularly careful after Sabrina had painted a very different picture of him.

To my great disappointment, Maria told me that her boss had left for a business trip and would return in a few days.

"Señorita Eileen, Señor Alfrenso said that if you come back, you're welcome to stay as long as you want and make yourself comfortable while you wait for his return."

Excellent. Now I could snoop around the castle freely. "Thanks, Maria. I will stay for a few days."

I was flattered that recently so many people desired my company. I thought that maybe since I had opened my third eye, I had some sort of charisma that attracted people to me.

Maria smiled. "Welcome back, Señorita Eileen. Make yourself at home. Why don't you walk around and see some more of the castle while I get the guest room ready for you?"

"But my luggage is at the hotel."

"Don't worry, I'll send the driver to pick it up."

"Maria, this castle is huge!" Actually, I was feeling a little scared in this nearly empty place.

"Don't worry. Adam the driver and the gardener are both nearby."

Soon she was back.

"Señorita, your room is ready and I've prepared a hot bath for you. I've left everything you need—soap, towels, clothes, hair dryer—inside the bathroom. Dinner will be ready at six in the dining room. If you're bored and want something to read, remember the library is five rooms down the hall from you. Now I'll go start dinner. What would you like?"

"Maria, *gracias.* I'm not a picky eater. I know whatever you fix will be delicious."

Looking happy, Maria left.

Soon my exhausted body was soaking in the steaming, scented water of the claw-footed tub. I sighed with pleasure as the therapeutic water eased the kinks in my muscles and joints, relaxing and rejuvenating me. Yet worries still lingered at the back of my mind like crawling spiders.

What would happen if I continued to be involved in Isabelle, Sabrina, Alfredo, and the unknown Nathalia's world? Should I cut off from them to save myself? But, with Isabelle at least, it was not as if I had intentionally sought her out. And what about finding the witches, seemingly by accident? And opening my third eye? There seemed to be reasons I had come here, reasons that had nothing to do with collecting materials for an academic book.

I fell asleep in the bathtub until Maria woke me up again. She handed me a towel and set out a blue silk dress for me to put on. It looked beautiful, but I had misgivings, so I asked her, "Maria, is this Señora Alfrenso's dress?"

She nodded. "Yes, we have many of hers. I picked this one out especially for you. You'll look lovely in it."

I didn't have the heart to tell her that the Chinese fear it will be unlucky to wear a dead person's clothes. Anyway, I'd worn Penelope's dress for the ball and nothing bad had happened, so I decided I'd wear this one and hope for the best.

"Señorita Eileen, as soon as you are ready, please come to the dining room. Dinner is almost ready," Maria said as she was leaving.

Before I had only eaten in the kitchen, not the main dining room. It turned out to be huge, big enough for formal banquets and decorated with old-style European elegance. The walls were covered with oil paintings of tables overflowing with food, handsome horses, bull fighters with red capes, and a huge landscape. The paintings were dimly illuminated by a huge chandelier hanging low over the room like a pregnant belly. A place was set at the end of a long table that was surrounded by chairs upholstered in crimson satin with gold tassels. There were pale blue plates, a delicate crystal wineglass, and heavy silverware adorned with a floral pattern. A cloth napkin and vase of fresh flowers completed the arrangement.

Sitting down, I asked Maria, "Don't you think this is too grand for a simple dinner?"

"Señorita, there are many rooms in this castle but not many guests. It's sad that all of these beautiful rooms are neglected."

The room truly was beautiful, but the truth was that it gave me the creeps. I felt that the big, empty room was actually not empty but filled with guests from the other realm. But I did not want to scare the housekeeper, so I said nothing.

I remembered Laolao had always told me that the "other beings" are everywhere and thus unavoidable. Those who died a peaceful death are mainly harmless—just passing by. But only people with *yin* eyes opened can see these entities—ordinary people can only see them when they are very sick and slipping into the *yin* world.

Laolao gave me careful instructions on how to handle these unwanted visitations. If I ever ran into a ghost, I should be careful to be polite in accord with the Chinese saying, "If you respect me one foot, I'll return your respect one yard." Of course, I knew this was not always true of living people, so maybe it was not true for ghosts either. In any case, if there was an "unclean encounter," I was to burn incense and recite a sutra to speed these beings back to where they belong. . . .

"Many rooms here have not been tended to for years," said Maria.

"Oh yes?" Perhaps it was in one of these neglected chambers that Alfredo stashed his hoard of cash and gold.

"Señor travels a lot and has no time to enjoy this place. So half of the time it's a waste, if you ask me." Then she stood up. "Excuse me while I get the food."

When she returned with a large tray laden with dishes and a bottle of wine, I invited her to sit and eat with me.

She looked startled, even alarmed. "Oh no, Señorita Eileen, that's very nice of you. But I can't eat with a guest!"

"Don't worry, Maria, I doubt Señor Alfrenso cares."

"But I'm a servant . . . Señor Alfrenso . . ."

"Maria, please. He's not here, and I certainly won't tell him!"

On the housekeeper's face appeared a what-the-heck expression. Then she disappeared for a few moments, returning with a plate, silverware, and a glass. She set these on the table and sat down next to me.

Maria poured us wine, and after she whispered a short prayer we began to dig in. The first course was a soup served with grapes and melon, too cold by Chinese standards, yet surprisingly tasty.

"The soup is excellent, Maria, what's inside?"

"Lamb stock, fresh bread, crushed almonds, olive oil, and pinches of garlic mixed with sea salt and vinegar." Her face glowed happily under the warm, yellowish light.

"All these ingredients—that's a lot of work."

She nodded. "Yes, if you want it to be good."

After finishing the soup, she served up various dishes—seafood paella, fried pork rinds, boiled octopus sprinkled with coarse salt, shredded flank steak in tomato sauce, pimento picante, and more.

"Hmmm . . . Maria, you're really a good cook!" I let out a long, satisfied sigh, then wiped up the sauce on my plate with a slice of home-baked olive bread sprinkled with sesame.

"Thanks, Señorita Eileen. It's because Señor Alfrenso loves to eat, so I always try to improve my skills. No matter how much he loves a dish, he gets bored quickly and wants new ones."

The red wine was good, too, and seemed well matched with the food. I drank only a little of mine, but I noticed that Maria did not hesitate to keep refilling her own glass. After her fourth her tongue loosened and she kept on chattering. It quickly became tedious, but then I realized her tipsiness might give me the opportunity I had been waiting for to pry into her master's and late mistress's lives.

"Maria, how long have you worked for Señor Alfrenso?"

"My mother worked here first. After she passed, señor hired me. I never married, so I plan to continue working here until either he's gone or I can't work anymore."

"Did you know Señora Alfrenso's wife well?"

"Yes, Penelope Alfrenso, a very beautiful but cold woman."

"So you didn't like her?"

"No one liked her except herself. But I don't blame her. If I were that beautiful, talented, and rich, I'd also love myself to death!" She laughed bitterly.

"How did they meet?"

"She was an opera singer. Señor Alfrenso always loved opera. Being poor as a young man, he would sneak into the opera house and stand behind a pillar to listen to her sing. One day he picked up his courage and went backstage to meet her. Despite his poverty, she fell for him. Señora's father found out and sent his servants to beat Señor Alfrenso up and warn him away from his daughter. As young lovers do, they found a way to meet and eloped."

"Did Señor Alfrenso tell you all this?"

"No, my mother. She knew everything that went on here." She quickly crossed herself. "God rest her soul. Maybe that's why I'm destined not to marry."

"Why do you say that?"

"I knew too many secrets, so señor will never let me go."

I thought Maria might leave, and quickly, if she could find some of the hidden cash and gold.

"How did Señor Alfrenso end up in this strange place?"

"He inherited it from his wife's father. After señora died, it passed to him."

"Does he really like living in this huge castle in this out-of-the-way place?"

"Oh, I don't ask the master anything like this. I'm sure he has his reasons."

"It's so big. . . ."

"Actually, I haven't been in all the rooms. I'm not sure even Señor Alfrenso has. There are rooms within rooms and more than one attic."

"Why was it built this way?"

"Some crazy count in the last century . . . that's all I know."

This made sense, sort of. In a way this place was as strange as Past Life Lake and Uncle Wang's temple.

Maria leaned over to me, and whispered, "Some rooms are not just abandoned—they are haunted!"

"And you're not afraid to be here when Alfrenso is away?"

"Not really. Because I stay far away from those haunted rooms. Also my mother's soul will protect me." She held up the small gold crucifix hanging around her neck. "She wore this every day of her life and gave it to me when she died."

"How can you tell which rooms are haunted?"

"There are noises. Sometimes pacing footsteps, other times singing. Opera singing."

Maria excused herself and returned with another bottle of wine. As she skillfully extracted the cork, I noticed that her hands were pale. I chewed meditatively on an octopus tentacle while she poured herself another glass of wine.

When she was done, I asked, "Please forgive me asking, but can you tell me how Señora Penelope died?"

"It was a motorcycle accident. She was still young and beautiful. A tragic waste."

Yet another death under bizarre circumstances! Anxiety welled up in me. "How did it happen?"

"Señor had an affair. Another singer, only worse—a whore."

"So Penelope found out. . . ."

"She always had a hot temper. She was utterly humiliated. Here her husband was married to a famous opera singer and then took up with a cabaret singer!"

Cabaret singer—it must be Sabrina. Now everything was beginning to fit together.

"Señora Penelope once said she could understand if her husband fell for someone young and pretty, but not someone low-class."

Maria didn't say the name, but it was enough to confirm my hunch that the other woman was Sabrina.

"After all, not only was señora beautiful, she was an opera singer who wore expensive clothes and partied with famous people.

"One evening they had a screaming fight and Señora Penelope left the house and jumped on señor's motorcycle. Later the police came and told us that the vehicle had plunged into the lake. She'd never ridden it before."

"Do you think she might have committed suicide?"

Maria held up her palms as if to block my question. "Anyway . . . she's dead and will never come back."

Suddenly the room felt chilly to me. I thought of Isabelle, another woman who had died horribly. What if Penelope also came back? I thought of her body, like Isabelle's, floating in Past Life Lake before being given a proper burial. Hoping to dispel this unpleasant image, I asked Maria where Penelope's grave was.

Maria swung her arm around and pointed toward the back of the castle. "Right here, just behind the castle wall."

I felt a jolt. Maria seemed to be pointing to the same place where I'd encountered Cecily and her band of witches.

To distract myself from this scary thought, I asked, "Maria, does Señor Alfrenso still miss his wife? He never remarried, right?"

"There are many things señor does not tell me. He worries that all women are after his money. He says he's waiting for one who doesn't care about his wealth. But I told him that's like waiting for a barren woman to bear a child. But that was before you came, Señorita Eileen. Señor Alfrenso likes you. Very much."

"Please don't joke."

"Many women have tried to get close to him. He only has ever invited you to stay—and for as long as you like."

"But why me? I'm not rich or beautiful. And I can't sing."

"I think it's because you never asked him anything about his money, about how much the castle costs, or his Bentley."

Maybe sometimes it's true that opposites attract. I needed money to live on like everybody else. But if that was all I cared about I'd already be married to Ivan. So I guessed I must seem different to Alfredo.

Just then, Maria got up to clear and I saw that she was quite unsteady on her feet. I worried she would fall as she tried to navigate the complex passages of the castle. I told her to clean up in the morning and helped her back to her room. She was asleep as soon as I set her on her bed. I tiptoed out, closed her door, and went to the library. There was a decanter of Madeira on the table, so I poured myself a glass and sat down. I was not in a mood to read. I just sat quietly to digest what Maria had told me about Alfredo and Penelope.

Between the revelations I'd just heard and the wine wearing off, I was too restless to sleep. I decided to take advantage of the situation and explore more of the castle. Since I was already familiar with the ballroom, music room, dining room, and a few others, I walked past those rooms and continued down the long corridor.

When I reached the end and was about to turn back I felt an odd sensation, a vibration emanating from somewhere. I turned around and realized it was coming from behind paneling at the end of the corridor. When I approached I realized that what I'd thought was decoration on the paneling was actually a door. As I approached more closely the vibration intensified, so I decided it must be inviting me to enter.

Both fear and common sense told me to ignore this vibration and go back to my room. Yet the pull of the energy and my curiosity would not let go of me. So I turned the knob, only to find that the door was locked. The more I twisted, the more I felt the urgent *qi* pulling on me. Finally, I just leaned my weight against the panel and, to my surprise, it swung open—like a desperate prostitute's legs.

Once I was inside, the door swung shut. I instinctively looked by the entrance for a light switch, found one, and flicked it on. The room was immediately filled with a dim light from a chandelier, revealing lace curtains, tasseled, bejeweled lamps, and delicate female figurines. A woman's room. Much was in shadow, but as I looked around, I was startled to see a beautiful young woman looking down at me from the wall. It was an oil portrait with an Egyptian scene in the background. Then I realized it was from an opera, *Aida*. I was in Señora Penelope Alfrenso's bedroom!

The whole room was covered in deep red silk, evoking elegance and authority, but also mystery and fear. All sorts of objects were placed on tables and shelves, neatly arranged but covered with dust, neglected. An abandoned room, once filled with love, warmth, and hope, once alive and vibrant, now forlorn.

Set against the far wall was an elaborately layered canopy bed with matching pink embroidered pillows. I felt very sad as I let myself imagine the young, handsome Alfredo and Penelope frolicking on top of the bed, sometimes lovingly, other times playfully, back when they still had eyes only for each other.

Next to the bed was a vanity with an elaborately gilded mirror. It was covered with perfume and cosmetic bottles, their contents long ago evaporated. There was a rack of lipsticks of different shades, now dull and cracked. A silver hairbrush and hand mirror set were tarnished to a dull black. Tortoise-shell combs were strewn about, with a few auburn hairs between the teeth.

This was a woman who had clearly lived for beauty. A woman of taste and elegance, but also arrogance. Perhaps in a way it was better that she'd died young. I wondered how a woman like this would react when one day she looked in her mirror and saw the first wrinkle or white hair. Life is cruel to all, beautiful or not.

I walked around, taking it all in—a chaise lounge for señora to take her nap, or read an opera score, or a fashion magazine. I wiped the dust off a framed photograph to see the prima donna herself, Señora Penelope Alfrenso, singing to a packed opera house, gloved hands raised, as if pleading for her life back. A woman who had everything—except a faithful husband.

It was with a sense of melancholy that I looked around her intimate, private room. On a dresser were framed pictures showing Penelope at parties, wearing dramatic makeup, elaborate gowns, and opera costumes. A few were of Penelope in exotic places, with or without her husband. She appeared in attention-grabbing poses, displaying her décolletage, slouching with a cigarette in a long holder, leaning seductively on the hood of a luxury car. A woman with a life of high drama both on and off stage. A controlling woman for whom everything had to be perfect—but wasn't.

I was starting to feel dizzy. This room, exactly as it had been in the young woman's last hours on earth, made her death seem like it had happened moments ago. Most distressing was a set of wine-glasses on a silver tray. Both had a crimson residue on the bottom and one had a faint lipstick trace on the rim. It gave me an uncanny feeling, as if the woman were still somewhere in the castle, or perhaps in the room, bitter at the intrusion of another woman—me.

23

Secrets on a Tape

As I continued to look around, I realized that this room had been Penelope's private sanctuary, one her husband could most likely enter only at her invitation. Or perhaps she retreated here to live as a saint, after Alfredo had lost interest in her.

Penelope had been rejected just like the out-of-favor concubines cast aside by the emperor to live in the *lenggong,* the "cold palace." A lonely, empty life. An imperial concubine could never go home, because she remained the emperor's property. And a celibate one, for no man would dare to love a woman who'd once been married to the emperor. She might even accept the gift of a white silk scarf with which to hang herself—if she was granted permission. The cold court was filled with these bitter concubines and their predecessors' even more bitter ghosts. I wondered if the motorcycle had been Penelope's substitute for the white scarf.

Seeing all her possessions, looking ghostly themselves in their abandoned state, I reflected how, despite having so much, a person could still be desperately unhappy. Here was a woman, rich, famous, beautiful, with thousands of lavish possessions, yet unable to possess her husband's heart.

To me, this room full of no-longer-cared-for objects proved the cliché that you can't take it with you. In the past, however, rich Chinese thought otherwise. They assumed that the more they possessed in this life, the more they could take to the next. The famous Lady Dai, now well past her 2,000th birthday, was found buried with over two hundred jade bracelets and other treasures.

In China, the grave goods were provided to ensure that the deceased would have as good a "life" after death as before. This was not generosity on the part of the living, but rather fear that disgruntled ancestors would return to wreak havoc on them. Nor were the dead easily satisfied—the least slight might bring them back from hell to punish the living.

When someone was sick or afflicted, it was assumed to be the work of ghosts. Of course, there was no easy way to know what would appease the deceased. So humans were employed to make otherworld journeys to ask the spirits what they wanted. If even more offerings did not satisfy them, a black magician would be hired to cast spells to keep them from crossing into the *yang* world to bother the living.

I sighed, thinking that relationships with the dead can be as difficult as those with the living. I wondered, had Alfredo done anything to appease the spirit of his deceased wife? If not, would she come back, asking for what was her due?

My eyes landed on an elaborately carved box in a corner. I went up, opened it, and found myself staring at a stack of newspaper clippings. They were mostly reports and reviews of Penelope's concerts, a few interviews and bits of gossip. Accompanying photographs showed the prima donna singing by a grand piano in front of a big orchestra, or doing an interview in her lavishly decorated music room. A few showed her and Alfredo smiling into the camera and looking happy. Who would have known that these were façades they put up for the public?

None of the articles seemed to be of particular interest until I saw one with the title:

Opera Singer Penelope Alfrenso Catches Husband with Another Woman

> Our beloved, beautiful, and talented opera singer Penelope Alfrenso's marriage may be in trouble. More than ten years after her lavish wedding, she was shocked to discover that her husband, Alfredo Alfrenso, has been having an affair. But even worse for the famous prima donna, this third party is also a singer—in a shady cabaret!
>
> According to rumor, Penelope wants a divorce, but her husband adamantly refuses, his reason being that Catholics cannot divorce. Of course everyone knows a very generous donation to the church can lead to an annulment. Most likely, Señor Alfrenso just wants to hold on to his wife's immense family fortune.

Hmmm . . . interesting, Penelope had died tragically *before* she could start divorce proceedings. Upon her sudden death, Alfredo became the heir to her fortune. Hard to believe there wasn't something fishy going on. I remembered Sabrina's suspicion that Isabelle had been murdered by Alfredo. Was this refined man actually a serial killer? If he'd killed Isabelle to cover up his affair with her mother, he could have killed his wife as well. If he truly had his own money hidden somewhere in the castle, why would he kill for even more money? Then I thought of Ivan—for the greedy, no amount is ever enough.

As I was currently staying in Alfredo's castle, these thoughts were horrifying to me. I had no money that anyone would want to kill me for, but being under the same roof with a possible murderer was terrifying. He seemed a considerate man, but I hardly knew him.

The rest of the newspaper clippings were of no interest, just glowing reviews of Penelope's many performances. I put the clippings back and returned the box where I had found it. I did not want any trace of my visit because the state of the room suggested it was unchanged since the day of Penelope's death. Either Alfredo wanted it left untouched so he could remember his wife as if she were still alive or he'd shut the door and never reentered the room, trying to forget her.

I spotted another carved wooden box almost identical to the first one. When I opened it, I found a stack of letters inside. Despite feeling somewhat ashamed to be prying into someone's most personal matters, I could not resist unfolding the first letter. Letters expressing someone else's uninhibited expressions of affection are usually embarrassing, but reading these was even more uncomfortable since I knew their love had ended tragically.

The first letter, from Alfredo, had none of the reserve he'd shown with me.

> *How can I live without you? It was the grace of God that led me through the thorn-filled path of my life to happiness with the most beautiful woman I have ever seen. . . .*
>
> *As the days and years pass, like the mountains and the sea, my love for you will never change.*
>
> *Every day, I am happy, just thinking of you.*
>
> *Please, never doubt my undying love. . . .*

It went on, but I felt poignantly how changeable is a man's heart, so I stopped reading. Those letters written by Penelope, in contrast, seemed to express an undertone of anxiety.

> *I never hoped to meet anyone like you. You are handsome, courteous, and give me a love that is truly rare on this earth.*
>
> *I hope you won't let me down, that we'll hold hands and watch the sunset till our hair turns white.*
>
> *I know that the bloom of my youth and life will eventually fade and the fresh colors turn to gray. If you truly love me, I will feel young even into eternity.*

From Alfredo's declarations, it seemed that he truly loved Penelope, at least in the beginning, but it was not impossible that his flowery words were intended to conceal his real interest—her money. After reading these bits of the love letters, I wanted to leave. I had shared enough suffering with Alfredo's wife. But then I spied one last chest, obviously antique, perhaps a treasure of Penelope's family. This object seemed to stand out in its significance, almost as if Penelope was somehow wanting me to notice it.

I felt myself slipping into my altered state as I walked over and opened it. Inside was a cassette tape and a small player. I had a sensation of another hand taking mine and guiding it to pick up the cassette. I searched for an outlet and saw one on the wall right next to the chest. To my surprise, the dusty cassette player came to life as I plugged it in. I inserted the tape and pressed the play button.

After a brief interval, a high-pitched, resonant voice began singing an aria from *Madame Butterfly.* I turned down the volume just in case, even though Maria was unlikely to wake up anytime soon. Despite the low quality of the tape player, I could hear the passion and nuances of the singer's unfulfilled love. After the aria finished, the tape went silent. I would have liked to hear more of Penelope's voice, but this strong sense of the dead woman's presence gave me a queasy feeling.

Whether it was the leftover effects of the wine I had consumed or my overwhelming emotions, I could not tell, but I felt myself drifting off into sleep. I turned off the tape and sank down onto the chaise lounge. I realized it was not sleep but the same sensation I'd felt at Past Life Lake and also in Uncle Wang's temple. My limbs felt as if they were melting as my consciousness seemed to leave my body.

This time, instead of the sensation of being underwater, it was as if I were sinking into the cold earth. Frightened, I imagined I would be forever trapped in this tomblike room. I sensed an uncountable number of people who had also been trapped here long ago. Despite my drowsiness, I seemed to hear a voice like that of Penelope on the recording I had just listened to.

I strained to hear her words, but they were muted by the earth surrounding us. I sensed a beautiful face in front of me, but unlike her portrait, she bore an expression of inconsolable grief.

"Are you Penelope?" I asked, voice trembling.

She nodded.

"You still live in this room?"

This time she spoke, her voice soft yet powerful. "This is my home, my room."

This was quite scary and now I regretted having entered her room. But I could not move, so I just asked, "How did you die?"

"You already know—of a broken heart."

"How is it over there?"

"It's cold, especially without my husband to embrace and warm me."

I felt a shudder, thinking of those ill-fated concubines withering in the cold palace.

She stared into my eyes with her doleful, long-lashed ones. "You must do something for me."

"Just ask."

I hoped she wouldn't, like Isabelle, ask me to find who'd killed her. One death was more than enough for me to handle. Even with my *yin* eye opened.

But her request both surprised and saddened me. "Please make a paper boat, write my name on it, and set it out onto the sea."

Since we were on an island, this wouldn't be hard for me.

As if she'd read my thoughts, she said, her voice cracking, "I mean the underworld sea between the two realms."

"Why do you want me to do this?"

"It is my only hope to reach my husband, so I'll be with him, at least in spirit."

So in spite of everything, she still loved her husband and wanted to be with him, even after death.

"I'll certainly do that. But where are you now?" I asked.

"I can't tell you. It's too horrible. Also please help me find an evil woman."

"Who?"

"The witch who helped the prostitute steal my husband, then took him for herself."

First a ghost appears and then she asks about witches. I was beginning to doubt my sanity.

"Her name was Nathalia, but I think later she changed it to Cecily," said the apparition.

Cecily? Either she meant the witch I knew or I was really crazy. But still, what was happening seemed real, so I went along, asking, "What do you want me to do after I've found her?"

Instead of answering she suddenly vanished into the mirror just as she'd appeared—from nowhere.

24

There Is Always One Near You

I didn't know which was more frightening, Penelope appearing or her disappearing. Either way was enough for me. Once she vanished I was able to move my limbs again and I bolted to my room. Back on my own bed, I felt some relief, though I was still in a cold sweat from the "unclean" visitation. I muttered a prayer for protection, then tried to remember everything Penelope had said to me, lest it vanish from my mind like a dream.

Paradoxically, I felt deeply touched by Penelope's attachment to Alfredo, despite his betrayal. Even in hell, she still wanted me to make a paper boat, write her name on it, and set it out on the underworld sea so she could cross from the *yin* world to visit her husband. For all her arrogance, the prima donna had at least one noble quality—she truly loved her husband.

What to make of what a ghost tells you in a dream? If it was a dream. But if not, what? Anyway, it did explain some things—like Cecily being Nathalia, or vice versa.

I massaged my temples, hoping, but failing, to clear my head. So the witch had changed her name and lived underground to avoid her victims' vengeance. I wondered if she ever thought to amend her wrongdoings, rather than spend most of her time in hiding. Surely she would be worried that Penelope's ghost was unappeased.

Hoping to sleep, I closed my eyes and took deep breaths. I must have been asleep because Laolao came to me, not like a ghost but as a memory.

"See, Eileen, I always told you that your brain is different from the others, but you didn't believe me. You should know that at the back of our brain there are five doors opening onto different paths. But unlike ordinary people, you're gifted with one more door, one that opens to the other side."

"What other side?" I asked her.

"The side that everyone fears to enter, but are also desperate to peek into, especially when their loved ones have gone there first."

"Is it dangerous to go there?"

"Not if you're respectful and do it with good intentions. If you show respect, you'll receive it in return."

I nodded as if I understood.

After that I couldn't close my eye—I mean my *yin* eye. Images floated before me: Penelope and her fading love letters in her cold, forbidden, haunted room. Isabelle underwater. Sabrina mourning at her daughter's grave . . .

Then I remembered an article I'd read a long time ago in a metaphysical magazine. Entitled "There Is Always One Near You," it explained that because people are dying every minute, ghosts are all around us. But normally, only those few people who possess the *yin* eye can see them.

After reading the article, I asked Laolao, "Do you have the *yin* eye?"

"I do, but not like my mother—your great-grandmother—had."

Laolao went on to tell me how her mother saw impure beings everywhere. At the cinema, even with only a few people in the audience, Great-grandma would tell her daughter that it was a full house—to the latter's nervous giggling to hide her fright.

Once when they were having dinner, Great-grandma told her that "someone" was tasting the food on her plate. When Laolao asked what ghosts look like, her mother's answer was, "Just like us, but their faces are very pale. The bitter ones—those who died of murder, suicide, or violent accidents—have bloody tears dripping from their eyes!"

Great-grandma also told Laolao that every room in every house is crowded with them, but only those of us who are blessed—or more likely, cursed—with the *yin* eye can see them.

Laolao said, "So as not to disturb them, whenever we entered an old building or temple, your great-grandma would bow, and utter politely, 'Please excuse our intrusion.' "

Once when they visited a family in a very old Chinatown building, Great-grandma told Laolao that on the couch she saw a ghostly woman holding a baby and staring at them with sad eyes. When Laolao asked if she could sit without pressing on the mother and child, Great-grandma said, "Right here. The mother sees you and has already moved to the side."

Growing up hearing these ghost stories, though Laolao clearly considered them to be real, I was intrigued by them but regarded them skeptically.

But when I argued with Laolao, she always said, "If you don't believe in ghosts, how do you answer the question, 'Then where do all the dead people go?' "

Now I seemed to be finding out where they went—the Past Life Lake, Uncle Wang's temple, Penelope's boudoir—and probably everywhere else.

Things were happening too fast for me to keep up. I felt I needed some sage advice. Giving up on trying to sleep, I took out from my backpack an old tortoise shell, three ancient coins, and the *Book of Changes,* also known as the *I Ching,* and arranged them on the desk.

These were Laolao's tools for divination, reserved for the most important situations. She'd given them to me before she died, since she would no longer be around to advise me and wanted me to carry on the family tradition. Laolao liked to quote from the *Book of Changes* that in this world, from moment to moment nothing remains the same. She was always quoting the famously incomprehensible Chinese classic.

Once I asked her, "Then why bother with fortune-telling?"

"To predict the unpredictable, what else?"

What kind of logic is that? But I was not going to argue, for

Laolao was the authority in the house, and it was her fortunetelling that put food on our table.

Many times Laolao had made me sit with her and taught me how to do it. Although I went along, it was hard for me to feel much in this 3,000-year-old book of inscrutable advice. However, I did know how to use it, at least in theory.

Laolao had always told me, "No challenges, no need for divination," which means that you only do divination when faced with an unusual dilemma. For if you have no challenges—that is, a good marriage, happy, healthy children, lots of money, a fulfilling job—why would you go to a diviner to have your future told? To hear that your luck is about to change? But I had none of these things and since I'd arrived here, there was something peculiar to deal with nearly every day!

Although I didn't have Penelope's birthday, I knew the day she'd died, so this should be good enough, at least for a brief consultation. For now, what I needed was some hints to the mystery of this whole thing, like: How had Penelope and Isabelle died, murdered or accidents? What had actually happened between Cecily and Sabrina?

My hands were a little shaky as I manipulated the coins. Although Laolao had demonstrated and taught me how to do this many times, now I would be on my own without her guidance. But of course since Laolao was much better and sophisticated than I, if she did this the result might be quite different. But anyway I had no choice but to use whatever I got.

The three coins are cast to obtain the six lines that make up the famous hexagrams. For thousands of years in China, the various arrangements of the six *yin* or *yang* lines were believed to represent all possible situations in life.

I shook the coins in my hand as I muttered my inquiry. The coins dropped onto the table with dull thuds, like three heavy bugs. Consulting the chart at the back of the book, I learned that I had obtained hexagram #33, *Dun or Retreat*. Next I flipped the pages of the *Book of Changes* and found the beginning line of *Pull Back*:

At the end, pull back,
Situation dangerous.
One should not try to undertake anything.

It was obvious that this was not a favorable reading. With my heartbeat accelerating, I continued to reflect on these lines. It seemed to be saying that going back was dangerous, but so was going forward. A trap with no apparent way to get out. This prognostication did seem to apply to poor Isabelle and Penelope. In the end, nothing had worked out for these women. Isabelle should not have gone diving by herself, and Penelope should have stayed off the motorcycle until she calmed down. But they did not have the advantage of the *Book of Changes* to warn them.

Laolao had taught me that the first hexagram you get shows the present situation when it is already receding into the past. To find what to do next, you use another hexagram. This time I obtained #46, *Sheng, on Pushing Upward*:

Pushing upward brings great success
It's the right time to see an important person
Do not be afraid
Going to the south
Is auspicious.

This seemed to me a lot better than the first one. I assumed that pushing upward meant prevailing in difficult tasks—and my research had turned out to be far more arduous than I'd anticipated. It was telling me not to be afraid—good news, though it did not fully dispel my anxiety. And all my adventures had been on the southern part of this island, so continuing here would be fortunate.

I was half persuaded by the famous book, but it was clear I would be "pushing upward." Nothing ahead would be easy, not like reading about ghosts and witches in the brightly lit university library.

More than my book was at stake now. I could not give up my compulsion to resolve all the mysteries I had stumbled upon: the circle of witches, headed by the sinister Cecily; the tragedy of the talented but cold Penelope; the death—or murder—of Sabrina's daughter, Isabelle. And most puzzling of all was the opening of my *yin* eye and its uninvited visions. . . .

Also puzzling was the reading stating that my stay in the southern part of this island would be fortunate. Because as for now, the only fortune it brought me was meetings with ghosts!

25

An Unexpected Proposal

After my disturbing discovery of Penelope's boudoir, with its air of desperation and decay—and her even more disturbing emergence from the other world—I decided I needed to be in normal, even dull, surroundings for a while. I wanted to eat, go for walks, read, sleep, and gather my thoughts. Then I hoped I would be calm enough to decide on my next move—unless it would be decided for me by additional visits from the other world.

I said good-bye to Maria, thanked her profusely, and pressed a red lucky money envelope into her hand. Then I asked her to give my regards to Alfredo upon his return.

When I entered the lobby of my small hotel back in Santa Cruz, the young receptionist waved at me.

"Señorita," he said, and smiled mischievously, "there's a man waiting for you."

"Where is he?" I asked.

He gave a quick glance around the lobby before answering. "He's not here. Went to eat, I guess. He arrived early this morning and was very disappointed that you weren't here. But I told him you were on your way back."

"Did he say anything?"

He shook his head. "No."

It was getting more frustrating and annoying.

"Don't worry, señorita, I'll call your room when he is back."

A half hour later, as I was unpacking, the phone rang.

"Señorita Chen, the man came back; he says he knows you. He's waiting in the small garden."

Should I go down to meet this mystery man? But I had already taken a quick glance in the mirror, then dashed to the garden, full of anticipation. The face that greeted me was a familiar one—Ivan.

Even though it warmed my heart to realize his devotion, I was not entirely pleased.

"Ivan, what are you doing here? Why didn't you call?"

"Eileen"—Ivan's face fell like a sack filled with stones—"I thought you'd be happy to see me. . . ."

"Of course I am, but I'm also shocked. I'm not prepared for this."

"I was on a business trip to Paris and wanted to stop by for a surprise visit."

Feeling guilty, I smiled sweetly. He pulled me into his arms and kissed me.

"Are you happy to see me now?"

"Of course I am," I mumbled, then blurted out, "how long will you stay—and where?"

Ivan let go of me, looking very upset. "I'm going to stay with you, of course!"

"But that . . . will really complicate matters," I said calmly, not wanting to spill oil on fire.

"What matters will it complicate, may I ask?" His tone held an angry edge. I feared he was about to explode.

"We're supposed to be in a trial separation, remember?"

He didn't respond but held my elbow and pressed me forcefully toward the elevator. I could see we were beginning to attract attention, but, fortunately, there was a waiting elevator so we were quickly out of sight.

Once inside my room, he paced around, obviously trying to calm down.

Finally, he spoke, this time gently. "Eileen, after some serious thinking, I have decided that I love you and I want to spend the rest of my life with you. I will do everything I can to make you happy."

He seemed to take my silence as consent, because he sat down beside me on the bed, smiling dreamily, and asked in a formal tone, "Eileen, will you marry me?"

"But, Ivan—"

I was about to say that I wasn't going to make such a big decision right here and now, but he had already pressed his lips against mine.

Ivan was a skilled kisser. I was sure he could melt many women's hearts, as well as any resistance between their thighs, not only with his swollen and powerful you-know-what, but also his equally swollen and potent wallet. I often wondered why, out of all the other women, he wanted me. Perhaps he sensed I was different from all of the airheaded, gold-digging bimbos that I suspected frequently shared his bed. Those women who'd practically have an orgasm by seeing him in his Ferrari or setting down his black Amex card at a fashionable eatery.

It took some effort to disentangle from him. Just as I was about to say something, he held up a small red velvet box. With the right man I suppose I might have been ecstatic to see this, but now all I could think about was how to extricate myself.

After he opened it, I saw a huge ring, its diamond sparkling ostentatiously.

"You like it?"

"Ivan, let's cool down first, please."

He didn't look very happy. In fact, he looked like a punctured balloon.

Putting the box down, he said, "We've been cooling down for almost four months now. Eileen, I know you like me, so why do you keep putting me off?"

Now his swagger was replaced by a scolded puppy expression. I had never before seen the wealthy, relentless Ivan with such a vulnerable expression. I wondered, was it an act, just to manipulate me into marrying him out of pity, or had I really broken the heart that I'd not even known existed?

"Ivan, we really belong to two different worlds. I like money, but not as much as you. You're a businessman and I'm just a professor, not even a tenured one. I spend my time in dull libraries, not nightclubs or yachts. It wouldn't take long for you to get bored with me. I really don't want to end up spoiling my life with a bitter divorce."

"Eileen! You talk about divorce and we're not even married! I love you exactly because you are not money crazy. And even if God forbid that someday I'll lose what I've achieved, you will still love me and be there for me, right?"

I put a finger across his lips. "Don't say unlucky things. You're not going to lose anything, okay?"

"Not including you? Anyway, Eileen, marriage is not as bad as you think. Sometimes you're too pessimistic about life."

"At my age I have to be careful."

"You'll be safe with me. Promise." He sighed, looking sad, manly, vulnerable—and seductive.

I needed to harden my heart. I couldn't let myself fall for the affection-craving little-boy persona that was tugging at my maternal instinct. Nor for the vision of an easy life with all his money.

That night, no matter how much Ivan wanted it, I insisted there would be no sex. It was the first time that we slept together and didn't make love. It felt strange. I was too tired and confused, and making love was the last thing on my mind.

I needed to have a clear picture of recent events in order to decide what to do with my life. That was why I didn't want to be distracted by Ivan and his proposal. I felt as if I were treading on a tightrope. This was not the time to make a decision that would affect the rest of my life.

The next morning when I woke up, Ivan was sitting on the edge of the bed, staring at me with sad, bitter eyes. I immediately sat up, then pulled the bedsheet to cover my half-exposed breasts and bare shoulders. Ivan had seen me naked a hundred times. We'd tried all kinds of positions—"auspicious" and "inauspicious"—or even "criminally obscene." We'd experimented with what we'd seen in esoteric Chinese sex manuals: Flirty Eyes, Willow in the Wind,

Banquet in the Backyard, Evening Sailing, The Drunken Return, The Turning Dragon, The Monkey's Attack.

I wondered why I suddenly felt so awkward with him. Then I realized, sadly, that for whatever reason, what I'd felt for him before was now gone.

Ivan stood up. He was stark naked and as hard as Grandpa's stone statue. I felt bad that he wanted me but I did not want him. It was nobody's fault but my own, because I'd let him sleep next to me.

Despite my loss of romantic feeling for Ivan, I still had some affection for him. He was an expert manipulator, so I had to harden myself to refuse giving him what he wanted. But I knew him well enough to be aware that he could not tolerate anyone turning him down.

Ivan started to do his morning exercises, having always liked to show off his toned body. Finally he dressed, though very slowly, perhaps to better show me what I would be missing. In a way I regretted my loss of feelings for him. I could remember not long ago when, like a cat eyeing a bird, I would ogle every inch of his body and his every sensuous move.

Once he was fully dressed, he said sarcastically, "I'm going back to San Francisco. You take care of yourself."

I knew his feelings were hurt, not only because I wouldn't make love with him, but because in Ivan's dictionary, failure was a word to be spat and trod upon.

"Ivan." I tried to be friendly. "Do you want to have breakfast together before you go to the airport?"

"No, I don't have any appetite. Besides, I don't think you enjoy my company anymore."

"Ivan, don't be childish."

"Childish? I think you're the one who's childish! On a whim, you just dumped everything in San Francisco and came here to gather material for your book, about witches—of all things.

"Do you really think you can find real witches? Have you written anything so far? Can you show me some finished pages? I'm leaving you alone now so you can be pursued by those famous hot European lovers. Good luck with these penniless Casanovas!"

"Let's not quarrel just as you're leaving. I want you to know that I'll always care about you and treasure our time together."

"All right," he said curtly, then gave me a peck on my forehead. "When you realize you've made a big mistake, come home."

Hearing his words I felt a sudden surge of homesickness, but I wasn't ready to go back yet.

As I was about to reach out for him, he said, without looking at me, "I thought you really loved me . . . my mistake." Then he shut the door with a bang.

I wasn't happy to have it end this way, but I wasn't going to chase after him. The day might come when I would regret this decision, but no point to worry about it now. I flopped back onto the bed, feeling a headache coming. Just then, my eyes landed on the red velvet box on the nightstand.

I opened the box and took the ring out. It was a huge, sparkling solitary diamond set on a gold band. The diamond had at least five carats. I wondered if he'd forgotten it in the heat of the moment, or deliberately left it to remind me of what I'd given up. I could not imagine that he would buy something that expensive unless he really cared for me. Of course I'd have to return it to him. But he might refuse to take it back—it would, after all, be a reminder of his humiliation. If so, maybe I would give it to charity. Not only because it was the right thing to do, but because it would always remind me of what might have been—if I'd been different, or he had.

I sighed at having to turn down this once-in-a-lifetime catch.

26

A Letter of Heartbreak

I did feel sad now that the trial separation from Ivan was permanent. Not that I really wanted to be back with him, but it did leave an empty area in my life. Now there was one less person to welcome me when I finally returned to San Francisco. Craving friendship, I decided to visit Sabrina again. I pushed thoughts of Ivan to the back of my mind and set out for her house.

Despite Sabrina's eccentricity and her heavy drinking, I was looking forward to seeing her. But as I was ascending her steps I felt extremely apprehensive, as if a huge boulder was about to crash down. When I reached the door, I hesitated. Instead of knocking, I turned toward the setting sun. It was a bloody orange disc, about to sink into the sea like a huge, suicidal tortoise. I felt a chill, as if it were me slipping into the ocean. I turned back and braced myself to knock.

The maid opened the door and made a gesture for me to come in. I noticed that her eyes were swollen and bloodshot.

"Is Señora Sanchez here?" I asked.

She shook her head.

"Can I wait until she gets back?"

"No." She shook her head mournfully.

"Then please tell her that I'll come back soon, maybe tomorrow."

"Señorita, I'm sorry to tell you that Señora Sanchez has passed away."

"What? What happened?"

"Two days ago. Alcohol poisoning. You know she had a problem. She wouldn't tell anyone, but she had also been suffering from stomach and liver cancer. So she knew it would be soon."

Though it had been obvious to me that she was ailing, I didn't realize that her ill health was so advanced. I had assumed that I could just knock on her door and see her again.

The maid pointed outside the window. "If you want to pay your respects, señora is buried there next to her daughter."

For the moment I just wanted to sit down, so I sank onto the couch.

"What will happen to this house?"

"It's Señor Alfrenso's house. He let Señora Sanchez live here and paid me to look after her."

So perhaps Alfredo was not so bad after all. Unless it was all done just to keep Sabrina quiet.

"Oh, señorita, she said if you came back again, I was to give you something. Please wait." She left and returned with a wooden box.

I opened the box and saw a letter enclosed in a sealed envelope of expensive paper. There was an object underneath it. I did not want the maid to ask me about what was in the letter, or to see what Sabrina had left for me, lest she claim it for herself, so I took my leave of her and went outside.

As I walked down the stairs, my eyes moistened. The tragedy of Sabrina's wretched life filled my whole being with sadness. At the foot of the hill was a tiny grocery store and I made my way down to it. There I bought a bouquet of white roses.

I swept Sabrina's fresh gravestone, which in Chinese culture is a gesture of respect, then Isabelle's more worn one. I knelt down and intoned a quiet prayer for both of them. Sitting beside the new grave, I took out the envelope. Under it, to my surprise, was a gold bracelet, from which dangled several little amulets: a red heart, a lamp, a violin, a bell, a cup, a stone inscribed with a sword, another heart with the number "13" inscribed on it, and a blue bead—to protect against the evil eye.

I tried to understand the symbolism of this interesting combination of charms. The red heart must be Sabrina's passionate, fiery love for a man; the kerosene lamp maybe referred to illumination, or a lit path; the ringing of a bell announced something happy; a violin makes beautiful music, to lighten up a depressing life, or to accompany her singing and dancing; a cup to hold water to quench thirst, but thirst for what? The red stone inscribed with a sword stirred a memory in me, but I could not think of what it was.

Most puzzling was the unlucky number thirteen, written on a heart. I thought how well it described her life, always unlucky in love.

Why had Sabrina left this bracelet to me? Perhaps it was all she had left and I was the only friend left to leave it to. But most likely it was simply a generous act to mark my kindness to her.

I took several deep breaths to calm myself, then took out her letter. My heart began to beat faster when I unfolded it and saw my friend's untidy writing, perhaps written during her last hours.

> *My Dear Black-Eyed Friend from Afar,*
>
> *It was such a pleasure to have known you, my friend, even for a short time. In life, because there's death, time is never enough, as we are all rushing toward the big* UNKNOWN.
>
> *Of course I've known all along that I'm dying. It's deliberate—drinking myself to death. My eyes have turned yellow, I look like I'm pregnant because my stomach is filled with water, and sometimes I vomit blood. Not very pleasant to look at me now. That's why I've been eagerly waiting for my liberation from this terrible world filled with heartless people—except you.*
>
> *Even as I write this, I'm a walking corpse. My husband killed himself, Alfredo left me, Isabelle died, my baby son stolen. I'm heartbroken when I look in the mirror now and remember how I looked during*

my youth. I was a beautiful, vivacious woman. I boast, yes, but it's the truth! I was happy that my daughter was equally beautiful, but like my own youth, she was taken from me.

MURDERED!

Here was the accusation of murder again. But despite my investigations, with both my normal eyes and my third one, I seemed no closer to discovering what had happened. Now I felt even more obligated to get to the bottom of this—to put Sabrina's spirit at rest—at least so that her ghost wouldn't also visit me.

You may not believe me, but I know. Isabelle's murderer is none other than her "father," my handsome lover, Señor Alfredo Alfrenso!

I shook my head. There were all these terrible rumors about Alfredo, but how to know what was true? Sabrina was obsessed, understandably, and I knew she was inclined to embellish and dramatize things. Distressed by all the misery and uncertainty, I continued to read.

I am partly at fault. True, we were nearly starving, but I told my daughter that things would work out. I also made the mistake of telling her about Alfredo's secret stash of money inside Heartbreak Castle. The foolish girl went behind my back to demand money from him. She didn't know who she was up against!

That day, she came back seeming depressed, and frightened. She wouldn't tell me anything, but a mother knows. Alfredo must have feared that Isabelle would rat on him and the government would confiscate all his illegal money. And then tell his wife, the beautiful and cruel prima donna, Penelope!

My naïve Isabelle must have thought that being his adopted daughter would protect her. But obviously she was wrong. So wrong.

I kept reading, thinking that Sabrina was as rambling when she wrote as when she talked.

You were very kind to have visited me so often. I miss my beautiful daughter, her dog too. She raised a Lhasa Apso from puppy. Unfortunately it was swallowed into the earth—I know you heard about this and figured out I was the woman who witnessed it. I was not surprised because that dog was very old and suicidal. This was exactly the spot where Isabelle often took the dog to play, so I think, sensing his own pending death, he wanted to be reunited with his mistress.

Your high spirits and resemblance to my daughter brought me back to life, though for a short time. In my heart, I believe you are my Chinese daughter sent by Heaven to comfort me during my last days on earth.

I want to die knowing that you will find out the truth. Not only about Isabelle, but also my stolen baby son. Soon after he was born, I put a pendant—a red stone inscribed with a sword for protection—just like the one on the bracelet I am giving you. I like to think that he still wears it around his neck.

Thank you for reading this, my friend, it means a lot to me that someone would actually listen to an old, worthless, dying woman.

Dear child, may you live a long, happy, fulfilling life.

I also hope you'll wear the bracelet to remember me. This was my last piece of jewelry. I had to sell all the others.

Your Green-Eyed Friend,
Sabrina

Instead of explaining things, this letter made them murkier than ever. That Alfredo had murdered Isabelle just didn't ring true to me. But then neither did his callousness toward Penelope. Clearly there was more to the man than I'd realized. It seemed that he hid his true self like a camouflage-skinned snake, fooling even my third eye. Anyway, there were so many flaws in this whole thing. Isabelle said in her diary that Sabrina had pushed her to get Alfredo's cash. But Sabrina's letter said something different. Maybe neither was telling the truth.

I put on the bracelet, hoping to feel closer to its previous owner. My eyes fell upon the red heart with the sword. I suddenly remembered that Luis always wore a pendant that was also a red stone inscribed with a sword! Could this mean that Luis was Sabrina and Alfredo's son? If this was true, then not only was their son still alive, he lived almost next door to his father! But father and son had never known each other.

I knelt and muttered another short prayer to both Sabrina and Isabelle, then stood up and walked toward the road, leaving mother and daughter behind forever as tears coursed down my cheeks.

All the way back to the hotel on the bus, I kept rereading Sabrina's letter, wondering how much was true and how much was alcohol-fueled imagination. And what about Alfredo—was he the gentleman he seemed to be, even if he was a bit of a womanizer, or a murderer? A womanizer I could handle, but not a murderer.

Alfredo was part of all the mysteries I'd become preoccupied with, but better leave the mysteries unsolved than put myself under the power of a killer. Laolao would have told me that with my third eye, I would see evil in his aura if he had killed anyone. I had seen nothing of the sort, so Alfredo was probably okay. But could I trust my life to my third eye? To add to my confusion, there was the question of Cecily, aka Nathalia. Seeing her again was essential to my research, but for all I knew, she might already have cast a spell on me.

27

Another Proposal

Putting caution aside, the next morning I went to visit Cecily. When I arrived at her underground dwelling, I yelled down, “Cecily, are you there?”

After more yelling with no response, I climbed down the ladder. Reaching the floor, I saw that the witch was nowhere to be seen, nor were any of her possessions. It was apparent that she had moved out, but I could not imagine why. Perhaps some of her evil doings had finally caught up with her.

As swiftly as I could, I climbed back up to the open air and headed straight for the witches’ market, hoping to see Cecily, or at least her followers.

When I arrived, I glimpsed someone at a booth who looked like her, but was disappointed when I realized it was not Cecily but a frumpy middle-aged woman hawking cheap jewelry and prayer beads.

I went up to her and smiled. “Señora, isn’t this where Cecily and her group are?”

“Not here.”

“You know her?”

“Maybe.”

I was quite sure she knew something, so I decided the best way to loosen her tongue would be to buy something. I held up a bracelet made of evil eye dispelling beads and asked the price.

"Two thousand pesetas."

About thirteen dollars, which was an absurd price for the beads, but not for the information I needed. I handed over the cash.

"So what about Cecily? She's my friend and if she's in trouble I want to help."

At the word *friend,* she gave me a suspicious look. "I don't know where she's gone. They say she's afraid for her life."

"Someone wants to get her?"

"Maybe a few, maybe a lot, maybe none but just her fear."

This was either very confused or very subtle. Was she a Zen master disguised as a witch to give me advice through a riddle? Or was she just a crazy witch herself?

"Does it involve a rich man?"

"Señorita, please"—she cast me an annoying glance—"I'm not a psychic, so how do I know? Go ask someone else. I come here to do business, not chitchat with a stranger. You Japanese, Korean, Chinese, Vietnamese?"

Now she looked at me curiously. "You're a tourist. You should buy more gifts for your friends at home."

I was hoping that I might find her in a better mood later, so to build our "relationship," I bought some loose beads, then walked away. Looking around, I did not see anyone I recognized. I was reluctant to buy more trinkets and get no answers.

I knew that sooner or later I would question Alfredo more about Isabelle and Penelope. I decided to not put it off any longer, so I hailed a taxi and told the driver to take me to Heartbreak Castle, full of apprehension.

I feared what would happen if Alfredo figured out how much I knew about these unfortunate women. My excuse would be to say a few words of condolences about Sabrina's death. Even if he was secretly relieved that she was gone, a few words of sympathy would still be in order. Of course I was hoping he'd inadvertently reveal something about his relationship with Sabrina and her daughter.

Maria opened the door, invited me in, and led me to sit in the living room.

She smiled. "I'm glad you're back, Señorita Eileen. Señor Alfrenso is just back from a trip and is taking a nap. Please wait here and I'll bring you some tea and biscuits."

After I had sipped some tea and munched on a cookie, I fell into a reverie. When I emerged, I was startled to look up and see Alfredo sitting on a high-backed chair across from me.

"My dear Eileen," he said, and smiled, "you seemed far away. . . ."

I sat straight up and nodded, feeling a burning sensation on my cheeks. Strange, this man was not my lover, but it was already the second time that he had seen me dozing in front of him.

"Sorry, I must be exhausted." I certainly could not tell him what I'd been thinking about.

"No need to apologize, Eileen. I'm so happy you're here. Do you have plans for more sightseeing? Any place you want to see, let me know and I'll take you."

His seemingly polite offer seemed ominous. I realized no one back home in San Francisco knew anything about Alfredo or the castle, so I could disappear without a trace. What if he'd take me to some isolated place and then . . . I couldn't finish my thought.

"Thanks, Alfredo," I said quickly. "What about if we just have a nice chat?"

"Of course, whatever pleases you."

"You know that Sabrina has passed away?"

"I was the one who paid for her burial."

"So you knew her well?"

"It was a long time ago. She was a troubled woman. Let's hope she is finally at peace." He stared at me with his penetrating eyes. "I am so happy to see you again. Eileen, let me be frank. I really like you and hope you can stay."

I didn't know what to say to this.

He paused to sip his drink, then continued. "I mean long term. You can be mistress of this place instead of a professor with a meager income. I will give you a luxurious and glamorous life. Please think about it and . . . don't say no."

This reminded me of Laolao telling me that for my whole life I wouldn't have to worry about money, because rich men would be attracted to me. But . . . why? I thought I was nice looking but not stunningly beautiful. Besides, I was probably not sophisticated enough for a rich guy—I didn't care about drinking hundred-dollar bottles of wine, nor did I wear designer brands—unless I found them at a thrift store.

I was as happy eating a bowl of shrimp mei fun in a Chinatown dive as I was at a trendy, high-end restaurant. And if taken to a nightclub, I'd likely doze off. So I didn't consider myself trophy wife material. But maybe it was because I didn't care about any of these things that some rich men found me refreshing. Like a breath of clean air in Beijing or a Buddhist temple in Las Vegas.

Anyway, it was not quite clear to me what Alfredo had in mind. I never considered myself the mistress type. But when he continued I was taken completely by surprise.

"Eileen, let's get married and have a child together. I'm sure he or she will be very handsome and smart."

Whoa, slow down! I thought. It seems rich men were always impatient to get what they want. First Ivan and now Alfredo.

But Alfredo was not getting any younger and so he might think this was a rare opportunity for true love, and with someone he must assume did not know about his past.

"I'm extremely flattered, but I don't know what to say. I didn't come here thinking I'd get married, but to write my book."

He laughed. "But you can still write you book . . . without having to worry about tenure."

I chewed on what he'd said, feeling distressed, not sure how to get myself out of this uncomfortable situation. Tenure, yes, an unpleasant reality, how nice it would be not to have to worry about tenure. And what progress had I truly made with my book? A few pages of notes, that was it. I had mostly occupied myself poking my nose into other people's business—jilted women, witches, and the dead.

"After Penelope's passing," said Alfredo, "I've been waiting in this Heartbreak Castle hoping to find someone to mend, or better, capture my heart. I believe you came here in answer to my prayers."

Was he really that lonely, or did he want something else from me? He was an appealing man, but given what I'd heard about him I did not want to be further entangled with him, let alone share his bed or his life.

Seeing that I was not about to answer, he smiled. "Eileen, take some time to think about my proposal. Our future son will be very fortunate. As my heir, he'll get my business, this castle, and everything else I can give him."

I was quite tempted, but what if our baby was a daughter? And though Alfredo seemed not to know about Luis, Sabrina's stolen baby might show up and complicate matters.

He went on with a philosophical air. "You know, Eileen, women are like ships who need a safe harbor to moor. No matter how fancy or gorgeous a ship is, if she can't find the right harbor, she will drift aimlessly forever. Think of all the dangers one faces in life."

I wondered if this was some kind of threat and was not reassured by him saying, "Just think of all the hazards one might encounter at sea—sharks, giant squids, towering waves, hidden rocks, typhoons . . . Excitement and adventure seem tempting, but eventually a woman needs a place where she is safe."

He paused to see my reaction, then went on. "And I can give you a secure life."

Like you gave Penelope, I thought. Her ghost had asked me to write her name on a paper ship. She'd wanted the paper ship to bring her back to Alfredo, even though he had treated her badly. I sighed inside.

Other women would have already jumped at this once-in-a-lifetime bonanza dropping from Heaven. But if I believed the rumors, it wasn't a bonanza and certainly not from Heaven. Probably all of us do need a safe harbor eventually, not just women. But before coming to the harbor there should be a voyage—and that's where I was in my life. I believed my sails were lifted by the wind and my ship had a long way to travel before it was time to seek the shore.

"Well, think about my proposal before you give me your answer. In the meantime, Maria has set a table for us outside, so let's enjoy our lunch," Alfredo said.

During the meal we talked small talk, but there was tension due to his still-unanswered offer of marriage. Laolao seemed to be right that rich men would want me, but she had not warned me that I might not want them. Before I could even imagine considering Alfredo's proposal, there was something I knew I had to tell him.

There was no easy way to bring up the subject, so I said bluntly, "Alfredo, maybe you already have a son somewhere."

I could see that this caught him off guard. To compound his shock, I went on. "Sabrina told me she had a son with you."

It took a few seconds before he answered. "Yes, she said it was mine. A few months after we'd split, she brought a baby boy to me and claimed I was the father. Since you know Sabrina, you know it may have been another man's child. Because I'm rich, she'd pick me as the father over some Bohemian wastrel. But I didn't know for sure so I paid for her house—they were cheap in those days—and also gave her a little money every month."

Although this sounded like a kind gesture—it could keep her quiet about his illegitimate child.

"However, one day she told me that the baby had been stolen by Nathalia. When I confronted Nathalia about it, she said she'd never even known about Sabrina's pregnancy. Most of what that witch says is a lie, however. So who knows?"

"What happened to the baby?"

"No one knows. I was young then and I didn't really care. However, I did ask around and try to track him down. But no one knew anything. Or so they said. Nathalia has a very fearsome reputation as a witch and people here are superstitious. Anyone who thought she was involved would be terrified to say anything."

He shook his head and let out a sigh. "It makes me sad so I try not to think about him. Even if the baby is still alive, I have no idea where—or how I could tell if he's really mine."

"Alfredo." I looked him in the eyes. "I think I know where your son is. . . ."

He looked at me as if I had just arrived from a UFO—these islands were famous for alien landings.

"Eileen, please don't joke about this!"

"I wouldn't joke about it, Alfredo. Let me explain." I told him about my stay in the soon-to-be-vanished village. I went on to tell him about the pendant that Sabrina had told me about and that seemed to be the same one I'd seen Luis wearing.

When I had finished, Alfredo exclaimed, "Yes, I know about the village. But I thought it was completely deserted a long time ago."

"It will be soon, but there are six people who still live there: Luis, his grandpa, Father Fernando, Juan, and the two widows."

"Could this Luis really be my son? How could he have ended up in a place like that? That pendant sounds like a gift I gave Sabrina when we were together. For protection—she believed in things like that."

He stared intensely into my eyes. "So you made friends with Luis—who may be my son—in that tiny village?"

I nodded. "He's a nice young man. Good for you if he's your son."

From his dazed eyes came a spark of hope. "I want to go to the village as soon as possible. Can you come with me?"

I nodded. "Alfredo, can I ask you another question?"

"Go ahead."

"You also had a daughter?"

"She wasn't really my daughter. . . ."

"What do you mean?" I already knew the answer, but I wanted to hear his response.

"I adopted Sabrina's daughter, Isabelle, but informally, not legally. Anyway, it all happened twenty years ago, and Isabelle died in an accident. She drowned while diving."

"Were you close to Isabelle?"

He didn't respond. Maria had told me that Penelope had also died of a freak accident. There seemed to be one too many convenient accidents. I was scared now that he'd realize I knew too much, so I decided to change the subject.

"Can you tell me about Nathalia? I've met her, but I need to know more for my book. You know, it's not easy to run across a real witch."

"I know her, but I don't know her well."

"She's now called Cecily. I have no idea where she's gone. A woman at the Witches' Market told me she left because she fears for her life."

"How's that?"

"Because Sabrina's ghost may come after her."

He laughed. "If a ghost is coming after her, there's no way she can hide. It's much more likely whom she fears is not a ghost, but a human."

"But whom?"

"That I don't know. She's a wicked woman. She cast spells on many innocent people. She has many enemies."

After that, my potential husband abruptly stood up. "Let's not talk anymore about unpleasant matters. Why don't we put aside these past tragedies and enjoy our lives? Eileen, please seriously consider my proposal. Perhaps you think I am too old for you, but a mature man knows how to make a woman happy."

Of course his age was not my main concern, but it was easier if that was what he thought.

"Maria has made up the room for you," he said. "You look tired, so feel free to take a nap. And don't worry, I will give you time to decide."

28

Cecily's Ritual

I'd slept soundly all afternoon, but as a result was unable to fall asleep again when night came. So I put on a sweater and stepped outside to see if a walk in the cool air would relax me. It was overcast with only a few stars pathetically shining through. A light breeze blew from the sea, soothing my frazzled nerves. The silence was occasionally broken by birds' cries, or distant barking. Walking for minutes I spotted the pond where I'd encountered Cecily and the other witches.

Through the trees surrounding the water I saw a figure, indistinct in the moonlight but substantial enough to be a human rather than a ghost. As I approached I saw that it was Cecily, this time by herself.

Cecily. Formerly Nathalia.

I slipped behind a tree to watch. On the ground was an area in the shape of a five-pointed star outlined by candles stuck into the earth. In the center, revealed by the flickering candlelight, was a crude wooden doll of a mother holding a baby. Cecily wore a cape and also a black hat, pointed like a traditional witch's hat, but with a wider brim that partly concealed her face.

She threw some powder on the doll and began to dance around the altar as she chanted in a low voice what seemed to be names of ancient gods. She continued this weird performance, then paused and from a basket extracted a live chicken. I knew what would come next and was tempted to look away but decided I needed to observe the sacrifice for documentation in my book.

Cecily lifted the bird up to the sky, then brought it down toward the earth. Mumbling another spell, she took out a sharp knife and, with a practiced hand, cut off its head. Blood spurted onto Cecily's hands as she set the poor bird—still quivering—on the altar, no doubt as an offering to some unknown, likely evil deity.

Next she took out a small jar of water and sprinkled it over the space. She continued to chant and pray, then flopped on the ground, rolling her eyes so only the whites could be seen. This was creepy, for she looked like she was transforming into a living corpse. All her strength seemed to have been consumed by the unpleasant ritual, but I still feared to approach, because I suspected she had endless reserves of evil energy.

I didn't think Cecily would be well disposed toward me when she realized that I had seen her ceremony, chicken sacrifice included. Her reaction was likely to be quite unpleasant. But this could be my opportunity to question her, and being caught in the act might loosen her tongue. I approached, making some noise so as to warn her of my presence.

When she spotted me, I said, "Cecily, is that you? I was just out for a walk. How are you?" Then I looked down at the lump of feathers and blood.

Even in the faint light I could see that she was not at all happy to see me here.

"Eileen! What are you doing here! Spying on me, are you?" She jumped up, glaring at me.

I didn't like her rudeness, but I didn't want to tangle with her either. I backed away, holding my hands out in a placating gesture.

"I'm staying at the castle, so I often go out for walks."

"You know this is my special place for rituals. When I met you the first time I invited you here, but I never said you could come back."

"Well, I'm here. Actually, I looked for you in your cave, but you moved out."

"Because I want to be left alone. But since you are here, join me in the ritual."

"I can't, not with a sacrificed chicken. . . ."

"Ah, Americans, so concerned about animals—except when dinnertime comes."

"Maybe. For Chinese, blood sacrifice is to appease the dead. So who are you trying to appease—someone you wronged?"

I surprised myself by talking back to her like this. Previously I would not have dared. This made me realize how my stay here had changed me. With my third eye opened and having conversed with ghosts, I seemed to be getting braver.

"If you're bothered by a dead chicken, just leave. There are curses. . . ."

I ignored her threat. "This is someone else's property, so you're trespassing. And I know why you're here."

"Really?"

"My third eye opened. Now I know a lot of things . . . that you used to be Nathalia, for example."

I was pleased to see that I'd actually succeeded in scaring her.

"I think I have a pretty good idea of what you are doing here," I continued. "Something to do with the woman you drove to drink, which killed her. Your one-time romantic rival, Sabrina Sanchez, right?"

"Just leave me alone, will you?!"

I didn't know where my courage came from as I went on. "Sabrina told me about your stealing her baby boy. That's what this carving of a mother holding a baby is for. To keep Sabrina from coming after you from the *yin* world! Good luck—it's not going to be so easy for you.

"And there's her daughter, Isabelle. I bet you had something to do with her demise too. She's now a restless ghost. She came to me again. However, it's not me she's after, but you." Especially, I thought, if Cecily was the one who'd pushed Isabelle into the lake.

I could tell I'd gotten her attention because she asked, almost pleading, "What did she say?"

"Isabelle's ghost is looking to find out if she was murdered. You better do some more rituals and hope they'll leave you alone."

"You weren't here when it happened. Everyone knows that Isabelle drowned, period. And I had nothing to with it!"

Maybe Cecily didn't. But I also noticed she didn't deny contributing to Sabrina's ruin. I was no closer to an answer, but since Cecily was so vehement in her denial, she moved to the top of my list. Alfredo moved down, but was still a suspect.

"How are you so sure she drowned if you weren't involved?" I asked.

"It was in the newspaper and no one said otherwise."

"Or you arranged it to look like an accident. And if you didn't do it, who did?"

We remained silent for some minutes.

She vigorously shook her head. "No, it's been twenty years and there's no evidence of foul play. And why are you so interested anyway? You're just a tourist; it has nothing to do with you. So forget about it and go back to your little tryst with Alfredo!"

"I made a promise to Isabelle."

"Ha, to a dead person? In your dreams?" She chuckled nervously.

"As a witch, you should know these things are real."

She had no answer for this and remained silent, looking scared and worn-out. Since I seemed to have succeeded in intimidating her, at least for now, I pressed on. "Cecily, did you steal Sabrina's baby son?"

I could tell by her expression that I'd hit home.

"How did you know?"

"Hahaha!" I laughed mirthlessly. "So what Sabrina told me is true!"

"What did she tell you?"

"Everything. You're the witch she hired to cast a love spell on Alfredo. You took her money, then took her man, and then her baby boy too. No wonder she took to drink."

"You think you know everything? There's nothing you can do."

"What was the baby's name?"

"How do I know what the priest named him? He was messed up, that baby!"

"So you just threw him away!"

"No, I didn't. I left him at a church so he'd get a good Christian upbringing."

"That's a laugh. When's the last time you were in a church? You'd be afraid to go, after all you've done."

There was actually an expression of fear on her face. For all her paganism, she'd been born Catholic in a Catholic country and must have some residual anxiety after going over to the dark side.

But fortunately Luis, if he was the abandoned baby, had grown up healthy, handsome, and hardworking. But I was certainly not going to tell the witch. She was quite capable of using a spell to take him back.

"Miss-Asian-knows-it-all, leave me alone, right now!" Cecily screamed angrily.

Again, I didn't know where my courage came from, for I replied, "Or what? You'll cast spells on me? Use black magic?"

She cast me a dirty look instead. "You're just a crazy woman! I don't have time to talk to someone like you!"

With that, she turned her back on me, gathered up the candles and the doll, and vanished into the night.

PART FOUR

29

The Long-Lost Son

Now that I was certain Cecily had taken Sabrina's baby, I had the difficult task of informing Alfredo. Perhaps he would be happy to hear that his son was alive and had turned out okay—but then again, he might be heartbroken because of the lost years.

When I returned to the castle, I told Maria I needed to speak with Señor Alfrenso about something important. She brought me into the study and soon Alfredo arrived, looking worried. When I reminded him that I'd found his son, his eyes became as round as two kumquats.

I explained that Sabrina's baby had been stolen by Nathalia, but that for some reason she had abandoned him at the village church.

"Oh, God, why would she do that?"

"Because she thought he was sick and would bring her bad luck. Maybe she'd thought if the baby died she'd be accused of murder."

He seemed lost in thought for several minutes, then asked, "How do you know all this?"

"I started asking around and was able to piece it together."

He put his head in his hands, looking very upset. For a minute I was afraid he would cry and embarrass himself in front of me.

"Oh, God! Oh, God! I still can't believe this! I have a son living right next to me and never knew about him? How did that happen! These women . . . no end of trouble," he exclaimed.

Finally he lifted his head, but now he was smiling. "So you really think my son is alive and well?"

I nodded.

"What does he look like?"

"You're lucky, Alfredo. Luis grew up to be a very nice and handsome young man. He's a skilled furniture maker, and he also loves to read and learn."

"A reader and a furniture maker?"

"Yes, he may have been sick as a baby, but he's strong and healthy now."

"So after all, it's good that I was with Sabrina, as now I have a son and an heir! Tell me exactly how you found Luis."

"It really was just by chance. I wanted to find Past Life Lake and on the way I walked through the little village. Luis was working in his backyard, so we struck up a conversation. I ended up staying with him and his grandpa, who taught me sculpting."

"But how do you know he's my son?"

"Oh, I learned that later. Sabrina told me that she'd put a silver chain with a pendent around her baby's neck. Her description matched the pendant I saw Luis wearing."

"Yes, I know the pendant you mean. Take me to see him as soon as possible. Tomorrow morning?"

"Yes, of course."

This time my trip to the village was comfortable because we were driven by Alfredo's chauffer. However, I insisted that we should walk the narrow path leading to the village, so as not to alarm anyone with an expensive car and roaring engine.

As we were approaching the village, Alfredo took my hand. I knew he was extremely nervous to meet his long-lost son. When we were still some distance from Luis's house I signaled the driver to stop.

"Look," I said to Alfredo, "we need to figure out how to handle this. You can't just arrive at his house and tell him you're his father.

He and his grandpa will be even more shocked than you. You'll shake up their life completely. Maybe they'll think it's some kind of scam."

"Would it be that bad for me to be someone's father?"

No, I thought—who wouldn't like to discover they had a rich father? But even though Alfredo probably was not at fault, he'd have a lot of explaining to do.

Soon Grandpa came out from the house and sat at the table, followed by Luis holding a tray of food. This seemed as good a time as any for Alfredo to meet them, so I suggested that we get out and walk toward the little house. As we approached, they began to dig into their food, talking and laughing. I glanced at Alfredo and saw distress written all over his face.

Finally, he said, his tone tender, "So this is Luis, my son?"

I nodded.

"I need some more time to get used to this. Let's not disturb them yet."

I gestured Alfredo to conceal himself with me behind a tree.

When they were finished eating, Luis cleared the table as Grandpa picked up a stone and start to sculpt. Luis went to saw wood. Minutes later, he wiped the sweat off his face and took off his shirt.

I leaned over to Alfredo. "See? He's wearing a pendant. When we go up to meet him, take a look at it and see if it's the one you gave Sabrina. Now let's go up and say hello."

"Let's wait a little longer."

"Why?"

"I . . ." he stammered, looking very nervous.

Just then Juan came out from the church, walked over to Luis and Grandpa's house, and sat on the front stairs. He picked up a stick and began to write on the ground with it.

"Who's that?" Alfredo asked.

"That's Juan. He's a mute and somewhat slow, but a nice kid."

"Mute and slow? That must be why he stays in this place."

"There are nice people in the world who are not smart and rich like you."

"I know, I know. I'm sorry."

Just then Luis waved to Juan and the latter walked over to sit on a stump to watch Luis work. Grandpa stood up and went back inside the house, staggering slightly.

"I'm worried that Grandpa is not well."

"Not surprising; he's an old man."

Alfredo would soon be also, I thought. Now that he was out of his element, Alfredo's genteel veneer seemed to be slipping.

"Now let's go and say hello. These are my friends—and one is your son. So be careful what you say."

As we approached, both Luis and Juan looked very happy to see me, but puzzled when their eyes landed on Alfredo.

As I introduced everyone, they all seemed a bit awkward. Luis quickly excused himself and came back with a pot of tea and fruit.

"Grandpa is taking a nap. Do you want me to wake him up?" Luis asked.

I saw that Alfredo was giving his son an intense inspection, while the young man seemed only mildly curious about Alfredo.

I thought Grandpa's presence would only complicate what was already a difficult situation, so I said, "No, let him have his nap. We can all chat."

I only introduced Alfredo as a friend because I thought the first step was for them to get acquainted. I had come to take Alfredo's suave manner for granted and so was a little surprised that now he seemed awkward and at a loss for words. He just watched Luis and me as we conversed. I guessed he was thinking what it would be like to have Luis as his son, maybe even the future head of his business.

The young man was honest and forthright, but had none of Alfredo's sophistication. Juan did not pay attention to our conversation, but occupied himself scraping words on the ground. Alfredo did not even look in his direction.

Luis smiled at Alfredo. "Señor Alfrenso, thank you so much for coming here to visit."

Alfredo nodded but did not speak.

"Alfredo, did you notice Luis's pendant? It's an unusual one." I leaned toward him. "I wonder if you will recognize it."

Luis held it up proudly while Alfredo leaned over to examine.

"Very nice," Alfredo said. "I remember seeing one like this years ago. Luis, are you interested in moving out of here someday?"

"That's my dream. I read books in the library about other countries and would like to see them sometime. Eileen told me I should see the U.S. first, especially San Francisco, and then go to China. Eileen also told me that Chinese say to read ten thousand books and travel ten thousand miles. I like that."

"What about business and making money? Does that interest you?" asked Alfredo.

I could tell he was shocked to see his "son" shake his head.

"I make good money selling the furniture I make. I can sell that cabinet over there for twenty thousand pesetas."

Alfredo was clearly unimpressed, not surprising as this large-sounding number was only about one hundred and thirty U.S. dollars.

Luis smiled. "Someday I would like a girlfriend. To get married and have a family."

"Twenty thousand pesetas won't get you very far if you want a woman," Alfredo cut in.

Luis ignored this and went on. "Someone like Señorita Eileen." A deep blush spread over his face.

Alfredo was irritated by this. "Eileen already has other plans. Just look for a pretty local girl who can keep your house for you and grow some vegetables. Or if you really want to travel, someone who has some sense about business."

"The girls here . . . don't know much. I want a professor, like Eileen," insisted Luis.

Now Alfredo looked angry. "You will have to find someone else, young man. Eileen is not available and, anyway, she is not suitable for you," he said firmly.

I didn't think things were going in a good direction so, hoping to soothe the situation, I said, "Of course Luis knows I am very fond of him, but that's all. He needs to learn more about how the world works—and I cannot imagine a better teacher than you, Alfredo."

This flattery seemed to work, at least a little, because Alfredo's expression softened a bit. I realized that it would be difficult for him to accept that this simple country boy was his child—if he'd ever imagined his stolen baby grown up, it would be as a lawyer or businessman, not a furniture maker. I decided this would be as good a time as any to break the news.

"Luis, I have something very important to tell you."

"You're going home soon!?" Luis looked alarmed.

"No, nothing like that. I brought Señor Alfrenso here because we think he is your father." Then I explained to him about his pendant.

Luis looked completely stunned and our little group fell silent. Finally, he opened his mouth, but no words came out.

Juan looked up, probably sensing the tension, but, not understanding, went back to drawing on the ground.

"But, Señor Alfrenso, I . . . don't have a father."

"Of course you do! Everyone has a father and I am yours. I'll have my driver get your things and you can move into the castle tomorrow."

Alfredo was used to having things his way without any argument. But his authoritarian personality was at a loss here. You don't barge into a stranger's house, claim to be his father, and expect him to immediately hug you and call you Daddy.

I pulled Alfredo aside, and whispered in his ear, "Slow down. Give Luis some time to know you first."

"But I'm getting old and don't have a lot of time!" he answered in a heated whisper.

"Calm down! Take some deep breaths. Put yourself in his shoes. Suppose you met a strange man who claims to be your father. Would you just leave and go with him? Luis doesn't know you. He'll probably be angry that you did not search harder for him. I would be angry, too, if it were me."

Alfredo nodded, like a toreador who's just missed being gored by the bull. We went back to Luis and Alfredo maintained a sullen silence while I patiently explained everything to the young man, about how Sabrina had given birth to him, only to have him stolen by the witch, who in turn abandoned him.

After I finished, he said, "Let me ask Grandpa. Maybe he can tell me if Señor Alfrenso is really my father."

"Luis, please don't wake Grandpa up right now. I do think Alfredo is really your father; otherwise I wouldn't have brought him here to meet you. Why don't you take some time to think it over. Then you can tell Grandpa and see what he says."

"All right," he said softly, but I could tell the young man was totally confused. His life to date had been simple, with the little house, his grandpa, and his craftsmanship. Now he was connected to the larger world outside and his life was completely unsettled.

Alfredo was probably as confused, but he hid it better. I suggested to him that he go home so I could stay behind to talk to Luis alone.

After the older man left, Juan continued to draw on the ground, seemingly oblivious to the father-and-son drama unfolding in front of him.

After Alfredo's silhouette disappeared down the path, I told Luis to sit down with me at the table and began to explain.

As I did so he kept shaking his head, and asking, "Is it really true?"

I nodded and told him everything—about Alfredo, Sabrina, and Cecily, about how Sabrina gave birth to him, only to have him stolen by the witch, who in turn abandoned him.

When I finished, he was unable to respond as tears coursed down his cheeks.

"It's all right, Luis," I said, and put an arm around his shoulder. "Now you have a father, not to mention that he's very rich. So from now on you could live a very good life with every luxury you'd ever dreamed of."

He wiped his tears. "I don't know what to think of this. You say I have a father, but I also had a mother, and now you tell me she's just died. Why didn't you tell me when she was alive?"

"I only found out from a letter she left me. I'm so sorry, Luis, but I didn't know."

"Will you tell me about my mother?"

This was not going to be easy. I liked Sabrina, but it would be hard to describe her character in a positive way.

"Of course, but let's wait for another time, when we are all calmer."

"If I really go to live with Señor Alfrenso, will you come with me?"

"It's nice of you to invite me. But I don't belong here. This is your country. Mine is far away."

He sighed heavily. "I . . . I'm afraid . . . I'm in love with you, Eileen."

I can't say it was a complete surprise—it had been pretty obvious that he was attracted to me. But I knew it didn't mean much, given that there were no other women of interest around. It was a sticky situation for me to extricate myself from.

"Luis, I like you very much. But let's just be friends and not complicate matters," I replied gently.

"How can true love complicate matters? It's pure and simple."

I had no particular reason not to return Luis's love. But we would have no future. As recounted in the 3,000-year-old *Book of Changes,* "Everything changes." Especially love, even though the ancient sages did not think to mention it. I couldn't possibly bring him to live in the U.S. He spoke only Spanish and couldn't earn a living making furniture.

I put my arm around his shoulder again, trying to comfort him. He pulled me against him and I surprised myself by not putting up any resistance. I felt as if I were a newborn chick in a child's hand, although Luis's own hand was large and big-boned. His heart was that of a child, but in a big, muscular body. I closed my eyes, letting all my inhibitions slip away.

He lowered his head to kiss me. His thick lips were warm and soft, but his kiss tentative. Maybe it was his first kiss.

"Eileen, stay with me tonight."

"Alfredo expects me back. You shouldn't antagonize him right now. Besides, Grandpa is right here in the house."

"We'll go to Past Life Lake. So you can see our future underwater. We'll be a happy family."

I sighed. "Luis, slow down, all right? I'm older than you. Much older."

He looked like a child told not to swing too high, lest he fall.

"Let's just stay friends, all right?" I said.

He remained silent for a while, then asked, "What would it be like to be rich?"

"I don't know. I've never been rich."

But that wasn't completely true, for Ivan was rich. But I was not going to get into that with Luis.

"When we first met, you told me the story of *The Butterfly's Lovers,* remember?" said Luis.

So he was back to the subject of love. I'd have preferred to stay on the subject of being rich.

"You are the one who told me a story that shows love conquers all," he said.

"Luis, that's just a legend. Real life is not that simple." Of course, life had been simple for him. No doubt this was part of the problem.

"Eileen, please answer me honestly. Is there any chance we can be together?"

"I'm afraid not."

And that ended our conversation.

As I was about to leave, I noticed Juan was nowhere to be seen. But the word he'd scraped on the ground surprised me.

Father.

What did that mean? What did he actually know? Did he want Alfredo to be his father?

But if that was the case, he'd be greatly disappointed.

When I arrived back at the castle, Alfredo was waiting for me. He told me he was eager to see Luis again and hoped I would encourage the young man to visit very soon. I told him that he was still in a state of shock and it would be better not to push.

"But he has a rich life waiting for him here. Why would he want to stay in that no-place village?"

It would be of no use to explain. Alfredo, like Ivan, could not understand why someone would want other things in life than money.

I told Alfredo I had a headache, went to my room, and locked the door. I needed to be left alone to try to think clearly. Bittersweet memories of Luis's kiss kept floating up in my mind. Turning him down had made my life simpler, but I did have second thoughts.

I couldn't yet tell if I loved him, but after Ivan and his ilk, Luis's naïveté and kindness were extremely appealing. So was his physical beauty—beauty derived from honest work, rather than an expensive gym membership and a personal trainer. But being attracted to him did not undo the fact that there could be no future for us as a couple.

That night Laolao came to me in my dream, and said, "It's good to follow your heart—but be careful."

30

Farewell, My Beloved Village

When the sun shining through the window woke me up, my chest was tight and my throat dry. I had a premonition that a disaster was about to happen, but what, I had no idea. I thought if I did intense meditation I could open my third eye and "see" what was coming, but I was afraid.

Laolao had always advised me to follow my heart, but also to be careful. Should I follow my heart and give in to Luis's love? Or should I be careful and marry Alfredo—or even Ivan—for their money?

I kept driving myself crazy with second-guessing. Had I made a mistake connecting Alfredo with Luis? They lived in such different worlds, I doubted true affection could develop between them. But after I learned that they were father and son, how could I just let the matter go?

I thought it best to leave Luis alone for a while, but after a week, I gave in to Alfredo's urging and brought him back to the village. There was no answer when I knocked at Luis and Grandpa's house, which was strange since they rarely went anywhere. We sat by the table in the courtyard and waited until three hours had passed. Fearing something might be wrong, I suggested we go to the church and ask Father Fernando for their whereabouts.

Only Juan was at the church, dusting the altar. Once he heard our footsteps, he turned and hurried toward me, his bad leg thumping heavily on the floor.

I gave him a peck on his cheek. "Juan, you're okay?"

He smiled, nodding enthusiastically.

"Juan, remember this is Señor Alfredo Alfrenso, the father of—"

Before I could finish my sentence, to my utter shock, Juan threw himself at Alfredo. Looking completely disgusted, Alfredo roughly pushed the young man away.

"Please tell him to go away!" Alfredo said to me.

I signaled Juan to leave and he did, looking completely crushed. I hated to do it, but I also didn't want Alfredo to hurt the young man any further. Juan must have been hoping that Alfredo was his father. Of course, that was why he kept writing the word *father* on the sand after I took Alfredo here. But I knew Alfredo only cared for those who were attractive—or rich. I told Alfredo to wait and hurried around to the back of the church.

Juan was sitting precariously on a broken chair, sulking. "Juan, I'm sorry. I know you want Alfredo to be your father, but he's not."

He just stared at me with his sad eyes.

"We're looking for Luis and Grandpa. Do you know when they'll be back?"

With his stick, he wrote on the sand, "Gone."

"What do you mean gone, like gone shopping or for a walk?"

He made some gesture and sound that I failed to understand.

"When will they come back? We can wait."

He waved his hands frantically.

Did he mean they were gone for good? It seemed unlikely, but I needed to wait for Father Fernando to find out.

I went back to join Alfredo to wait for the priest. An hour later Father Fernando finally returned and I asked him about our friends.

The priest looked uneasy. "I'm sorry to tell you that they left. I'm worried that they will not come back."

"What do you mean?" Though fearing the answer, I had to know. I realized I'd forgotten to introduce Alfredo, but it almost seemed that the two knew each other, though there was no warmth between them.

"Please come to my office and talk," said Father Fernando.

Alfredo and I followed him. Juan wanted to join us but was stopped by Father Fernando, who gestured him to sit in a pew and wait.

After Alfredo and I settled into the priest's small office, I explained to him how I'd found out that Luis was Alfredo's son.

Before Fernando could respond, Alfredo said eagerly, "Father, please tell us where Luis has gone so I can find him."

Father Fernando held up his hand. "First, I must tell you the sad news. Grandpa passed away two days ago."

"How can this be possible?" I cried.

"He was in his nineties and had a weak heart. I think he'd had an argument with Luis, then collapsed. I rushed over and gave him extreme unction, just as he was dying. Yesterday we buried him. He was a good man and a good Christian."

"I'm so sorry to hear that. Do you know what they fought about? Luis is such a gentle man."

Father Fernando didn't answer me, but instead turned to Alfredo. "Señor, please excuse me, but I need to speak to Eileen privately." He cast me an uneasy glance.

I followed the priest out of the church and around to the churchyard. Leaves and earth whispered under our feet, as if telling a long-kept secret. Nearby I could see the fresh grave. Tears came into my eyes. At Father Fernando's suggestion I followed him in saying the Lord's Prayer. Afterward we walked through the small cemetery toward a cluster of trees.

"Eileen, I'm afraid that you may be setting off a personal catastrophe for Señor Alfrenso and Luis," the priest said in a worried tone. "You see, it is not Luis who is señor's son, but Juan."

It was another shock to my already overtaxed mind. I'd wondered about the effect of telling the two that they were father and son. But my concern was about disrupting their lives, not the worse possibility that I would be telling them a falsehood. And just when Luis had lost his grandpa, and me telling him that we would never have a relationship.

"You sound like you're sure."

"I'm sorry, Eileen, it would be easier for everyone if you were right. But there is no question—Juan is Señor Alfrenso's son, not Luis."

Father Fernando took something from his pocket. It was the red stone pendant on a silver chain.

"That's Luis's!"

The priest shook his head, then gazed into the distance. "Many years ago our village was prosperous and there were many young people. But even then, some of the women didn't wait to take their vows in church and tried to hide their condition. Babies were sometimes abandoned at our church's doorstep. Luis and Juan came to us that way. Luis was a vigorous baby, so Father Ricardo was surprised that his parents left him. As for Juan, he suffered from a palsy and no one would want him. So Father Ricardo took him in and took good care of him. When Father Ricardo found him, around his neck was this silver chain and pendant."

"Then how come Luis was wearing it?" I asked, my confusion growing.

"When Juan was little, he had frequent tantrums and would bite on his pendant. Father Ricardo feared that he might swallow it and choke on it.

"Since Luis was such a calm child, Father Ricardo decided to lend Luis the pendant, knowing he would keep it safe. If the mother ever showed, Ricardo would explain and return the pendant. But she never came."

Of course the mother never came. Sabrina had no idea about her son's whereabouts and Cecily wouldn't want to reclaim the afflicted child. Nor, I thought, would Alfredo want a son unless he was perfect. I thought of Confucius' famous saying that parents should act like parents and children like children—in other words, care for each other. But the Chinese sage would not have said it unless it was often not observed, even in ancient times.

I decided not to tell Father Fernando who Juan's mother was, nor about the witch who had abandoned the child. The priest was a kindly man, but I feared even he might shun the boy if he knew about his connection to witchcraft.

Father Fernando sighed again, shaking his head. "The human heart is so fickle."

It is said that the heart has its reasons—but unfortunately, too often the reasons are bad ones. The priest hadn't said anything about Luis so I asked, but with trepidation.

"Since Grandpa's death Luis has been heartbroken. He decided he was ready to leave. When he came to the church to ask my blessing and say good-bye he gave me the necklace to return to Juan. I saw him off to the ferry yesterday. You just missed him by a day."

I suspected that it was not only Grandpa's death, but also my putting him off that led to Luis's abrupt departure. Despite what I thought had been good intentions, I had caused nothing but trouble for my friends.

I wondered if things were even worse than I knew. Worried about Luis, I asked the priest, "Did you tell him he's not Alfredo's son?"

He shook his head. "No, I didn't have the heart, although I should have. Someday I'll have to tell him. Meanwhile he's trying to start a new life."

"What does Luis plan to do?"

"He didn't tell me. I'm not sure he knows himself." He paused, then looked at me. "You may have already guessed that Grandpa was not Luis's real grandfather?"

"Of course. He was a foundling."

"Yes, Grandpa and his wife took a liking to the boy and took him in. When the wife died, the old man and the boy continued to keep house together."

"Luis didn't say where he was going?"

"No, but he left a letter for you. He likes you."

"You can tell?"

He laughed. "Oh, yes, even as a celibate Catholic father. The day he met you, he talked about you nonstop, saying how smart and learned you are, a professor, and friendly too."

I was about to ask, "What about pretty," but suppressed myself.

The priest stood up. "All right, let's head back. You can read Luis's letter. As for Alfredo, I'm afraid you'll have to explain, since it was you who told him Luis is his son."

When we were walking back to the church, he spoke again. "Eileen, I'll be leaving the village too—"

"When?"

"In a month maybe, or even less, as soon as social service comes to help the two old people into a nursing home."

I felt bad that the elderly man and the widow would end up in a nursing home. And Juan's situation seemed even worse, as I was pretty sure Alfredo would not acknowledge him. It was Juan who seemed to get the worst of everything.

The priest must have known what I was thinking because he said, "I'm being reassigned to a larger church back in Spain. They won't need me here. And Juan will be a verger, so he'll be looked after, even after I am gone."

As expected, when we went back to Alfredo and I told him about Juan, he became agitated. I could tell he was completely heartbroken. He'd unexpectedly gained a son, lost him, then gained one he did not want. Nor did he have a woman who cared about him. He was an aging, rich man with bad karma.

Back in the car, his self-control slipped. He pounded on the seat back and shouted over and over, "What did I do to deserve this!?"

"Alfredo, you found your son, even if he's not as you expected. Why don't you take Juan back? Maria can take care of him, or with all your money you can hire more help."

"No, absolutely not, I won't have a son like this! Who knows if he really is mine? Sabrina was famous for sleeping around! Of course, she wanted my money. I want a DNA test on Luis. Juan could not be my son, absolutely not."

He reached into his pocket and pulled out an envelope, inside of which was a toothbrush.

"What's that?"

"My driver got it from Luis's house. It's for a DNA test."

I felt very sorry for the man. I could not blame him for wanting a normal son, though this did not excuse his intolerance toward Juan. The DNA would not come out as he hoped, but maybe that was the only way he could move on.

When the car reached the castle, Alfredo invited me to go in, but I declined. I wanted to read my letter from Luis in private. I asked the driver to take me back to Luis's house.

Once inside the house, I sat on the long chair and tore open the letter. Even before I read a single word, tears coursed down my cheeks. *Please, let me have some good news from Luis,* I thought as I began to read.

My dearest Eileen,

I am sure you want to know about Grandpa. He died suddenly, but I knew it was coming. The day after you and Señor Alfrenso visited, Grandpa was not feeling well. He warned me that Señor Alfrenso is an evil man and couldn't be my father. I'd never seen Grandpa so upset. I fear it brought on his death.

There's no reason for me to stay on here without Grandpa. The only thing I know how to do is carpentry. You know I want to see the world, so I decided to be a sailor. Maybe the sea will help me forget.

Please take whatever you like from our house, even the furniture. I put Grandpa's sculptures for you in the first drawer of the closet next to the bookshelf. I'm not sure I will ever come back because everyone I know will be gone.

Maybe someday I'll have made enough money to go to San Francisco to visit you.

Whatever happens, my love for you will never change. I believe you love me but can't bring yourself to admit it.

I'll miss you, my dear Eileen.

Good-bye and good luck.

The furniture maker who'll never stop loving you,
Luis

I fought tears as I read the letter. I felt sad and guilty. Had I given in to Luis's romantic longing he would have stayed. But despite my third eye, I had no idea if either of us would have been better off that way.

Being a sailor didn't seem like much of a life to me. But neither did living out one's years in an empty village. At least Luis would earn a little money, have free meals, and maybe, as the expression has it, a girl in every port. The latter made me a little jealous, but also a little less guilty.

If I had accepted Luis's love, what sort of life would I have—especially when the passion wore off? If I had married him and remained on the island, I couldn't be a professor anymore. The only work I could imagine doing was as a shamaness—just as Laolao had always wished. I could sell herbs, tell fortunes, and conduct underworld tours. But I doubted there was much need on the island for an exotic, Chinese witch. The other witches certainly would not like competition and were expert at spreading malicious rumors and casting spells. I was sure they'd do everything they could to drive me out of business.

Even if our love lasted, as the Chinese say, "Couples with no money have a hundred things to be miserable about." At first a couple may be in the phase of "they're so filled with love that they can survive just by drinking water." But pretty soon they'll need real sustenance. And then the quarrelling begins.

I got up to look for the package Grandpa had left me, and found it waiting in the closet, just as Luis's letter described. I set it on the table and inside found several of Grandpa's sculptures. I could see that either these were done some time ago or he'd gotten his muse back. I ran my hands over the clean contours and subtle molding. Was he a crazy old man or a wise one—probably both, I thought.

I sensed the set of sculptures were intended to tell a story, but my mind was too clogged with emotion to figure it out. At the bottom of the box was an envelope. Expecting another letter, I was surprised to find a crumbling newspaper clipping instead.

> A diving accident took the life of a local young woman, Isabelle Sanchez. Though her body was found in Past Life Lake, police were baffled because they had never heard of anyone diving there, due to local belief that it is inhabited by ghosts. A geologist studying the lake some years ago noted

> that there is a severe undertow, making it dangerous for swimmers, particularly children.
>
> While it has been suggested that the death was not accidental, the police will not comment further at this time. They do, however, deny the possibility of ghostly involvement.
>
> A source who asked to remain anonymous told this newspaper that her death was related to a falling out with a close friend, local businessman Alfredo Alfrenso. He and Señorita Sanchez were overheard quarrelling about money the night of her demise. When questioned by police, Señor Alfrenso said the quarrel was of no importance and that he was shocked and saddened to learn of the young woman's death.

I knew Grandpa had a reason for saving this article, and also for being sure I would see it, most likely to warn me about Alfredo. I placed the article next to Luis's letter and turned my attention back to the sculptures. There were five and they resembled, or at least I imagined they did, Alfredo, Penelope, Sabrina, Isabelle, and myself. Suddenly I thought the figure representing Alfredo was pushing Isabella. The one I thought was me was just watching, a puzzled look upon her face. Or perhaps they were just sculptures after all.

I folded Luis's letter carefully and put it away in my purse. Then I took a last look at the little house and said another prayer for both souls—the one in the earth and the one under the sea. After that, I turned to make my way back to the hotel.

31

The Proposal, Again

Back at the hotel, the receptionist handed me a message. It was from Maria asking me to go to Alfredo's castle immediately. Anxious that there was yet another disaster, I called Maria from my room and was told señor had taken ill and was asking for me. I grabbed a taxi in front of the hotel and asked the driver to hurry.

Maria opened the front door, her face pale as she let me in.

"What happened, Maria?"

"Señor Alfrenso had a stroke! The doctor has just left and señor is now resting in his bedroom. Follow me."

Alfredo looked weak and depressed, but he was awake and able to sit up, so I guessed the stroke wasn't too severe. I felt a wave of relief.

I sat next to him on the bed. "Are you all right, Alfredo?"

"Thank you for coming to me so quickly, dear." His eyes filled with tears. "Eileen, I . . . want to tell you something."

"Don't worry, I'll stay here to keep you company."

He smiled faintly.

I remembered Grandpa's warning, but in Alfredo's present state he couldn't do me any harm. As I waited for him to speak, Alfredo had fallen asleep, so whatever he had to tell me would have to wait.

I went into the kitchen to ask Maria what had happened and

was told that the doctor had said it was not serious and Alfredo just had to rest. I didn't have a lot of confidence in a country doctor, but there was little I could do. My guess was that the stress of discovering that Juan, not Luis, was his son had brought on the stroke. But of course I said nothing of this to Maria.

"The doctor says he needs to stay in bed for at least a week. Then he'll be weak for a couple of months," Maria said.

Maybe I'd be gone by then—away from this island filled with the dramas of life, death, love, loss, greed, jealousy, heartbreak, infidelity, witchcraft, and revenge.

"Señor is not taking it very well. You know, he has always been very strong and active. He can't accept being sick," said the housekeeper.

Of course, none of us wants to accept that life, health, and everything else are transient. Only death is permanent.

"Where are señor's friends? Has anyone come to see him?" I asked.

"Señor doesn't have friends, only business associates. But they live far away and only travel for business deals. Anyway, señor insists I not tell anyone but you about this."

"Then why tell me?"

"He says you're the only one who doesn't care about his money. He doesn't trust anyone else."

This surprised me but gave me a glimpse of the world Alfredo inhabited—a heartless one. For this reason I felt I should stay and comfort him, despite his unkindness to so many of the people who had cared about him in the past. I never fancied myself a nurse, but Laolao had always told me that her supernatural abilities were to help others who did not have her gifts. And this was true—no doubt many shamanesses were charlatans, but I had never known Laolao to cheat anyone.

"You're kind, Señorita Eileen. But señor just needs you to stay with him. A nurse will come soon to care for him and his lawyers will take care of his business matters."

"Good." I wondered what these matters were. A will? But I was not going to ask, lest Maria think I too cared only about her boss's money.

"Don't worry too much, señor has the best doctors and lawyers," she said.

It was sad that he could afford the best doctors and lawyers, but not friends.

"I can stay for a few days; hopefully he'll get better soon," I said.

"Good. I'll go and prepare your room."

Along with the nurse, a physical therapist came from the hospital in the city twice a week. The stroke had left Alfredo's speech very slightly slurred and some weakness in his right leg. He was very frustrated and irritable with the nurse and therapist, but I cheered him on and he gradually improved.

I went to the temple on Grand Canary and bought herbs to prepare healing soups for Alfredo. Chicken with ginseng, red date, ginger, and astragalus to improve his speech and strengthen his heartbeat. Tortoise soup brewed with medlar, gentianae root, and radices rehmanniae to improve his dry mouth and weak pulse. I was going to cook snake soup, which improves circulation, but Maria screamed when she saw me bringing the wriggling reptile into the kitchen.

The soups Laolao had taught me to prepare seemed to work, because after a month Alfredo could go outside for walks, though he still tired quickly.

Maria and I were happy to see that he was well on his way back to normal. Now I felt I could in good conscience go back to the hotel to work seriously on my book. Also, I needed a break from caring for the crotchety patient. I knew Alfredo did not want me to leave, but one morning when we were sitting on his luxurious white leather sofa in the living room I broke the news to him.

"Eileen," he said, taking my hand and kissing it tenderly. "Thank you so much for staying with me during my most difficult time. I've known many women in my life, but none like you. You have a natural goodness, something rare. I hope I can make it worth your while to stay."

"Alfredo," I said, subtly withdrawing my hand, "I'm so glad that you've recovered. But I have to get back to my book, my career. I've already used up most of my leave. I can't stay much longer."

"You can have a good life here. I'll give you anything you want."

I felt sorry that this proud man now looked so desperate.

A long silence passed before he spoke again. "Eileen, let me be honest with you. I've done a lot of harm in my life."

I thought tears were forming in his eyes. His voice strained, he asked, "Do you think God will grant me the chance to do something right before I die?"

"Of course, Alfredo. There's a Chinese saying: 'Put down your butchering knife and you'll instantly become a Buddha.' It's never too late to right the wrong. Do you want to tell me what sort of wrongs you did?"

"You know, Eileen, in business, especially my kind of business, you have to be ruthless. Otherwise, you'll be beaten. If you ever show weakness, you won't be trusted, and you won't get investors. Your former associates will shun you."

I supposed this was true. Certainly professors who don't win tenure are despised. The business world must be even crueler.

"So you've harmed a lot of people on your way up?"

"Quite a few. Some were friends too."

"What did you do?"

He looked upset. "I married Penelope mainly for her money. My wife was a beautiful, accomplished woman, but it was Sabrina who excited me. I treated both of them shabbily. I'd been an officer in the army, so I had the contacts to become an arms dealer. I never asked my customers what they wanted the guns and rockets for. I have many deaths on my conscience."

Taking advantage of his vulnerability, I blurted out, "Did you also kill Sabrina's daughter, Isabelle?"

Seeing the horrified expression on his face, I immediately regretted my words. His mouth opened, but no words came.

"How can you think this? I would never kill anyone myself. If I caused deaths, it was only indirectly!" he finally said.

Of course every criminal has an excuse. Their only regret is getting caught.

"That's what Sabrina thought," I said.

"She was just bitter about me."

"Then who did kill Isabelle?"

"I can't tell you."

"So you know, don't you?"

"Yes, but too many people would be harmed if I tell you."

I couldn't think of a good reason to protect a murderer. And he was my last chance to find out—no one who might have known the truth was left. I feared Alfredo himself might not be long for this world. But I could tell it was no use to press him.

"Let's put away talk of these long-past, unpleasant matters. Please come outside with me for a walk," he said.

We strolled slowly over by the pond. Then, in this place where so many strange things had happened, Alfredo proposed to me yet again. It began with an apology.

"Eileen, I know I am far from being a perfect man. But I love you and would treat you well. If you aren't happy you can always go back to the States." He took both my hands into his and looked into my eyes. "I still hope I have a chance with you—please marry me. If we act quickly, Father Fernando can perform the ceremony."

"Alfredo, I like you, too, and I like it on the island. But your life is here and mine, soon, will be back in San Francisco. I wish it were different."

He planted a kiss on my hand, looking very sad and desperate. "I know you're not after my money, but I won't live much longer, and you would inherit my fortune. Then you can do whatever you want."

It wasn't a very romantic basis for a marriage, but common enough.

"You're unique, Eileen," Alfredo continued. "Even strange. It makes me love you all the more. But all I can do is wish you a happy life and hope that you'll visit me now and then while you are still on the island."

I promised I would.

"And please don't tell anyone about my stroke. If word gets out, lots of women will flock to my bedside, hoping it's my deathbed."

"So it's not all happy being rich?"

"I'm afraid not. Now that after all these years I've met a woman who's willing to be my friend . . ." He shook his head, not able to finish his sentence.

Although I would feel lonely without him, I would at least be able to focus on my book. Even though I might be able to extend my unpaid leave, my savings from the little bit of money Laolao had left me were running low.

Despite his questionable character, I was grateful I'd known Alfredo, a gentlemen of the old European style, quite unlike the American men I'd known. If he were a murderer, he was the most refined one I could imagine. I thanked him as graciously as I could for all his hospitality. He in turn thanked me for my care when he was sick. Then I took my leave.

Back at the hotel, I sank down on my bed, lonely, confused, and depressed. Needing someone to talk to, I had the hotel dial Brenda's number.

She recognized my voice immediately. "Hi, sis, what's up? Everything okay?"

My little sister's familiar voice was like a massaging hand comforting my eardrums.

"Things are okay here, Brenda, but also weird."

"How's that?"

"It's complicated to explain over the phone. I've met witches like I planned. But now I'm stuck investigating a twenty-year-old murder. And that's just the beginning of what I'm caught up in. The rest will have to wait until I'm back home to tell you."

"This all sounds very scary, Eileen. You sure you know what you are doing? A murder?"

"Oh, it was long ago, but I'm still working on figuring it out."

"You and Grandma were always doing strange stuff. Why don't you just chill? I hear they have nice beaches there. You're slim. Why don't you buy yourself a bikini and hang out?"

Brenda frequently offered this sort of advice, which would have been right on—if I were a different person.

"Speaking of weird things," said Brenda, "remember that animal skull on your birthday?"

"Yes, what about it?" That bit of unpleasantness had completely slipped my mind, given the much stranger events here.

"I found out it was a mistake."

My heart skipped a bit. "Who sent it? Not the devil, I hope."

To my surprise, Brenda laughed. "It's from a teenager—a boy!"

"A boy? You're sure?"

"Yes, he sent it as Halloween prank to his girlfriend who lives in Ivan's building. It was delivered to Ivan's apartment by mistake."

"That's odd."

"Ivan told me his neighbor asked about the package. He told me a while ago, but I forgot to tell you."

At the time it had seemed a malicious prank. Or perhaps it had been an omen for my trip and all the death waiting for me.

"I got a marriage proposal," I said.

"He's rich, I hope."

"Yes, extremely. And handsome, a sophisticated European."

"When is the wedding?"

"I turned him down."

"What!? Eileen, you're impossible!"

"He just had a stroke."

"Because you refused him."

I could see where this was going, so I changed the subject to her life. There was plenty of legal work for her, but no romance. In a few minutes we wished each other well and hung up.

As usual, Brenda hadn't offered much in the way of help, or sympathy.

Talking with Brenda made me think of Ivan. Now that he was no longer pursuing me I realized that he'd actually been pretty good to me, better than I'd been to him. So, with some misgivings, I called him.

He sounded reserved. "How are things going on the island? Is everything okay?"

"Hmmm . . . Yes and no."

"Eileen, you're not in trouble, are you?"

"It's a long story."

"With you, it usually is."

"I've had some very unusual experiences. And I still don't know how to handle them."

"You want me to come over and help? If someone's giving you a hard time I can beat him up—or buy him off."

"It's not like that." I realized too late that Ivan had taken my expression of uncertainty as an opening.

"Then tell me what's bothering you."

Obviously there was a lot I would not share with Ivan. I did tell him that I'd met witches, that they were strange, but made for good material for my book. I left out Luis's proposition and Fernando's proposal.

"Just as I thought," he said. "You send me away, then get yourself into trouble."

He was right, but hearing his voice made me realize that I preferred my kind of trouble to a life with him.

I sighed, realizing the call had been a mistake. "Ivan, I'm okay, really. Maybe we'll see each other when I get back. Not for a while, though. Don't worry about me, I'm fine. I hope you're okay too.

"All right, Eileen, be safe. And think about me sometimes. If you need help, let me know."

And that ended our conversation. For a moment I wondered if I had done the wrong thing in leaving him to take this bizarre trip.

Like Brenda said, "Don't waste a good catch, ever! Especially the big fish that has already swum inside your net."

But this just reminded me that there are many fish in the sea.

32

Digging Up Mud and Dirt

While I felt some comfort hearing Brenda's and Ivan's familiar voices, neither showed any understanding of my present turmoil. Nor was anyone helpful. Alfredo hadn't told me anything that clarified Isabelle's death. Grandpa's newspaper clipping only hinted at the solution, and Luis's disappearance was one more mystery. I wasn't getting any answers from the humans I knew, so it was time to consult the spirits again, though not without some misgivings.

While I didn't really believe the dire warning that channeling could shorten my life, it was hard not to feel nervous about it. And the atmosphere of the dim temple, the acrid incense, and the blindfold were pretty spooky, even though I was there to contact spooks. Which, according to Laolao, might hang around after I was done with them.

There were also stories about mediums going crazy. I didn't think I was crazy, but my months on the island had left me pretty confused. After mulling it over, I decided to go ahead, or otherwise I'd be haunted forever by the unsolved mystery of Isabelle's death.

During the ferry ride to Grand Canary I tried to relax by watching the waves. Once there, I got a taxi and was soon at the Luminous Spirit Temple. This time there was no crowd, only a few elderly Chinese people offering incense and muttering prayers in front of the altar. At first I was afraid Uncle Wang wasn't there, but then I spotted him seated at a table in back, writing with a brush.

He seemed to be surprised but pleased to see me. "Señorita Eileen Chen, what brings you here? Come and sit with me."

I got straight to the point. "Uncle Wang, I need to try ghost writing again."

"But we don't have a session today. You must need urgent advice?"

I nodded.

"Hmmm . . . in that case, we'll do a special session. However, the master of recitation and the scribe are not here. So I'll have to represent them both."

"Will this work?"

"Of course, I've done it hundreds of times."

"Thank you so much, Uncle Wang. You are very kind."

Since he was going to do me this special favor, I needed to pay him discreetly. I went to the counter to buy the biggest size bundle of incense, lit it, and placed it in the bronze burner. Under his watchful eye I also stuffed a wad of cash into the donation box.

When I went back to Uncle Wang, he asked, "You know, talking with the dead is no small matter. In fact, it is a very grave matter. Are you sure you're mentally prepared?"

I nodded.

"Good. Meditate now to cleanse your mind." He pointed to a corner. "Kneel down on the cushion and empty your head. I'll go to prepare things and 'open' the altar. When it's ready I'll tell you."

I did what I was told and tried to empty my mind until Uncle Wang's voice roused me. On the altar he had prepared the wooden tray filled with sand. The forked wand lay beside it. I noticed several people watching while trying to seem unobtrusive. Uncle Wang held his hand up to his mouth, signaling them to be quiet.

Next Uncle Wang gently wrapped the red blindfold around my eyes so I would not be distracted by anything in this world.

After that he said, his tone very serious and respectful, "Now invite silently the loved one, god, goddess, immortal, or whomever you choose, to come to the altar. Don't try to write in the sand yourself, but let the spirit do it."

I nodded and picked up the wand, mentally inviting Isabelle to come. I patiently waited but didn't feel any presence. Then after what seemed an interminable wait, I felt something. Not Isabelle, but someone else. I didn't know who this being was, but I could tell it was female.

She: Leave me and my husband in peace.

Me: Who are you, and who's your husband?

She: He loves you, but you refuse him.

Me: But I . . . haven't done anything. . . .

She: Yes, you have.

Me: What?

She: You have disturbed my rest.

Me: What am I supposed to do?

She: Don't dig up the mud and the dirt. Know this: Whatever I did, I have paid the price. It was many years ago. Please, you are living. Forget us dead until your own time.

Me: Did you murder her?

She: You're an outsider, so you don't know our story or our life. If we didn't get along, it makes no difference now.

Me: I'm just trying to help!

She: You can't. We will not come back anymore.

Then I was jolted back to the *yang* realm. Wang immediately untied the red cloth from around my eyes. I was dizzy and nauseous, so Uncle Wang had to help me to a chair. He and the few other temple visitors studied me curiously, as if I'd just returned from a hair-raising meeting with the King of Hell.

"You all right?" Wang asked with concern.

"I guess I'm . . . fine."

"But you're pale and even trembling. Now come sit in my office and have some hot tea."

Once settled in his small office, Uncle Wang poured me tea and handed me an almond cake. "Señorita Chen, you don't look well. Your face is paler than a ghost's."

"I almost saw one."

"I see them all the time. You need not be frightened of ghosts. They're more scared of you."

I wasn't so sure about that last statement, as I was pretty scared myself.

"So, have you also seen *her?*" I asked.

"Yes, I saw the one who just appeared to you."

I almost choked on my tea. "Did you really? What did she look like?"

"I just felt her presence, couldn't see her face clearly. She was haughty! Above everybody and everything—including the law. I think I knew this woman. She died in an accident. She comes back because she is still bitter. Miserable *qi.*"

"Did she also see you?"

"Of course not."

"Why not?"

"You're the one she came for, not me. I didn't hear any words, just a loud buzz."

"Were you afraid when you saw her?"

He laughed. "At my age, what do I have left to do? I don't need to plan for the future, so I do whatever I want. If she wants to take me with her to the other side, she can be my guest. I'll soon join her anyway. I'm prepared."

"How do you prepare?"

"Señorita Chen, you're too young to understand. If you really want to know, come back in fifty years."

But then he wouldn't be here anymore. Unless like Laolao and Isabelle, he would come to me in my dreams. Perhaps he would. Though I'd only met Wang twice, I felt a great affection for him, perhaps a karmic link.

He handed me a sheet of paper covered in Chinese characters. "This is what I copied from your sand writing. I think it has the answers you've been seeking."

After I took the papers, he added, "Don't look at them now,

when you're still agitated. Wait until you have meditated and stilled your mind.

I thanked him profusely.

"May I ask if you had some unpleasant experiences lately?"

I debated telling him about recent events. He was, after all, an old man and shouldn't be troubled by the dirty and bloody affairs of this world.

When the word *dirty* entered my mind, I involuntarily gasped.

Uncle Wang looked at me with concern. "Are you all right, Señorita Chen?"

I took several breaths, trying to calm myself. "I'm . . . okay, don't worry."

Should I tell him I'd just had a realization—was the "dirt" buried with Penelope's body twenty years ago the fact that she had murdered Isabelle?

But I kept my mouth shut.

"I will give you some advice," he said.

"I welcome any advice you can give me, Uncle Wang."

"Good. You can come back for a chat with me anytime. But don't come back for another channeling." He stared at me to see my response.

"But why not?"

"Most cross the boundary between the realms of life and death but twice—at birth and at death. To do so more will severely damage your body and mind, or take years off your earthly life. You are young; enjoy the life of this world and forget the next for now.

"Señorita Chen, you're a brave woman to come to this remote island by yourself. I know you seek truth with great determination and stubbornness. But even the strong have weak moments. The evil wait for these moments to drag you down.

"Let me tell you a true story. Many years ago there was a man—let's call him Señor Ho—who claimed to possess the *yin* eye and boasted about the spirits he saw. No one knew if he made it all up or if he really did see those unclean things. He fell sick, but one day, feeling better, he went to see his friend.

"He got into a taxi and saw a puny man sitting in front next to the driver. He thought to ask the driver to let off the other passenger, but decided against it because the driver was speeding and looked ferocious. Señor Ho feared that the man was the driver's friend, and that if he complained, the driver might spite him by speeding even more and endangering everyone's lives.

"When the taxi pulled to a stop at Ho's destination, he finally chided the driver, telling him it's against the law to take another passenger when he was the one who paid.

"The driver looked completely shocked. 'Señor, what are you talking about? There's only you and I in the car! You're the only customer—of course you pay the whole amount!

"Then Ho realized something terrifying: The extra passenger was not a human. Though the driver didn't have the *yin* eye to see it, he was nevertheless affected by the creature—who had caused his crazy, reckless driving. Ho didn't go meet his friend, but turned back to go home—this time by bus, because the other people would provide protective *yang qi.*

"Once home, Ho immediately knelt in front of Zhong Kui, the Chinese ghost queller. Ho burned incense and made offerings of tea, wine, and food. Then he muttered a prayer, asking for the invincible hero's protection."

"What happened to Señor Ho? Did he die of fright?"

"Ho was fine, but he was extra careful to avoid getting sick. When one is healthy, one possesses abundant *yang* energy, so the spirits can't cause trouble, because they are *yin.* They'll pick another victim, a sick and weak one."

When finished, Uncle Wang asked, "Señorita Chen, you understand why I told you this story?"

I shook my head.

He continued. "Because you don't look very well, my friend. I'm sure you're not sick like the man I told you about. But you've had many spirit visits lately and, even though you are young and strong, you cannot help but absorb some of their *yin* energy."

"But the spirits have told me about important matters—they wanted my help."

"Sometimes knowing too much is not a good thing, even for a professor. Save your help for the living. You understand?"

I thought I did, so this time I nodded.

* * *

As soon as I was by myself back in my hotel room, I said out loud, "It was Penelope all along! She killed Isabelle, not Alfredo." I struggled to rearrange my thoughts, having been thinking that maybe it was Alfredo.

Suddenly everything seemed to fall into place. In the temple I'd invited Isabelle to come to me, but it was not her presence that I felt. Penelope must have pushed Isabelle aside so she could approach me instead. She'd tried to shut Isabelle out of her husband's life, and now she was trying to shut her out of mine as well, by pushing her back to the underworld. A heartless woman, both in this world and the next.

Given that Penelope had committed this terrible crime, her motive remained obscure to me. If it was jealousy, why hadn't she killed Sabrina instead? Perhaps she felt the younger woman would become a greater threat. And what about her own death—was it an accident, suicide, or murder?

I could go back to try to channel her again. But there was Uncle Wang's warning and I sensed he was right. As I stared at the blank wall of my little room, I realized that gratifying my curiosity was not worth another visit from the other world. I wanted to be done with the dead and go back to living my own life. Maybe the dead really are bitter, but I'd done as much as I could to solve their problems.

And even if I channeled again, how could I tell what was the truth? Ghosts were once human and probably as likely to lie. And what about if the three parties involved—Penelope, Isabelle, and Sabrina—all came to the altar at once and had a big quarrel? How do you settle an argument between ghosts? Would they kill each other in front of me and die all over again?

33

Hidden Treasures

I was not done with death; I've learned that one never is. Although I was done with channeling the dead, I could still question the living, that is, Alfredo. After that, I hoped I could put all of the mysteries behind me and go back to the U.S.

When I called Maria to let her know of my impending visit, I was dismayed to hear her say, "Very bad news, Señorita Eileen. . . ."

"What happened? Did Señor Alfrenso . . ." I couldn't finish.

"He had a heart attack. This time it doesn't look good."

"Where he is now? I'll be right there."

"Hospiten Sur here on Tenerife. It's very close to the bus routes, but please don't waste time; take a taxi or hire a car. I'm with him now. I'm sure he'll feel great comfort seeing you."

"Don't worry, Maria. Tell him to hang in there."

In less than an hour, I was in the lobby of the hospital, asking for Alfredo Alfrenso's room. The instant I saw him, I sensed that this time death was not far away. His voice was faint and his hands plucked ineffectually at the sheets. As soon as Maria spotted me, she shook her head and pulled me outside the room.

"Señorita Eileen," she said in a heated whisper, "I'm so glad that you're here. Señor has been calling your name, asking for you."

"How's he doing?"

"Not well. Not well at all. The doctor says this time it would take a miracle for him to recover. Even if he does, he will be very weak. I can't imagine—Señor is so strong and proud."

Maria started to cry. I put my arm around her shoulder.

"Maria, let's not give up hope. We just have to take very good care of him. What else did the doctor say?"

"Just that his heart cannot pump his blood properly. The medicines will help, but only a little."

If Maria was going to lose her calm, I could not. "I'm so sorry to hear that. Now we need to stay strong for señor so we can help him recover, okay?"

She nodded, wiping her tears.

Back inside the room, I went up to Alfredo's bedside. Close up, my friend looked even worse. My heart sank. Now, instead of a late-fiftyish man, he looked like an octogenarian, almost as old as Uncle Wang, though without the older man's spirit and energy.

Alfredo looked as if he were about to enter the underworld, or was almost there already. Under the bedsheet his body, so recently big and powerful, looked like a sick child's. His cheeks were so sunken that I believed if I put water there, it'd stay. His hands, once fleshy like a bear's paws, were now skeletal claws. For the first time, I noticed that his pinky was slanted, just like Juan's, proving now that the unfortunate young man whom he'd refused to acknowledge was indeed his son.

Just then Alfredo opened his eyes. When he saw me, his face lit up with a half smile. I hid my tears as he reached up to touch my face. I held on to his wrist, feeling his pulse, as weak as a kitten's.

"Alfredo, how are you feeling?" I asked, my question as limp as his hand. How could he feel except horrible and pathetic?

He tried to speak but coughed instead. Maria immediately held out a glass of water and helped him sip.

"Alfredo, maybe you shouldn't talk. . . . You need rest."

"Soon I'll have my eternal sleep."

"Alfredo, I'm so sorry how you feel. But please don't say unlucky things like this. . . ." I stopped, not knowing what more to say.

His voice faded like incense smoke. "Eileen, thank you so much for coming. You're a good woman."

He rolled his head toward me and stared at me with sad eyes.

I leaned toward the housekeeper, and whispered, "I think señor wants some words with me in private."

Maria left, obedient as ever, and I turned to the sick man. "Alfredo, I'm here to care for you. Maria too. Just concentrate on getting better."

Another well-intended but meaningless sentiment.

My friend shook his head. "Eileen . . ." He sighed. "You really think that I'll . . . recover?"

I had no choice but to lie. "Yes, of course. See how well you did last time?"

"I appreciate your encouragement, but this time is different; I'm not going to make it."

I shook my head.

"You're a good person, Eileen."

"Not everyone is evil in this world, Alfredo. Most are good."

"But I'm not. I harmed a lot of people on my way up. I cheated on Penelope with a prostitute and a witch. This is my punishment."

"Don't worry about that now. What's done is done."

"Don't you think it's too late to make amends for my bad deeds?"

According to Chinese culture, a person's life span and deeds are all recorded in the *Book of Life and Death* by the King of Hell, who decides life and death. What we did, good or bad, in each of our lives is set down in detail. The time of everyone's demise is prerecorded in this terrible book. Our allotment of years is set by what we did in our previous lives. To live longer, we should look in a karmic mirror and discover our past bad deeds, then try to neutralize them by doing good in this life. Then the King of Hell might cross out your original death date and write in a later one.

But it seemed that Alfredo's chance for redemption was slipping away with each beat of his damaged heart. There were no postponements. As the Chinese say, "If the King of Hell wants you to be present at two in the morning, he's not going to wait until three."

But of course I did not recount these gloomy Chinese beliefs to him.

Alfredo's faint voice woke me from my reverie.

"Eileen, I need to tell you something and I have very little time. Please listen very carefully. You must also promise never to tell anyone what I am about to tell you. Keep it to yourself to the grave. Can you promise?"

I nodded, then blurted out before I could stop myself, "Are you going to tell me that Penelope killed Isabelle?"

My friend looked so shocked and disturbed that his sunken eyes rounded like two huge coins, his irises gold-flecked, ironically mimicking his life's pursuit of wealth.

"How did you know?" he exclaimed as if he'd just run into a ghost.

"I had a chat with Penelope."

Now he looked like he'd just been hit by lightning. "How? Please don't joke; my unlucky wife has been gone for many years!"

"I spoke to her ghost."

"Eileen, please!"

"Alfredo, it's my third eye. I think I told you, since I was at Past Life Lake, I can see things, things normal eyes can't see.

"You may think I'm crazy, but I went to the old Daoist Luminous Spirit Temple on Grand Canary and channeled someone. She seemed to be Penelope and she confessed."

He didn't reply at first but looked even more miserable. Then he nodded weakly. "So you figured it out."

"How come you didn't do anything, like tell the police?"

It took a while for him to speak, his voice pained. "The police did come—I bribed them to cover up the whole thing."

"Then what about Penelope? She killed herself out of guilt—or maybe it was Isabelle's vengeful ghost?"

Alfredo looked totally exhausted by my questions. "You're really psychic, aren't you?"

"When Penelope died, you inherited everything, didn't you?"

"It's my fault in a way. She found out about me and Sabrina, then Isabelle. It was because of Isabelle that she took off on the motorcycle. What else have you 'seen'?"

"That's it. Don't worry, Alfredo, I won't use my power anymore. It might shorten my life to keep using my *yin* vision. At first I didn't believe in my own power, but then when I tested it, it told me the truth. Sabrina believed you killed her daughter and I have to admit that I believed her at first. But you didn't seem like a murderer to me. It was only when I channeled Isabelle and Penelope came instead that I knew for sure.

"I judged you wrongly and I am very sorry. You've been nice to me, Alfredo. I could have been hurt by the witches had you not taken me in your castle and had Maria care for me."

"Why would Sabrina think that I killed her daughter?"

"She said that Isabelle threatened to expose your illegal arms dealings unless you gave her money. Is that right?"

"Since you know so much, I might as well tell you everything. . . ."

He sighed, then took a few labored deep breaths before continuing. "Yes, I've hidden a big hoard of cash and gold in my castle. Let me tell you where."

"It's best not to tell me, Alfredo."

He looked at me curiously. "You're really one strange woman. Most women would jump into my bed—or now my deathbed—just to get this information. And you don't want to know. Why?"

"I don't want to have anything to do with illegal money. And I don't want to deal with the police!"

"No need to worry about that."

"Why not?"

"Because the police are my friends. The best kind of friends, the ones you pay. Besides, when money is illegal, it's because the government can't get its hands on it. Governments are the biggest gangsters. You think what they do is legal? Only because they make the laws, you understand?"

It made sense, though I'd never thought of it this way. But it wouldn't help with the police to tell them that they were gangsters.

"No one cares about Penelope or Isabelle. After all these years, they're like out-of-print books. But I want to tell you where my treasure is because I want you to have some. It's under a floor panel, beneath the grand piano in the music room. There are several thick piles of musical scores. The loose panel is under the Wagner pile. I picked that because no one in Spain cares for Wagner but me.

"But there's more under Past Life Lake . . ." he quickly added.

"Past Life Lake?! But it's haunted!"

"That's exactly why I put it there. No one will dare to look for it."

"How did you put the treasures under the lake?"

He took a slow sip of the water, then went on. "I used my connections in the arms trade. It was expensive, but completely secure. A company that makes missiles placed everything in thick steel barrels with noncorrosive coating and welded the tops onto them. There is a hidden lever that opens them, but only I know how to do it."

He laughed a little. "Of course I watched the entire process. The barrels were smuggled here in a fishing trawler, and I paid a team of divers from France to bury them in the lake bottom. . . ."

I couldn't quite follow the technical details, but I let him finish his boasting, then quickly asked, "You weren't afraid your hired help would dive to Past Life Lake to steal the treasure?"

He shook his head, letting out a chuckle. "Hell no! I told the divers that the canisters were filled with nuclear waste that I had been paid to hide. That way, they wouldn't dare try to open them.

"It's evil money and if anyone goes after it, they'll be buried along with the wages of my sin. Maybe a hundred years from now the lake will dry up and the treasure will be found. The paper money will be worthless, but the gold will hold its value. So, one day it might be used to do good. If so, perhaps I'll attain redemption—a century or so from now."

We remained silent each in our own way contemplating this strange turn of events.

Finally, he spoke. "I told Isabelle about this and the poor innocent girl, having no idea what it'd involve, went to dive there. So she was a victim of her own greed."

I suspected that Isabelle was more needy than greedy.

"So, did Penelope kill Isabelle or was she drowned trying to get the treasures?"

"I'd say both."

Maybe that was the truth. As the Chinese say: "People die for money, birds die for food."

A long story and depressing from beginning to end. Greed, stupidity, and maliciousness—an unholy trinity.

"Why have you told me all this, Alfredo?"

"I have no one to whom to pass on my wealth. You have been good to me, even despite your suspicions. Of course there's no way you could get the treasures in the lake. But you can take those under the piano."

"But you have Juan, your son!"

"My son?" He looked unbearably sad. "Why was it him instead of Luis?"

Then I suddenly remembered something. "Did you ever get Luis's DNA tested?"

He nodded. "My lawyer took the toothbrush to be tested in a lab. Luis's DNA doesn't match mine, so it must be Juan. A retarded son, how cruel is fate. Anyway, even if I give Juan all my money, what could he use it for? He'd be cheated out of it in no time."

I had nothing to suggest. Juan would always be dependent on the kindness of others, never a sure thing.

"Where is he now?"

"He's in good hands. Father Fernando took him back to Spain. But if you want his address, let me know."

He went on. "Now listen. The money—"

I interrupted. "Please, Alfredo, I don't want anything to do with your finances!"

"You won't, not if you just inherit. Anyway, I've recently changed my will. You'll get five percent, Maria will get some, and the rest will go to the church to use for the poor. You can get what's under the piano, but swear to me that you will not go after the treasures under the lake. Too many women have died there already."

I had my own reasons for staying away from this unhappy place. "Alfredo, you are too kind to me. I really haven't done anything to deserve it."

"You've done far more than you realize, Eileen. If you don't take the money, a thief will, or worse, the government, who are thieves themselves."

This was my excuse to look for his money.

"I hope someone can have happiness from what I've done. I've harmed nearly everyone else I had anything to do with."

I nodded. "Your women, your business rivals and partners . . ."

"Nathalia too."

"You mean that evil witch? Because she stole your son with Sabrina?"

He sighed. "I told the police that Nathalia killed Isabelle. . . ."

"Then why didn't they arrest her?"

"They said they had no evidence. Anyway, nobody here will testify against a witch—they're all terrified of curses. And maybe they are right—look at my misfortunes. My life has been cursed."

I was remembering that Nathalia lived underground and kept herself out of sight, except when she wanted to be seen. Likely this was not the only crime she was hiding from.

Alfredo went on hurriedly, no doubt because he sensed his time to make amends was running out.

"But curse or not, I've deserved my misfortunes. Do you still have compassion for this old sinner? Will you stick with me for my last few days on earth? With your third eye, will you watch over me in the other world?"

I was thinking that human nature is too complicated for my little brain. Right now I wished I was back in the library, pouring over obscure metaphysical manuscripts instead of trying to comfort an old man departing a far from exemplary life. In my heart I could not completely excuse him, yet I had no wish to further discomfit his last hours or days.

"What about where I'm headed. Do you think I will arrive in hell?"

He'd obviously had a severe Catholic upbringing, though he'd never referred to it. None of my visions had revealed anything like the old-fashioned hell. Rather the ghosts seemed obsessed with righting wrongs. That's what Laolao had always told me: try to be on as good terms with the dead as you are with the living. So I told him the best thing was to acknowledge the harms he had inflicted and ask for forgiveness. I thought this would be the only way he could ease his troubled conscience now. And I did want to comfort him. He'd never done anything bad to me, so I had no qualms about helping to ease his last days.

Just then a fiftyish, bespectacled doctor came in with a nurse. I discreetly left the room so they could tend to Alfredo. But to my surprise Maria was gone.

A few minutes later when the doctor and nurse came out, I asked, "Doctor, how is my friend doing?"

The doctor studied me for a few seconds, then said in a near-whisper, "I'll give him at best one to two weeks. So if you're his daughter or wife, be prepared."

So cold talking about a person's few remaining days. Besides, how could I be Alfredo's daughter; did I suddenly look Spanish?

"How come he can still talk so well if he's so sick?"

He didn't answer me directly. "My advice is, since his mind is clear and he can still communicate, you had better discuss important matters with him as soon as possible, before he sinks into coma. You understand?"

"Certainly, and thank you, Doctor."

But he was already headed away, down the hall.

When I went back inside Alfredo's room, he was sleeping. I wanted to go back to the castle to look for the money but felt I should stay by his bedside. I imagined what it must be like to wake up, remember you are dying, and have only the four white hospital walls for company.

So I stayed by Alfredo's bedside and dozed off until his voice awakened me.

"Eileen, Eileen . . ."

I rubbed my eyes and saw my friend's ravaged face.

"You're still here?"

I nodded.

He sighed. "I'd have never imagined that on my deathbed the only one who cared enough to stay with me would be a stranger, a Chinese woman from across the sea."

"Alfredo, I wish I could do more. . . . I can't leave you by yourself."

He looked out the window, then turned back to me. "Eileen, this has been hard on you too. You need rest. I'll be fine. Please go back to my castle, have Maria cook you a nourishing meal, and sleep on your comfortable bed. But I hope you will come back here tomorrow."

I nodded. "Of course."

As if suddenly realizing something, he asked, "Where's Maria? She's supposed to be here."

I'd been wondering the same. "She's probably gone back to the castle to rest; she's worn-out too."

"Maybe. But she should have stayed. When you see her, tell her to come back tomorrow. Get a good rest, Eileen."

"I will."

"Your kind face is what motivates me to stay alive, at least for as long as I can."

I stooped to kiss his cheek and felt his tears.

34

A Rich Old Maid

Back at the castle, there was no response to the doorbell, so I pounded on the thick wooden door, without result. Then I picked up a stone and pounded even harder. Still no Maria. Suddenly I felt so stupid that I tapped my head, a traditional Chinese way of waking up one's brain. Alfredo must have the key and I should have asked him for it!

Maybe Maria had taken off to spend the night with a friend or go out somewhere to have fun. I was feeling a little panicky because I had no idea where I could spend the night. I decided to try one last time. I threw myself against the door shoulder-first and was happily surprised to have it swing open with a loud squeak like a ghost's cry.

Just in case it was a ghost who'd helped me, I muttered a thank you. After all, Laolao had told me that wherever you are, there's always a ghost nearby. Maria was usually in the kitchen so I walked there first, but there was no sign of her. Nor was she in her room. I checked the other rooms we usually used, but they were all empty.

It was a relief to have a roof over my head for the night. But given the stress of the day, I could not imagine being able to fall asleep. And despite my shame at suddenly realizing that I did want the hidden money after all, I found my legs dragging me toward the music room. I needed to see if those legendary stacks of cash and gold actually existed. Real or imaginary, so far they had caused only misery.

Walking toward the music room, I was all too aware of being the only living being in this huge castle, surrounded by the black night. Laolao had always warned me that after midnight, any dwelling place, especially old ones, is filled with denizens of the other realm who'd silently watch our every move. I'd never believed her, at least not back in our cheery apartment in brightly lit Hong Kong.

Supposedly, these entities usually don't mean any harm; they're just curious—apparently the other world is a pretty boring place. Whether or not their spirits were really near me, my mind was obsessed with unnerving thoughts of Isabelle, Sabrina, Penelope, the supposed hidden treasure, and the witches. And Alfredo, too, now on the threshold of the other world himself—or maybe already there.

Laolao had told me if I was careful not to provoke otherworldly entities, they'd leave me alone, out of mutual respect. But what would offend a ghost? I had no idea.

Still, to be on the safe side, I muttered a soft, respectful, "Hello, all of you, hope you're all having a great time. I'll go ahead with what I came for and won't bother you. I hope you'll also respect my space and leave me alone."

After that, my heart beating fast, I stepped inside the music room. Before I switched on the light, I saw, or at least thought I saw, a woman sitting by the piano. Feeling icy water seeping down my spine, I flicked on the light and looked again. There was no one there. Had it been Penelope's ghost waiting for me? I was sure that if she'd been alive, the woman would have bitterly resented me, and if she was really a ghost, would resent me even more, since I knew she was a murderess.

Despite my pounding heart, I was resolved to complete my mission, so I approached the huge grand piano, which looked forlorn under the eerie light of the grand chandelier. My eyes searched the space underneath the musical instrument and saw the piles of musical notation covered with dust. It was indeed a clever hiding place, for no one was going to move such a massive object and sort through the piles of moldering books and papers.

As I started to move the papers, I noticed that some seemed to have been recently disturbed. Coughing due to the clouds of dust I created, I removed the piles and began to tap on the floor. I easily detected where there was a hollow space. I hurried to the kitchen and returned with a big knife, then started to pry and lift the planks. As I did so, I noticed places where the varnish seemed to have been scraped off the wood.

After a few planks were lifted I saw a deep space underneath. But my happiness at find the hiding place was short-lived. I saw no cash or gold, just an empty space. Then I noticed a few torn banknotes stuck between planks. So money had been stored there.

Someone had beaten me to the treasure!

But who? Not Alfredo for sure. Not Isabelle, nor Sabrina, nor Penelope. As far as I knew, ghosts could not steal anything material. But Nathalia was still alive. I noticed that despite my chill, I was soaked with sweat, whether from the exertion of clearing the floor or plain fear, I couldn't tell.

Just then I was startled by the phone ringing insistently. Chinese term such a phone call *zuihuan*—a ghost call to lure your soul to the underworld. But I didn't have time to think, for my feet had already brought me to the phone and my hand had snatched up the receiver.

"Hello, who's this?"

"Señorita Eileen, it's Maria."

I fervently hoped that she would not come home before I'd had a chance to straighten up her master's music room. But I also felt relief that I might not have to spend the night at the castle alone.

Maria's voice was uneasy and I could hear her heavy breathing on the other end of the line.

"Where are you, Maria? Señor Alfrenso has been asking for you. He wants you to be at the hospital early tomorrow morning."

"I'm afraid I can't do that."

"Is something wrong?"

"No, but I'll no longer be working for Señor Alfrenso."

"Why now? It's the time señor needs you the most."

"Because I no longer need to work for him."

She paused to breathe again before blurting out, "I took all his money and gold from under the piano."

It took a few seconds for this to sink in.

"So it was you who took everything?"

"Yes, Señorita Eileen."

"How did you know he hid his money there?"

"I overheard your conversation when I was outside señor's hospital room."

She went on. "Since what I took under the piano will be enough for me for the rest of my life, I'll leave what's under the lake for you."

This was certainly not unselfishness on her part. She knew that neither of us could get to this money.

She went on. "That's why I had to leave so quickly. . . . Remember I told you that my mother also worked for señor?"

"Yes, I do."

"She worked her butt off; then she died and I had no choice but to take her place. Stuck in this castle in the middle of nowhere, I never had a chance to get married. Now no one will want me, it's hopeless. So I believe that señor owes me the money. Finally I can have a life."

I was puzzled by her confessing to me. "Maria, why are you telling me this?"

"I know you're kind and won't hurt me. You, a stranger foreigner, are the only one who's been nice to me. Penelope was the worst. She was mean and treated everyone as her inferiors."

This didn't surprise me, she was a murderer after all. "What about señor?"

"He never cared about me or my mother, we're just servants. I called because I don't want you to think señor lied to you—no reason for you to keep looking for what's not there anymore."

She paused to take her breath, then said, "I also want you to tell señor that I took the money."

"Why?"

"To spite him, that's why. Also, I don't want him to think you took the money and pretended that there was no money there."

"You're not afraid I'll call the police?"

I doubted I would report her, but she wouldn't know this.

"It's all illegal money anyway. But some others may know about it. Cecily, she's a sneak. She's been in the castle; she probably knows where it was, so watch out for her."

"Are you sure?"

"Pretty sure. I saw her snooping around with her witch friends when señor was away. She probably knows about what's under the lake too."

"How come Cecily and her group know about the lake?"

"I think she hypnotized señor. She even hypnotized me once, but I didn't know anything useful for her. She's just been waiting for the right time to act."

"But even if they know about the valuables under the lake, how can they get at it?"

"Just look at her followers, all big and muscular."

"Even so, I don't think anyone can get it without hiring professional divers."

"That's why they wanted to get the treasure from the castle first—so they'd have the money to hire workers to bring it up from the lake. Why do you think they were always hanging around the castle here?"

My thoughts were interrupted by Maria laughing crazily. "Hahaha! But it's me who is lucky, not those bitches!"

I didn't respond and she spoke again. "All right, I've got to go. Don't change your mind and report me to the police. They'll never find me anyway. Farewell, Señorita Eileen; I hope we'll never meet again."

She added. "One last thing, I already told the driver and gardener they could leave. So they're no longer working for Señor Alfrenso either."

"And they listened to you?"

"I told them señor is not going to make it and his lawyer will contact them about possible compensation after his passing."

After that she hung up.

I made my way to my room, locked the door, put a chair against it, and collapsed on the bed. Despite these precautions, I was too afraid to sleep, not so much of ghosts as of human evil.

* * *

I must have finally dozed off because I was awakened by the sound of the phone ringing ceaselessly. Sun was streaming in as I ran down the hall to answer. Glancing at my watch, I saw it was already two o'clock in the afternoon. In my groggy state, I wondered if it was Maria calling again. I even wondered if her earlier phone call had been a dream.

I snatched up the phone. It was not Maria, but a man's voice. "Can I speak to Maria, Señor Alfrenso's housekeeper?"

"What do you want from her?"

"Whom am I speaking to?"

"Señor Alfrenso's friend."

"Were you with him at the hospital yesterday?"

"Yes, that's me, Eileen Chen."

"Then I'm sorry to tell you that Señor Alfrenso has passed away."

I felt bad I had overslept and lost my chance to see my friend once more.

"When did that happen?"

"Just about an hour ago. I am Antonio Mendez, his lawyer. Fortunately Señor Alfrenso was able to change his will before that. He left most of his fortune to charity."

"I'm coming over to the hospital right now."

"There's no need. You're not a relative, so you do not need to sign anything."

Anyway I didn't think I should go to the hospital. When I'd kissed Alfredo good-bye, though weak he looked peaceful. I felt sad enough without having to look at his empty bed. I did not know what would happen here, now that the Heartbreak Castle had broken another heart—mine.

Outside the castle, I took a last walk around the grounds. Then I spotted a familiar creature—the white horse Lonlon, looking handsome yet melancholic. Do animals know when their master has just passed? It seemed that he did. I went up to caress his muzzle and mane reassuringly.

In response, he looked deeply into my eyes, seemingly saying, "Don't be sad, señorita. This is life, things come and go, prosper and whither. . . ."

I did not know what would happen to him either. I thought out loud. "Poor creature, Alfredo and Maria are both gone. Who's going to take care of you now?"

He leaned his head close to mine as if saying, "Don't worry, the lawyers, they'll take care of everything. . . ."

I stroked his mane one more time, then walked away, my heart as heavy as the rocks on the bottom of Past Life Lake. The castle was not a happy place, and I knew I would never come back. Now it was in the hands of the lawyers, the category of humans closest to undertakers.

That afternoon while having tea at the hotel café and reading the local newspaper, I saw an article about Alfredo.

Prominent Local Businessman and Owner of Heartbreak Castle Alfredo Alfrenso Dead of a Heart Attack

Businessman, socialite, and man-about-town Alfredo Alfrenso was one of our most prominent citizens. In his youth he was married to the glamorous opera singer Penelope Ramirez, but she died in a tragic motorcycle accident. He never remarried but had many companions, including socialites, a cabaret singer, and a woman locally considered to be a witch.

Despite his wealth and prominence, his life was not free of tragedy. A young woman with whom he was frequently seen drowned in a diving accident in the notorious Past Life Lake. Rumors that she was actually murdered were never verified.

The source of the late Señor Alfrenso's wealth remains unknown. Though some speculated that he was an underground arms dealer, he was never seen with a rifle or pistol.

> Apparently, most of his vast fortune was left to the Catholic Church to benefit the poor. Sadly, he never remarried and so had no heir to whom to pass on his estate.

After I finished reading, I felt a deep sadness. Without being direct, the reporter had managed to completely defame the dead man. He was far from perfect—who of us is?—but he deserved better.

35

My Young Sailor Lover

Two days later, Alfredo was laid to rest next to Penelope in a little private cemetery behind the castle. As far as I knew, he had not received last rites, but his body was interred in sacred ground nonetheless. Perhaps Father Fernando put in a good word for him, and his bequest to the church would certainly have helped.

Only his lawyer, a Catholic priest from a nearby parish, and myself were present for the burial. Though the ceremony was simple, his coffin was lavish, perhaps specified in his will. Rich Chinese also are buried in ornate coffins. This does nothing for the dead; it only gives their family a chance to show off to the living. Sadly, Alfredo's coffin had no one to impress—his lawyer didn't care, and the display meant nothing to me.

After the funeral, I walked over to Grandpa's grave and said a quiet prayer for him, then took the rickety bus back to my hotel, feeling acutely lonely.

Once I was inside the hotel lobby, the young receptionist rushed over. "Señorita, there was a man asking for you earlier, but we couldn't find you."

I couldn't think who it might be. I feared it was Ivan, here to propose again. Yet, embarrassing as that would be, I almost wished it were him just to have someone to dispel my loneliness.

"Is he still here?" I asked.

"No, but he left you this." He handed me an envelope, then returned to the hotel desk.

I tore it open and recognized Luis's handwriting.

> *Dear Eileen,*
>
> *I'm back for two days' shore leave; then I'll be sailing again. I hope you will come visit me in the village. Everyone is gone, so I am all alone here. I'll be waiting for you—forever.*
>
> *Luis*

I didn't wait for the elevator, but ran up the stairs to my room to change, grab my bag, and dash to get a cab to the village. When I spotted Luis's house in the distance, its owner was sitting in the courtyard by the table, looking toward the path leading up to this little bit of paradise. Once our eyes met, he ran over to me, scooped me up in his muscular arms in one smooth movement, and then carried me into his house.

Without any exchange of words, we began to undress. More precisely Luis pulled off my clothes, then his own, in swift, cursive calligraphic movements. Quickly we began to explore each other's bodies and emotions. As our hands played mischief, I had a sudden awakening to our having been lovers in past lives.

I was certain that my young lover felt the same. Luis knew exactly where my body liked to be touched—inside my mouth, underneath my tongue, behind my ears, my armpits, nipples, and of course the valley between my thighs. And I also knew his favorite places, which was anywhere a sexual explorer could get her hands and tongue on.

Our lovemaking moved from tender caressing to titillating wrestling and, finally, fusing. Soon we both let out loud, satisfied, animal cries.

If things didn't work out for us, at least I'd tasted a man's purest, rawest, most genuine love.

Afterward, we lay on his bed, savoring each other's emotions, desires, and scents. Luis's sky blue eyes penetrated mine as his large, furniture-making hand tenderly caressed my hardening nipples.

"I love you, Eileen. You make me the happiest man on earth."

"Thank you, Luis. You also make me the happiest woman in the world."

"Let's go to the lake!"

"What for?" I wondered if he also knew about Alfredo's treasures.

"To see both our past and future."

"Can you see them?"

"I don't think so. But you can."

Could I really? Luis was already putting on his clothes and so I did also. Then he dragged me out of the house, toward our karmic destiny.

Past Life Lake looked like a pregnant belly from one angle and a socket swollen with tears from another. Tears of sadness or joy? Probably bittersweet, just like everything else in life.

We walked to the shore and without a word, knelt on the sand together. I peeked at Luis, suppressing an urge to kiss those still-innocent lips of his. Gazing at the lake, he seemed mesmerized, as if being pulled by a powerful energy emanating from the water.

I felt the same energy but was inspired by it to open my eyes wide so I could *see*—I didn't know what I was looking for, my future or Alfredo's fortune, sealed away in barrels somewhere on the lake bottom.

Soon I saw light moving on the surface of the water, making abstract patterns as if of an alternate universe—watery, dreamlike, enthralling. Then the patterns coalesced before my eyes, surprising me. The vision looked nothing like barrels of treasure, but rather a very familiar-looking woman. I sensed her busily engaging herself in different activities: doing divination with the *Book of Changes* or tea leaves; interpreting dreams; picking lucky days for weddings or funerals; blessing houses; concocting and selling herbs; performing magic tricks.

As if in a trance, I stared intensely, trying not to blink because I feared that once I did, she'd be gone from my vision. Then she spotted me and waved! Her waving caused the water to spread out in circles, ever widening into infinity. Who was this unknown woman who seemed to possess magical powers, and what was she doing underwater? Could she be Sabrina, Isabelle, Penelope, or Cecily?

Then I realized that she was me!

Was I seeing my future or my past?

Just when I was about to yell to Luis, "Look! That's me underwater!" he averted his eyes from the lake, calling out, "Eileen, let's go back home."

And the vision was gone.

"Why?" I could hear the sharp edge of disappointment in my voice.

"I should have listened to the villagers not to come here."

"How's that?"

"I don't know. It's . . . too weird."

"Are you scared?"

"Maybe it's just superstition. I only like positive things and happy endings. Somehow this lake doesn't feel right to me. It holds things dark and unfathomable, and I don't like that."

"How's that?"

"Because I only like honest things and people, like Grandpa and Juan—and you."

I didn't think I was totally honest, nor totally dishonest—just human. But anyway, I was pleased that Luis felt this way about me.

"This lake has been here for centuries, they say. I think it has absorbed too many people's bad deeds and bad energy," Luis said.

"What do you feel?"

He scratched his head. "I don't really know. Whatever it is, it's too much for me." He took my hand. "Coming here was a bad idea of mine. I want to be with you at home, in bed, not here with a cold, gloomy lake. Let's go."

Back home, we again made love, this time more slowly, savoring it, and then again for a third time. Luis was like an orphan in an abusive orphanage where all he experienced was hunger, so all he desired was food. And now I became his exotic, yummy dish. He savored every part of me like I was steaming dim sum. He couldn't get enough, even though he was already overstuffed.

I failed to resist. But I did take revenge. Instead of attacking him like a tigress, I adopted the strategy of retreating in order to conquer, until we both moaned and groaned and lay back exhausted on the rumpled sheets.

After our lavish feast of lovemaking, Luis kissed me tenderly, his big hand caressing my swollen breast.

"Eileen, will you marry me?"

"Let's just be happy together. As for marriage, who knows? There's no rush to decide."

"We can move to the city, and I can make and sell furniture."

"You need to finish your contract as a sailor first—"

He looked upset. "I know. After I sail, you will disappear from my life and go back to your rich boyfriend, marry, and live an easy life."

I had not expected that this young man had already mapped out my whole life for me. However, I couldn't absolutely rule out the possibility. So I remained silent.

"Eileen, I love you."

"Maybe it's because you've never loved a woman before."

"No, I know I want to spend my whole life with you."

"Because you're too young to understand what love means."

"Then tell me."

"Hearts can be fickle. Real love is more than just great sex. Or physical attraction. A lot more. What about when we're old?"

"So you think we're not suited to each other?"

"I didn't say that. I'm just saying love is . . . Anyway, why don't you go back to the ship, finish your contract, and then we'll talk about this, okay? It's only a few months."

He sat up, looking very upset and very handsome. "I understand. You don't really love me."

"Luis, let's face the facts. I'm thirteen years older than you and admit it, we live in two totally different worlds."

He shook his head. "When we first met, you told me the story of *The Butterfly's Lovers.*"

"Yes, so?"

"It means that love conquers all."

"But don't forget the ending is tragic, Luis."

Now he looked completely crestfallen. "Then there's no hope for us?"

I was getting a little exasperated. A hot afternoon in bed did not guarantee a lifetime of happiness together.

"Eileen, am I just a cute puppy in your eyes?"

"Luis, how could you say this? You're not a puppy. But at thirty-three, I also can't jump into marriage just like that, you understand?"

"So you don't want to marry me because I'm poor!"

At that moment he really did look like an injured puppy, his vulnerability softening my heart.

The next morning I woke when dawn broke, only to discover that Luis wasn't next to me in bed. Nor was he in the house or working outside in the yard. Only when I reentered the house did I see his note on the nightstand. Picking it up, I read:

> *My dearest Eileen,*
>
> *Sorry, but I had to go; the ship is about to weigh anchor. I wanted to wake you up but didn't have the heart—you slept so deeply.*
>
> *I have the feeling that you're still not sure about me. I think you really do love me, but you have too many worries about everything and that affects your love for me. I know you think I only trust love because I'm too young to know better. Maybe when I'm older I'll think like you, but I hope not. Love is too precious to be doubted.*
>
> *I hope when I come back that your beautiful face will be the first thing I see. If my little house is empty, I'll always think of you and wish you the best of luck forever.*
>
> *If I come back and find you gone, I'll know it's forever, so you don't need to leave a letter for me.*

Thinking of you and loving you,
Luis
PS: I stayed up the whole night carving something for you; it's on the nightstand.

On the nightstand was a small wooden carving of a crib. A not too subtle hint that he wanted a family with me.

I sighed heavily. He wasn't giving up.

Luis had left, just like that. Sadness welled up in me, bringing to my mind Li Yu's poem:

I dream, forgetting I am just a trespasser on life.
Now, after an evening's stolen pleasure,
Alone, resting against the fence
The rivers and mountains going all the way to infinity,
It's easy to part, harder to meet again.
Spring is gone, like flowing water and fallen petals. . . .

I didn't know if Luis and I would see each other again, but I was glad that we'd met, though briefly. He was certainly not my first lover, but he was my first virgin. The little house, a short time ago filled with lovemaking, was now empty and lonely, so I decided to go back to the hotel.

No sooner was I was back in my hotel room than the phone rang.

"This is Antonio Mendez. I'm Alfredo Alfrenso's lawyer. I'm glad you finally answered the phone, Señorita Chen."

"Señor Mendez, please just call me Eileen."

"I must extend my sympathy, Eileen. But there is some good news for you!"

"What's that?"

"You're going to be a very well-off woman."

Although Alfredo had told me that he had mentioned me in his will, I hadn't entirely believed him. Now, it turned out to be true. I felt elated but also a little guilty benefiting from his untimely death.

"Alfredo has left you almost five million dollars."

"I can't believe it! I never imagined anything like this." And I hadn't, not in this life nor any previous or future ones. For a moment I wondered if all the strange events on the island had caught up with me and I was losing touch with reality. I shook my head to clear it, and stammered, "It's very generous of him. I'm grateful and thank you, too, Antonio!"

"You're a fortunate woman."

"Did Alfredo leave anything for his son, Juan?"

"I'm afraid not. But he left two million to Luis."

Luis? I couldn't believe what I'd heard! So Alfredo still wanted Luis to be his son, despite knowing the truth!

"Luis is not his son, so why would he get anything?"

"Of course it's not a free lunch. To inherit, Luis has to agree to take care of Juan for life. And the money will be paid out to him over time."

I felt a wash of relief. "Don't worry, I'm sure Luis will agree. He is very generous and always kind to Juan. But right now he has left to be a sailor. I think he'll be back in a few months. What if he doesn't return, though?"

The lawyer laughed. "Ha, Eileen, don't you worry about this! We're a big law firm and can find anyone we want. That's what people pay us for."

Hanging up, I remembered what the *Book of Changes* had told me after I'd left Penelope's haunted room:

Pushing upward brings great success
It's the right time to see an important person
Do not be afraid
Going to the south
Is auspicious.

So the "great success" and "going to the south is auspicious" lines must have been referring to this five-million-dollar inheritance!

Epilogue

My time on Tenerife had been filled with new experiences, but they had been taxing ones. After all the misfortunes I had encountered I felt a need for closure, so I took trips to pay respects to the five departed souls: Alfredo and Penelope, Sabrina and Isabelle, and the only one who'd led a full life, Grandpa.

Standing at Sabrina's grave, I told her the good news that Juan, her son with Alfredo, had been found safe and sound. I also told her not to worry about her son, because his best friend Luis had inherited money from Alfredo to take care of Juan for life.

At Isabelle's grave, I told her the truth about Penelope but also asked that she promise not to enter my dreams again. For whatever reason, she kept her promise.

I never again visited Past Life Lake, for I believed I had learned whatever it had to teach me, and now wanted the unquiet dead out of my life.

Since our confrontation I had not seen Cecily, nor heard anything about her. I wondered if she'd gone to the lake in search of Alfredo's hidden wealth. Unexpectedly, my question was soon answered when I read the morning paper over breakfast a few days later.

FOUR WOMEN DROWN IN PAST LIFE LAKE

> Four women drowned while diving in Past Life Lake, a notorious body of water that has claimed many victims in the past. Pending an autopsy, official identification has been withheld. However, sources have informed us that one of the deceased was Lucia Cruz, thought to be in her forties. Another victim was an older woman, while the other two are twins, probably in their twenties.
>
> The source also said that the four women were considered by some to be witches and were sometimes seen selling products in the Witches' Market. Why they were diving and the exact cause of their drowning remains under investigation.

Had the witches overtaxed themselves trying to bring up the treasures?

Or was the lake really haunted with ferocious ghosts eager to pull people down to the depths?

Either way, what really killed them was their own greed.

Imagining the women drowning, I suddenly felt like I couldn't breathe. I forced myself to take a deep breath, only to have my head start pounding. Needing to lie down, I quickly signed the check and left the dining room. As I crossed the lobby, the receptionist called me over and handed me a package.

"Who's it from?" I asked.

"I have no idea; it just came in the mail."

Instead of waiting for the ancient elevator, I rushed up the stairs to my room. Once inside I tore open the package and found a DVD. I inserted it into the player and pressed the play button.

At first I saw nothing but a park with tall trees. Then I recognized it as the place where the two brothers, Ed and Kyle, had claimed they'd witnessed the earth swallowing the homeless man and a dog—Isabelle's dog.

I really was not in the mood for any more strange happenings but, my heart beating fast, I steeled myself to watch.

Onscreen, a very old man dressed in rags appeared, accompanied by a feeble-looking dog anxiously sniffing the ground. Suddenly a gust of wind blew, stirring up a cloud of dust. Then the dust seemed to form the image of a woman whose face I had come to recognize—Isabelle!

I rubbed my eyes to have a clearer look. Though she was only in silhouette, I was sure I was seeing an apparition of Sabrina's daughter. The dog must have seen it, too, because it began barking excitedly. What followed was even more unexpected. Another silhouetted form, its expression elegant and arrogant, tried to snatch the dog away. Just then the dog and man were pulled down into the earth, as if by some unknown geological force.

At this point, the tape ended, leaving me agitated and sweating. So the story was true after all. Not only did the earth truly swallow up a man, but also the ghosts of Isabelle and Penelope were there, still fighting over a dog from beyond their watery graves.

While I strained my mind, trying to make sense of the whole thing, a voice in my head interrupted me, saying, *"Let go of the other world and focus on your present one. The only way to counteract evil is to do good."*

I began to gather up the packing material when I noticed there was a letter. I unfolded it and read.

> *Dear Eileen,*
>
> *You will see that Ed and I didn't lie—the earth truly did swallow an old man and a dog. We felt a ghostly presence, and the dog certainly could sense it as well. I'm sure you're the only person who'll believe in our story. Maybe you will even be able to tell who that ghostly presence was.*
>
> *I could feel the presence with my sixth sense, but I think because you're a woman, yours is stronger than mine. I do know that there really are ghosts—and the*

dog knew it too. I hope this tape won't scare you, but help you solve some of the puzzling happenings here on the island.

Ed and I will go back to the U.S. this afternoon, so this is good-bye.

Perhaps our paths will cross again. In the meantime, best of luck in all your adventures.

Kyle

The tape had scared me—how could it not? But I was also relieved because now I could include this strange event in my book, and I had video evidence of it as well.

I had to conclude that the people whose paths I'd crossed on the islands—Alfredo, Sabrina, Maria, Cecily and her friends, Luis, Father Fernando, Juan, Uncle Wang, even the long-deceased Penelope and Isabelle, and the brothers Ed and Kyle—had been my teachers, however unwittingly. I wouldn't have chosen the lessons, but felt better off for them. And I was richer too. Laolao had always told me that everything that happens to us is for a reason and I was beginning to think she was right.

Even though I was now financially secure, I had learned the price of greed and resolved to be satisfied with what I had. Alfredo was hardly a model, yet in the end he had redeemed himself by trying to make amends—including supporting the young man he'd rejected as his son.

Luis seemed to be the only one without greed. He was perhaps the most decent man I had ever met; yet even so, I wasn't sure that I would be content to spend my life with him. With or without me, I hoped that his beginner's heart would never be defiled as he journeyed through this world filled with smoke and dust, wind and frost.

Luis reminded me of a fictional character, the protagonist Jia Baoyu in the great Chinese novel *Dream of the Red Chamber*. Living amidst endless temptation and evil, Baoyu forever retains his innocence and undying love for Lin Daiyu.

Like Baoyu waiting for Daiyu, I decided to go to Luis's house and wait for his return.

While waiting, I could finally start to write my book. I'd had more than enough adventures to fill a book, whether nonfiction or fiction.

Now that the evil witches were out of the way, I decided to revisit the Witches' Market. I considered even setting up my own booth as a professional, but an honest one. There were many things I could do: use my third eye to discover secrets, enhance luck for the unfortunate, prepare traditional Chinese herbs, not only familiar ones like ginseng, but authentic ones like swallow soup, live frog wine with animal blood, and water mixed with burnt talisman ashes. Or, like Laolao, maybe I'd even beat the petty people. But I decided that practicing witchcraft could wait while I worked on my book. So I sat in my hotel room, scribbling furiously.

The days and weeks passed until I thought it was about time for Luis's return. So I packed and checked out of my hotel. The bellman managed to squeeze all my luggage into a taxi and after the long ride I arrived at Luis's house. There was no sign that he had come back yet. Once my luggage was safely inside, the first thing I did was start a fire and heat water for a bath. Soothed by this, I went to Luis's bedroom and took a long nap. Waking up and feeling refreshed, I went to sit in the courtyard with my pen and a notebook.

I forgot about the passing time, until I noticed the sunlight was fading and I looked up at the setting sun. The huge disk rested on the horizon, dyed a stunning orange-red. Watching it slowly submerge into Past Life Lake, I thought back on all that had happened since I'd come to the little village.

There were sculpting lessons with Grandpa and my talks with Luis about love and books, our simple good times, and Luis's plain but tasty cooking. Happy and sad moments, all evoked by this stunning twilight, far from home in a remote village next to a haunted lake.

The setting sun marked the end of this phase of my life; but when it rose the next morning, I was sure it would show me new adventures, maybe with Luis and maybe not.

Lines of Lu You's poem came into my mind:

> Nothing stains me with the world's dust
> Wherever I go, cares do not follow me.
> When it rains, I just wait for the rainbow. . . .

I knew this was the real gift of the opening of my third eye, not to look back on the dead but to see the world of the living with a new perspective.

A READING GROUP GUIDE

THE WITCH'S MARKET

Mingmei Yip

ABOUT THIS GUIDE

The questions and discussion topics that follow are intended to enhance your group's reading of this book.

Discussion Questions

1. Surveys show many people still believe in witches. Are you one of them? If so, why?
2. What is the difference between a shaman and a witch?
3. Do you believe that some people possess supernatural powers such as the ghost-seeing *yin* eye?
4. Should Eileen continue to be a professor of witchcraft, or should she follow her *laolao*'s footsteps and be a shamaness?
5. Do you think Eileen would be happier with the poor furniture maker Luis or with her rich ex-boyfriend Ivan?
6. Each character in the novel teaches us a different life lesson. What do you think these lessons are?
7. Alfredo's maid, Maria, is loyal to him until his death. What do you think of what she does after?
8. Laolao and Uncle Wang both seem to have supernatural powers. Do you think these powers are real? What do you think about how each uses them?
9. The protagonist, Eileen Chen, learns much of importance from her dreams. Do you learn from your own dreams?
10. Divination (fortune-telling) plays an important role in the novel. What do you think of using divination to make important life decisions?